Dedalus Europe 2014
General Editor: Timothy Lane

Before & During

Vladimir Sharov

BEFORE
&
DURING

Translated by Oliver Ready

Dedalus

The publication was effected under the auspices of the Mikhail Prokhorov Foundation TRANSCRIPT Programme to Support Translations of Russian Literature and the Grants for the Arts Programme of Arts Council England.

Published in the UK by Dedalus Limited,
24-26, St Judith's Lane, Sawtry, Cambs, PE28 5XE
email: info@dedalusbooks.com
www.dedalusbooks.com

ISBN printed book 978 1 907650 71 0
ISBN ebook 978 1 909232 99 0

Dedalus is distributed in the USA by SCB Distributors,
15608 South New Century Drive, Gardena, CA 90248
email: info@scbdistributors.com   web: www.scbdistributors.com

Dedalus is distributed in Australia by Peribo Pty Ltd.
58, Beaumont Road, Mount Kuring-gai, N.S.W. 2080
email: info@peribo.com.au

First published by Dedalus in 2014
Before & During copyright © Vladimir Sharov 1988-1991
Translation copyright © Oliver Ready 2014

Printed in Finland by Bookwell
Typeset by Marie Lane

The Author

A historian of late-medieval Russia by training, Vladimir Sharov (b. 1952) is one of the most distinguished and uncompromising novelists of the post-Soviet period. The publication of *Do i vo vremya (Before and During)* in *Novyi mir* in 1993 led to an unprecedented rift among the editors of that celebrated journal. Undeterred, Sharov has continued in his distinctive groove, writing an ongoing commentary on Russian history, philosophy and the sacred texts. He disputes the characterization of his novels as 'alternative histories': 'God judges us not only for our actions, but also for our intentions. I write the entirely real history of thoughts, intentions and beliefs. This is the country that existed. This is our own madness, our own absurd.'

Sharov lives in Moscow and is the author of eight novels, including *The Rehearsals* (1992), *The Raising of Lazarus* (2002) and *Back to Egypt* (2013). His books have been translated into several languages, including French, Italian and Chinese. *Before and During* is his first book to appear in English.

The Translator

Oliver Ready is Research Fellow in Russian Society and Culture at St Antony's College, Oxford. His translations include Dostoevsky's *Crime and Punishment* (Penguin , 2014) and, from contemporary fiction, *The Zero Train* (Dedalus, 2001; 2007) and *The Prussian Bride* (Dedalus, 2002; Rossica Translation Prize, 2005), both by Yuri Buida. He is Russia and East-Central Europe Editor at the *Times Literary Supplement*.

This translation is based on the edition of *Do i vo vremya* published by ArsisBooks in 2009, with minor modifications made in agreement with the author.

I first set foot in this hospital in October 1965 – the eighteenth, if I'm not mistaken. They weren't supposed to keep me in. The plan was for a certain Professor Kronfeld to see me privately and choose a set of pills to match my particular 'profile'. From the metro I followed a diagonal path, as instructed, across wasteland and unfenced building sites; the path was well-used and the previous night's snowfall so well-trodden that here and there it had turned to ice. You couldn't imagine anyone living here: foundation pits and uneven piles of concrete slabs immediately gave way to vegetable depots, garages, warehouses. The once navigable Yauza flowed nearby, the railway line passed right through, and everything else had just clotted around.

This shortcut should have been a twenty or twenty-five minute walk, but I'd been going for more than half an hour and the street I needed was nowhere to be seen. The path was narrow, slippery, and of course I was walking more slowly than usual, but still, it was high time for it to end. I wasn't prepared to walk like this for ever, in fear of falling, like a clown on stilts. I was tired and annoyed with myself for not taking the other route, the easier one. What was I doing trudging from one warehouse, one job site to another, when I could have skirted them all along two broad streets that were swept and kept safe for walking? Convinced I was lost, I cursed myself mercilessly; I was almost in tears. The situation hardly warranted such a reaction, but I was on my way to a doctor, to a mental hospital; I didn't know what he'd say to me, what fate held in store. I was a bag of nerves. If only I hadn't cut it so fine, if only I'd given myself enough time to take the longer, more reliable route, not this uneven, uncertain path.

But God exists. There I was, wandering blindly among the garages, doing my best to avoid the potholes and the mud, when suddenly the ground, and the path along which I was walking, and this whole half-built labyrinth, and even the snow, all gave off the scent of vanilla and fresh hot bread. Ahead, a stone's throw away, was the bakery I'd been told to look out for. Apparently, it was on the same street as the hospital, three buildings before it.

The scent of vanilla is the scent of my childhood, the scent that surrounded me when I was conceived, brought to term, brought to life, the scent of my mother, my grandmother, our house, of all that was good and kind in my life. I spent my first six years on Pravda Street, not far from Soviet Hotel, famous for its gypsies to this day, and right opposite the huge 'Bolshevik' cake factory. That was where the smell came from, and I've always been convinced, for as long as I can remember, that the reason the factory bears its proud name is that this is what the Bolsheviks were like: soft, rich, sweet.

My mother was terribly fond of chocolate. Her fingers were long and slender, her nails painted violet, and when, over a cup of coffee with one of her numerous lady friends, she took a diamond or turret-shaped chocolate from a brightly coloured box, the effect was beautiful. At three I discovered that these chocolate selections were produced by the 'Bolshevik Girl', a different factory, and this made my mind up once and for all about the Bolsheviks, men and women, and resolved that vital

8

childish question of where they came from and how they were born. My picture of the world was complete.

We all know how durable the first impressions of childhood are: even after university, as a grown man and a seasoned journalist, whenever I was asked to write about the Bolsheviks I couldn't help making them out to be soft and tender, then I'd tie myself in knots trying to revise what I'd written, but to no avail – they never came out as they were meant to. It's hardly surprising: I was still living in another world, and there, it seemed, I would remain. Thanks to those Bolsheviks, I was taken for a bit of a fool at the paper, though I was liked well enough. Needless to say, my sketches could never be published in their original form, but they had one undeniable quality: the heroes were described with a love and a tenderness so genuine that our old newspaper hounds openly envied my sincerity, which, alas, would dissipate the moment someone tried to improve my text.

I knew this couldn't go on forever: it was hardly fair that someone else had to do my work for me, and a couple of years later I resigned. It was a painful step; I loved everything about the paper, the very smell of it, and anyway, I had nowhere else to go. By then I'd accumulated a vast quantity of unpublished sketches and stories, and I slowly drifted about – a bit of freelancing here, some hackwork there – in search of publications that might find my view of life congenial. In the end, there was probably only one place I could find them, and find them I did, by returning with my Bolsheviks to my childhood, to the place where they and I both came from.

Ten years have now passed since the time when editors were only too glad to publish me in *Pioneer's Truth*, *Bonfire* and, especially, *Tiny Tot*. Those first books which are read to children at home, in the crèche, at the nursery, are mine, because they contain my own childhood, kindness, tenderness, because my Bolsheviks are like mummy, kind, tender mummy, and children love these stories and want to hear them again and again. Then, like everyone else, my readers grow up, discover the world, realize that communists weren't always kind and soft, but their love for them remains. I don't think I have anything to be ashamed of; I wrote honestly, and I wrote what I thought, even if now, perhaps, my stories look a bit naïve.

My little books about Lenin eventually made my name, and shortly before the story I'm about to tell I suddenly received two very flattering offers. Offers I could never have dreamt of earlier. Many years before, while still at university, I wrote my thesis on the wonderful French writer Germaine de Staël. I'd continued to collect material about her and even dropped off a proposal for a book about her at Young Guard Publishing House, for their series *Lives of Remarkable People*. Nothing came of it, of course. But just recently, when I'd forgotten all about it, Young Guard sent me a letter declaring, amidst a flurry of obeisances, that, if I hadn't changed my mind, the publishing house was ready to sign a contract with me: the book on Madame de Staël had already been scheduled.

A month later to the day (I had only just got started on the project), Politizdat invited me to contribute to *Fiery Revolutionaries*, an equally popular series. It was mentioned, moreover, that my reputation was so irreproachable that the choice of both hero and era would be left entirely to me. Well, so much for grand plans – these past three years I haven't written a page, and but for the royalties from reprints of earlier books I'd have had nothing to live on.

*

The hospital grounds were extensive. Buildings in different styles and different, though faded colours were grouped haphazardly around a large central flowerbed, which now, at the end of autumn, was covered with yellow, patchy grass already sprinkled with snow and the remains of flowers planted in clumps. The building to which I was headed, a recent pre-fab, stood directly opposite the gates, and I reached the sixth floor in good time. I needn't have hurried. Kronfeld was busy on his ward round, which had been held up by a ministerial commission, and a nurse told me that it would be at least an hour before he could see me. Thereupon the door to the ward was shut, and I was left alone in a small, bright space, almost like a conservatory, that could equally have been a corridor or an ante-room.

I felt trapped: I couldn't take the lift or the stairs. The window looked out on to the Yauza, which at this point was extremely narrow; its embankment – a high granite wall – all but blocked the water from view. The parapet had recently acquired a cushion of snow, and the arm of a floating crane protruded from the depths beyond, like a well sweep. I stood and watched, convinced that any moment now it would start bowing, or at least turn, but it never did.

I'm only forty-five, but after a head injury three years or so ago – I slipped on ice near a bus stop and fell – I began having blackouts. Two or three times a year I'd leave home and not come back. My family would go from morgue to morgue, queue up in police stations, be told they'd never see me again, but then, after several weeks, sometimes months, I'd eventually turn up, whether in a detention cell somewhere in the South (since childhood I've been drawn to the South, to the sea), with no papers or money, having been arrested for vagrancy, or in one of the local psychiatric clinics. Usually I'd be badly cut and bruised after another beating at the hands of policemen or hospital attendants (I was told I could be troublesome, even violent in that state), or of nameless companions on my wanderings (how I wished I could see myself, at least once, at such moments). Then I'd be laid up in bed at home for weeks at a time, but I'd always recover in the end: I have a strong constitution. Even my memory would return, though at first I could remember neither my Christian name nor my surname.

For the time being, then, everything came back to me, and I found it neither hard nor painful – as if I were unspooling a length of thread. I could see how much my mother and aunt enjoyed talking to me, recalling what had happened, and once again I felt like a child whose recovery after a serious illness fills everyone around him with joy – how nice to see him get better. But the outlook was bleak: according to the doctors, people like me ended up murdered by criminals or crippled so badly they never walked again, while a third group – the police tried to avoid having anything to do with us – would go missing for a year or more; and above all, after each new episode my memory would be slower and less likely to recover until, in the end, complete amnesia beckoned. It was this terrifying prospect that had brought me to the hospital to see Kronfeld.

On the other side of the door, in the ward, a new drug was being tested, a drug said to have a radical, even miraculous effect on the circulation of blood in the brain (my illness was directly linked to the fact that many vessels had been damaged by my fall and the blood no longer flowed through them). This new medication was my lifeline: I understood that. And yet that hour, hour and a bit, of waiting for the ward round to finish was torture. I hadn't really been there all that long, forgotten in the ante-room, and it wasn't really so frightening – lifts came and went, people kept flitting past behind glass doors, I could have called out, asked someone to open up, even, if it came to it, shouted, and the doctor would have interrupted his ward round and come – but I'd worn myself out to such an extent over recent months that I had no strength left.

For the first year or two I put a brave face on my illness and even managed to see the funny side, joking about the cathartic benefits of memory loss: all the scum and dross was being washed away, leaving me pure again, like a babe. And in fact, that's precisely how it was. Besides, I was having a far easier time of it than many with similar problems; I recovered my memory quickly enough, with no loss of intellectual function. Perhaps I had my mother to thank – every day she fed me endless vitamins – but whatever the reason, my thinking was unaffected. In short, life, even after my fall, was perfectly tolerable, but then, all at once, exhaustion set in. I found myself waiting for the next episode, the next attack, trying to anticipate it, feeling ever more scared; a few months like that and I soon reached breaking-point. The doctors said I mustn't tire myself out, and I did whatever they told me to do: reined myself in, freely acknowledged that this or that was too much for me, that I hadn't the strength, until I suddenly realized: I'd become an old man.

I was still just about clinging on when several people dear to me passed away all at once, dying such lonely deaths that it was as if I were the only person they had. This human solitude, this obligation I now felt to remember them all, almost to rescue them all, was too much, and I cracked. I was found somewhere beyond Tula, at a station, mugged and beaten to a pulp, and it was a month before I was identified and brought back to Moscow.

It took me another six months to recover: my kidneys had

been damaged, albeit not too severely, and the doctor who'd treated me all through my illness and knew me better than I knew myself said that at first, after this latest episode, I didn't want to come back, didn't want to remember. I'd lost so much that now I just wanted to remain as I was, without memory. Previously, he said, I'd been an incorrigible optimist, as if all this were nothing serious, some misunderstanding, but now he could see that my brain had adapted, as it were, to the illness, learned to take advantage of it, to make itself at home in it, and treating me would be far more difficult, because I myself was no longer on his side. And there was something else. I understood that pills would not be the end of the story, that sooner or later, unless someone killed me first, I'd end up on a dementia ward, hardly the nicest place in the world. I suddenly took in the prospect that the doctors had been dangling before me for some time: senility, and soon – for that was precisely where my illness was headed. Previously, the notion of 'me among the morons' had merely served to amuse me, and I'd even used it to amuse others. I was only forty-five.

Now, in touching distance of my hospital bed and with nowhere else to go – I'd forced myself to come here, after all – I suddenly understood that step by step I was becoming someone to whom you could do whatever you wanted. Yet only recently, until the last attack, none of this had scared me: neither the hospital, nor complete dependence on attendants and doctors, nor even death among old men enjoying their second childhood. Oblivion was all I'd feared. Memory was my sore spot and I feared only that which was directly linked to it. It was the most I could manage.

I suppose that right from the beginning of the illness, from the very first attacks, my life had begun to close in on itself, to turn backwards. I increasingly valued that which had already happened, which I had already lived through. Memory had become the centre of my world, and I would lose it so quickly, in a flash, that it resembled nothing so much as death. Death was waiting behind me, not in front of me, and almost instinctively I too set off in that direction – back, to the past. This about-turn, this redirection of my life backwards, upstream – something which had become ever more obvious both to me and to those close to me – was not, as I initially feared, an empty and pointless repetition of what had gone before. For whatever reason, perhaps because I was coming at it from the other end, this life was completely different and completely different things mattered in it. I discovered almost immediately that so much of what I'd lived through I'd lived through provisionally, without joining the dots, with no real comprehension or appreciation. But now it was all coming back to me.

This was, of course, a lavish gift. For a good few years I drew from it day in, day out, and it never diminished; in fact, it grew, and there were times when I almost rejoiced at my illness. My doctor was right: I'd adapted, got used to it, accepted it with barely a murmur. And yet, something within me still longed for a return to ordinary life, a bulwark of sorts, and it was there that the idea was hatched – perhaps it was my doctor, knowing the reasons for my breakdown, who prompted it – that I didn't actually need my memory, that I could just as well do without it (the months or more I'd spent in a state of oblivion had shown me as much), but I should, and above all, still could, preserve the memory of those whom only I had known or, at any rate, whom only I was prepared to remember. In real life the shoots of altruism are not so numerous for me not to have seized on this idea: the duty I had to remember all these people, to prolong them, at least for the duration of my own life. It became the banner under which I continued to fight my illness. There was also one other story from the distant past that played its role here.

*

When I was twelve, I took communion for the first time – on May 3, my name day. A week or so after this event, an event I still fondly remember in its every detail, I happened to hear a conversation between my father and one of his friends about a recent article on the subject of Ivan the Terrible's 'Memorial Book of the Disgraced'. I remember how astonished I was by the very idea, the very possibility of such a Memorial Book. For thirty years a human being murders other human beings without compunction and now, on his death-bed, he begins to recall them and to set aside a certain amount of money for prayers in their memory. Some he recalls himself, others are recalled by his accomplices, but there are many, needless to say, they can't recall: they didn't even know their names when they killed them. And so, Ivan leaves money for monks to remember even those whom, as he writes, "You know Yourself, Lord."

The night after that conversation a strange thought occurred to me: a man can kill another man, even an innocent, sinless man, precisely because there is such a thing as Resurrection, because there is someone to recall and resurrect the victim. And I suddenly understood another thing, too: death is a return to God, a return after long and difficult trials, after responsibility and freedom of will. Father always liked to talk to me about such things, ever since I was seven. It was like returning from adulthood to childhood, or even to the maternal womb, as if such a return were really possible. And above all, for the Lord nothing was in vain, nothing vanished, nothing was lost, and

He wanted the same for us too, as people.

That was the conclusion I drew from the Memorial Book, but why, and for what possible purpose, the memory of each victim should remain on earth, why their names should have been recorded, instead of simply saying about all of them equally, "You know them Yourself, Lord," was beyond my understanding, and to some extent still is. At the time I merely thought, "Will we really all remain here? Will we really not burn in the flames or drown in the waters? Is it really impossible for us, too, to be killed off for good?"

By the time I'm describing, I'd already loved Christ for many years, for as long as I could remember, and, strange though it sounds, my love for Him did not remotely interfere with my love for Lenin. I can't name the exact year when I first learned about Christ, learned of His sufferings and martyr's death, but I loved Him at once, loved Him with all my soul, my flesh, my blood, my thoughts, and it seemed to me that this was how it had always been, that I'd always known Him and loved Him, and that He had always been with me.

Since then I've heard many sensible arguments about the impossibility of loving Lenin and Christ at the same time (it's either one or the other), about how Lenin himself didn't like, and even hated, Christ, and that Christ, were He to have met Lenin on His way, would hardly have taken a shine to him either. But that's their business, and it shouldn't even concern me. Laugh all you like, but I really do love Lenin and I really do love Christ, and I believe Christ, just as I believe Lenin, and I thank God for giving me this gift of love, and for giving me that other gift – the gift of analysing, changing my mind, asking why I love him, and does he deserve my love anyway? – to a much lesser degree.

Only one thing clouded my love for Christ during

my childhood: the thought that I was too young and too untouched by sin to keep turning to Him, though I wanted to do so constantly, that I shouldn't even pray too often, since by doing so I was depriving other people of Him, people far worse off than me. I knew there were many such people, far more than there were cheerful and happy ones, but my own childhood contained so little evil and grief that I couldn't really understand those unfortunate souls whose one hope was Christ, and the person who helped me, strangely enough, was Ivan the Terrible.

Every day after that conversation about the Memorial Book, sometimes many times a day, I would imagine his death, or rather play it out in my own mind. I would picture this dreadful man on his death-bed, repenting of his deeds before God, understanding that his victims were innocent. He'd be crying, begging God for mercy and forgiveness, confessing, donating money for the memory of those he murdered, while himself realizing perfectly well that the scales could not be balanced. He'd been granted only one ability in life – to work evil, to kill thousands upon thousands. Resurrecting even a single one was beyond him.

How much would he have given now to save at least one of his victims? At the very least, he'd have renounced his right to kill without a second thought – but alas! For the first time ever he sees himself in all his foulness, in all his sin, and it's like a celebration: of his own repentance, of faith in God and fear before Him, before His might. There's humility here, and trepidation, and not because he fears eternal damnation – at first, perhaps, he does not even think of it –but simply because he understands the full greatness and righteousness of God, and his own complete worthlessness.

I pictured Ivan's torments to myself very vividly, with great relish, and these inventions, I suppose, were what I understood by Christianity; at any rate, they were the most striking feature of whatever I knew about faith at that time. Ivan's prayers and appeals to God were more colourful and more convincing than my own, and when I prayed it was usually not for me, but for him, and often in his name. I enjoyed it and believed that I, a child, a pure soul, would save him, rescue him from Hell, but there was also another, more important reason: the idea had lodged itself in my mind that repentance was commensurate with sin, and to the extent that I could not compare with Ivan in evil, nor could I compare with him in repentance and faith.

These childhood prayers left their mark, of course, and, I dare say, more than a mark. They've kept their hold on me to this day. Even now, when, setting out on this labour, I stop to consider what to call these notes of mine, the first thing that comes to mind is that Old Russian genre, the Lament. What follows, I expect, will also be a lament, a lament for people I knew and loved. For people who, sad to say, died before their time, leaving nothing behind except in my memory. And when I go too, so will my memories. Not one of their lives fell into place; in none of them was there much love, joy or, at times, even meaning; and not one of these people accomplished much while they still could. We like to say that a peaceful death is granted only to those who've fulfilled themselves – they hadn't. They went through agony before dying and departed in sorrow. Dying, they felt hard done by, disgraced, cheated. So, in memory of my childhood, I have every right to call this my own 'Memorial Book of the Disgraced'.

*

19

The first person I want to include is Nikolai Petrovich Pastukhov, a former public prosecutor in Moscow. We met about seven years ago, on the road. We were both on our way back from Kiev to Moscow, travelling first-class in an unbearably hot two-berth compartment. The train, as usual, was running hours behind schedule, and with nothing better to do we finally got talking as we were nearing Moscow. Pastukhov had a friend, dead for some years, who'd also been a prosecutor. They'd studied and risen up the ranks together, neither trying to get ahead of the other; they'd treated each other like brothers, as Pastukhov put it, and the older they got, the closer they became. That friend – his name was Savin – had got married, second time round, to a woman twenty years younger than himself.

'Her father was in trade, was falsely accused and received almost the maximum sentence. But Lena, his daughter, made a nuisance of herself, and the case ended up on Savin's desk. The girl was nothing short of heroic: she wasn't even eighteen, there wasn't a penny in the house, all their property had been confiscated, and she'd been told by every half-competent lawyer that there was nothing they could do (her mother had died giving birth, so her father was the only family she had). Savin immediately warmed to her. Important people were mixed up in the case, and helping her was no simple matter. But together they almost rescued him. They got his sentence reduced first to five years, then to three, in time for the next amnesty, and then, just a month before the amnesty, he died. Heart failure, the girl was told, but Savin learned through his channels that he'd been beaten to death by his cellmates.

'Lena lived only for her father, to save him, to bring him back; now, nothing mattered. Up until the day when Savin finally made up his mind to propose to her, she hadn't left the house for two months. He'd fed her like a nurse, even cooked for her. Lena had no one but him, and he was a loner himself; in short, she agreed. They'd known each other for about eighteen months, more than enough for Lena to grow fond of him – she was a kind, affectionate sort of girl – and there was something else as well: he was the same age as her father, and even resembled him, or so Savin told me (I never saw Lena's dad). It seems unlikely she loved him to begin with, but she loved him later and loved him deeply – there's no doubt about that.

'They had a good life together – surprisingly good, in fact – until the last two years. He already sensed that he was seriously ill, though he didn't know the cause, or how long he had left. He understood, of course, that he'd die well before her, but what suddenly mattered to him most was not what sort of wife she'd been to him, but how she'd live without him once he'd died – this beautiful young woman (he only ever thought about her now in this peculiarly detached way). Savin, I believe, was overwhelmed by the thought that he'd be gone and Lena would remain. I'm sure he often wondered who she'd sleep with and who she'd marry, but that wasn't the point; he didn't intend to get in her way, he just needed to know how she'd get on without him and how any of this was possible: her still here, and him gone.

'Later, when he already knew he had cancer and a year left to live – eighteen months at most – there was only one thing he could talk about: what she'd do once she'd buried him. Everything else was secondary, and even the thought of his own death would only occur to him now as the precondition for her separate life. He spent his last months hastening his own end, refusing all medication except painkillers.

'His wife knew what he was thinking, of course, and Savin

seems to have succeeded in infecting her with his madness. At any rate, whenever I went to see them Lena was just as incapable of talking about anything else and kept trying to persuade me that Savin was wrong to want to know what would happen to her later, and that if he started following her every move from the other side it would make her life impossible, intolerable: how can you live a normal life when your ex-husband – your dead ex-husband, at that – is constantly spying on you?

'So he was already dead for her as well, and she too was living that future life; she even spoke about him in the past tense. Only when I came by to visit Savin did she remember he was still alive and set about trying to win my support. She was always on edge, though superficially her behaviour was reasonable enough; you could see how careful she was with her words, how keen she was to make a favourable impression. She'd tell me she'd been a good wife to him, loyal and caring, that she'd never once betrayed him, even though he was a difficult man and twenty years older. But the moment he was dead and buried, her obligations towards him would cease: you could hardly expect her to go on living for him and him alone. She insisted that I, his very best friend, explain this to him and convince him that he was wrong.

'I'd tell her that Savin was dying, that he had only weeks left to live, that you can't explain anything to anyone on their death-bed, that it would be disgraceful to talk to him about this now; he'd die and she could do as she pleased. But Lena wasn't taking much in any more. She'd tell me who she would sleep with, what offers she'd had: trips to the Caucasus, fur coats, precious jewels – all true, of course; she was beautiful, after all. Once she even put her arms round me, kissed me on the lips and drew me to the sofa, when Savin was wide awake and the door to his room stood open. I don't think Lena had opened it on purpose, or that there was any kind of plan here: him not yet dead, and her sleeping with his friend before his very eyes. It was all much simpler than that – she'd long ceased to think of Savin as a living being, much less a man, and she wanted to buy me off, bribe me to ensure that he didn't get in her way after he died. Lena, of course, already hated him – as a dead man, I mean – but he still loved her, reached out to her, kept trying to take her hand and wouldn't let go. He wasn't really asking her for anything; perhaps he just wanted to know, as a father (for he wasn't just a husband to Lena: he'd taken the place of her dad as well), how she'd get on without him.'

At that point, the train stopped once more. I asked Pastukhov: 'And then what? She was right, wasn't she? And even if she wasn't, you could hardly force her to lie down next to him in his grave.'

'Yes,' he agreed, 'and the first thing Lena did when Savin died was to draw up her will, saying that she should be buried in a different cemetery entirely, next to her mother.'

In Moscow, Pastukhov and I continued to meet regularly, if infrequently. I saw how attached he'd become to me, how offended he was if I didn't call or drop in, and this became especially obvious during his last year, after he retired. Yet the thought of how much I meant to Pastukhov never even crossed my mind. I could see he was lonely, since the only name that ever seemed to come up in our conversations was Savin's, yet for some reason I was completely convinced that he'd remained on close terms with his old colleagues. Then, one morning, I got a call from Pastukhov's ninety-year-old mother, who told me that he'd suddenly died overnight.

This took my by complete surprise, and I recall the bewilderment in her voice as well. She just couldn't understand it: hardly ever been ill, thirty years her junior, retired – so much life still ahead of him. (Those may not have been her exact words, of course, and there was certainly no irony in them, just surprise.) I started bumbling away in reply, when she suddenly said that I was his only friend and that even when he was dying the only person he talked to her about was me, and the only people he ever mentioned were me and Savin – and Savin, of course, was dead.

She also told me that Pastukhov had named me his executor, so she was obliged to hand over his papers to me and leave me to it. At the time I just couldn't believe that Pastukhov had no one else in the world, but the funeral put an end to my doubts. There were seven of us: his mother, myself, a trade union representative from the office where he'd worked and paid his Party dues, and four trainees from the same place to carry the coffin.

After that first conversation on the train about Savin's wife, her name often cropped up during our subsequent meetings. On two or three occasions, when something unexpected happened in Lena's life and Pastukhov didn't know what to do, he came to me for advice and we'd have a long chat. All in all, I had a pretty good idea of the shape her life had taken since Savin's death. I knew, for example, that a few days before Savin died, Pastukhov had given his word not only to help Lena and do everything he could to see that she was comfortable, but also to keep Savin up to date with her life. Every week, at a regular hour, Pastukhov would make a special trip to Savin's grave.

Then the visits to the cemetery suddenly ceased, or at any rate became rare and non-compulsory. When Pastukhov suddenly arranged a meeting with me for the precise day and time when he used to see Savin, I asked him why. He said that for several months already he'd been going to Savin only on anniversaries and only for his own sake; after all, everything he'd promised Savin was happening anyway, without him. Six months before this conversation he'd told me that Lena was happily married, that her husband treated her like a queen. He was in trade, just like her father, and Lena felt happy to be among her own crowd; he hadn't seen her looking so beautiful for years. Pastukhov was clearly pleased and even relieved to have carried out this part of Savin's will: Lena was comfortable.

That time we got talking about trade and the corruption that was plaguing it from top to bottom. The trials of the directors of Moscow's largest food stores were already into their second year, and Pastukhov, who was involved in the investigation, knew all the ins and outs. He was extremely pessimistic about the whole affair: it was impossible not to steal if you wanted to survive, but the worst thing was that the most competent people were all at the top – lock them up and everything would fall to pieces. As a result, far more would be lost than was being siphoned off now. He mentioned that Lena's new husband was also mixed up in one of the cases, though only a little. He was one of the competent ones, and he didn't actually take all that much for a man in his position, so it was unlikely he'd end up in jail. But Pastukhov would help him just in case, in memory of Savin; what's more, he'd do so with a clean conscience, because in our lousy conditions Lena's husband did more good than harm.

Things weren't so simple, though. Pastukhov was a stickler for rules, a real fanatic, and having to break the law for Savin's sake, having to hush up this case without any justification at all, did not appeal to him in the slightest. True, Pastukhov and the trader were getting on wonderfully at that point – just as they had at the beginning of their acquaintance. During the first few weeks of Lena's new marriage, Pastukhov was a frequent guest at their home, as if in the place of her father; once, the three of them even made a trip to Savin's grave together, but Pastukhov's relationship with Lena soon took a turn for the worse. It's not hard to see why: she knew all about the obligations he'd taken on towards Savin, and having to see this man day in, day out, while he followed you and squealed on you, was hardly pleasant. She insisted many times that her husband kick Pastukhov out of their home, but the trader seemed to know that he might need Pastukhov one day, and quickly changed the subject.

Pastukhov told me that he'd let him in on all the circumstances relating to Savin's death just as soon as he and Lena had got together, but I can't imagine the trader immediately agreeing to help, and certainly not of his own free will. Essentially, Lena had begun a completely different life since their marriage, and the only person who could supply regular reports about this life for Savin was him, her new husband. Pastukhov spent a long time trying to make him understand how crucial it was for him, Pastukhov, that his closest friend's request be carried out, trying to persuade him that Savin was entitled to this, as Lena's first husband, and that it was only right, by any moral criteria, that a dying man's last request be heeded. But the trader refused to understand him, was deaf to every argument, and merely repeated that he knew how much he owed Pastukhov, that he was ready to go to great lengths for his sake, but that he wasn't prepared to share the intimate details of his married life with an outsider.

At a certain point, Pastukhov – in whose apartment the conversation was taking place – miscalculated and pressed him too far. After leaving him, Lena's husband, who was virtually teetotal, hit the bottle and had to be escorted home. He spent half the night swearing and calling his wife a 'slut'.

'Do you know what your police chums want from me?!' he yelled at her, before breaking down in tears; after all, his friends had warned him never to welcome a prosecutor into his family. She was crying too, kissing his hands, saying that she would tell Savin everything herself, that they wouldn't breathe a word to anyone, and that there was no need for him to be scared of Pastukhov – he wouldn't dare do a thing. She managed to reassure him, and he fell asleep.

She really did start going off to the cemetery on her own, but then Pastukhov said that she shouldn't, that it was hard on everyone, and that he felt sorry for Savin in particular: why did he need to know how much she hated him? This conversation took place just before Pastukhov went away on holiday, so it was only much later that I found out that Lena's husband, on hearing from her that Pastukhov would be the one visiting the grave again, gathered his things and left without a word. Lena thought that was that, and about time too. She was tired. But two weeks later – Pastukhov was still away on holiday – the trader came back: he was madly in love with her and realized he couldn't leave her, come what may.

Returning to Moscow, Pastukhov found a broken man, ready to agree to anything. He explained to me once that this is what happens during investigations as well: the accused breaks down all at once, the moment you pierce his shell in that one and only spot; the shell disintegrates and before you sits a man literally begging to confess.

'He was scared I might have him locked up, of course,' said Pastukhov. 'He'd known that before as well and he'd acted bravely enough then, but now he'd realized he couldn't live without her and that if he was put away he'd lose her, so he got scared. It was really her who broke him, not me.'

And another thing: he'd suddenly begun to understand Savin.

After all, it was the same situation – he'd be gone and she'd remain. Pastukhov told me that the phone rang the moment he walked through the door and he immediately guessed who it was. After saying hello, Lena's husband told him he'd been calling every hour for the last day, and then, plunging straight in, started telling him all about Savin, repeating what Pastukhov himself had said earlier, only putting it better. That Savin had made a woman of Lena, and nothing would ever change this fact, whatever happened afterwards. That Lena and Savin had lived an entire life together, which couldn't be crossed out just like that, at one stroke. That he understood now what Savin meant to Lena, and Lena understood what Savin meant to her, and that from now on he would stop encouraging her when she pretended that there had never been anything between them. Naturally, he would visit the cemetery conscientiously, but the reason he was calling now was to discuss the urgent matter of what he should say to Savin, so that Savin and Pastukhov would permit him 'to carry on enjoying Lena'.

'What do you think?' he kept asking. 'Is it worth me telling Savin about this or that?…'

'You could hardly discuss such things on the phone,' Pastukhov told me, 'so the next day he came round and we went through it all in detail.'

Much later, I asked Pastukhov whether he'd checked up on Lena's husband. Three times, he said, though there was no real need: they were still meeting up regularly and it was obvious from his behaviour that their agreement was being honoured in full.

'Once you've broken a person,' Pastukhov would say, 'they're no longer capable of lies, only of trivial deception. They have a constant urge to confess, whether or not it's appropriate, and they're only too ready to bare their souls to the first person they meet. It would seem that he himself told Lena about his visits to Savin's grave (until then, she'd been convinced for some reason that I'd left them in peace). What's certain is that one way or another she discovered that her husband was informing on her and she wasn't about to forgive him. She thought of breaking up with him – Lena knew her own worth and could easily have found someone no worse and no poorer – but by this point Savin or me (it amounts to the same thing) had begun to frighten her, and she'd realized she couldn't get rid of us just like that. Her husband knew this too, knew that in a sense we were saving Lena for him; but it wasn't so much that he felt indebted to me, more that he could no longer do without Savin. He complained to Savin about Lena, sought his sympathy, got everything off his chest, and felt better for it afterwards.'

Savin was only too happy to share the pain and hurt which Lena dispensed so freely, and their bond grew stronger with each passing day. There was one period, though, when the trader overstepped the mark. Lena had begun to cheat on him. She'd always been a free spirit, blind to convention, and the need to have an independent life, hidden from her husband and Savin, had developed into an obsession – a way of trying to save herself and of getting away from the pair of them. It would seem that she consciously acted in such a way as to make it exceptionally unpleasant for them to encroach on this separate life of hers. Yet, despite her various subterfuges, her husband soon learned the details of her adulteries, and on one occasion he even walked in on her and her lover. Armed with all this intelligence, he'd go straight off to Savin and tell him every last detail, however sordid. He evidently wanted to intimate that the only person being betrayed here was Savin, while he was neither here nor there – just a private detective.

'The trader quickly acquired a taste for surveillance. Detective work, after all, is terribly addictive: who doesn't want to get to the bottom of what others are doing their damnedest to hide from you? And anyway, he wasn't doing this for himself, as it were, but for me and Savin,' said Pastukhov, 'and this, of course, resolved many ethical dilemmas.'

He carried on like that for two months or so, and then (without Pastukhov even needing to step in) suddenly came to his senses. At bottom, Lena's husband was a decent enough man and he soon realized he was out of line; whatever he called himself – a *locum tenens*, a temporary replacement, or just a pleasure-seeker – she wasn't just cheating on Savin, she was cheating on him as well. But the key point was this: he and Savin really were drawing closer and closer year by year, needing each other more and more, and to say that he had become an extension of Savin (I'd heard Pastukhov say similar things) would not, I believe, be a great exaggeration; they really did seem to have merged into one.

There's no doubt that for Lena's husband this outcome was nothing short of providential, but it wasn't clear whether he himself understood this, and now, when Pastukhov had died, I was alarmed by the thought that he would waste no time in destroying everything. I was scared – very scared – that it would fall to me, as the executor of Pastukhov's will, to try to prop up the construction he'd built through blackmail and threats. This was the last thing I wanted; I've always tried to avoid responsibility, always been unable and unwilling to tell people what to do, and besides, I was already ill by then, so I probably wasn't up to it anyway. And there was one other thing troubling me. Despite all his efforts, Pastukhov had failed to get Lena to rewrite her will and agree to be buried with Savin. So this, too, might fall to me, and I hadn't the slightest idea of how to talk her into it.

Just as well, then, that Pastukhov appeared to know my limitations as well as I did: stuck to the bulging envelope containing Lena's husband's file was a note addressed to me requesting that the envelope be destroyed, since it was no longer required, and, furthermore, that it not be read, barring exceptional circumstances (this last phrase was underlined). And indeed, Lena's relations with her husband did not seem to change with Pastukhov's death; in fact, nothing changed at all. He continued, at any rate, to make weekly trips to Savin's grave.

I'm fairly certain that Pastukhov knew all too well how durable the edifice he'd created would prove: it was precisely the durability and stability of this strange love triangle that must have led him to the thought that there was in all this something exceptionally important and just. So important that it could justify both his own violation of the law and the fact that Lena and her husband were, beyond all doubt, deeply unhappy people. He thought that here, perhaps, one could find the key by which to understand the mutual obligations of husbands and wives, the law which imparts equilibrium and harmony to their relations. Pastukhov was very influenced by the fact that he'd never been married, so he had no personal stake in the matter and, as befits a lawyer, could take a calm, impartial, independent view of all these questions. He saw things from the outside – the only way of seeing them as they are.

Similar justifications of his right to formulate a law on marriage – often very subtle ones and, as far I could tell, technically irreproachable – were to be found all over Pastukhov's papers and I anticipated that he must have carried most of his work on the law to completion. All I discovered, however, were a few not especially original propositions. Still, it wasn't hard to grasp from them what Pastukhov wanted. He clearly believed in life after death, though for him it played a subservient, dependent role. People continued to watch us from there, and especially the life of their family, which absorbed them, touched them and moved them just as much as before, but they could no longer influence it in any way.

That being the case, Pastukhov thought, the dead possess one inalienable right: to know. Nothing, however bad or good, should be concealed from them. He also wrote that the first marriage is sacred, that those who enter into it, whatever may happen to them subsequently, ought to be buried in the same grave when they die; then, interrupting his text, he mourned the fact that he would not be able to ensure the same for Savin. He recognized that a widow's rights should not be limited, but he thought that if a woman was aware that her husband knew the details of her life and that she would be lying next to him after her death, she would restrain herself. And that was about all.

Sorting through Pastukhov's archive, I was expecting revelations, perhaps because, in fact almost certainly because, I felt guilty towards him – we met up far too rarely. Needless to say, I was disappointed by what I found. Only later, after quite some time, did I realize how little Pastukhov actually wanted: all that mattered to him was that I, or somebody, knew what he'd been thinking about and then went on thinking about it for themselves and remembered him. The whole point was that the labour had only been started; the dots were not yet joined. All he'd wanted to do for the time being was to bring me into his game, to explain its rules, its laws, and then we'd have sat down together and started discussing the details, thinking and talking it over. We'd have taken our time, gone into everything thoroughly, as the gravity and importance of the topic required. He didn't even mind this labour being put on hold, for years and years, because for as long as the labour was not completed I would keep remembering. And there was something else: he loved Savin.

*

The second person I want to enter into my Memorial Book is Vera Nikolayevna Rozhdestvenskaya. She was the wife of my grandfather's brother – if there's a shorter way of saying that, I'm afraid I don't know it – and three years ago four volumes of her memoirs fell into my hands. At the time it didn't even occur to me that she might still be alive, or indeed anybody else from their generation. Not long before then I had, for very specific reasons, begun taking an interest in the history of my family, its origins, occupations, character. This happened shortly after the death of my father and, as I now see, was an attempt to appropriate, along with the rest of his legacy, everything that tied him to his relatives. My father's death had snapped thousands of lines and bonds, suddenly cutting me off from the past.

My father, when he was alive, never said much about his childhood, his father, his mother, or his relatives in general. Sometimes this would annoy me, and I'd badger him to tell me about this or that, though on the whole I understood that he was simply looking out for me: so many dreadful and unforgivable things had happened, and I was only a child. I've no doubt I'd do exactly the same if I had children, but when he died and when, after the funeral, I began to understand my new place in the world – his place, essentially – and make myself at home there, it turned out that I was a kind of impostor. There wasn't even anyone to tell me who I was or where I'd come from.

For a long time all efforts to establish anything concrete about my family led nowhere; either there was a conspiracy or it really was the case that no one knew anything about it. I'd unsuccessfully interrogated all my distant relations (all my close ones had already died), everyone I thought might know something, when suddenly I got a phone call from a second cousin of my father. She told me about a certain Vera Nikolayevna Rozhdestvenskaya, still with us: if anyone knew about us, it was her, and if I wanted, she could try speaking to Vera Nikolayevna's daughter to arrange a visit. There was only one problem: Vera Nikolayevna had been in poor health recently and it would be hard to make conversation with her. Three days later this aunt called back, dictated the address to me and said they were expecting me the very next evening.

Between Kurskaya and Taganskaya metro stations, on the side of the Garden Ring closest to the centre, on sunken ground behind a big block of flats used by scholars – there were stairs leading down – was the five-storey Khrushchev-era prefab I needed. My aunt had described both the route and the major landmarks in great detail, and with total accuracy, but I still managed to get lost and arrive half an hour late. I was met at the door by Vera Nikolayevna's daughter, Anya, and an old, affectionate collie called Nastya. After making my apologies, I learned that this was the fourth building in which they'd lived, all four of them situated on one and the same spot. First, there was a log hut here, then a large building also made of wood, then a stone house for the clergy of the two nearest churches, and now the prefab from which they were currently being evicted – only they had no desire to leave their neighbourhood and this was already the third year they'd been holding out.

Anya told me all this while I was still taking off my coat and shoes; then she showed me through to her own room and started bemoaning the fact that her mother had been ill since the summer and found it difficult to be around strangers, or indeed anyone she didn't know well. I could see that Anya regretted having invited me over and didn't know what to do about it. Frankly, this was the first time I'd ever found myself in such a situation. Getting up and leaving without even seeing Vera Nikolayevna seemed stupid, although it wasn't hard to guess the nature of her illness: Vera Nikolayevna was almost certainly senile, and why my aunt hadn't just told me straight out, without resorting to euphemism, was beyond me.

Anya and I seemed to understand each other without words: no sooner did it occur to me that Vera Nikolayevna was senile than she immediately abandoned the subject of abstract ailments and, almost guiltily, rushed to say what a wonderful memory her mother used to have, like many in the family line. Besides, Mama, like her own mother, had been brought up to keep a diary from the age of five, to record every little thing, every single day. So she never forgot anything, never lost anything; whatever she'd live through stayed with her.

When, three years earlier, Mama turned eighty, she decided to write her memoirs, and for some unknown reason Anya gave her support to the idea, although it was clearly a bad one. After all, the diaries had survived, and any unmediated impression is inevitably fresher and more sincere than a memory that's been polished and touched up. But she only realized this later; at the time, she strongly encouraged her mother, who managed to write four whole volumes before falling ill. It was these volumes that devoured her memory. Her family eventually noticed that no sooner did Mama write down some episode or other from her life than she immediately forgot it, or rather, she remembered it very vaguely, as if through a haze.

'It makes sense, I suppose,' Anya explained. 'Everything that hadn't ended up in the diaries was stored in Mama's head, and she knew that it would all just die if she forgot it, or, if you like, wouldn't even be born; but now she had no need to remember anything.'

Then Anya started telling me what a hard and terrifying life Mama had had, but she'd kept her dignity and managed to bring up three daughters single-handedly. It was obvious that Anya loved her very much, that she was proud of her and was afraid I'd ruin everything. I was an alien presence in their home, capable, in a matter of hours, of wrecking everything they'd been through, their whole life together. From the outside, nothing would change, yet, were Anya to look at her mother even once through my eyes, everything would become false and insincere. For me, the visit had become completely pointless: Vera Nikolayevna was in no fit state to tell me much, and in any case four volumes of memoirs were much more valuable than any conversation. I was just about to ask for them, when Anya suddenly decided that her love for her mother should not fear being tested: she got up and said in a firm voice that we'd kept her waiting long enough.

After all I'd been told, the impression Vera Nikolayevna made on me was very favourable. She was slim, straight-backed and, despite her eighty years, there was no mistaking her breeding. Before me sat a truly beautiful old woman, whose only flaw, most visible when she threw back her head, was a large, dangling goitre. At first, I didn't even realize she was unwell.

I was introduced and welcomed very warmly, like an old friend. Anya served tea and brought in a beautiful pie which, as she stressed more than once, had been baked by Vera

Nikolayevna herself in my honour. She was always trying to say nice things to her mother, and wanted me to follow suit. So I praised the pie after every mouthful; and actually, it was perfectly edible.

It was a hard life, of course, for Anya. Later, once I'd convinced her that I really was enjoying myself – by then, Vera Nikolayevna was already at the piano, playing her favourite waltzes ('The Waves of the Amur', 'On the Hills of Manchuria') and reminiscing about her childhood and the Russo-Japanese War – she suddenly said that Mama had always been an excellent cook and still tried to keep her hand in now, only she'd get the sugar and salt mixed up, so Anya would have to throw everything into the bin and start all over again.

Just how serious Vera Nikolayevna's illness actually was became apparent only after an hour, when she tired and began repeating herself and getting confused. Before then she'd been speaking perfectly normally and there was nothing untoward about her tone or facial expression; yet our conversation was peculiar all the same. She spoke about my father with great enthusiasm and vividly remembered the time they first met, on New Year's Eve, which was always our family's favourite holiday, celebrated as lavishly as possible. Vera Nikolayevna recalled the fir tree, the decorations and the presents received by others and even by her, so soon after being made welcome in the home.

That great-uncle, her husband, loved my father very much; they were almost the same age. My father was the most light-hearted and jovial member of our far from jovial family, and she, following the example of her husband, soon grew fond of him. Even now she spoke of him with rare affection. At the start of our conversation I mentioned that my father had died two months before, but for her the world was closed, complete; the dead and the living were fixed in it once and for all, and there was no place in it for this piece of news.

I soon noticed that Vera Nikolayevna was taking me for my father, even calling me by his name: Andrei, Andryusha. Anya had already realized what was happening and, frightened lest I take offence, tried to correct her mother, to explain that I was Andrei's son and that Andrei himself had recently passed away, but her mother wouldn't accept this, not even from her. Deep down, I didn't mind and told Anya not to worry. Later, I caught myself thinking that I liked being taken for my father; I liked others to see him in me and to recall him so tenderly. Still, I told Vera Nikolayevna once more that my father was dead, but once again I was ignored. Father and I really did look alike, not to mention the fact that the last time Vera Nikolayevna came to our home – back before the war – Father was only a few years older than I am now. To her, news of his death sounded like a not very clever joke: how could he be dead if he was sitting right there in front of her, drinking tea?

All evening long, I put them in one awkward situation after another: first Anya, who didn't want to show me through to see her mother but didn't know how to say so, and now Vera Nikolayevna. She took pleasure in recalling where she and my father had been together, but when I asked separate questions that concerned only Father, she was surprised: she thought I was asking about myself and it must have seemed very strange to her that I remembered so very little and was so very curious. Several times she marvelled at my forgetfulness, before reproaching me: 'Andryusha, do you really not remember?'

Only then did I change the subject. I asked Vera Nikolayevna about her childhood, and she replied with gusto. Secondary school, her first pair of dancing shoes, the dacha and the amateur performances they held there, the boycott of German shops in 1914 and the thoroughbred collie she was given not long before the war – her memories of all these things were sharp, detailed and above all joyful, and I was glad to have got her off the topic of our family. She spoke for twenty minutes or so, until she got stuck on two things, both of which, it was clear, still depressed her. Stumbling on them, she would start repeating the whole story all over again. Usually she would do so word for word, and only when Anya, seemingly forgetting her mother's illness, reproached her for it did she deign to add a few details.

The first story concerned her beloved elder sister, an unusually gifted mezzo-soprano. While still a fourth-year student at the Conservatory, she sang twice at the Bolshoi, and it was thought that a brilliant career lay ahead of her. But in '19, during the famine, her sister went off to the Volga for grain with the Turkish student renting the room next door. Somewhere near Samara both she and the Turk disappeared, or rather, Vera Nikolayevna's father received a certificate six months later confirming her death from typhus in a Samara hospital, but both Vera Nikolayevna and the whole family were convinced that the Turk had abducted her and sold her into a harem in Istanbul. Such things, apparently, were not uncommon at the time. Later, she tried more than once to find some trace of her sister, travelling twice to Samara, but with no success. For her family, this was a shared cross, a shared sin: any of them could have gone in her place.

The second topic to which Vera Nikolayevna kept returning was linked to my great-uncle. They married in '23 and spent fifteen years together, until the end of '37, when my great-uncle was arrested and shot three months later. By common consent, theirs was an unusually happy marriage. She bore her husband three daughters and was madly in love with him; in fact, she undertook the writing of her memoirs for no other reason than to ensure that the story of their love would not be forgotten. All the years spent with my great-uncle were preserved – or rather, ought to have been preserved – inside her with total clarity, because immediately after his arrest and death Vera Nikolayevna's life ended.

From Grozny, where they'd been living and where her husband was in charge of the oilfields, second in size only to those of Baku, she immediately moved with her children to Moscow and literally hid herself away in her parents' home. That previous life in Grozny was not only filled by my great-uncle and her love for him, it was also a life in which she herself had played a worthy role, equal to his. In particular, she'd been one of the organizers of 'Wives of Engineers and Technical Workers (ETW) Are a Great Cultural Force', a movement that had gained exceptional popularity in the thirties. She'd run a host of clubs and societies in Grozny, lectured in the factories and factory schools, and a few months before her husband's arrest was even presented with the Order of the Red Banner of Labour (a rare award at the time) by Kalinin himself in the Kremlin. Because of this, she never took her daughters to Gorky Park, at the entrance to which, almost right up until Stalin's death, hung her portrait with that same award – she feared being recognized and arrested.

Leaving Grozny meant an abrupt and permanent break with that life and all it contained. Despite her university education she spent the rest of her working life as a typist in a run-down office – a difficult, joyless existence in which it was hard to make ends meet. This new life contained nothing that might over-shadow or push back the years she'd spent with my great-uncle.

She and her daughters often went hungry, but she managed

to raise them all the same. She found the strength to do so, she told Anya, only thanks to that other life. Her love for my uncle was as pure as any woman's can be, but one thing troubled her and gave her no peace. She'd been married once before to a high-school teacher, though it only lasted a year and she left him before ever meeting my great-uncle. Now, talking to me with her daughter in the room, she didn't want Anya to find out about the teacher. In fact, she didn't want there to be a single extra man in her life – it was an affront to her love, made her guilty before her husband, as if she hadn't waited for him. To erase this marriage, Vera Nikolayevna pushed her meeting with my great-uncle further and further back in time, until she was no more than a girl. Their affair had begun in the most ordinary way. She was walking her dog not far from her home, on Yauza Boulevard, when she sat down on a bench where my uncle was reading the papers, and they began talking. First she told me she was twenty-one at the time, but with each repetition her age decreased. By the end she was insisting she'd been a mere sixteen.

And here's the main reason I've included the name of Vera Nikolayevna in my Memorial Book. All evening long, she was more than happy to recall the details of her childhood, but when I asked her about my family she gave evasive and reluctant replies about everyone bar my father, saying she couldn't remember much and there was no need for her to do so anyway – after all, she'd written everything down, and Anya would give me her memoirs if I wanted them. Anya did indeed give them to me and I devoured them, volume by volume, in the space of three days. In places they were written stunningly well, in others you could already sense her illness, but that wasn't the point: except for that meeting on Yauza Boulevard, there wasn't a single mention, anywhere, of her husband, of the man in whose memory and for whose sake it had all been written. At Yauza Boulevard the notes broke off; afterwards there was nothing, not a single line.

I've been thinking about this story for some time, but one thing still eludes me: if Vera Nikolayevna is right and whatever is not written down really does drift away and die, then will nothing remain of her love for my great-uncle? And was her belief that the memoirs were complete no more than an exercise in self-defence, a kind of madness? Or is it really the case that somehow, someone – God, perhaps – is preserving the bond between them, and it shall, therefore, be spared, not sink into oblivion?

*

The third person I'm going to write about is Tolstoy. I'd known for some time that I ought to commemorate him, but only now, in the hospital, did I realize I was ready, after a long conversation with two of his disciples, Morozov and Saburov, who, at their teacher's behest, had lived for nine and twelve years respectively in a farming commune in the Altai. But it would be wrong to think that I learnt most of what's written here from them: I learnt the main facts of Tolstoy's life in our block of flats on Pravda Street from our neighbour, Semyon Evgenyevich Kochin (to whom I will shortly return). But only now have I been able to set to work, after meeting them – Tolstoy's followers.

Our conversation, in which many other people took part besides Morozov, Saburov and myself, revolved for a long time around two well-known interpretations of Tolstoyism. One maintained that Lev Tolstoy had created a doctrine so ethically pure and irreproachable that it was simply impossible for it to be put to bad use; the other held that among the cruellest NKVD investigators there was no shortage of former Tolstoyans. Kochin, who in 1936 passed through the hands of just such an investigator in Moscow's Lefortovo Prison, once explained to me how this came about.

'Say what you like, but Tolstoy's disciples are the best people I've ever met. There have been others, of course, who, taken individually and judged on their own terms, were no worse, but if we mean people who bear the same stamp, made good by what they've been taught, then there's no one to touch them, except, perhaps, a few sectarians. And the communes in which they settled were also blessed, though the Tolstoyans wandered off much too far from everyone else; still, they made sure not to burn all their bridges, and for many this became a dreadful temptation. Tolstoy, their teacher, had taken a massive leap in his moral principles, almost completely remaking himself; and so, however voluntary it may have been, his school was still an act of violence against ordinary human nature.

'Essentially, the Tolstoyans pursued almost identical aims to those of the Bolsheviks, though by very different, incompatible means: absolute freedom. You could leave the commune any day you liked and return to it any day you liked, if the commune had no objections. But the fact that the Tolstoyans were remaking themselves – through their communities, their communes – into new people whose refuge was the collective, and the fact that their aims were so similar to those of the communists meant that they quickly made themselves at home in Soviet Russia, as if among family. They'd experienced this new life before and they knew it was beautiful. Under Tolstoy's influence they'd severed their ties with ordinary existence, with all its compromises and weakness, its lies, filth and abasement, and they really had built heaven on earth. Heaven, it turned out, was near at hand, it was attainable, feasible, and above all, there was no need for miracles, no need for God.

'It was this – their previous life in heaven – that was their contribution, their dowry, when they entered the Soviet commune. The reason they joined, or why so many of them joined, was simple: to bring closer the transformation of earth into heaven. The power held by the Bolsheviks, the entire machinery of the State, could hasten the entire process to such a degree that not only they, Tolstoy's disciples, but everyone else would receive a share in the earthly paradise, in which, as in the celestial one, blessings could never diminish, however many you distributed. On the contrary: the more righteous people that joined, the more each of them would have.

'The Tolstoyans who re-entered our life to bring everyone the good news of heaven, to tell us that it was just as the ancient prophets had said it was, and, above all, that it was near at hand – these men who wanted to lead and guide us possessed, if they became investigators, far more inspiration and idealism, far more enthusiasm and ruthlessness, than any others. They had no doubt that they were right, no doubt that those who had fallen into their hands really were common, communal enemies, enemies who were blowing the new collective off its course to heaven. And another thing: these people, who'd already remade themselves once, were disgusted by ordinary life. They too had once clung to it, but they'd managed to make a clean break, and the fact that others continued to hold on to it seemed wrong to them – this was weakness, cowardice, deserving contempt, not pity. In general, those who feel the imperfections of this world most keenly are disinclined to set much store by the lives of others.'

Tolstoy, said Kochin, when creating his doctrine of

goodness, happiness and justice, failed to notice that if he wanted to attain them fully, without compromise, such as only saints can achieve, he should either be God or go away for ever and live on his own. In the past, people seeking peace and solitude used to go off to the desert, then later the monastery, and this made perfect sense.

There used to be a rule, observed by some if not all, that when a man was intending to abandon 'the world' for the monastery he had to obtain the consent of his family first, because to choose a sinless life by causing pain and grief to your loved ones is itself a sin – good must not be the cause of evil. But times changed, and fewer people chose the monastic life. Meanwhile, attempting to turn a new page while changing nothing around you turned everything into a lie; so it had always been, and so it would remain. To avoid this lie, people who remained in the world had only one option: to make a clean break with the past, strike it out of their life, erase it for its imperfection. A man leaving for the monastery can leave his past at the same time; not so the man who remains. Yet neither have the right to touch the past, if it is not theirs alone.

A man holds no power over another man's past, Kochin would say; or rather, even if he does have this power, he cannot and must not use it. It's wrong to destroy a past shared with others, wrong to clear a space for a new truth. And another thing: God has arranged things in such a way that the good you want to bring to all will never redeem the evil you bring to those around you. Goodness depends on distance. The good directed at those you love is always greater than the good distributed among all. If you cause pain to your loved ones for the sake of everyone else, the evil will outweigh the good; it's as simple as that.

Of course, it's not easy, Kochin would say, to accept that

you have to leave, that everything you've understood has meaning only for you, that even those closest to you, those you've spent your entire life with, those you've loved, who've borne your children, don't want to share your joy with you, shove it back down your throat, stop up their ears, anything so as not to hear what seems to you most pure, most beautiful, most bountiful, what you dream of giving to everyone, keeping nothing in reserve, knowing that your gift will never run dry, that these are the loaves which, however much you break off, will never diminish – but your loved ones shove piece after piece back down your throat and refuse to understand. So then the practical fulfilment of the idea begins. Why do they reject something so beautiful? Why won't they accept it? Why won't they exchange evil for good? Or are they just foolish children and isn't it your duty – as father, as teacher – to take them by the hand and lead them onto the path of righteousness?

There's nothing more dangerous than teaching, Kochin would say. A father doesn't answer for his son, nor a son for his father, but a teacher answers for his pupils. You must renounce teaching. People say it's a sin not to pass on the good that you know, but they're wrong. If you're a teacher, you must have power. Power increases the efficacy of your lessons many times over, and you should want to have more and more of it, you should want to exploit it, enjoy it.

Such a terrible thing: to reject your past, to write off all, or almost all, of your life; whatever was in it is declared evil and false, chopped off and torn out by the roots, and no one can emerge from this intact. Yes, the thrill of a newly discovered truth may suppress the past, may allow it to be forgotten, but behind you lies emptiness. And another thing: being born from an idea rather than a mother's womb makes everything artificial and unnatural, and the world created by those who've rewritten their life, who've managed to sum it all up at the midway point and deliver their verdict, who've managed to purify themselves and be reborn, is equally artificial. That world, of course, can be easily adjusted, taken apart, put together and moved about, but other people – people incapable of casually rejecting what came before – can't write their way into it; it's too fast and they can't keep up.

Tolstoy, Kochin would say, was a very good man: he fought against the death penalty, dreamed of moral self-perfection, of everything on earth being exactly as Christ wanted it to be. But for this to happen, he was ready to renounce his past, and not only his own; to cripple the lives of those closest to him, those who loved him.

I knew myself that Tolstoy's family struggled for many years, that from the 1880s onwards he and his wife drifted ever further apart, that the children took the side of the wife, bar a single daughter, and that his disciples took their place. I knew that for a long time he tried to make peace with his family and when this proved impossible, when whatever he did or said only served to pull them further apart, he left Yasnaya Polyana, the family estate, and died ten days later at the railway station at Astapovo, in the home of the stationmaster who picked him up on the platform.

Kochin's father spent 1901–1907 in Canada, first as a correspondent for the *Libération*, then as an ordinary factory worker. He wrote many articles for the paper about the Doukhobors who'd left Russia to settle in Canada, sent them off to Yasnaya Polyana, even received a short note of thanks from Tolstoy himself, and then corresponded regularly for several years with Tolstoy's confidante, Chertkov. By then he'd already become a Social Democrat, drifting to the far left of that movement, which was why, after 1917, he joined the communists. But his views resembled Bogdanov's more than they did Lenin's; at any rate he was convinced that Marxism was a religion, and revered Christ as Marx's precursor.

It was through his father that Kochin became interested in Tolstoy. His father worshipped Tolstoy and was entirely on the side of his disciples; Kochin, meanwhile, thought that Tolstoy was essentially kidnapped from his family and from Yasnaya Polyana, that this kidnapping dragged on for almost thirty years, and only in the last days of his life, gathering extraordinary speed, did it kill him. Usually, disciples kidnap their teacher after his death; these ones kidnapped Tolstoy while he was still alive. He died because of them, but he himself had come running to them, and in the end it was they who were proved right. Like so many other teachers, Tolstoy was the victim of his disciples, but he spawned them himself.

To prove this, Kochin even drew up an outline of the Tolstoys' family life from diary entries and letters. The first seventeen years of marriage between Lev Nikolayevich Tolstoy and Sofya Andreyevna Bers were, he wrote, happy, almost ideal. They loved each other – more than that: they were in love with each other, and it was very hard to find a single crack between them. In his bachelor days Tolstoy had dreamed of a mother-wife, not a lover-wife, and the woman he married bore him children almost every year and fed them herself. But after her tenth delivery she began to fear new pregnancies. By this point their marital crisis was already far advanced.

The relationship began to break down as early as 1879. In a letter to his friend Strakhov, he wrote: 'My cause will benefit from my death.' At the same time Sofya Andreyevna writes about him to T.A. Kuzminskaya: 'Lyovochka has thrown himself into his work, into visiting jails, village and district courts, conscription centres, into the most extreme compassion for the ordinary and the oppressed. It's all so incontrovertibly good, grand and high-minded that it merely makes you feel your own worthlessness and vileness more sharply' (1880). In '84 she writes to her sister: 'Yesterday Sergei Nikolayevich returned from Tula and saw Lyovochka in Yasnaya Polyana. He was sitting there in a peasant's smock and dirty woollen stockings, dishevelled and dirty, making clogs with Mitrofan for Agafya Mikhailovna... I'm so repelled by all this holy foolery, this indifference towards the family that I'm not even going to write to him. Even after producing all these children, he's incapable of finding anything in the family to occupy him, any joys or even duties, and my contempt and coldness towards him just grow and grow. We never argue – please don't misunderstand me – and I shan't tell him any of this. But it's become so hard for me with the boys growing up, a huge family and another pregnancy that I'm desperate to fall ill or be run over by horses – anything to have some respite, to escape this life.' That same year he writes in his diary: 'Cohabiting with a woman whose spirit is alien – i.e., with her – is truly foul.'

Relations between Tolstoy and Bers recover more than once, and for long periods at a time, but then comes the final split. At the end of the '80s, Tolstoy does not just sever their ties, he even renounces the past that he shares with his wife. Until then he always thought – in fact, nothing was more important to him – that (from a letter to Chertkov, 1888), 'procreation in marriage is not lechery... Not a sin, but God's will... Not for nothing did Christ praise children and say that theirs is the Kingdom of Heaven... All hope rests on them. We are already befouled, and how hard it is for us to cleanse ourselves, but every generation in every family brings forth new, innocent, pure souls, who can remain unstained.' But now he started telling her that marriage is not a form of service to God. Marriage is always a falling away and a retreat from God. Many of his late works – *Kreutzer Sonata, Devil, Father Sergii, Resurrection* – are about precisely this. She writes: 'Here I am copying out Lyovochka's article "About Life and Death", where he points to a quite different good. I remember how when I was young, very young, before I was even married, my entire soul craved the good of complete renunciation, of living only for others – I even craved the life of the ascetic. But fate sent me a family, I lived for it, and now I should suddenly admit that somehow that was all a mistake, that that wasn't life? Will I really end up thinking such a thing?' (Diary, 1887)

She writes: 'And if the salvation of a man and of his spiritual life consists in destroying the life of a loved one, then Lyovocha saved himself. But isn't that the death of two?' (Diary, 1890). Perhaps, Kochin would say, Tolstoy was waiting for his children to become his disciples, too, for his wife to give birth to followers. But she didn't know how to give birth to disciples, only children, so then he walked out on his own family, left it to join his disciples.

But the greatest scar Tolstoy inflicted was not on his wife, but on his eldest son, Lev Lvovich Tolstoy. They resembled one another to a quite extraordinary degree, like two drops of water. When the father started drifting away from the family, the son began to compete: their similarity forced him to be his father's equal. At one time he even responded to the themes of Tolstoy's late novels with talented counter-novels of his own, but then he cracked, developed a nervous disorder and left Russia. One can only regret the fact that he stayed sane and knew, to the end of his days, that he was Lev Lvovich Tolstoy, not Lev Nikolayevich Tolstoy. Subsequently finding himself in America, on his uppers – 1917 had come and gone – Lev Lvovich began playing his father in Hollywood films and, being a competent artist (he studied in Paris for several years in his youth), began painting his father's portrait, taking himself as the model. A more complete capitulation would be hard to imagine.

Kochin's words contained a great deal of truth, of course, and there are good reasons for citing him here; but the history of the relationship between Lev Nikolayevich and Lev Lvovich was even sadder than he thought. The fact is that Tolstoy's eldest son was actually Tolstoy himself, or else his brother. There's no room for doubt here. The Tolstoys' family doctor, Glyuk, told colleagues that he was convinced that Tolstoy *fils* was Lev Nikolayevich's monoovular twin. For unknown reasons his development had been delayed, and he matured only in the womb of Tolstoy's wife, Sofya Andreyevna Bers.

Glyuk said that he had always been astonished by Bers' love for Tolstoy. It was a classic example of a mother's love for a son, and the fact that Bers essentially bore Tolstoy another Tolstoy, that she brought to term the same Lev as had Lev Nikolayevich's own mother, explained everything beautifully. Of course, any other man, especially one with Lev Nikolayevich's desperate fear of death, could only dream of a self-continuation of this sort. Indeed, few others have been so blessed: to prolong your own life by another entire human life, to watch yourself grow and develop, to see how you became the person you are; while remaining yourself, to see yourself from the outside, to know that this is you, that this is how you really are. Lev Nikolayevich had the good fortune to be resurrected without dying, to be given two lives, both very long – but he failed to appreciate this gift.

And so, when Lev Lvovich began to grow up and it

became obvious to everyone that he was none other than Lev Nikolayevich, Tolstoy started claiming that no, he wasn't, he was merely his and Bers's son; naturally, there was something of his father in him, as in any child, but no more than that. By now the elder Tolstoy was an egoist to the core, and felt as if he were the last link in the chain. Everything had been building up to him and he was the summit, the end of the line; any attempt to extend him was blasphemy. There could only be one Tolstoy.

One shouldn't think that such cases among twins are so very exceptional. Not long ago in China, for example, in the course of an operation on a man complaining of constant stomach pains, doctors removed part of a jaw, a rib and a clump of hair, all belonging to the man's twin brother, whom he'd eaten in his mother's womb. There was a similar story last year in India, where doctors even managed to extract soft tissue from a patient's stomach, not to mention an entire, undamaged occipital bone.

The stories about the Chinese and Indian patients excited the Tolstoyans greatly, especially Morozov. Constantly interrupting one another, they began discussing the fraternal conflict and competition that begins in the womb and proves as cruel and as bloody as that between Cain and Abel. The others were also shocked by these two cases of cannibalism, and everyone in the ward agreed that you could hardly go on living once you'd found out you'd eaten your own brother – otherwise there can be no morality at all. The second Tolstoyan, Saburov, forgetting that the topic of conversation was his teacher, Tolstoy, said: 'Isn't the human psyche amazing – the way people manage to forget what they want to? Come what may, you're as pure and chaste as before! These people probably don't even feel any guilt, don't experience any remorse, as if it wasn't them who did the eating. How foul and disgusting it all is!' But not everybody took Saburov's side.

Another patient, Rogov, said that perhaps it was a ritual murder: whoever kills his brother and enemy, according to popular belief, inherits his strength and intelligence. But there's also another possibility. Tolstoy was starving, or rather both of them were starving and realized that only one of them could survive, so they drew lots. This was a dreadful tragedy for them both, but the one who got lucky vowed to his brother to live for the pair of them. They embraced and kissed. So there can be no talk of disgust; on the contrary, we have before us an example of supreme morality, a model of heroism and self-sacrifice, and only time could show whether or not the survivor was worthy of the gift.

'We should use such examples,' added another, 'for the education of our children, rather than cast them aside in shame. Apart from anything else,' the same man said, 'we have no real grounds for accusing Tolstoy of murder; after all, he didn't actually consume his brother, he just delayed his development. What saddens me so much more is the way Tolstoy reacted when his brother was finally born. Why did he need to tell Lev Lvovich that he wasn't Lev Nikolaevich? It's like a mother who, dreaming of a son, gives birth to a girl and brings her up as if she were a boy. As a result, the daughter grows up with male gestures and manners and spends her life miserable, or even commits suicide, unable to cope with her split identity.

'By bringing his son up differently from how he'd been brought up himself, Lev Nikolayevich thought that he would turn him into someone else entirely. Tolstoy always tended to think that the environment plays a far greater role than heredity. To wean Lev Lvovich off literature, he packed him off to France to study sculpture. And after his son's return to

Russia, though it was already obvious that he had none of the makings of a sculptor, Tolstoy would explain to Lev Lvovich, at every available opportunity, that a writer is formed by life; it was the experience of war and his time in Sebastopol that had turned him, Tolstoy, into the writer he was. And besides, an author of prose needs inner tranquillity, something Lev Lvovich lacked: he was nervous, neurotic and would never be a real writer like Lev Nikolayevich.'

The counter-novels of Tolstoy *fils* were a particular bone of contention between us. Morozov thought it simply impossible for Lev Lvovich to have come up with plots distinct from those of his father, so the son, by foisting a different – sometimes radically different – interpretation on his heroes, tried, as his father wished him to do, to detach himself from him, to leave no one in any doubt he was his own man. That is, he accepted the rules imposed by the elder Tolstoy and behaved as if he were his son. But Tolstoy didn't appreciate this, didn't wish to understand it, and thought he was being mocked.

But I don't agree with Morozov's interpretation: as we know, Lev Lvovich, unlike Lev Nikolayevich himself, didn't deviate an inch from the line of the young Tolstoy. In my opinion it was actually the elder Tolstoy who consciously ceased to be the man he'd been, who artificially remade himself. One day he understood that he was in the wrong before his brother-son and, stepping aside, left him to prolong himself. From that time on the genuine Tolstoy was Lev Lvovich: it's him we should be studying.

But the problems between the brothers did not end there. Eventually, Lev Lvovich – now, the real Tolstoy – left for Sweden, where he underwent lengthy treatment for his neuroses under the renowned doctor Ernst Theodor Westerlund, while the elder Tolstoy ran away from Yasnaya

Polyana, ran away, you might say, from himself. After the death of Lev Nikolayevich Tolstoy, and especially after the Revolution, everything gradually settled down. In Hollywood, Lev Nikolayevich was played, logically enough, by Lev Lvovich, who, gazing at his reflection in a period of acute penury, painted self-portraits of the great Tolstoy.

And lastly: perhaps it was the sight of the flourishing, fecund Tolstoyan communes that made the Bolsheviks decide on their policy of collectivization.

*

The fourth person I'd like to commemorate here is the previously mentioned Semyon Evgenyevich Kochin, our neighbour in the communal flat on Pravda Street where I lived with my parents for the first fifteen years of my life. Then we received our own apartment in a completely different district, on Lenin Prospect, and I only saw Kochin twice after we moved, the second time just over a year ago, a month before he died. So I suppose I managed to say goodbye. Both during and after our time as neighbours, Kochin lived with his sister, a quiet old maid who treated her brother like a child; in fact, everyone treated Kochin like a child. Certainly, I always thought of him as my peer, from my earliest years.

Kochin had the largest room in the apartment, though its shape was very strange indeed. The side with the window, facing south, was extremely narrow – in fact, the window was all it contained – but from there the room, or 'auditorium', as Kochin preferred to call it, broadened out, forming a trapezium. By the same token, his bed, which he rarely left, was called 'the royal box', and the old linen curtains were known as 'the drop'. Following Kochin's logic, everything beyond the window should have been 'the stage', or even 'the theatre of life', but I doubt he saw it that way: life beyond the window didn't interest him very much. After his release from the camps he probably never made a single attempt to leave his room, to look beyond the pane of glass with which it ended. He liked things to be complete and bounded; his world was as flat as a cinema screen, and he deliberately renounced the depth of the stage for the sharpness and clarity of the image; or perhaps he just couldn't cope with scale. He once told me that in his youth he'd trained as an artist and was considered a fairly gifted colourist, but he could never get the hang of perspective – that deliberate distortion of dimensions for the attainment of truth.

Kochin would start his day by searching for human faces in the uneven surface of the curtain's fabric. If the faces were kind, his mood would instantly lift, he'd get out of bed, and be smiley and cheerful all day long. But if the faces were bad, he'd be depressed, lie in bed for hours without moving, and look every inch the invalid. It was a serious condition and many years ago, before I was even born, his sister tried to cure him by taking him to the best doctors and getting him admitted to hospital, but there was nothing to be done and eventually he was left in peace. All these trials did bring some benefit, though: he was registered disabled and began to receive a miniscule pension.

From the age of about five, after my grandmother died, I would go round to the Kochins' room several times a day, sometimes hanging about for hours at a time. From morning until evening, when everyone got back from work, the flat would be deserted and I didn't like being on my own, so I'd go over to Kochin, to the only room that was never empty. It goes without saying that he soon infected me with his passion:

each of us would boast about the faces we found, until Kochin himself put a stop to it all. The problem was that often, when he found good faces, I found bad ones. He became gloomy and took to his bed again, while his sister showed me the door. Kochin, I suppose, was the first person in my life who took everything more seriously than I did; I quickly learned to pity him, and deceive him.

Kochin would begin his better days by drawing open the curtains, but the room became no lighter. This was because almost the entire window, if memory serves, was glued over with thin strips of paper covered in a dense scrawl. As a result, the room remained murky even on sunny days, and the light was always on. That was fine by me: I like electric lighting. Kochin claimed that, taken together, the strips constituted an autobiographical novel which, thanks to the dearth of events in his life and, thereby, of cause and effect, was entirely made up of discrete thoughts and scenes. Thoughts, after all, come to one without system or logic, at least on the surface; discovering them afresh, over and over again, was his daily labour as a writer. In reality, of course, logic was present here, but it was internal, inconstant and fickle.

In practice, Kochin's notion of how a writer should work took the following form. On days when he was not depressed, Kochin would spend the whole morning sketching a detailed outline of the novel's development: namely, how and in what order the lines stuck to the window should be read on that particular day. This was usually done in red pencil and was very reminiscent of diagrams showing the circulation of the blood. Such an association must have suited Kochin, because he himself was fond of repeating the idea that a novel is a creature which, like a human being, lives and breathes, develops and grows. Then, when the outline was complete and somebody came by to visit, he would leap up onto a table placed against the windowsill and – walking, squatting, sitting down or standing on tiptoes – read out the text in accordance with his plan. A more engrossing spectacle would be hard to imagine. Kochin needed an audience, a pair of eyes behind him, and though he read quickly and fluently he always found the time to glance over his shoulder. Fortunately, he wasn't fussy – he was happy to read to anyone, except, perhaps, his sister. At any rate, he was quite satisfied with me, a five-year-old kid.

Kochin explained more than once why it was that he stuck his words to the window; no two explanations were ever the same, nor did one ever contradict another. It all began, it seems, during the war, when, to protect them from bombings, window-panes were plastered over with paper ribbons in criss-cross patterns. Kochin let his sister cut out several pages from his novel and started claiming that his writings were saving the world from destruction and disintegration. He also liked to say that his novel kept his sister and him warm and stopped them from freezing, that a novel should be tempered by the sun, that it should be transparent, and that until electricity was no longer required his work would not be done. He also said that he couldn't keep it in the drawer: you can't deprive a living thing of light, and anyway, a novel is photosynthetic, no less than a plant.

Being a child, I had little idea of what Kochin's text was all about, although the first novel I'd read, *Oliver Twist*, led me to suspect that no comparison was possible. But I was fond of Kochin – you could even say that I loved him – so I never voiced my doubts.

Now, I have a much better idea. On my last visit to Kochin – I'd received a telephone call from his sister, who said that he was terminally ill and that it would be a good idea for me to say goodbye – he really was chained to his bed, but he was in good spirits and unmistakably glad to see me. I'd barely said hello and taken off my coat when he handed me a new and, it seemed, freshly completed outline, and ordered me up onto the table to read. This was far from easy. His thought was encoded in arrows and figures; following its train required some highly elaborate contortions, though he was always there to help me, gesticulating vehemently and guiding me up or down, left or right, to the corner and back, etc. The real problem lay elsewhere: many of the scraps of paper had faded, nearly all of them had been glued on two or three layers thick, the letters showed through each other, one line was superimposed on another, and I kept losing my thread. Nevertheless, I still managed to read out the bit he wanted; afterwards, I even asked permission to copy it down, which he found deeply gratifying. As a result, I still have some of what he wrote. You could hardly call these notes a novel, of course; a more accurate term would be a cycle of poems in prose or, perhaps, a chain of extremely microscopic stories. No: better call them poems.

'I was walking to a village. To reach the village I had to cross three streams. I crossed the first, crossed the second, entered the third. When I entered the third stream, I heard a noise. It was the water splashing against my legs. I decided to look at the water splashing against my legs. It splashed beautifully. I was in no hurry and decided to carry on looking. Since that time seventy-two years have passed. So that was before the Revolution.'

'One man thought that my life was a cup. By accident he dropped the cup and broke my life. He broke my life, apologized and left. All night long my wife picked up the pieces. Picked them up and stuck them together. In the morning she put the cup out of harm's way. Then she left me for that man. When it's about to rain my old wounds begin to ache, like a soldier's.'

'The bog dried out and the moss began to resemble sheep. Many people saw the moss and they all said that it was sheep. Sheep give wool, give skins, give meat. Sheep give all these things. Give all these things to us. And what do they keep for themselves? They forget about themselves. They are altruists. They are good. If moss has turned into sheep, that's good. Hooray! I've got a job now. They made me a hut and told me to guard the sheep. This will be my home till the winter.'

'The windows of my room face the roof of a nine-storey building. For some time this roof has been a hive of activity. People are forever walking on it. Some are out on errands, others are just out for some air. My sympathies are entirely on the side of the former. People who are out on errands always walk straight. When they reach the edge of the roof, they jump. Their jumps have strength and force, they are well thought through, swift and business-like. On reaching the edge, those just out for some air turn back. Or they sit on folding chairs and look down. I often wonder whether these two groups of people have anything in common. My wife says they do. My wife says it would be easy to cross them. She says that in less than a year the roof will be jam-packed with little mules. If so, I'll owe her a chocolate.'

'All afternoon and evening, the snow melted. By morning it froze. Became slippery. People looked as if they were walking the tight-rope. Started clutching at the air, like old men. Started falling, like children. Became softer.'

'When Christ walked on water, did he leave traces? If not, then it's easier to leave traces on earth than on water. If not, then earth and water are not one and the same. Then God really did divide them.'

'The trees in the alley are lined up in a row. Like soldiers. An alley is a regular forest. Growing an alley takes time and effort. But there is a more innovative method. Bury soldiers in the earth. Water them every day. Then, in spring, they will grow and put out shoots.'

'Today I wrote a manual for birds. An adult bird that wants to become a nestling should grow smaller. Change its perspective on life. A bird that wants to be reborn should abandon this idea.'

'I'm standing on high ground. It's dangerous here. There's a deep drop below me. I look down. My head spins. But I carry on looking. Down below, trees are growing. I'm standing over them. I'm a bird that flies while standing. Below the trees is a bog. The underworld is flooded.'

'A man fell as if he'd been scythed. He'd realized he was grass. He'd realized he was in a meadow. He'd realized it was time. Time to make hay.'

'A bird perched on a branch; the branch swayed. The bird flew off the branch; the branch swayed. I think: not for the first time. I think: all this has happened before.'

'A deep lake in the woods. Its bottom is decked with fallen trees. Fish move slowly among the branches. Amongst themselves, the trees call them birds.'

'All winter long I courted a snowgirl. I fell in love with her. I was glad she had a simple face. Glad she had a big tummy. On the whole, I'm not too fond of dainty young ladies. In March she finally agreed to be mine. I was happy with her. I was glad she became so jealous when other snowgirls were around. When the warm weather came, I took her north. My love saved her life. In winter we'll come back again.'

'I was ill for a long, long time. I'd come to terms with my illness, got used it. It became a part of me. I grew old and my illness grew with me. But it still died before me. I buried it inside me.'

'1936. Moscow. In a first-floor window stands a naked woman. She's beautiful. She's a good mother. She's waiting for me. She's waiting for whoever sees her in the window. Anyone can put into her whatever he has. And take it back whenever he wants. It will all be returned to him safe and sound. With interest.
    "What's this woman called?" asked the teacher.
    "Sberkassa,"[1] I yelled from my desk.'

'"Ice," said the teacher, "is organized water. Water that possesses a settled way of life. Ice is a good production worker and a reliable comrade."

---

1 The common Russian word for a savings bank – outlets, at the time in question, of the Soviet State Bank. (Tr.)

"And rivers?" I asked. "What about rivers?"

"Rivers," said the teacher, "are also good production workers, if they flow downhill.'"

'A desert. Yellow-grey takyr. The earth's shroud has cracked all over and disintegrated. The cracks are deep. Too deep for glueing. The wind scatters the sand. From the foot of the dune to the top, gently and slowly. Power should be trained. Then, a steep drop. Everyone who gains power deserves to be forgotten. If you want to make a revolution, make one. Scattering sand is a lovely way to pass the time. You could spend your whole life doing it.'

Right at the end, when I was already in the doorway, Kochin said to me: 'Tolstoy foresaw that his teachings could lead to evil. He told Sofya Andreyevna that disciples are children, too, but damaged ones, brought up without a mother's warmth. He urged his wife many times to treat them like their shared children, or rather, even better, with even greater care, the way people treat sick children or orphans. And there was one other way of avoiding evil: Sofya Andreyevna should agree to feed Tolstoy's disciples as if they were her own children, with the breast. Tolstoy, moaning and in tears, implored her to do this, but she, according to Chertkov, coldly replied that she hadn't enough milk for everyone and then, to spite him, she even bound her breasts with bandages, so their last child was fed not by her, but by a wet-nurse. That was the last straw. A few years later, anxious that his disciples should not feel unwanted, he went over to them for good.'

*

I got to see Dr Kronfeld eventually. He came out to meet me himself, took me into his office and, after hearing me out, told me to settle any urgent business by the start of next week: a bed would be freed up on the ward on Monday and he was ready to admit me. I was in for a long stay, half a year at least, because the course of treatment, given the dosage I'd be receiving, would be very drawn out. Perhaps he could take me in some other time, though beds for trying out new drugs didn't come round very often, and it would probably be months. If Monday suited me, then I should call him the day before, on the Sunday, on the number he was about to give me.

The five days given to me for deliberation were spent calmly enough. My fears were quashed by his upbeat tone, and even the length of time I'd be spending in hospital didn't frighten me. He looked like a good doctor: not once in our conversation did I doubt his sincerity, for all my paranoia. And he didn't deceive me. On Sunday, as agreed, I called to confirm I'd be coming in, and on Monday – the twenty-fifth – my mother and my aunt accompanied me to admissions, where I changed into hospital pyjamas; then they handed me over to a nurse, kissed me and left. Mother cried, but mainly because that was the thing to do. Waiting for my next fit to strike had worn her down, as had the fact that she could never let me go off anywhere on my own. But now the hospital had agreed to give her a rest, a breather, and there was even the hope they might help me recover. My mother, of course, was desperate to believe this. At any rate, they confidently promised her that I wouldn't get any worse, so she left me there with her mind at peace.

The admissions department was housed in a building right by the Yauza, behind the twelve-storey block where Kronfeld had his office. It was old, dating back to pre-Revolutionary times. It looked as if it had been planned as a country house, but halfway through the job someone decided to convert it into a medical facility, and the central, most elegant part was extended on both sides with wings that were disproportionately long, not to mention tall, after which the entire construction immediately began to resemble a military barracks. Later, numerous alterations – cosmetic improvements, as they say – evened everything out for good. The ornaments, animal heads and other decorations in stucco had either fallen off or been broken off; even the columns, which had once jutted out from the wall in a semi-circle, had gradually been plastered over and could now be distinguished only by their colour. It was a historic site, built by some gold merchant for the psychiatrist Korsakov.

The twelve-storey block and admissions department were connected, almost umbilically, by an underground tunnel, and I was convinced that the nurse preparing my papers would take me off to the now familiar sixth floor, but Kronfeld, it turned out, was truly ubiquitous and ran not just one, but two whole departments; the one we needed was right here. The nurse had plenty of nice, cheerful things to say about Kronfeld, before abruptly lamenting the fact that I was so very young. She did this at great speed, almost running the words together, in a way that was strangely reminiscent of how old women say their prayers and lamentations in church. Eventually, her paperwork and commiserations both came to an end, and she calmly took me by the hand and led me to my room. As we walked over, she explained how lucky I'd been with my bed: it was by the window, and the window looked out onto the park. There could be no more desirable spot and the bed should really have gone to one of the veterans on the ward, but this was no ordinary department and she felt sorry for me – almost a child, but already under Kronfeld's care.

So it was that I become a lawful denizen of this world. Now I just needed to make myself at home here. Hospital life, it turned out, took a lot of getting used to, much more than I expected. I was, by any criteria, a privileged patient: I'd got in by the back door, and above all, my condition was less serious than everyone else's; but this was scant consolation. Just the opposite. The fact of the matter was that I was about the only patient who actually perceived himself as ill. The law, the norm, was to feel the pain, not the illness. The pain would come and you'd be in agony, but then it would weaken and abate; you'd forget all about it, as if it had never existed. For me, forgetting was impossible. My illness was always with me, always in my thoughts: how it was evolving, how it was changing, how the drugs were affecting me, whether I felt any better, or worse.

From my own or any other point of view, the life of my fellow inmates was horrific, and nothing would have persuaded me to swap places with them; but it was hard on me as well. Particularly hard, I suppose, because I had no one around in a comparable situation, no one who could understand me. A high fence separated me from everyone else, throwing me back on my own resources.

Ultimately, life on a dementia ward or, as the euphemism goes, geriatric ward, is a trial for anyone, anywhere, whatever his sickness and however far advanced; everyone – patients, doctors, nurses – is infected with a sense of total hopelessness. Nothing can be done. In fact, it's not even possible to maintain a semblance of order: patients soil their beds and the sheets on our ward, despite its privileged status, were changed every other day at best (and no more than once a week in other hospitals). As a result there was a permanent, pervasive smell of sour urine, not to mention the usual hospital odours of rancid oil from the kitchen and chlorine from the toilets. The damp sheets and the filth left many of the patients with ulcers and bed-sores, but since these ailments were so visible, efforts were made to deal with them: the dressings were changed regularly – the doctors made sure of it – and then, on top of all the other smells, the ward began to reek of ointment and alcohol.

The building was set aside for the old élite, though not all of it – only the central part and the left wing. The right part of the building started being done up after my arrival. The plan was to divide it off from us and assign it to the emergency services – for people picked up off the street, as I had been in the past. The makeover was meant to last a year, if not two, but it was clear that the decision to hand the wing over had already been signed off 'upstairs'. Some of our old beds had been freed up, and the start of the works coincided with the first patients being brought in. They were put in rooms where the builders had not yet started, and then, after several days of fighting and swearing, were transferred to other clinics. This absurd situation was the result not only of our usual chaos, but also of the longstanding lack of beds in psychiatric care (about one for every two required). What beds there were went to chronic cases, and no one wanted to spend a penny on the rest.

That the patients in our part of the building were not run of the mill was obvious enough from their conversation, even without Kronfeld telling me, in the course of one of his ward rounds, that virtually all the residents here were either Old Bolsheviks or former Party bosses; just being around them made him feel like a General Secretary. It was Kronfeld who told me that ending up here was considered a respectable final career move. It's not hard to see why. Living in the same flat as an old man who's lost his marbles is exceptionally demanding. He needs his own room, constant care, someone beside him at all times, or you won't be able to move for the dirt and the stench, not to mention the likelihood of the gas being left on or the flat being flooded. But finding a woman who would agree to look after him is no simple task.

There's also the old people's home, but that's tricky too: there's a waiting time of several years, and even people without families can die before they move in. Besides, few are prepared to consign their mother or father to such institutions: their grimness is an open secret. The hospital's a different matter. Officially, people are admitted there on a temporary basis (though if you try, you can draw things out indefinitely), and in theory, you're being treated, not simply maintained. Say what you like about conditions in a geriatric ward, but it's a far cry from an old people's home. In fact, it's the best solution for all concerned – families and patients. Consequently, you need impressive connections and an impressive career just to get in.

But according to Kronfeld, things were just about to change: several nursing homes – half-hospitals, half-hospices – were being built all at once in Moscow for chronic cases, and in a couple of year's time most of our patients would be transferred. If the nursing homes really did get built, there would be fewer patients and the hospital would finally begin to resemble a hospital. But now, with just one ward attendant for every two rooms, you could forget about bedpans and new sheets being brought on time, not to mention the fact that no one on the ward could afford a bribe.

All this was true, of course, but still, it wasn't just a question of tips and bribes. There were some attendants – old women themselves – who, when I went to call them over to one of the patients (shouting from your bed got you nowhere) would explain in the most rational, ruthless terms that to prolong the life of these old dogs was pointless and a waste of national resources. It would be better for the country if they were put down and the staff transferred to normal hospitals – to maternity hospitals, say, where there was also one attendant for every two rooms and where clean linen was just as much in demand as here. I often heard them telling the man who'd summoned them that he wasn't a human being – an animal, at best – and that it was hardly the job of ward attendants to look after animals. There was no one to complain to, so the women, convinced they were in the right, would try to win over the doctors as well.

*

My first two months in hospital were basically spent on preliminaries. Day in, day out, a bewildering variety of drugs was poured into my muscles and veins, most of them cognitive and memory enhancers. Along with vitamins, they were meant to prepare my organism for the treatment itself. I certainly felt their effect and remember those sixty days of my life more sharply than any others. The contrast is all the more acute in the light of what followed, when they began administering Kronfeld's drug; there, my memory becomes bitty and hazy. Especially for the first few weeks. I slept day and night and only gradually, as my brain began to adapt itself to the medication, did anything begin to stick. Meanwhile, that preparatory period of hospital life seems unparalleled in its vividness and colour. Even now I'm incapable of seeing those two months from a distance, from the outside; time hasn't healed a thing and I still fear the same terrors I feared then, still harbour the same faith, the same hope, that nothing has been decided, while knowing that we are doomed.

At first I came and went as I pleased, felt bright and youthful, was hardly ever in bed; there was a sense of almost forgotten well-being, of bodily joy – I must have shed ten years at least – strangely combined with humiliation and fear. That fear, even when I was calm for weeks at a time, never left me; it grew and grew. So the sleep, that long, almost unbroken sleep induced by Kronfeld's injections, was a deliverance. Ever worried that the fear would return, I learned to draw it out for as long as I could.

Thanks to the surplus of life poured into my veins, I was extremely active; a busybody, some might have said. At any rate, those two months before lethargy took over were enough for me not only to meet everyone on the ward, including some very strange people, but even to get know some of my fellow inmates very well. About ten of them seemed to be outsiders, and this bothered me for a long time until finally, at the end of my first month, I plucked up the courage to ask Kronfeld. By that point I knew many of them by name, such as the Tolstoyans Morozov and Saburov, and Nikolai Semyonovich Ifraimov, on whom more below. I'd been accepted into their circle, you might say, but no one's proud of ending up in a dementia ward and it seemed indecent to ask them how they'd got there themselves.

Kronfeld readily understood my curiosity and why it was that I'd turned to him in particular. He replied, with perfect courtesy, that they weren't under his care and that he knew little about them. Rumour had it that in the twenties, and perhaps later too, the building was given over to a boarding-school attended exclusively by children of high-ranking functionaries, both Soviet and Comintern (or so he was told by the nurses who'd been working here for twenty years or so). When the fathers were dispatched on distant and dangerous missions, abroad or to a war zone, they left their children here; on their return, they took them back. You could even call them hostages. In any case, Kronfeld promised to try to explain it all more precisely, if I wanted him to; he found it interesting, too.

The next day he came round to see me again, but I didn't learn anything new. All he said was that, for reasons unknown, some of the alumni had spent their entire life in the boarding-school; perhaps their relatives had died, perhaps they'd betrayed them. Only a decade ago there had been about thirty of these old-timers, but now only eleven were left; none of them were below sixty, and each year two or three passed away. No one could say what was keeping them here. The authorities had long lost all interest in them.

Apparently, he added, the boarding-school was simply forgotten during the war years, then someone suddenly remembered (these were the Khrushchev years) and wanted to shut it down. The order had even been signed. But none of the inmates fancied living outside, where no one was waiting for them. Strange though it seems, an explanation for all this was found and accepted, the decision was withdrawn, and they were left where they were.

But it was a waste to maintain the whole building for thirty people, so other patients started being transferred here – just ordinary convalescents. The result was a kind of rehabilitation centre. A natural process set in: one group shrank, the other grew, and by the end the two were completely mixed up and the boarders ended up without a single room of their own. All the same, he said in summary, they were the patriarchs here, the old-timers. The preferences and privileges they received were taboo; everyone, even the nurses, had to reckon with them.

Complete clarity was still a long way off, but I suddenly came to my senses: my conversations with Morozov, Saburov and other boarders had been the only chink of light for me in the hospital, I'd tried not to miss a single one of their seminars, was grateful they'd accepted me without asking any questions, and here I was sticking my nose into their lives. I was in the wrong, no doubt. If they'd wanted me to know their past, they'd have found the time to tell me.

This line of thinking quickly developed into self-flagellation (here in hospital, I was always making mountains out of molehills). Then I realized that Kronfeld hadn't told me anything new and thank goodness for that: my intentions may have been iniquitous, but God had kept me from sin. Still, human curiosity is indestructible and a couple of days later, assuring myself that Ifraimov was a boarder too – so this time everything was out in the open – I went to him with exactly the same question.

Ifraimov wasn't in the least surprised. There was no great mystery here, he said, but it was a long story – and he bowed, as if to apologize. He was fond of grand gestures. At first we were going to make ourselves comfortable in the hall, in front of the TV, which was switched off, but there was already somebody there, so instead we just paced the corridor from one end to the other.

*

'For exactly a decade,' he began, 'from '22 to '32, this building was home to the Institute for Natural Genius, or ING, a top-secret operation at the time. It was signed into existence by Lenin, in his role as head of the Council of People's Commissars (CPC), which invested the highest hopes in the ING. We, those ten men who from force of habit, or inertia, continue to hold weekly seminars, are the last of its alumni. The rest have either died, or been killed.

'In '32, as I've already mentioned, the Institute was disbanded at the behest of the same CPC, which by now had a quite different make-up. Purportedly, it was closed down as a waste of resources; the reality was something else entirely. In 1932, for the fifteenth anniversary of 1917, our director, the charming and exceptionally clever Professor Khristofor Innokentyevich Trogau, read out the semi-theoretical opening chapter of his newly completely study of the Revolution to his learned colleagues at the ING.

'He'd used his own, highly unusual sources, and the resulting picture differed so much from the official version that it led to a scandal. The manuscript was confiscated, Trogau was imprisoned and perished soon after, while the majority of those in the room at the time also met their end. Among us, for example, there is not one man who heard him. But 1932 was still a relatively liberal time. The materials gathered by Trogau continued to circulate in the Institute even after the manuscript was seized and we had a good idea of what his study contained – but more on that later.

'It was no accident that Trogau became the Director of ING,' Ifraimonv continued. 'He'd been studying genius for some time. The 1890s witnessed the birth of the HEURO group, consisting of politicians, philosophers, plenty of scholars (mainly biologists), doctors and psychiatrists, several entrepreneurs and engineers – in short, as motley a crew as could be imagined. The conclusion they came to was that in the twentieth and twenty-first centuries the power of a state would be measured not by its territory or by the quantity of its citizens, but exclusively by their quality. They deemed the human brain to be the chief natural resource, ahead of all others, whether taken in isolation or together: gold, coal, oil, minerals, etc. Consequently, the task of every Russian government, in their view, was to augment and enrich the brain.

'It should be noted that Germany, as so often, got here first; a similar group appeared there several decades earlier. It was led by the outstanding psychiatrists Kraepelin and Kretschmer, but they understood the health of the nation in a quite different way, so on this question too Russia and Germany soon became mirror images of each other. Germany considered health to be something utilitarian and, in essence, purely physical. The eugenicists, who in the German group were in the majority, were convinced that the main problem was the enormous quantity of retards, freaks and above all mental cases who, by reproducing themselves, rotted the nation. The conclusion was clear: the good of society demanded their mandatory and forcible sterilization.

'A different view triumphed in Russia, one based on a slew of scholarly studies. In the last decades of the nineteenth century the lives of every Russian genius and their closest blood relatives were studied in detail; in parallel, as a control group, the Jewish population of the empire was also analysed, and in particular, the combination in this nation of self-evident talent and no less evident imbalance. The outcome was identical in both cases. Genius, it turned out, was inextricably bound up with one or other form of mental pathology. In contrast to the Germans, the Russians were not prepared to part with their geniuses even for the sake of the mental health of the nation; on the contrary, in Russia both government and society agreed that geniuses were the very salt of the earth: only by begetting geniuses did the people justify its existence. From this there followed not only a tolerant attitude towards the mentally sick, but also the first steps towards analysis of their ideas, their ravings and other anomalies, lest a single instance of talent be neglected.

'Although the group's activity was concealed from public view, some of its findings still floated up to the surface. The public, as is usually the case, received them in caricatured form. One Pyotr Tkachev, who'd done a brief stint as HEURO secretary, published, under his own name, a treatise arguing that history is made not by the masses but by those capable of critical thought; that is, by geniuses who have managed to look at the world without bias, to see its imperfection, defects and sin, and to lead millions of people set on destroying its foundations. As you well know, Alyosha, geniuses aren't only to be found in politics – in fact, it's astonishing how very few of them that particular field contains. But Russian society in those years was naïve. Convinced that it would be enough to overthrow the monarchy for everything to fall into place, it gave Tkachev's theory an ecstatic welcome.

'This extraordinary coupling of pathology and genius,' Ifraimov went on, 'demanded explanation, and a good deal of time was devoted to this question. The findings? Any given society is rigidly structured to ensure that each generation reproduces it without aberration. Thousands of things are forbidden, thousands are taboo. Any given man knows almost from the cradle what he can and can't do, what's bad and what's good. The norm is implanted in us all; not one of us is forgotten. From birth to death we live beneath the gaze of a censor from whom nothing can be hidden, not even the pettiest little trifle – for we ourselves are that censor. And we are terribly vigilant, Alyosha. Geniuses are society's sworn enemies. They alone are capable of destroying it, for they understand that it could be otherwise. Often one exceptional individual is all it takes for everything to collapse with a deafening crash.

'Defending itself, society tries to persuade the genius that his thoughts, ideas and theories are folly, delirium, madness, that they are senseless, disgusting, depraved, filthy, and that, for his own good above all, he shouldn't share them with anyone, not even his loved ones. He should remember that all this is his curse, his cross, his disgrace, and pray to God that it remains a secret, that it follows him to the grave. Society's arguments are certainly persuasive. Most geniuses don't even put up a fight against the censor; quickly, even joyfully, they accept the situation and live a life which, if not always happy, is entirely normal. The only chance a genius has to fulfil himself is if society is deficient within him, if it's sick and weak. First, he kills it off inside himself and then, having set himself free, he summons every last ounce of strength, life, hatred, and destroys it outside himself too.

'How and when does society sicken inside a man? Sometimes these are mild ailments that soon pass: a dream, say, or hallucinations induced by thirst, hunger, heat. Sometimes they're more serious: hysteria, hypnotic trances, narcotic hallucinations, illusions, especially so-called *déjà vu*; autism, synkinesis and much else besides.

'Faith in justice and the justifiability of the ordinary world can be destroyed by some tragedy that befalls us, or our dear ones, or which we merely witness: we keep returning to it, again and again. The loss is so great that accepting it and resigning oneself to what's happened is more than anyone can bear. A world that permits such a thing cannot be just. Such an experience is often a source of mental illnesses, its origin – though not, of course, the only one.

'Who are these people we place in the madhouse? What unites schizoids, paranoiacs, epileptics, cyclothymics and so on? Yes of course, their illnesses are completely different, but they also have something in common: their sufferers have rejected our norms, our laws, our entire universe. They've taken the same bricks and built everything anew, and now none of the old taboos can restrain their genius; their "good" and "bad" are not the same as ours, and in our world they are completely free. This, in a nutshell, was the HEURO group's main conclusion.

'On this basis, two programmes were developed for Russia by the end of the century, which, in line with current fashion, were called the "minimum programme" and the "maximum programme". In reality, they were simply different stages of one and the same programme, whose ultimate aim was the return – by the efforts of man, not God – of all humankind to heaven and its union with the Lord. To this end, the common programme envisioned the resurrection of all the dead, beginning with Adam, as well as the endowment of personal immortality, eternal youth and the fullness of happiness for each and every man.

'The minimum programme required that the Lord's gift to Russia be realized. The Jews, in their sin, had been deprived of God's grace; the new Holy Land was Russia, whose people had been chosen by God to gather around themselves all the forces of goodness and light that exist on earth and to prepare for the final, decisive clash with the forces of darkness and sin. The group was so far-sighted that even then, in the 1890s, it could assert with confidence that the forces of darkness would be led not by England, mistress of the seas, nor by Germany, whose influence was rising year by year, but by the provincial, distant United States of America.

'The HEURO members thought that to fulfil the mission with which she had been entrusted Russia would need to increase the number of its geniuses by a factor of tens, hundreds or thousands; that is, to implement the "geniusification" of the country. There was only one way of doing this: to shake up society by every available means (in politics – socialist parties of every hue; in religion – sects and theosophical societies; in art – modernism and above all futurism; in morality – sexual perversion and homosexuality: the support of all of these would radically weaken censorship and lead to an equally radical increase in the quantity of geniuses). The anticipated outcome of this labour would be a change in the nature and circulation of mental illnesses: where once they were non-contagious or barely contagious, now they could escape the confines of the patient, launching an epidemic that could no longer be stopped.

'This epidemic (which later became known as the Revolution), by razing society to the ground, by leading it through unthinkable calamities, grief and suffering, by shaking it up from top to bottom, so that not a single man, even the most ordinary, lived the life he expected to live, would lead to a mass flowering of genius (the HEURO prediction proved accurate: the number of geniuses really did increase exponentially during the Revolution, but hunger, cold, Spanish flu, typhus, cholera, death in combat during the Civil War, mass execution and the even more widespread exodus of geniuses to other countries, naturally corrected the statistics), which in turn would make Russia the leader of the forces of good.

'The maximum programme would be the final battle between darkness and light, between sin and righteousness. It would be lengthy and fought on both sides with unprecedented ferocity; the scales would tip one way then the other, as if God was still undecided; and it would end precisely as described by John in the Book of Revelation. The catastrophe that would befall mankind would be so terrible that not even the rubble would remain from the previous life; nobody and nothing would be spared.

'That previous life was a vessel of sin – sin oozed from its every pore, pervaded it, possessed it; now, that life would perish, together with sin. So too would people's notions of good and justice, everything they loved and believed in, everything they revered. Children would perish in front of their mothers, torn to pieces by wild beasts, and children would see those same beasts mauling their mothers; and if, heeding their pleas, the beasts should leave someone untouched, he, too, would be consumed by the flames. In short, nothing would be left, not even faith in God.

'People have to pass through unthinkable suffering, or they can never be purified and resurrected. Calamities and grief have to drive them insane, all of them, to the last man, and only then will they make a clean break with their former life, only then will their souls be freed. We will be so filled with freedom that, however small the abilities of any man among us, he too will become a genius and, as such, open himself to God. Man, for the first time, will see His true majesty and beauty, the perfection of the world He created, and, seeing it, will return to God. Yes, that's exactly how it was all meant to be,' said Ifraimov. He paused, then added, unexpectedly: 'So there you are, Alyosha; I think I've satisfied your curiosity…'

We were standing by the door to his room; he half-embraced me and, before I could even say goodbye, went back in.

*

Apart from the eleven boarders, there were five other patients on the ward who stood out from the rest. Three of them were young lads, soldiers by the look of them, all apparently nursing injuries to the brain; their memory, at any rate, had gone completely. They were treated as chronic cases, and one or other of the ward sisters attended to them round the clock. As it happens, the soldiers were a blessing for the entire ward.

The reason was simple. God may have deprived the soldiers of their reason and memory, but their flesh was unusually strong, and the three Sisters who worked shifts in our building and treated them as they saw fit (Kronfeld was torn between two departments and only dropped in on us occasionally) decided, on learning this, to divide the soldiers among themselves, so that each of them could have their own lover. I saw, for the first time in my life, three women who were constantly pleasured, constantly satisfied, and who, let me add, repaid the joy they received a hundred times over. The couples were indefatigable. It was as if, in addition to their own lives, they'd been given what remained of ours. From dawn till dusk, with barely a break, cries and groans could be heard from the soldiers' room: bodies sobbing in a torment of joy. Sometimes all three Sisters would go in there together and, excited by what was happening in the next bed along, begin a kind of joust, to see whose lover was the strongest. On such days even our oldies, poor souls, nearly went mad with lust.

The care shown by the Sisters for their chosen ones was touching indeed: not only did they always change their sheets, they washed them, shaved them, trimmed their hair and even splashed them with scent. They were, unmistakably, in love with the soldiers, and we have this love to thank for the fact that our dear Sisters, having come to the end of their shift, never hurried off home. On the contrary, they felt so good here, so happy, that they sought every possibly pretext to stay. In fact, they loved the ward in general, and loved us, its patients. We were the witnesses to their joy and they wanted us, too, to feel happy. They had this urge for the whole world around them to rejoice and be merry, to be as young and beautiful, as full of passion and love, as they were themselves.

Only rarely did they tear themselves away from their lovers, but when they did they were always patient, kind and considerate, almost radiant. Any one of us felt privileged just to exchange a few words with them; we, too, I suppose, were in love with them, and they must have known it. If our relations with the nurses were strained, the Sisters were 'angels' and 'doves', and rightly so: I don't remember them ever refusing anyone their help. For whatever reason, they rarely closed the door to the soldiers' room; perhaps the openness of it all added zest to their vigorous couplings, excited them even more, or perhaps the Sisters were convinced that, fenced off by our sickness, we weren't aware of anything anyway. But even if they didn't think of us as people, it hardly mattered: for us their love was the last morsel of real, living life. And we were grateful that they chose not to hide it.

The hall where we assembled was opposite the soldiers' room, and just as soon as we began to hear the Sisters whispering 'my darling, my sweet, my bird, my berry, my dearest, my one and only,' and then, 'yes, my lovely, yes, yes, like that, yes, yes, I want you, I want you,' our meetings seemed to break off of their own accord. We weren't exactly elbowing our way to the doors, but still – behind those doors was life as God had made it, while we were just old men. Whatever energy we still possessed was sufficient merely to argue; next to them, that seemed dull. Even after they finally quietened down, it took a while for our symposia to resume.

Aside from the soldiers, the ward contained one other entertaining couple. A man and a woman. Everything suggested that they, too, were from the first cohort; at any rate, they certainly enjoyed the same rights and the same privileges. The couple were some twenty years older than

Morozov, Ifraimov and the other boarders, and, as a rule, kept themselves to themselves. They were very peculiar. At times, they seemed almost no different from most of the other patients here, but that impression soon passed. Their intense but to me largely incomprehensible activity – despite their age, they had more energy than anyone else who dwelt here – clearly carried some meaning. Occasionally it brought the entire ward together, gave it a point around which to gather; it was a sort of performance, which they carried off with rare expressiveness, not to mention the fact that each of us was given a role, a purpose – no spectators, no extras. Most of the inhabitants of this world had turned inwards once and for all, no longer noticing anything outside them, but this couple, like skilful public entertainers, drew even them into their act; they clearly had a thing for old men.

The theatre arose out of nothing, spontaneously, always led by one and the same couple, who had eyes only for each other. In this sense the duet was just as closed, just as self-contained, as all the other patients, but there was so much intensity, so much passion in their performance that it pulled in whoever was near them, without the slightest resistance; everything around the couple came alive and continued to live for as long as it remained united. Afterwards, the ward settled down all at once and returned to normality. I can't say that the couple fascinated me from day one – I spent most of my time in the company of the boarding-school alumni I'd asked Kronfeld about – but you couldn't help noticing them.

*

I've already spoken about how frightened I was, how wracked with indecision, when the prospect of hospitalization first arose. In fact, were it not for the insistence of my mother and my aunt, I might never have committed myself to Kronfeld's care. But the first few days in hospital went better than I'd feared; I was flush with optimism, and above all, I immediately felt a kind of inner harmony and calm. Finally, after a long break, I began working again. Sadly, this sunny period soon passed.

Even before leaving for hospital, I'd vowed to revive my Memorial Book. I'd resolved to work on it every day, whatever conditions I found myself in, and drew up a clear plan detailing whom to include and in what order; now, the words were just beginning to flow. Even those whom I'd intended merely to touch on briefly, since they'd left so few traces inside me, came alive on the page and I kept remembering new episodes, new phrases, new gestures and facial expressions; the work came easily, with barely a pause, and I could have written reams about each and every one of them – they really did seem to be coming back to me, returning to life. These were happy days indeed: I felt a force inside me, almost as if I'd been granted the gift of resurrection, but then, at the end of the second week, everything ground to an abrupt halt.

In hospital I prayed more assiduously than ever. I had so much to ask God for, so much to thank Him for. I prayed as I'd once prayed as a child, at home: with tears and endearments. Luckily, no one on the ward paid me the slightest bit of attention; and then, on the twelfth day of my life in hospital (I remember the exact date), I had the sense that no one, absolutely no one was listening. In fact, it was as if there was no one at all, as if everything was empty, deserted, dead. And that was when fear set in. It was already night, I lay down to sleep without finishing my prayers, and when I woke up in the morning I could no longer work.

Three days or so later I attended another of the boarders' seminars. I was late arriving, so I don't know how the topic had been formulated, but it was perfectly clear what everyone was talking about. At issue was the historicity of famous people, specifically Stalin and Christ. Stalin was the subject of a monotonous, colourless lecture by a certain Sergei Prochich, who described himself as a pupil of the celebrated scholar of Russian folktales, Vladimir Yakovlevich Gustavs. This was not the fruit of his own research but an exposition of a major opus, completed in draft, by Gustavs himself. Despite his dull voice, it was obvious how much Prochich admired his teacher, how proud he was of him, how he loved him, and how hopeless he was at expressing it. All that came of his efforts was a redundant portentousness, the mere repetition of the words of his mentor.

Gustavs began collecting materials on Stalin back in '23 and went on doing so until the day of his arrest and death in '38. He left no stone unturned: according to Prochich, he copied out more than ten volumes' worth of text. The evolution of Stalin's image was examined by him in every genre and every art form, from ditties to symphonies, and in every region of the country, even Kamchatka.

There's no need for me to describe Prochich's lecture in detail, especially since the main conclusion of the study, founded on the analysis of thousands of sources, was accepted by us all – at any rate, nobody argued with him. I'll repeat it here. Gustavs was convinced that Stalin was an entirely mythical figure. 'Such a man never existed,' Prochich quoted him as saying. 'A real Stalin, a Stalin who eats and drinks, is as nonsensical a notion as a live Phoenix.'

Stalin, in Gustavs' estimation, was the great achievement of the popular genius. 'I always said,' he wrote, 'that the only true artist is the people. Who can be set alongside Stalin? We love him as the creation of our hands.' He went on: 'How much inspiration, wisdom and love was needed to create him! Hundreds of thousands, even millions of nameless talents created him day after day, year after year, with sensational results. This, truly, was a national task.'

None of us, I repeat, disagreed with this thesis and the lecture was heading nowhere, but then, for reasons unknown, Prochich suddenly began shouting in a heartrending, womanish voice: 'There was no Stalin! No! No! Never! He never existed!' He went on like this for some time, then his words became breathless and confused, merging into an unintelligible lament, and only then were we able to drag him away.

As I've already said, our gatherings took place in a small hall on the first floor, where palm trees growing in pots framed the television. In our hospital, unlike others, this was the quietest spot, for not one of the patients could understand the pictures on the screen (apparently, this was something to do with line frequency, or the fact that the images changed too quickly for the patients to keep up). The only thing they could watch was cartoons. Actually, they quite liked cartoons, and the doctors, believing that the greater the resemblance of the patients' current life to their previous life, the better, herded them over every evening to watch 'Good Night, Little Ones!' While they watched television, we enjoyed a leisurely stroll along the corridor. After lights-out, we returned to the hall and resumed our scholarly labours. Stalin was never mentioned again – there was no mystery here – but he did become a kind of foil to what followed.

The conversation began with a discussion of the latest sensation: the 'Turin Shroud', in which Christ's body was wrapped when he was laid in the tomb and on which His appearance was imprinted and preserved to our days. Its discovery convinced the last remaining sceptics that such a man or God-man really had existed, that two thousand years ago he'd lived and walked in Palestine, before being crucified and buried; in short, that everything had happened exactly as the Gospels describe. And, following the Gospels, His grave stood empty on the third day: He had ascended into heaven and taken his appointed place at the right hand of the Father.

Strange as it may sound, I wasn't amazed by the fact that I'd lost Christ only the day before. Everybody was speaking calmly, even indifferently, in the tone that was usually struck at these meetings. Whether or not there were any believers among the boarders was simply impossible to tell. The Turin Shroud wasn't the only thing they discussed; they also analysed other evidence of the historicity of Christ, the apocrypha in particular. A man I'd never met, who was affectionately called Matyusha – I couldn't remember him from the previous seminar on Tolstoy: either he wasn't there or I just hadn't noticed – remembered some late and relatively rare testimony about Christ, known as *The Man Who Was Hanged*. Only two of those present had read it, and the rest begged Matyusha to at least summarize the main points and explain what all the fuss was about.

He began by saying that *The Man Who Was Hanged* was a Jewish novel written in the tenth or possibly eleventh century; the earliest copies, at any rate, date from that time. The book, which is almost carnivalesque in its brutality, proved wildly popular in its day, and many copies have survived. Its merits as a source about Christ are harder to gauge, but probably modest at best. Most write it off as an anti-Christian pamphlet of negligible interest. On the other hand, there are theologians who deem it to be based on ancient oral sources and thereby credible, at least in part.

In this tale, the story of Christ and Christianity is set out as follows: one extremely self-assured young man, Jesus of Nazareth, secretly enters the Temple's Holy of Holies, where the Ark of the Covenant is kept, and takes from it a talisman; he sews it into his thigh, and the lions guarding the Ark suspect nothing. The talisman gives him the power to perform miracles and to out-argue even the most educated rabbis. All this earns Jesus hundreds upon hundreds of devotees, who claim him as the Messiah, the God-man, sent to earth to redeem the sins of humanity. Immaculately conceived by the Holy Spirit, He, untouched even by original sin, changes the world with His birth: if previously evil on earth has multiplied and multiplied, and people have drifted further and further away from God, then now, having been sent to them by his Father, He will bring them back, like prodigal sons.

The new heresy spreads like wildfire. Followers of Christ can be found in almost every village in Israel, and communities begin to form even beyond the Holy Land. So then the Sanhedrin, with barely a second thought, takes a very strange step. It decides to oppose miracle with miracle. In essence, this is the capitulation of faith, an acknowledgment that faith is weaker than miracle. An identical talisman to the one stolen by Christ is given to a rabbi famous for his virtue, and soon he begins outdoing Christ both in miracles and in quarrels about faith. The pupils of the new Messiah turn their backs on him with astonishing speed. He is abandoned by almost everyone, seized by Orthodox Jews and, after many humiliations, hanged. Hence the title of the tale: *The Man Who Was Hanged*, not *The Man Who Was Crucified*.

'So,' Matyusha continued, 'the Sanhedrin celebrated its victory, but it proved merely Pyrrhic. Faith in Christ was resurrected with his death. And he himself was also resurrected by popular rumour. There was not a single house where at least somebody did not believe that on the third day he rose from the grave and was taken up into heaven by God. The revived heresy became a terrible threat to that faith in the One God which the Sanhedrin was meant to preserve. And there was worse: thousands upon thousands of foreigners across the Greco-Latin world instantly put their faith in Christ, and their numbers grew and grew. People sprinkled themselves with water, were baptized, and began to think of themselves as Jews. They believed, with the zeal of converts, that they had joined God's chosen people.

'There was no doctrine yet, only faith in the death and resurrection of Christ, the Christ who took upon himself the sins of the world; but not one of his followers doubted that he had become a genuine Jew. The rabbis considered Christianity as something akin to vernacular Latin: those who had recently come to know the One God found it hard to observe all the laws and precepts and had convinced themselves that none of this mattered when set against faith. Such a tendency had existed previously, too, but now that it had received the highest sanction it risked overwhelming those for whom faith without Law was unthinkable. The community of Christ's followers, swelling by the day, was deemed heathen by the judges, who were terrified that it would sweep over them like a wave. In other words, the judges were frightened not by the doctrine of the Christians, but by their number. They were scared by the fact that the Christians did not even suspect that theirs was an entirely different faith, that they and the Jews were strangers to each other.

'From earliest times the Jews had lived among pagans far more populous than they, and by now they had accustomed and adapted themselves to this state of affairs. Everything was clear, and everything made sense: there were Jews and non-Jews (*goyim*), who had nothing in common, who sought neither compromise nor agreement in matters of faith, and this absolute separation suited everybody. Christ changed the world. Suddenly there appeared a great quantity of people who considered themselves Jews, but the Jews themselves were not prepared to recognize them as their brothers. They had lived far too long in isolation – it was already a part of them, their mark of distinction – and now the thought of coming out into the open filled them with terror.

'The Jews wanted to turn back, and demanded that the Sanhedrin lead them back to the place where everything was as it used to be, where they knew how to live. This was the voice of an entire people, the voice of all those who had not followed Christ, and the Sanhedrin could not fail to hear it. For a long time the rabbis did not know what to do; meanwhile, the number of Christians grew and grew. Any moment now, it seemed, God's chosen people would dissolve and disappear amongst them. The threat to the Jews was even greater than during the years of Babylonian captivity, as both Levites and men of the soil acknowledged – so then one of the junior members of the Sanhedrin, Ananias by name, took the plunge and proposed the following to his elders.

'"Let our two most educated rabbis," he said, naming names that have not come down to us, "go over to the Christians and create, from all that is known about Christ, an entire doctrine, a new faith by which it would be clear to every Jew and every Christian that they are people of completely different faiths, that they are strangers to one another. Then they will have no choice but to go their separate ways and leave each other in peace. Order will be restored."

89

'To judge from the tale,' Matyusha continued, 'the unknown rabbis were the apostles Peter and Paul. They took up residence in Rome, in a specially built tower which they did not leave until the day they died, lest contact with Christians forced them to break even one of the laws of the Kashrut. To remain unsullied, they ate only that which the Law permitted Jews to eat during the strictest fast. That is, creating the doctrine of Christ and building the Church, they lived and died as Orthodox Jews. The tale mentions that they even managed to be buried as Orthodox Jews.'

This story, and in particular, it seemed to me, the way in which Matyusha told it, incensed the Tolstoyan Saburov, who said: 'But that means that the Jews deliberately created a false faith?' 'Hard to say,' Matyusha replied. 'From the point of view of the Jews, then of course it was a false faith, and it would be hard, if not impossible, to imagine a greater sin than the one that Peter and Paul took upon themselves, but Christians themselves would hardly agree that their faith is false. In fact, anyone who accepts that the path by which man comes to know God is slow and difficult, that it is gradual, would agree that the doctrine of Peter and Paul is genuine. Never, before or since, have such a quantity of people abandoned paganism all at once, and placed their faith in the One God.'

'But can't you see,' Saburov insisted, 'how this tale delights in evil? Can't you see, whichever side you take, how filled it is with hatred, ingeniousness, inventiveness, how neatly it all fits together? Besides, it was written by Jews, so this is their point of view, so the faith, therefore, is false. Matyusha, just think what you've told us: first, Christ is made to suffer humiliations and murder, a murder even crueller than that described in the Gospels, then two rabbis, like some Ivan Susanin, leads astray those seeking a path to God, while holding these trusting souls in such contempt, and taking such pride in never violating the commandments, that not once do they break bread with a single one of their followers. One cannot, one must not, speak calmly about this. I can't imagine any of us having ever heard anything more outrageous.'

'You may be right,' Matyusha agreed, 'but still, as I've already said, one mustn't rush to judgment. Yes, there's a great deal of invention in this tale, there's a mind that, having occupied itself in its youth with annotations to the Halakha, has broken free. But that's not the point. The point is that the tale is a lie, a self-incriminating lie, whatever the author himself may have thought of it. And I'll tell you why the Jews incriminated themselves in this way. For them the tenth and eleventh centuries *anno domini* were a terrible time: one horror after another. Many communities in England, Germany and God knows where else perished in their entirety. Everyone was killed, from babes at the breast to old men. Please understand,' he said in a strangely muffled voice, 'even faith cannot endure when every last man and child is being butchered. Even faith cannot endure when pregnant women have their stomachs ripped open and sewn back up, their foetuses replaced with live kittens. It's beyond anyone's endurance!

'So then the Jews decided,' he continued in an even quieter voice, 'that either there simply is no God, because no God could have created such a world, or the cup of sin is overflowing and tomorrow everything will be destroyed. And they wanted to save the Christians who were killing them and save the world, because the purpose for which it had been created was yet to be fulfilled. No longer could they let themselves die in innocence – so they slandered themselves. The sin they took upon themselves was so great that no sufferings could ever atone for it. They restored justice, balanced the scales. Now, once again, evil did not simply exist in the world – it was recompense for sin. They told God that they themselves were guilty, and said it in such a way that He believed them and forgave the Christians.'

*

Somehow, having lost the ability to pray, deprived of all support, I began seeking protectors here, on earth. Earlier, too, I'd tried to help the other patients, especially my roommates, in so far as I could: I ran after the nurses when sheets needed changing or a bedpan was wanted, ran after the Sisters when my neighbours were in agony and needed an injection to fall asleep. Sometimes I even interceded for them: not one person here, with the possible exception of Kronfeld, viewed the sick as human beings, and this was done so frankly, so openly that at times I could barely restrain myself. I suppose that the nurses, the attendants, were the only real authorities here, or at any rate, the only authorities with which we had any contact, and no one was closer to them than I. Because of my requests, my habit of interceding, I was always at the centre of things and very quickly learned how best to exploit my position.

This all began on the third day of my life in hospital, when I couldn't stop thanking the nurse who brought me to the room for the entirely unmerited bed by the window. I wanted her to know that I appreciated the favour, that I wasn't some ungrateful pig. Needless to say, it wasn't gratitude that moved me, but fear: I was scared of them all, scared of the time when I would be at their mercy. Any aggravation of my illness meant an increase in their already enormous authority; the power they wielded, in other words, was the measure of my illness. Nevertheless, for as long as I was praying to God, I could still cope with my fear, as if He were a bulwark against it. For as long as I had Him, I did not permit myself any utterly unforgivable actions, any unforgivable expressions of fear; some taboos still held. But He had left, while the fear remained.

The fact that I was helping my neighbours, in so far as I could, brought me the keenest joy; these were tangible good deeds, and I couldn't help feeling a sense of satisfaction. Especially as there was an element of risk here. I knew that my relationship with the nurses was at stake: they had plenty of work as it was and adding to their load was unlikely to please them. But I still ran after them, still called them, until suddenly it dawned on me: I had my reasons here as well.

I realized that I was interceding for others because I wanted to have the right to the same sympathy, pity, assistance in the future, when I would find myself in their position. I wanted to show the nurses how good I was, how deserving I was of sympathy. And another thing: I was trying to make them better, for them to remember that with me, and because of me, they were once better, for them to feel thankful towards me. I felt a constant need to talk to them; when they were not around, I did so in my own head; when I slept, I dreamt of them. There was something drawing me towards them with irresistible force, my fear notwithstanding. I needed them to notice me, single me out, consider me one of them, view me as a defender of the sick, as a kind of dignitary in their midst, and a very accommodating one to boot. There was endless fear here, endless cunning, but there was also the most ordinary pity towards those lying next to me, so for a long time I managed to convince myself that my sin was not so great.

What frightened me most was the nurses' total lack of any sense of guilt. So complete was it that, talking to them, I felt like weeping with helplessness. They made fun of me, said that soon I'd be just like my neighbours on the ward, and when that moment came they'd be only too happy to discuss questions of morality with me. I wasn't just scared of them, perhaps: I was affected by what they were actually saying. At any rate, I caught myself thinking that if they agreed to do what I was asking them to do – whether for myself or for another patient was irrelevant – then it meant I was going along with them, agreeing, at least to some extent, that saving the life of a child or a woman in labour was more important than extending the life of any of my roommates. The former, after all, were just beginning to live, their energies yet to be spent, while our lot, say what you will, had already lived the better part of their allotted span.

Once I described to them, with no hint of disapproval, a tradition observed in some tribes: how old men unable to feed themselves leave the community and go away to die, so as not to be a burden. Moreover, everything is arranged in such a way that the community bears no guilt for their death, nor does any individual within it, not even their children; the old men, meanwhile, die in the knowledge that they have proved strong enough to help their people survive.

The nurses, I should add, received my support with no great enthusiasm, never forgetting that I was a patient and, by that token, no match for them. But they still welcomed my understanding and exoneration. They listened gladly to stories taken from Japanese, Yakutian and other books about old men who take to the hills to end their life's journey in solitude. They asked questions and debated it all amongst themselves; after all, they, too, were old, and death was never far from their minds. In pursuing such conversations I was well aware, of course, that I was betraying my fellow men, that I was essentially denying them the right to life, but I consoled myself with the thought that there could be no other way. It was the price, if you will, for bedpans and sheets.

At the end of the first month of my hospital life I caught a nasty cold, ran a fever and barely left my bed. After a week of lounging about I was still ill, but there were signs of improvement, and I could no longer bear to lie in bed day and night in the company of my roommates. It so happened that the boarders had a meeting planned for that day, and, just to see some normal human faces, to hear some normal human speech, I decided to sit with them for a while in the hall and then, when I tired, to go back to bed.

The conversation had come back to Tolstoy. Clearly, this was an inexhaustible topic for them, one that, for whatever reason, had long been troubling them, to no avail. This latest exchange, like the previous one, reconciled nobody. No agreement was reached and nor could it have been, for the simple reason that the conclusions all but incriminated Tolstoy's followers. Serpin, the Tolstoyans' perpetual antagonist, swiftly dismissed, not without flair, their entire life and everything they believed in. They could hardly have been expected to go along with this. Any man, even in his youth, finds it hard to resign himself to the fact that any part of his life has been misspent – but this was their life from start to finish. Agree with Serpin and there would have been only one thing left for them to do: hang themselves. Logic and reason are by the bye in such cases; a basic sense of self-preservation is enough to find a thousand arguments in one's defence.

Still, Serpin's thesis was undeniably elegant. He began by saying that he himself could see the futility of this conversation, that it would be better to end it there and then since nothing good could come of it: those he was addressing could never be changed, and there were no new disciples of Tolstoy among those present, as far as he could see, so there was no chance of any serious debate. Here he pulled a gruesome face, called the Tolstoyans masochists for putting up with him, and proceeded to make the following argument:

Disciples, by their very birth, are abnormal, defective children. Where ordinary children, in their own time and in the natural course of events, take the place of their fathers and become their equals, disciples, by contrast, are doomed to inequality. Only the very rarest of them attain, at the end of their lives, what children are granted without the slightest impediment. Perhaps it's because they are not carried for nine months, not fed at the breast. Essentially, they are children who belong to no one.

They must have left their parents once, abandoned them and come to their teacher. Their choice, their rejection, is a heavy burden to bear. It's hard to blame them, but these are broken people. To reject those who brought you into the world is an immense trauma, one that can never be overcome and that leaves its mark on everything. And another thing: a child does not choose his parents – they're like a gift from God – while a disciple finds his teacher-father himself, and the result is the most appalling pride. A disciple is conceived in his teacher's womb without sin, without vice – a terrible temptation that few, teachers or disciples, can resist. Their relations seem so pure to them – after all, even original sin has not touched them – that the gates of heaven stand open. Accordingly, a disciple, having been born without sin, is permitted a great deal, far more than is permitted to ordinary people; hence the evil that they work with such peculiar ease.

And lastly: children resemble their parents: everyone is used to this, everyone accepts it. A disciple, meanwhile, striving to be a copy of his teacher, is always afraid of someone saying that he's a fake, that he has only pretended to be loyal, that in fact he is a heretic and a traitor. So once again he has betrayed: first his father, now his teacher. This 'once again' is more terrible than anything. The world, after all, is always changing, and today is not equal to yesterday, but what disciples inherit from their teacher has no progeny, it freezes, solidifies into dogma and faces one way only – backwards. Disciples can add to it nothing but their own fear. Soon, fear will be the only life that remains in the doctrine, the only thing that breathes and grows in it, until all else is obscured.

*

By the end of December my strength was returning and I was feeling better. My body had adjusted to the injections, and although Kronfeld kept increasing the dose I no longer felt the difference. I was sleeping better, too. The standard eight hours were more than enough for me. Mood-swings had long been a part of my life: before coming to hospital and during the first two months on the ward, a sense of impending tragedy had rarely left me, as if everything had already been decided, all hopes abandoned. Now, this fear subsided once more; I was calm and placid. For the first time in a long time I could take my mind off my own problems; I suddenly felt bored to be continually monitoring myself, bored without new impressions, so once again I began taking an interest in my companions on the ward, and not just some of them, but all without exception: both those who were senile and those who'd been at school here. It was Ifraimov who prompted my curiosity, and I realized that my attention was drawn first and foremost to the people he'd told me about, the people he'd named.

Observing life on the ward proved instructive. I sensed that this muddled, nervous bustle, this peculiar mixture of people, concealed something important, but what that was remained a mystery to me for a very long time. I often thought I was on the verge of solving it, but each time my answers proved false. Perhaps I was simply burnt out, or perhaps this life was too much for me. In any case, a week had not yet passed when Kronfeld, on one of his ward rounds, suddenly said that he'd become much less happy with me over the last two days: I was too excitable and, unless something changed, he'd have to increase the sedatives. For a doctor of his experience this was a gross mistake; the dose should have been increased there and then, but he waited too long. The next day, on top of my excitability, my old fear returned, that same sensation of impending catastrophe, and now I could no longer control myself. It all happened so quickly that I didn't even realize that my reprieve had expired.

Just before this I'd been thinking of resuming work on my Memorial Book, sat down to write, then immediately realized I was doing so out of sheer inertia. I'd remembered having once kept a Memorial Book, and now, having recovered a little, felt able to continue. But the reason I'd kept it, the purpose – all that was lost. It suddenly dawned on me, in a flash, that the life I'd led, the things I'd done, had not simply been interrupted – they'd gone for good; and, perhaps, not just for me.

The world around had changed and my writings were devoid of meaning, whether for those I'd known and wanted to preserve, or for myself. For as long as the world was, at least in part, the world in which they'd lived, it needed them as its precursors, as the root and explanation of what followed. They represented tradition, a reliable reference point, proof that even now nothing had changed, or sunk into oblivion. They'd had a share in that world, but it had gone, and remembering them became redundant. This was utterly obvious and I suddenly realized (I'd had an inkling even before, of course) that God was the sole pivot of the world, its sole justification, and now that He'd left me, now that He'd gone, everything had to end.

I felt sick and scared stiff, because I saw that nothing could be retrieved. Now that God was no longer at my side, now that perhaps He was no longer at anyone's side, I realized how close to me He had always been. Even now my memory of this sensation is as fresh as ever, the sensation that God was with me wherever I was, that there was no need for me to call him. Now I continued to feel God, but only as one feels an amputated limb. I recalled that even after that nocturnal prayer of mine, so many weeks before, I tried appealing to him more than once, tried to bring him back, but for whom, and to whom, were my prayers being said?

Stranger still was the fact that when I was praying I never once had the feeling that God had retreated specifically from me, that it was precisely me who had enraged Him – or else I would have found the right words. I believed in Him and I loved Him, and has it not been said that 'Your faith will save you?' No, I felt that He had left us all. For good. I was seized by despair the like of which I had never known. As if there were nothing around me but cold, as if the world had expanded to infinity, as if it were no longer enclosed, as if everything in it had become alien to me. I could neither fill it with people, nor warm it. God had filled it but now He had gone, and everything instantly lost all sense and meaning, leaving a vast, empty space, through which one could only fall and fall.

Now I found it easy to draw a circle around the space that God had once taken in my life, for it remained unoccupied. The world's external forms remained the same as before, but the core had been ripped out, and there was no way of understanding what was holding it all together, or how. A sense of the fragility of the construction, of the imminence of collapse, was always with me. At times it was as if the world had become nothing more than its own image, mere form and appearance, while life itself had gone. Like in winter, when a puddle freezes over and the water beneath the ice sinks into the soil. Step on the ice and there'll be a dry crack, a hole.

Everything suddenly became irrelevant, pointless. I'd no idea how to carry on and gradually I fell into a stupor. I felt dreadful but there was nothing to be done, no pill that could help, no sign of any change in my condition, no response to any outside stimulus. This peculiar state was, however, interrupted by an almost week-long interval. Previously, I'd always been very cautious when it came to talking about God – it was all so obscure that I distrusted myself, or rather wanted to distrust myself – and yet I knew at once, and for certain, that I was not the only one who'd been abandoned, not the only one who couldn't pray. I could feel in my bones that a terrible, unparalleled disaster was approaching, that the world was forsaken and doomed to ruin. It had nothing to hold on to.

One day I could stand it no longer and began sharing my fears with Kronfeld during one of his ward rounds. I'd wanted to do this for some time, to warn the others through him, but I hadn't dared. I chose him because I liked him, but Kronfeld decided that the hospital had got to me, that I was merely looking for sympathy. He viewed my apocalyptic forebodings with irony, said that he hadn't been feeling quite right either, though there was a perfectly tangible reason for that: two departments had become too much for him. As for me, there was no mystery here either: I knew I might lose my memory at any moment and I was scared of his treatment – after all, my fellow patients offered few grounds for optimism.

Kronfeld said all this in his characteristically calm, even indolent manner, and he must have infected me with his mood. To say that he convinced me that I was blowing my sickness out of all proportion would be incorrect, but hope, for some reason, began to flicker once more. I had a sudden fancy that not everything had been decided. That God was still waiting for something. And almost immediately the idea occurred to me – as it had before on a couple of occasions – to begin a different Memorial Book, the Book of my fellow men on the ward. It was a mad idea, and I suppose I was just tired of being afraid, tired of waiting, so I remembered the task that had occupied me for so many months and which I had grown used to as a kind of justification of my life, a licence. But the past was cut off, it was over, and it suddenly struck me as acceptable, even creditable, to write about those under Kronfeld's care. There were so many things mixed up in this: above all, my knowledge that I was guilty before them, before them all, and that I would go on being guilty. After all, I often looked at them as if they were already dead; I just couldn't help myself. These people really did face in one direction only – backwards, to the past, upstream. For them, nothing new existed. There was something exceptionally reminiscent of death about all this, and it gave me the right to include them in my Memorial Book. It even outweighed the fact that they were still among us, that I was burying them alive.

Not all the above, I dare say, is beyond reproach, but I can hardly be faulted for the way in which I would have gone about describing the old men. Had I managed to include them in my Memorial Book, they would, without a shadow of a doubt, have been first among equals. I knew how wrong it would have been to write until I came to love them, until I reached the point of wanting to preserve them like my own nearest and dearest. Lord, I really did want to love them for what they were. And this, of course, was difficult: nobody had loved them for ages, not even their own children. The seal was already upon them – nobody would ever love them again. So I had to start from nothing, had to take the first step of love towards them, but there was nothing to grab hold of. I was prepared for this, I understood that love would not come easily, that immense effort, immense strength, would be needed to love them; but did I have such strength, and did I have enough? I didn't know. I suppose I was still counting on God, counting on His coming back to help me; then the two of us, together, would certainly be able to make them loved.

I even remember the plan I had to attain this love. I understood that nobody loved them because everyone thought that as people, as independent human beings, speaking one on one with God, they had died, disappeared. All that remained was an empty, enclosed space, like the inside of a shell, and only a miracle equal to resurrection could return them to their former selves. But working miracles was beyond me; I too was a man abandoned by God, a man whom God no longer heard.

And yet, I don't repent, don't regret anything that happened. My plan was as follows. Illness, and then the hospital, had erased whatever distinctions, whatever differences once existed between the patients. Their diagnoses, as it were, had made them all twins. They contained whatever was considered essential for them to go on living. Everything else was seen as irrelevant and trivial, mere aberrations and nuances that altered nothing. So I decided to find out their diagnoses – from Kronfeld, the Sisters, the nurses – and cut them out. Very little would remain, perhaps almost nothing, but so be it; at least what would remain would be them, and not the illnesses from which they suffered. These scraps would contain their life – after all, each of them had lived a long, long time – and from these tiny fragments I would begin to piece them back together, restore them as they once had been.

Ahead of me lay slow, delicate work. Bit by bit, the edges would draw together, the gaps would close, and I would become ever more bound to those I was writing about. And then I would love them. First I would love them because I'd invested so much in them, because they had become my own creations, the work of my own hands, but later even this prop would not be needed.

That was my plan. But I hadn't even got going – I'd merely told myself that they were worthy of love, merely realized that they were people – when everything began to change. I suddenly felt that God was watching me, waiting to see what would come of my efforts. He was still far away and was drawing no closer, but He was already here, unmistakably here. Perhaps I am being presumptuous and my words will sound like blasphemy, but it seemed to me that He had decided to follow me, to trust me. In other words if I, a man, were able to love them, to save and resurrect them, then He, God, would save and resurrect us all. I knew that God wanted me to love them, that He wanted this badly and could barely restrain Himself, could barely accept that for now all this came not from my heart, but from my brain, and my fear. After all, if an ordinary man, not Christ, not the Son of God, really can show love for his neighbours – and can any less be demanded of a living being? – then we really are worthy of life. Then, and only then.

I felt how important this all was for God, that He, too, was lost and unsure what to do next, unsure whether people were even needed in the world He had created. He was already tending to the view that we were not needed, that we were the source of all evil, that we were incorrigible, but if I learned to love my neighbours on the ward it would mean that He was wrong, that we were not so bad, that we could still be saved. I knew that if I managed to commit them all to paper, or even just a few, or even just one (like the righteous Lot in Sodom), if I managed to at least make a start, then this disaster, which I could almost touch, would be stayed, would cease to draw near.

*

Well, no sooner had I begun thinking about a new Memorial Book than everything bad stopped in its tracks and froze, as if waiting to see whether the book would be written. The people here, where death was a natural, daily, longed-for event, where it was seen as a blessing, ceased dying. As if they had put themselves in my hands. Doing their best not to get in my way, not to distract me, they lay quietly and meekly on their beds, day in, day out, but I could see that each of them believed and hoped that he was the one I would choose to preserve.

I knew, and never forgot, that my plan was sheer fantasy, that in my current state a labour lasting years on end was completely beyond me, but the sick wouldn't have any of it and waited as if I really were up to the task. Truly, they were like children who believed that for a grown-up – for me – nothing was impossible; or else they were like the people who followed Christ, begging him to resurrect, to heal, to feed. There was no pretence here, no acting on either side, and the fact that now I had once again felt God was proof that He, Who knew my true intentions, was in deadly earnest, too. But then I realized how much work, how much psychiatric training, would be required before I could cut out their illness.

After all, if I succeeded I would, in some strange way, have cured them, made them well again; but in order to make a start I had to learn reams and reams of new things, read a vast quantity of books, God knows where or how.

A couple of days later, for reasons I can't explain, I told Ifraimov everything, all about my plan, though without mentioning God or any of this apocalyptic talk, but simply: here's what I was working on before I was admitted, but now I'm getting nowhere, can't remember a thing, so I'm thinking of writing up the people around me. The difficulties of my venture are perfectly clear to me, but I want to try. For you, I said, this must sound childish and absurd (I played down every word, softened it with irony), but still, I continued, if you or anyone else – I just don't know who to turn to – can assist me, I'll be terribly, terribly grateful. After all, your knowledge of old age is obviously far greater than mine; you've been seeing and observing the sick for decades; and yes, of course, this is just a stupid whim of mine, but who knows, maybe someone will decide to help?

In other words, I was just throwing a line out, doubting, even fearing, that anyone would take the bait, because, while speaking to Ifraimov, I began to understand that I was calling out to God, that I was begging Him – He was ready to consider coming back to man, the sick had stopped dying – and I was suddenly appalled by what I'd taken upon myself. I was glad, of course, that God had agreed, or almost agreed, to come back, that once again He was in my world, but at the same time I could see quite clearly that before me lay the fate of some shameless impostor and trouble-maker. A trouble-maker who promised the world salvation, who promised people – so many people – that they would be healed and raised from the dead. So what if these promises were only of the vaguest kind? Hope had been offered, they'd believed in it, gambled on it, and now, if I proved unable to help them – and was I really capable of anything of the sort? – I would be evil personified, a man who deceived them about the very thing that mattered most, who deceived those who put their trust in him. I suddenly realized that it was through me, and only through me, that they hoped to be healed, that God was waiting precisely for me, for my love, to say whether or not He should save the world. My intentions were good and what I wanted was right, unquestionably so, but at the same time this was the most blatant imposture, for there was no way on earth I could carry any of it out.

And yet, powerless though I was, I set out on this path, set out because there was no place and no time to stop or turn, but I walked as if doomed, dragging my feet, and so it was that I ended my conversation with Ifraimov. I wasn't hurrying him in the slightest, wasn't forcing anything, and of course I could never have anticipated the reaction that followed. Ifraimov heard me out calmly and, I thought, without a trace of curiosity, but the following morning witnessed the start of a full-scale pilgrimage. By the doors of my room, before reveille, there assembled the entire local population, every nation and tongue of our hospital world. Lord, they came to me one and all, patients and boarders, nurses and attendants, Sisters and doctors, including Kronfeld himself: every last soul. They even formed orderly queues, while the attendants, without so much as a grumble, wheeled in the bed-ridden, who, to top it all off, were clean and dressed in fresh linen, as if they were expecting a visit from the Ministry of Health.

And so, one by one, they emptied out on me whole sackfuls of life, in which everything was mixed up: the illnesses from which I was meant to deliver them together with numberless vivid details, numberless trifles of lived experience – exactly what I was after. The sick soon realized that I was not a fence, not a dam, and speech burst and gushed from their throats like a river in flood. They spoke and spoke, literally unable to stop, while those further off waited their turn, calmly, patiently, meekly, and nobody hurried anyone else; they all understood how important it was for everyone to have their say. They even helped each other to remember their own pasts, added bits here and there if the speaker was too shy or too brief: don't you remember what happened to you there, what you said to us then, or how you surprised us. They themselves brought the most infirm to the front of the queue, but they would have readily yielded their places to others, too. They sensed, I think, that it made no difference which of them I included in the Memorial Book: either they would all be saved, because God would come back, or they all would perish.

Back in the day, at the newspaper, I spent a long time trying to learn shorthand – fruitlessly, as it seemed at the time; but in hospital I discovered that the basic skills had been mastered. As a rule, I managed to jot down all the key points, although what follows is not a transcript, nor even a first edit, and certainly not a Memorial Book. On the contrary, I began with generalities – their illnesses. From the jumble of fates, stories, impressions that were emptied out on me, that is what I tried to find, to cocoon, to calcify. I can see now how much self-estrangement this required, how much of the haughtiness that I used to possess.

To look at them like that was wrong; I think so ever more often now. In fact, it may have been precisely this that ruined everything: they should never have been viewed with a cold, inquisitive gaze. Right from the beginning they needed to be loved and saved, not analysed. Only love could save them. I ought not to have known, ought to have entirely forgotten, that they were sick, that their illness was the main thing about them. I'd tried much too hard to convince myself that only the rags of their previous lives had remained. I was scared of the pits, the gaps, the potholes that would need to be filled, of the delicate, laborious task of mending countless rips and tears, and when they suddenly presented themselves to me intact, capable of making even their illness their own, a part of themselves, different from anyone else's, I, guided by my previous plan, began once more to cut them into pieces, to dissect them. Lord, I should never have taken this path, should never have looked at them through a doctor's eyes. The medical gaze had long since delivered its unambiguous sentence of death, but I was still hoping to heal them. I had no idea how to cope with it all. I was lost.

What shocked me first and foremost was not that there was so much life in the stories they told about themselves, but that, as it turned out, the nurses were really put out by the old men, thought them sly and dishonest; they were scared of them and fought them as equals. They knew, in other words, that the sick were alive. Later, I wrote that ultimately all these people – both those who were normally carefree and those whom I knew to be gloomy and remote, like the shadows of cruel birds – rejected anything new: impressions, relationships, people. They didn't want their life to continue in any shape or form; they found nothing good in it, nothing worthy of their attention. There was only one reason they needed it, only one reason they prolonged it: everything around them recalled something from their past and brought it back to them.

For them, the life of the present resembled little flames that kept flickering, vanishing and reappearing again, as if from nowhere. The flames were like fireflies on a thick southern night, and the sick followed them as if they were following a leader, striving to understand something, to find something in their own past; they lost them, wandered about in complete darkness, kept bumping into each other, then found them again, and only then was there enough light for them to see that they were in hospital, that their life was coming to an end. In this refusal to look anywhere but backwards, to the past, in this deliberate rejection of the future, this recognition of its worthlessness and pointlessness – if anyone had asked them, they would have agreed with one voice that there was no reason to prolong life any further – there was a dreadful obstinacy, emptied of warmth.

Interweaving events and people from their own life with such ease, as if in a dream, the world they ended up with was so precarious that I couldn't help feeling sorry for them. Everything about them evoked pity: they were so fidgety and muddle-headed, forever preparing for some distant journey, to the past, no doubt, hurrying to pack their bags but unable to do so, mixing things up, losing things, forgetting things. At night they were especially restless: it was as if, in the world in which they lived, the lights were going out and it was time for them to leave, but just when they needed to hurry most they discovered that they'd been robbed, ruined, that their losses were enormous, irreparable, that whatever they'd earned was gone, and they had nothing to take back with them.

Deprived of all they had and forced to remain in the hospital, where the other patients, the attendants, the doctors and the place itself elicited nothing but fear, they became stubborn and suspicious. You couldn't argue with them, couldn't get them to do the simplest thing. Yet they were credulous to a man and continued to believe that everything was not lost, that hope still existed. Perhaps this was all just a joke, or the thieves would feel ashamed and bring back what they'd taken?

Meanwhile, once again they began to save up all they needed for their journey, once again made ready to set out, counting and checking their chattels over and over again, ever more rigorously.

A further illustration of their indifference to the present recurs in the transcripts. Along with everything else they also renounced their own faces and no longer recognized themselves in the mirror. Similarly, they mistook the faces of their neighbours on the ward for quite different people, those who had once surrounded them in the distant past, in their youth. It was a quite astonishing masquerade: the soul had already parted from the body and left, reviling the prison that had once housed it, quickly forgetting it and shedding it like an old skin, but the skin remained, still alive. The flesh, deprived of the soul, was laid bare, turned inside out, and all of them, especially the old women, had lost all shame, were plagued by desire and filth. They couldn't remain alone for a moment. Their emptiness had to be filled, and no sooner did you brush against them than they immediately began to want you.

The soul did not simply go away: leaving them while they were still alive, it violated them, and this very fact that the freedom of the flesh, its joy of liberation – for they felt this, too – was bound up in them with violence, interwoven with it, incited the sick to the wildest perversities. They needed orgies, they needed to be crushed underfoot, crucified, abandoned; they needed to suffer, to experience other people's revulsion, to know that they were sinful, guilty beyond redemption. These were the terms of their joy, the price they paid for it. But even in their lust they were pitiful: decrepit and feeble, they rarely went all the way. Weeping with frustration, they kept tormenting their impotent flesh and then, as if forgiven, forgot about everything and fell asleep.

They rejected not only the soul, but also morality, and in this sense too they returned to their beginnings, to childhood. Previously morality had smoothed and softened them, imbued them with the principles of compromise and tolerance, but now, in a flash, they turned coarse. Their faces, their behaviour, their speech – everything became more abrupt, more final. Often they resembled vicious grotesques, caricatures of themselves.

Returning to childhood, they left God and became pagan once more. No trace remained in them of remorse, of any acknowledgement of their guilt, nor did they expect any mercy. Their sufferings struck them as merely an undeserved and wholly unjustified punishment; they burned with a sense of injustice, injustice that had befallen them and no one else; and all of them, I believe, had long lost their faith in God. I do not and did not judge them, not a single one, but when on the first day I recorded their stories (or were they confessions? I don't know how best to call them) it was the stroke victims I pitied most.

Typically gloomy and spiteful, frequently violent (but listless and remote when tired), they wanted to reform the world with force and action, to shatter it and tear down every door and partition, open the world up once more, make it airy and spacious. Their struggle ended in failure and defeat, and as far as our world was concerned, they were as good as dead. They rejected it; it rejected them. The stroke victims' passage from normal, active life to irreversible illness and hospital was lightning fast; it really was a blow, a sudden break, and they went on living in the knowledge that there was nothing natural or right about their illness, none of what those who had lapsed into childhood possessed in abundance.

Clearly, some part of their brain was healthy even now, but it couldn't force its way through the damaged tissue, restore connections, find its comrades, just like in wartime: the family is scattered across the country, some at the front, maybe alive, maybe dead, or perhaps just wounded and laid up in hospital, or missing in action, and there's no news about the others either: bombings, evacuations, everyone vanishing without trace. Nobody knows whether they still have their wife, their children, or whether they are alone in the world and all is lost. A great deal of life remained in the part that survived and it hammered away, as best it could, on a door that was shut and sealed. It couldn't understand who had locked it up in this cell. Like a healthy man who has somehow ended up in a madhouse, it couldn't make head or tail of anything and slowly went mad.

From the very first day that I began taking shorthand, I always kept in mind the fact that the idea of saving the sick by including them in the Memorial Book had come to me by chance, and only because I myself had been struck, because I myself had suddenly seen that I'd been forsaken by God. There was little altruism here, little to justify me, and I knew that I deserved no reward, no credit. I was merely saving myself, and they were the buoy I was clutching to keep from sinking.

I hung on to these people, started thinking about them, started wanting to preserve them, and realized that I was just as forsaken by God and by men as they were themselves, that I was simply unable to continue as I was, on my own. Only once God had made us equal in our solitude and abandonment, only once He had brought me low, towards them, did I remember them and call them my brothers. But even then I did not actually feel them to be my brothers: it was a purely intellectual notion. I considered myself above them and for a long time I kept trying to describe them from on high, as it were, even though God had put us on the same level. I told myself that I was the first among equals, like an eldest brother: the father had died and I was taking his place. I, needless to say, was not prepared to merge with them, I just wanted to bring them to the light, like a leader, for God to see them and take pity on them. I thought, in other words, that I alone knew where to find the light, that I alone knew God existed.

To tell the truth, I was changing in so many ways that I no longer understood or remembered how I'd failed to see that the new Memorial Book was my work, the reason I'd ended up here, the sole reason, perhaps, why I existed at all. My earlier lists were just practice, rehearsal, apprenticeship. And there was something else, too. In a flash, my future was revealed to me: my role, the actions I would be granted, or rather permitted, and what might ensue from them. Suddenly I saw with complete lucidity the entire path ahead of me; the one thing I didn't know was whether I would be able to heal a single person. Either way, the consequences were clear. I saw everything very coldly and sharply, as if it were a late autumn evening, when the leaves have fallen, when everything is transparent and bare, and winter and snow are on their way; when there will be no more warmth, no more Indian summer. You can see far into the distance, with no illusions, no hopes – only resignation.

It seems to me that the way I looked at the world then was close to the way it was seen by God. He had distanced himself, almost to the point of hopelessness, from the human race that He Himself had created. Now, He thought about it in the round, from its beginning to its end. His love for man had cooled; gone was the warmth that had prevented him for so long from seeing us as we are. He had loved us so much. We were all His children, God's children, and He forgave us, caressed us, and above all, indulged us. For a long, long time He managed to convince himself that we were still children –

and what can you expect from children? But all that was gone. He had tired of us, understood that we were adults and beyond help. The way he looked at us resembled ever more closely the way we were seen by doctors. For Him, we had become varieties of illness, a sort of cabinet of horrors, a collection of the most diverse deviations, disturbances, deformities.

Previously He considered each one of us His worthy interlocutor; after all, He had created not masses, not crowds, but one single man. In other words, He had arranged things in such a way that we took one man as our measure, while everything else – the families, classes, nations, states and who knows what else into which we had grouped ourselves – was our own invention, because we were scared of speaking one on one with Him.

He watched people, watched them hiding behind each other's backs, always wanting to retreat into the shadows, to make themselves invisible to Him, resulting in an endless circular pattern of very slow, wary movement. But if they didn't manage to hide, they would immediately start pushing each other, swearing, even fighting; they would burrow into each other, as into a hole, deeper and deeper, digging one another out in the process – and this was their life, their story. They weren't ready to talk to God, and not only because of the many sins that each of them bore; no, it was more that the life they had been leading for so long, for so many generations, was a life without God, and now, when He suddenly appeared before them, He became a nuisance to them all, and they didn't know, didn't remember, how to talk to Him, or what about. In short, they were already strangers to Him, they perceived Him as a kind of spy who had suddenly walked in to this life of theirs and started playing havoc with it, disturbing everything, altering its aims, its meaning, even its rhythm. The past had suddenly become pointless and wrong. Why, for what purpose, had He taken everything away from them?

They couldn't understand why He'd come to them. After all, their own lives, their sacrifice of eternal bliss, should have shown Him how they wished to live, or rather, that they couldn't live any other way. They'd already given up, accepted that they had no right to anything, that they were weak and unworthy of His mercy or favour, of anything more than a drop of pity for one or two. But now here He was, ready to talk to them, though He knew there was nothing to be said. So they hid from him and merely got angry and annoyed that, try as they might to take cover behind each other, one would always end up directly before him. It seemed to them that this was a special trick of His, to keep one of them always before him, and an unworthy trick at that; so, feeling sorry for the unfortunate one – the person, of course, not God – they let him back in, and somebody else would end up on the edge. And so, by saving themselves they drowned each other, and this went on for as long as He continued to stand there. What a mean joke to play on them: to have someone always out on the edge, one on one with Him.

*

A week after it became clear to me that I should start writing a Memorial Book of the people who dwelled here, Ifraimov came to see me again and, without any preliminaries or explanations, continued his story about the HEURO group, the Institute for Natural Genius and its remnants on our ward. Or at least that's what I thought he was going to talk about, until he amazed me with a sudden change of tack. 'Alyosha,' he said, 'as you yourself, I believe, know only too well, few writers were as widely read and revered in Russia on the cusp of the nineteenth century as Madame de Staël.'

For the rest of the evening – as if my notes, my labour, were no longer needed, and the only person who had to be preserved was Germaine de Staël – he spoke only of her. I had long been fond of de Staël; so, it now transpired, had he. I was curious to hear Ifraimov's thoughts on the topic, but also, given our location, somewhat surprised. I didn't argue with him or contradict him, but I was astonished to hear him talk about her as if she were a close acquaintance, and in such exalted terms. As far as I recall, I hadn't even said that I was planning to write a book on de Staël, yet this felt like a dialogue all the same. And to judge by the fervour with which Ifraimov spoke about de Staël, on this and subsequent days, he felt it too.

'Her contemporaries,' Ifraimov went on, sitting beside me on the bed, 'all said the same thing: that the role played by her not in literature, but in life was unique, and, which was even more remarkable, that she did not inherit this role but gave birth to it and nursed it herself; so it was truly her own, hers and no one else's. When you think about it, such enthusiasm for Madame de Staël on the part of her friends is hardly surprising: we all love ourselves and, as part of ourselves, those around us; but almost the same feelings for Germaine de Staël are shared by many people alive today.

'Although it was not given to her to rule countries or peoples, everyone agrees that without a treasury, an army or a court, she managed, all by herself, to achieve a great deal more: she became tutor to an entire generation, mistress of its minds. And perhaps other generations, too. The trail of her ideas, her lessons stretches far and wide; even now, when de Staël is little read, you would be hard put to find a book without a character that might be traced back to her. But back then, those whom God had decreed to be born female, from Russia to Spain and both Americas, couldn't put down her *Delphine* and her even more popular *Corinne*. Few of them succeeded in replicating the fate of Germaine de Staël's characters, still fewer derived any happiness from doing so, but there was no deceit here: her heroines are beautiful, but they are unhappy and they perish. Instead, she supplied an ideal dreamt of by all, one purified and preserved by failure. And the women who read her books in their youth passed it on, intact, to their daughters, which was why, as I've already said, so much has come down to us as well; the entire nineteenth century, or at least its female half, was built by her. De Staël soon faded, quite unjustly, into the background, but still, we would do well to remember her.

'As you know, Alyosha,' Ifraimov continued, 'Germaine de Staël had a very powerful, analytical, almost masculine mind; in fact she was more thinker, philosopher or essayist – especially the last, perhaps – than writer. Her *On Literature in Its Relation to Social Institutions*, in which, avoiding extremes, she continued to stunning effect the tradition of Montesquieu, had more life and talent than her novels. Her contemporaries saw this clearly, and so do we; time has not changed a thing. *On Literature*, a thoroughly rationalistic book, calm in tone, with its surfeit of brilliant, witty observations, its profound understanding of multiple, multilingual countries, peoples, individuals (de Staël was open to everything, absorbed everything), is the true expression of her gifts; the novels are secondary. In fact, as all who knew her agreed, she was at her very best in live conversation: she was quick, clever, precise, vivacious. In the salon which began to take shape in her house when she was still only a child, when her father's career in the French court reached the first of its three peaks, de Staël was one of a kind. She may not have created this institution, the salon, or invented the genre of salon conversation, but neither of us can be in any doubt that both the first and the second were modelled on her.

'She really was a marvellous conversationalist – she scattered aphorisms like peas – but without a hint of affectation or the slightest urge to dominate. People interested her for what they were; you felt it from the very first word. Memoirs describe her unusually fast reactions, her ability to see two moves ahead, but also to make startling, daring, reckless comparisons, thanks to which her remarks sounded almost strange in their novelty, never wearying her listener. There was good reason for this – she'd received an excellent education. Her knowledge, moreover, ran deep: she'd filtered it through herself, thought it through, made it her own. But she didn't stop there. In adolescence, while still a girl, she realized that it is not intelligence that makes life worth living, and this idea had also sunk deep inside her. So it's no wonder – and do forgive me, Alyosha, if I'm repeating myself – that generations loved, surrendered to passion and suffered with her books in mind.

'And yet,' said Ifraimov, 'Germaine de Staël was never happy. Yes, her life contained in abundance all she'd ever dreamed of in her youth, and yes, she was surrounded by remarkable people, kept falling in love, bearing children, was at the heart of all the intrigues, more or less, by which the destiny of France and Europe was decided, yet she died feeling cheated. Just like her contemporaries, we too have no doubt in setting her above the titled personages of her time, but she herself thought and desired one thing only, all life long: to be like them.

'I'm convinced that she dreamed of their lot, their fate, of all that was given to them, but not her; that what she wanted was power, power over other people. Not only that: she had always been convinced that this was what God had in mind for her. As if it were from Him, the Lord, that her right to power derived. There was no madness here. Surveying all she'd done with her life and her intelligence from her estate at Coppet, some five years before her death, she justly found her achievements incommensurably small, a senseless, pathetic waste of all she'd been given. She described herself as a puppet placed by fate not on the throne, but in the toy world of the Paris salon. The gifts she possessed demanded matching resources, a matching scale, but to the end of her days she'd been forced to remain a sculptor, an architect, who traded only in miniatures.

'Did the Lord really tempt her with power? That, Alyosha, is no simple question, even for those for whom the Lord is Holy, Most Good, and quite incapable of tempting anyone. But for de Staël – a believer, as you know, but also a doubter who counted many agnostics among her friends – the question was more difficult still. Had she been born in a different era, when the right to the throne was granted only by birth – by pure chance, the rarest fluke – then everything would have been perfectly clear, but she was raised on the Revolution, on its principle of universal equality. Things that until then had been said only by a handful of philosophers became, during her lifetime and before her very eyes, the basis of every right, not least the right to power. And this principle was observed in practice. After the execution of Louis XVI a good number of individuals, possessing no particular merits other than a thirst for power, climbed to the very top, affirming and reaffirming that anyone could gain power – the only question was whether or not they could hold on to it.

'Nor should we forget that the Revolution was the sole source of power at that time, which was why the king's cousin, Philippe d'Orléans, renounced his title, becoming

Philippe Égalité, as reward for which his son, Louis-Philippe, subsequently ascended to the throne. Philippe Égalité, it was thereby acknowledged, had been right to vote for the execution of his cousin. But she, Germaine de Staël, never received a thing.

'Yet it was her father, ultimately, who brought about this revolution. Every right to it, especially the right to dispose of it, belonged to him, Baron Necker, and by succession to her, his most beloved daughter. Through his addresses on the state of the country's economy her father, twice director-general of finances under the last Louis, created the Revolution out of nothing, and it was he, of course, who should have led it. Besides, he was honest and universally respected. There's no doubt he would have governed the country far better than those who subsequently gained power, from Robespierre to Napoleon. And the people of France wanted him in power: he was the one figure who suited everyone, who could have reconciled and becalmed the Republic, become the good ruler it needed.

'It seems unlikely that either she or Necker understood the speed with which he was pushed to the margins, into the shadows, he, the only person not to have compromised himself in the slightest – a shining example, by any criteria. Revolutions were a novelty at the time and de Staël could hardly have known – she could merely have guessed – that they entailed an almost manic acceleration of life, when generations of power replace one another with exceptional speed, in the space of days, months. What I'm trying to say, Alyosha, is this: perhaps she was wrong, and perhaps her criticisms of God were unjust, but a fact is a fact: she represented the élite, the crème de la crème, the highest-born élite of the Revolution, and she had every right to the throne.

'The arguments I've set out here attest to one thing: there was, undoubtedly, a logic to her position, but she rarely noticed it; she was no lawyer. Had she been summoned to prove her right to power in court, she would have changed the topic. She would have begun by saying that in her youth she had loved the following: Talleyrand, destined, after the defeat of Napoleon, to be France's saviour; Barras, a member, and for a time de facto head, of the ruling Directory; Napoleon's ally, Benjamin Constant; and numerous others who at various times held the fate of France in their hands, but whom, for various reasons, she couldn't name.

'It is a fact, and their own letters confirm it, that the political careers, typically meteoric, of each of these men began in one and the same way: a love affair with her, de Staël. All of them, without exception, were hers. All of them loved her, caressed her, possessed her. She was woman, and they entered her, stepped into her. She welcomed them all, hid them inside herself, gave them cover, gave them strength. She herself, like the Lord God, like the Revolution, was the source of power; it was within her, deep inside her, and those she allowed in gained power. Next, she would have told the jury: "For a long time I tried to deceive myself. I couldn't come to terms with the fact that power was inside me, yet beyond my reach. You must agree," she'd have said to them, "that I, Germaine de Staël, ever thirsting for power, was subjected to torments worse than those invented for Tantalus. I've lived my life, but never drunk my fill; do I really not deserve your indulgence?"

'A woman of resourceful intelligence, de Staël simply couldn't accept that there was nothing to be done. For many years she tried to persuade herself that her lovers were extracting power not from her, but from her salon, that the salon was the only ladder by which they could climb. De Staël adored her salon; she tended it, cherished it. On reception days, she greeted every visitor like her one and only friend. And this is not hard to understand: we both know, Alyosha, that only in the salon was she content, only there, among the brilliant, exceptional people whom she herself had chosen and invited, did she realize that her life was not in vain. Early on, almost immediately after the execution of Robespierre, when her traditional Tuesdays and Fridays resumed, she even created a myth about her salon. Its purpose was simple: that the source of power could be anywhere – however close by – but not in her. Later, in order to prove that power did not reside in her, that inside she was no different from any other woman, de Staël expanded this legend into an entire doctrine.

'Germaine de Staël,' Ifraimov continued, 'claimed that a very small, but well-organized and well-disguised group with an intelligent and strong-willed leader at its helm could seize the destiny of the world without the slightest difficulty. Just one thing was required – iron discipline, a readiness to submit oneself entirely to the needs of the organization. Her salon was a cover for just such a group. Behind the screen of fashionable conversation and philosophical abstraction, decisions were being taken about who would rule France and how. Thanks to Napoleon, this myth became very popular and spread far and wide. Fouché, who ran the French secret police and had many informers among Madame de Staël's friends, was a sober type, not given to flights of fancy, so de Staël's banishment first from Paris, then from France itself, is mystifying; perhaps he simply needed a conspiracy or two to cement his position.

'In general, Alyosha, it seems to me that the fate of Madame de Staël is somehow akin to the fate of Adam, the original man. As if their lives complete one another. As if Germaine de Staël was meant for a quite different time and the Lord wanted her to be Eve, wife of Adam, Mother of mothers, but she was born too late. Recall the episode from Genesis where the Lord tells Adam to name all the living things that He, the Lord, has created and with which he has populated the earth intended for man. But in order to give each creature its true, unique name, Adam has to know its nature; he has to discover, understand, who it really is. The Lord Creator knows all this, but Adam does not. And when the angels start bringing him God's creatures, one by one, he, in order to grasp who they are, enters into them, comes to know them, in full view of God, as he comes to know Eve, as a man comes to know a woman, as Barras came to know in Germaine de Staël the essence of power – and only then does he name them.

'If we are to believe her biographers,' said Ifraimov, 'Madame de Staël, after being banished from France in 1810 and abandoned by her closest friends, settled in Switzerland, in her ancestral estate at Coppet. For the first few months she was depressed, dispirited, didn't want to see anyone; but fate brought her an unexpected gift. A young Frenchman fell in love with her, the officer Jean Rocca, and, although he was only twenty-two and she forty-four, they married. A year later she gave birth to a girl, whom they christened with the same name that had been chosen for her – Germaine. Soon after the birth, Madame de Staël secretly left Switzerland and, travelling via Vienna and Warsaw, arrived in Russia. She spent time in Kiev, Moscow, St Petersburg, and was given an audience by Alexander I. Napoleon's troops were already crossing the Niemen and she, renowned as the Corsican's most dangerous enemy, received a rapturous welcome wherever she went.

'In the autumn of 1813 she left by boat for London, where a no less triumphal reception awaited her. Then she settled once again at Coppet, before returning to Paris in October, 1816. On

21 February, 1817, on her way to a ball given by Louis XVIII's Chief Minister, she tripped on the stairs of his mansion. The fall caused a haemorrhage to the brain, from which Germaine de Staël died five months later. The day of her death was 14 July – the day on which the French Revolution began.

*

'This superficial outline of events is uncontroversial and accepted by all the biographers, but the essence, as so often, is obscured. To understand it, we must go back five centuries. In 1492, on the ninth day of the month of Ab – that's to say, on the day of the destruction of both the First and Second Temples of Jerusalem – King Ferdinand II of Aragon issued an edict expelling the Jews from Spain. Six years after this edict two distinguished Jewish families reached Geneva and found refuge at the home of the great-great-grandfather of Baron Necker, Jacques Necker. It was with Jacques Necker, in fact, that the rise of the Necker clan began.

'The second half of the fifteenth century was a terrible period in the long history of the Jews. From one end of Europe to the other, many of their communities were obliterated or forcibly converted; in others, all the men were slaughtered and only the women were spared, for enormous ransoms. Some of the famous Kabbalist rabbis (among them disciples of the Rabbi Luria) claimed that the day was nigh when the annihilation of the Jews would be complete and the Lord's trumpet would herald the arrival of the Last Judgment. Consequently, in the *yeshivas* run by these rabbis, texts related to the Ninth of Ab and the Last Judgment were studied with particular zeal.

'Greatest attention was devoted to two problems. The first was entirely practical: what were Jewish women to do in those communities where not a single man survived, if they had no way of moving to another town? How were they to fulfil the Lord's commandment to "go forth and multiply"? How were they to continue their tribe? The second was a very eccentric Talmudic commentary on the twenty-second chapter of the Torah, claiming that when the nations presented themselves for the Last Judgment each would contain several *Kohanim* – that is, several direct male descendants of Aaron, whose veins flowed only with Jewish blood and who would act as intercessors. Moreover, the text could be interpreted in such a way that neither the *Kohanim* themselves nor their wives would know that they were Jews.

'Eventually, after lengthy labours, the key to understanding this commentary was found. The letters of the twenty-second chapter of the Torah, when arranged in a certain order, formed a new text which not only solved the mystery of the *Kohanim*, but also gave an answer to the Jewish women left without husbands and suitors. It contained, among other things, the recipe for a certain compound – its basic ingredient was the mandrake plant that helped Rachel conceive – after consuming which a husbandless woman, assuming the "custom of women" had not ceased in her, could fall pregnant and give birth to a child: herself. By giving the wretched woman another whole life the Lord, as it were, acknowledged her righteousness before Him and His guilt. Thanks to this miracle all that was perishable, all that was subject to age and decay, was wholly renewed in her, but neither grief nor misfortune could be erased from her memory, nor could she ever forget a single one of the murdered men. The woman was permitted to use the mandrake three times, after which both guilt and sin were passed on to the nation that had failed to help its fellow tribeswoman. Among the other things for which the Jewish refugees from Spain owed Jacques Necker their gratitude was the secret of the prolongation of life. To the best of my knowledge, the first Gentile to have used it was Germaine. Having been forgotten by the Neckers, the secret was discovered by her quite by chance when, with nothing better to do, she was sorting through the family papers in Coppet. After dithering and doubting about whether or not her action would be found pleasing to God, she decided to prolong her life.

'And so, Germaine's daughter, apparently born of Germaine de Staël and Jean Rocca, actually had nothing to do with Rocca at all – she was Germaine de Staël herself. For her second life Madame de Staël chose not France, by which she had been so cruelly disappointed, but Russia, with which she was extremely taken. Choosing three reliable women – a wet-nurse, a nanny, a governess – she travelled there with her one-year-old girl, bought a large, very beautiful estate in her name, south of Oskol, and, having made all the necessary arrangements, boarded a ship in St Petersburg bound for England. In Russia Germaine de Staël was given an Orthodox baptism and registered in the list of nobles under the name Evgeniya Frantsevna Stal, a landowner in the province of Tambov.'

After telling me that de Staël had settled in Russia, Ifraimov suddenly lost his thread and launched into a strange digression about the Franco-Russian War of 1812, about the softness and femininity of Russia… He went on to say that Gemaine de Staël lived in our country for a very long time and that he could tell me a thing or two about her, but not now – we'd been keeping everyone up for half the night as it was. He got to his feet and I walked him back to his room.

Knowing Ifraimov as I now did, I was convinced I'd

have to wait at least a week for this next conversation, but the following evening, as soon as the oldies in my room were asleep, there he was again, sitting down next to me, ready, by all appearances, to resume his account of the life of de Staël. There was something unusual about him, as if he'd resolved some important question overnight. Perhaps he'd been thinking about the Memorial Book. In fact, I was sure of it. In which case, the topic of Madame de Staël was far from accidental: Ifraimov wanted me to commemorate her as well. Though I suppose I may have simply imagined this.

*

Sometimes it would take Ifraimov a while to start talking and he could spend up to half an hour sitting motionless, bolt upright, his hands on his knees, his eyes half-closed. He'd held precisely this pose for the duration of the previous evening, too, only his eyes had been open and turned towards me. This time the pause lasted an unusually long time. I didn't want to be the one to raise the subject of de Staël and so, just as soon as he'd snapped out of his trance, I began by asking about Adam and the Tree of Knowledge. He replied at once, but not at all in the way I'd expected.

'When man was driven out of paradise,' he said, 'the Tree of Knowledge was banished as well, along with plenty of other trees. But trees proved better than people: they face upwards, towards God, and now only two things unite heaven and earth, preventing their final separation – prayers and trees. Having barely put down roots in the soil,' he went on, 'a tree begins reaching up into the sky, releasing one new shoot, one new branch after another, and this root system is stronger than that which holds it in the earth. Climbing higher and higher, it penetrates, pullulates air and sky, tying them to the earth as if by an umbilical cord. A tree, you see, is like the Tower of Babel, and although God understands that it is not pride that makes them grow, not one tree, however tall, is fated to return to heaven before the Final Judgment.

'Essentially, every tree repeats, as it were, the fate of the human race. It, too, is conceived in heaven, where its seeds ripen and gather strength and sap, before plummeting to earth like Adam. But their womb is in the sky, and it is to the sky that they long to return. Trees grow and climb very slowly, step by step, invisibly to the naked eye. In other words, the path by which man can be cleansed and saved is gradual, arduous, and not everyone can walk it. Out of thousands of fallen seeds a mere handful will sprout and put down roots, but they will cling on for dear life and, while God is with them, endure. There are trees that live many hundreds, even thousands of years, but even so, not one of them, as I've already said, is destined to return to paradise. Mould and rot eat away at them, as sin eats away at man. And yet, dying and enfeebled, the tree, in the last summer of its allotted span, brings forth in the sky a fruit as pure and chaste as a child born of the most sinful woman.

'You see, Alyosha,' Ifraimov went on, 'you have every right to ask me why the tree was punished. It's impossible for me to answer precisely, of course, and impossible for me to know, but I can hazard a guess. The tree of paradise had many fruits, and the point is not that Adam ate one of them too soon. The tree's sin lies elsewhere: the sweetest of all the fruits that grew on it was the one that I would call the fruit of the end, of the completed journey, the fruit of knowledge, answers, truth, and not of the path towards that truth. Having eaten it, man could no longer walk on his own without fear; he no longer believed he could ever reach God. Ever since Adam, callow Adam, plucked that fruit, we, his descendants, have also been much keener on answers than questions. It became so difficult to talk to God, so difficult to understand him, precisely because, after the Fall, He and we speak different languages. The world of God is the world of questions. Only questions are commensurable with the complexity of His world.

'Think for a moment of our doctor, Kronfeld: what kind of a man is he? I'm sure you'll agree that even if you know him as well as you know yourself and go to the trouble of explaining everything about him, your portrait will be incomparably simpler and more primitive than that same Kronfeld. The Talmud states that man, each and every man, is as dear to God as the entire world He created. And man is just as complex as the world, because the world is in each and every one of us. Whatever Kronfeld may be like, clever or stupid, good or bad, or neither, there will always be space for him in my question, but never in your answer. Answers have no place in God's world; they're inimical to it, artificial. They're simple and make the space around them just as simple and comprehensible as themselves, but this is an illusion, an imprecise, distorted, approximate world where everything is fuzzy, where the boundaries are blurred, where one thing is laid on top of another, to the point that even good and evil can no longer be told apart. Evil for the sake of good; good that turns out to be evil.

'This is no longer the world created by God; it's different, and we won't return to God unless we learn how to ask. The subtler and the wiser our questions, the sooner we will find our way to Him. And there is only one law we need to keep in mind – the law of tact. We need to know what to ask and what not to ask, because there are some questions so cursed that they are capable of destroying everything that exists. Some questions do permit approximate answers, others don't and never will; others still may be answerable – and we have every right to ask them – but these are answers we will never receive, or never understand. The world in which we exist is alive: it's changeable, mobile, and we should never forget this, just as we should never forget that our questions should not vie with the world, should not fight it; on the contrary, they should be in harmony with it, be acknowledged by it, accepted by it.

'All this, Alyosha, would seem obvious enough, but the language in which questions may be asked is disappearing: I mean the language in which the Five Books given by God to Moses were written, in the original, archaic Hebrew. Here, the words of the Torah have multiple meanings; the text brims with metaphor, imagery, simile. Try to understand, Alyosha: good metaphors are not merely games with words; they are true, they contain the real semblance of things, the unity of the universe created by the One God. Besides, people wrote without vowels back then, and words quite different in meaning often looked identical or similar on paper. All this allowed the text to breathe, to change, to open up to man each time anew, to be understood and explained anew. It was alive, as alive as the world. In translation, all this has been lost.

'The Septuagint and the Vulgate, by virtue of their languages and the nature of translation itself, narrowed and simplified the meaning of the Torah. A translation is never more than the translator's own interpretation, as if every phrase were prefaced by the words: I, such-and-such, living in such-and-such a place, at such-and-such a time, understood God's words like so. And all this – who he was, how he lived – ended up in the Bible. The translations of the Scriptures marked a boundary, after which a canon was formed and the words were left with one meaning only; but a language like that is fit only for answers.

'There was a time,' Ifraimov continued, 'when people didn't write words, they drew them. Man was in every symbol he drew; each one contained his thoughts, his prayers, his discoveries, or simply his speculations. Copying out a word, you drew your own understanding of it, and it was always new. When the Torah was given to man on Sinai, that age was nearing its end. Every nation, by and large, already wrote in identical letters, as alike to one another as twins; but there were still some who remembered and understood the old method. Egypt tried to renew it, or at least to prevent it from being forgotten. Then those people died and ever since we've been working away at a peculiar task: thousands of the best minds have written commentaries and interpretations of the Holy Scriptures, but the words with which they've written them are defined, finished and, as it were, fixed. Such was Esau: everything about him was perfect, complete; he could no longer change. So God took away his birthright.

'Monosemic words,' said Ifraimov, 'are a terrible disease. They are born of lies and the fear of being deceived. There is no trust, no freedom in a language like that. It's good for lawyers and bureaucrats, but you can't pray with it. And that's not all: more and more often now, we colour our words – "ours", "theirs", "good", "bad". The paint is bright, precise, full of contrast, and in the end it kills off sense. It matters little what a word means if you've already been told what to make of it. Letters, of course, were a great invention: they simplified the act of writing incalculably; but the losses, alas, were also considerable. The Kabbalists were wrong: the Torah is open to us in its entirety, given to us in its entirety; we are the ones who make it closed.'

It was late; everyone was asleep. Ifraimov was tired and sat slouched against the wall. I thought he must be waiting for me to get up and accompany him to his room again, like yesterday, and started feeling about for my slippers with my feet. I still hadn't found them when Ifraimov stopped me, as if he'd suddenly remembered about Germaine de Staël.

*

'After the first, tumultuous life lived by Madame de Staël in France, her second, spent in Russia, was almost a holiday. It was uneventful, especially at first, and there isn't a great deal I can say about it. Just one episode stands out, and only because its consequences, or even, you could say, the episode itself, have lasted to this day.

'We should give Evgeniya Frantsevna Stal her due: she wasn't a Necker for nothing, and she soon proved herself a very thrifty manager. In the middle of the nineteenth century, when the major landowners' estates in Russia were, as a rule, being mortgaged and remortgaged, rarely yielding income, the profit from her holding, which was virtually the sole estate in the province, kept growing. What was more – and this reflects especially well on Evgeniya Frantsevna – the peasants in her possession were considered the most prosperous in the region. She lived a very reclusive, solitary life, had little reason, unlike in Paris, to spend any money, and would immediately reinvest the fruits of the soil in the estate, enthusiastically trying out one improvement after another. Intending, at some point, to bring apples to Moscow, she laid out two huge orchards on the banks of the river, planted forests, and appears to have been the first person, outside Ukraine, to plant all her own land with beet, building a modestly sized, but eminently profitable sugar refinery out in the fields.

'Baron Necker told his master Louis XVI on several occasions that there was only one way of ensuring that your subjects paid their taxes on time – don't stop them making money from them. Evgeniya Frantsevna observed this principle assiduously, offering her peasants, in addition to other privileges, generous loans for the development of their trades. Country life fascinated her to such an extent that, contrary to her original intentions, she started wintering in her estate as well; indeed, after turning twenty-four, she no longer visited the two capitals at all. She even stayed away from nearby Tambov, other than for the occasional day trip; only during the annual assemblies of the nobility did she spend a week or two in town.

'Previously she had ventured out to Moscow or St Petersburg fairly often and stayed in hotels there, but never under her own name, so her series of tempestuous affairs remained secret and never compromised her reputation. She was, by any criteria, the catch of the province: rich, young, attractive, intelligent, and at first she was the object of numerous, persistent proposals, but she turned everyone down. She did so, moreover, in such a decisive and definitive manner that you immediately understood that her refusal was not directed at you personally and that she planned to remain unmarried for the rest of her days. People talked, of course, but she gave no further cause for gossip and the matchmaking efforts soon ended; even the suitors stopped visiting. Since she treated everyone in the same, respectful way, no one was offended by her refusals and her relations with all were unharmed. People thought her strange, but left her in peace.

'Life soon confirmed de Staël's conviction that if only Russian noblemen would spend more time on their estates than they did in St Petersburg, the soil, by virtue of its fertility and of the climate, would maintain them far better than any position in the civil service. In fact, she made this point on two separate occasions at the gentry assemblies, and on both occasions her speech was well received and broadly supported, but the result was always the same: her reputation for eccentricity was established for good.

'She stuck rigidly to her rule of never leaving the estate other than in exceptional circumstances. Alone among the local nobility, it seems, she chose not to abandon her estate, even during the cholera epidemic which ravaged the Russian south in 1851 and reached Tambov by September. She didn't even shut herself in, as was done by those who lacked the funds to up sticks and leave. Gratified by her own bravery, she continued her traditional daily tours of Pine Ravine, as her estate was called, keeping a close eye on all the works in progress. The sole precaution she took against disease was to order, in Oskol, a highly unusual palanquin of her own design. Aside from the wooden bottom, through which numerous small openings had been drilled for ventilation, its five other sides, which were joined to one another by hinges, were made of beautiful Bohemian glass etched with lead.

'This glass box – carried by four peasants and accompanied by her steward – was furnished on her instructions with a couch upholstered in light-blue taffeta, the only purchase she had brought with her from France, and now she reclined on it as she travelled about, wearing a long muslin dress, a white lace hat and dancing slippers, also white, which she was very fond of and which suited her perfectly. To make doubly sure of her immunity inside the box, she lit scented candles. It took no more than a day for her astonishing palanquin to become known to all in the neighbouring villages and estates;

to Staël's considerable amusement, it made a huge impression on everyone, masters and peasants alike.

'In the summer of that year, in the neighbouring province of Voronezh on the other side of the river, she acquired another village, Solovka, along with some woodland, and at the end of September, when all the paperwork had finally been approved, she set off to inspect it. Her palanquin had barely crossed the bridge to the other bank when Staël's attention was drawn to a young man walking ahead of them. Only later did she realize what it was that had caught her gaze, even from behind: the stranger's attire was patently that of a master, but his manner and his gait were more like that of a commoner, strikingly so. To confirm her impression, she was determined to see his face, but, without any baggage to weigh him down, he walked too quickly for her bearers to catch up with him. Eventually she grew weary of wondering who this man might be, and dozed off.

'She fell into a pleasurable and, so it seemed, lengthy sleep, until she was jolted awake by cursing and shouting, and, above all, by the fact that the palanquin had stopped. Having barely come to her senses, she saw kneeling in front of her that same young man from before. Staring straight at her, he alternated between crossing himself at great speed and rummaging frantically in his pocket, while somehow fending off the steward, who was trying to shove him off the road – a most amusing spectacle. Just as she'd thought, he was a perfect child, one of those who rarely feel rooted in this world. He had a sweet, well-meaning face and it occurred to her to strike up a conversation with him, perhaps even take him with her to her new estate. She'd already opened her mouth to call the boy over, but as she did so he finally found what he'd been searching for in his purse, and, try as the peasants might to stop him, adroitly placed a copeck on the rim of the glass box, after which he promptly took to his heels.

'Noticing that Staël had woken up, the steward set about explaining himself in a guilty voice, but she couldn't understand what he was saying and was simply incapable of working out what had happened for herself; only later did it suddenly dawn on her that the boy had mistaken her either for a statue of the Virgin Mary or for the Virgin Mary herself. It so happened that on that very day Orthodox churches were celebrating the Feast of the Annunciation, and in the morning peasants had come to the manor house to pay her their respects, bringing her bread and salt, as tradition dictated; she'd made the same gift in return and now they'd taken her for the Mother of God. This was all so impossibly funny – she, Evgeniya Frantsevna Stal, famous throughout the district as an old maid, being taken for the Virgin Mary! – that, recalling once more the mixture of decision and horror with which the boy had just offered up his copeck coin, she began to laugh like crazy and was quite incapable of stopping.

'Then the peasants moved off again with the palanquin; after this episode, though, she felt like doing something silly and could think of nothing better than make everyone to go back to look for the fallen coin. She calmed down only once the copeck was finally found on the dusty road and the steward handed it over to her. As a result, they reached Solovka when night was already falling and it was too late to inspect anything; besides, she was no longer in the mood for work. She merely remarked, in a lazy sort of voice, that the peasants' huts were in a poor state and some were even crooked; that the amenities were dilapidated and there would have been nowhere to put her horses for the night had she arrived by carriage; and that the manor house was made of stone, a rarity in these parts, and its condition, at first glance, looked reasonable enough.

'It was a two-storey house and she ordered her bed to be made up on the second, in a small corner room that had a fireplace and could be quickly and easily heated. In the absence of a shed, the palanquin was to be left in the large reception room on the ground floor. Just as soon as her room warmed up, she settled down for the night. Once again, though, she wasn't allowed to rest in peace. In the early hours the sound of shouting and swearing reached her from downstairs; it was all very reminiscent of her adventure the previous day. As nobody answered her calls, she got dressed on her own and went downstairs, where the peasants, still hot from the skirmish, told her that the same chap from before had just made two attempts to enter the house and destroy her palanquin. At the second try, he'd even got as far as the inner porch before they stopped him. They wanted to tie him down, but he fought like a man possessed, eventually broke free and ran off.

'When she asked them whether the stranger had happened to mention what it was about the palanquin that so displeased him, they confirmed that he had: he kept saying, or rather shouting, that he would break the spell, smash the crystal coffin and free the Sleeping Princess. She knew Pushkin's fairytale[2] and she suddenly felt very happy to have become the Sleeping Princess, glad that she was no longer being taken for the Virgin Mary. In that fairytale, if her memory served, the man who was supposed to free the princess and take her for his wife was a handsome prince, and it occurred to her that a proposal of this kind would be quite amusing, especially since no one had proposed to her for some time. Recently she

---

2 Alexander Pushkin's narrative poem, 'The Tale of the Dead Princess and the Seven Strong Men', which contains elements of both 'Sleeping Beauty' and 'Little Snow White'. (Tr.)

sometimes regretted the way she'd scared everyone off. Not that she was suddenly about to get married, but she felt bored, or weary, of her solitary life, and a suitor or two would at least provide some distraction. Agriculture was gradually losing its novelty, becoming mere routine, and she gave herself to it without her previous zeal. She felt the need for new faces, new impressions, and, for the first time in her two lives, perhaps, she felt frightened by the prospect of a lonely old age.

'Nevertheless, she decided not to do anything herself to encourage this boy, though he was sweet and she rather liked him; a boy, moreover, who had created such a magical and romantic role for her in his production. She was convinced that the action of this drama, fortunately, was not yet over, which may have been why she chose not to do anything. She'd immediately grasped the fact that this was his play, and she, at least at the beginning, must not interfere or try to change anything, but simply follow and obey. And another thing: she felt that his story contained some deep significance and that it would continue for an absurdly long time, far too long for any normal play, constantly acquiring new lines and twists, and the purpose for which it had all been invented would become clear – to the boy, to her, to the other participants – only at the very end.

*

'She'd expected to spend five or six days in her new village, setting the quit-rent and fixing the schedule of works for the autumn and winter. But now, after this nocturnal incident, it occurred to her that no one was waiting for her at Pine Ravine and that, if necessary, she could extend her stay here. If the boy needed time, she was not going to hurry him. In fact, she was prepared to help him in any way she could, though

138

her assistance was hardly required. The following night he reappeared and this time he was craftier. Knowing that the entrance was guarded, he tried to enter the house through a window and began opening the shutters, but he was clumsy and made too much noise; the peasants were on the alert and caught him easily. Eventually they let him go, but only after giving him a sound beating.

'Hearing about this in the morning, she tore a strip off the village elder and gave strict instructions that, in the event of another foray, the stranger should not be harmed but simply caught, bound and kept in the porch until she'd been informed; then, filled with pity, she wept the whole day long. Three nights passed without further incident – he must have been licking his wounds – but on the fourth, the attempt was repeated. This time, too, it ended in complete failure, but by then she already knew who he was.

'In these parts his sad fate was known to almost everyone. His father was Prince Pavel Ivanovich Gagarin while his mother, also of noble stock, was Elizaveta Ivanova, whose parents owned a very small estate nearby – actually, little more than a farm. Pavel and Elizaveta never married and their son, therefore, was illegitimate. As a result, he took his patronymic and surname from his godfather and was known as Nikolai Fyodorovich Fyodorov. His natural father died very young but, for as long as they were alive, he remained under the patronage of his grandfather, Prince Ivan Alexeyevich, a famous dignitary during the reigns of Catherine and Alexander, and of his uncle, Prince Konstantin Ivanovich. Their money paid for his education at a gymnasium in Tambov and half a course of studies at the Richelieu Lyceum in Odessa. Now that they, too, had died, he was left without means, and the most he could hope for, it seemed, was a teaching position in some village school.

'When the elder informed her that, in accordance with her instructions, this half-wit had been tied down in the porch, she sent him back to Fyodorov, with orders to persuade him that the time to free the princess had not yet come, that the spell was still upon her, and that if he smashed the coffin now, she'd die on the spot; she didn't dare go to him herself. She also told him to say that if he, Fyodorov, agreed to bide his time and wait for the magic to wear off, he might be admitted to the princess that same day. No sooner had the elder left than Evgeniya Frantsevna got up, put on the same muslin dress in which he had taken her for the Virgin Mary, the same hat and dancing shoes, and hurried downstairs. She lit four large wax candles by the four corners of the palanquin, lit another four – scented, black and slender – on the inside, doing all she could to make everything as it had been then, and, after one last check, lay down on the couch. Next, she drew down the lid of the "coffin" and set about waiting for the elder to finish admonishing Fyodorov before letting him in to see her. She knew that both her clothes and the candles, reflected in the crystal glass from within and without, made everything just as beautiful and mysterious as in a fairytale, and she was glad he'd see her and remember her just as she was then, whatever else might happen to them both in the future. Eventually the elder opened the doors before him and very slowly, squinting from the brilliant flashes of light, Fyodorov walked up to her coffin. He got down on his knees, made the sign of the cross over her three times and kissed the glass at the point closest to her eyes and lips. Then he sat down beside her.

'Although Evgeniya Frantsevna's eyelids were lowered, she succeeded, for the first time, in taking a good look at him. He was no longer a boy, of course, but he was still very young and his features reminded her of Rocca, with whom she had once been happy. For a moment she even forgot that this was not Rocca sitting before her, and once again she was upset on his and her own behalf, for not having borne Rocca a child. Perhaps it wasn't only Fyodorov who'd brought Rocca to mind now; for a few months already she'd been feeling that something inside her was beginning to change. Much of what had always seemed secondary and irrelevant was now coming back to her and every time she felt sad that she hadn't seen these things at the time, hadn't appreciated them, hadn't understood them. People, above all. She was used to hearing about Madame de Staël always craving new faces, about her being the sort of person who found other people interesting, so who could have ever taken offence? But it turned out that she had neglected a great many. Now she felt sorry for them, and for herself.

'Even so, the main thing here was probably still that boy, Fyodorov, not his resemblance to Rocca or anyone else. From the moment he entered her life, her position in the world had changed, and she herself suddenly saw it in a different light, as if she really were looking at the world from inside a coffin. Previously she was all movement, all action, always at the centre of intrigues and conspiracies, always surrounded by people whom she was either trying to win over or profit from – everything, in other words, flowed from her to them; but now, she was a changed woman. She lay without moving for hours at a time, scared of stirring and frightening him. Her body became numb, then sore, but she, unable since childhood to endure a moment's pain, took it all without grumbling. She just lay there, looking at this boy through half-closed eyes. When he talked, she would listen, but Fyodorov's diction was poor and his voice, in any case, was muffled by the glass, so for a long time she could barely understand a word; only later, by watching his lips, did she learn to work out what he was saying. And not once, of course, did she say anything in reply.

'She lay like that hour after hour, neither awake nor asleep, but in a strange sort of slumber. Time in her world had been slowed down by him, or even stopped completely. Everything, in fact, had been appeased by him, assuaged by him; after all, for the entire duration of these trysts – both the first and the second, when he spent an entire night by her side and left only at dawn (she didn't even know when: she'd already dozed off) – nothing ever happened.

'For nearly all that time he just sat there, looking at her with a kind of unimaginable tenderness. Often she saw tears in his eyes, and twice he even cried – why, she didn't know. Sometimes he began telling her about himself; she knew this even when she couldn't make out the words, because his voice became terribly sad. He would be telling her something when suddenly he'd get carried away like a child, start waving his arms about, jumping up and shouting, then break off all at once, as if his behaviour really were out of place, sit back down again and start staring at her once more, never taking his eyes off her. As the night wore on he would become tired, lie down with his face to the coffin and rest his head near her stomach; soon, she would begin to feel his warmth through the glass and also drift off. He trained her in stillness, patience, resignation; there had been too much strength in her, too much movement; now that had passed, and people came back to her all at once from the past, people who were just as slow as her trysts with Fyodorov, people who before had been unable to keep up with her. She was grateful to him for them as well.

'In Solovka, Fyodorov and Staël saw each other almost every day. Then, after a couple of weeks, having stayed twice as long as she'd expected, she went back to Pine Ravine and wasn't surprised to see him follow her; in fact, she'd assumed he would. Here, everything continued as before. When he came, the servants would leave him on his own – though not in the porch, but in the hall: Pine Ravine had a traditional manor house – and she would go downstairs, lie in the coffin and wait for him to be sent in. Sometimes, if she was feeling unwell or simply didn't wish to be with him, he was told that he couldn't see her now because the spell was upon her, and he left without grumbling. He was a quiet, docile sort. But this happened rarely. He had quickly – unexpectedly quickly – become part of her life, and should he fail to appear for a day or two, for whatever reason, she became bored, didn't know what to do with herself, became more and more worried about him as the day wore on and pestered the servants for information; when Fyodorov finally arrived, she breathed a sigh of relief, feeling happy and light at heart.

'It was clear that there was a terrible lack of love in this Russian life of hers, a lack of children, and a child was what he was to her, both in his stories and in the pity he aroused in her, and she listened to him as she would to a child, to her own creation; she felt sorry for him, loved him, pined for him as for a part of herself, for the flesh of her flesh. And so it continued for quite some time, two months or even three. Gossip began to reach her from the neighbouring estates: she was tormenting him, making fun of a poor madman. In fact, this whole episode made waves throughout Tambov Province and even reached the ears of the governor, perhaps on account of the glass coffin, whose construction, together with her pretence of being dead, struck everyone as the very height of cynicism.

'Whether it was all this talk that affected her, or something else, she suddenly realized that she could no longer listen calmly as he declared his love for her. She was finding it harder and harder to see him as just a child; she was constantly having to persuade herself that he really was a child, no different from any other; and it was hardest of all when he lay on the glass, and his heat, warming the coffin, began to reach her. This was the lightest of caresses, as if he were barely touching her, as if he were warming her with his breath, the breath of his body, and she would forget that they were separated by glass, as if he'd lain down directly on top of her, and she could feel him on her and began to want him, madly. She wanted him so much that her body could no longer be calm and moved beneath this warmth of his, as if he were dissolving the glass, coming nearer, lying down on her, and she was ready to part, to open, to let him in.

'He would fall asleep while she, unable to take any more of it, would lift herself up off the couch and, with her pubis, touch the glass he had warmed with his stomach and his groin, where he had made the glass not just warm, but hot, and moving her body this way and that she drove herself into a frenzy. Her senses were so sharp now that at night, when the house quietened down and the life went out of it, not even the burning candles could prevent her from identifying his heat; she could even identify it with words. It was completely different from any normal heat, she told her old French wet-nurse; it was alive and soft, and there was no need to keep your distance, because you couldn't be burned by it, stung by it. And when the candles went out she felt this heat more keenly than ever, flowing from him in waves, and she counted them, as if she were by the shore. She knew that Fyodorov could feel her too and she was grateful to him. At night, pressing her pubis to the glass, where his groin was, she could see his flesh respond to her, bulging through his tight trousers and he, trying to make himself comfortable, began muttering something in his sleep, tossing and turning, groaning, unable to settle down.

'It didn't take long for her to start thinking that it might be a good thing for the pair of them if she made him her lover, a kept man, or perhaps even marry him. But this was fraught with problems and she wavered, unable to make up her mind. She was so used to living on her own, to depending on nobody and answering to nobody, and held her reputation so dear, that agreeing to all this being destroyed did not come easily to her. Besides, she valued Fyodorov just as he was, she liked lying beneath the crystal glass, liked being the Sleeping Princess, being loved as the Sleeping Princess, and she didn't want to lose any of this. In other words, she'd have been happy to make him her lover but only on condition that nothing else in their relationship changed: the way he looked at her, the way he sat with her, the way she lay beneath him, close but inaccessible, unattainable. She liked the innocence of their relationship no less than before, and how this could be combined with him becoming her lover was beyond her comprehension. Nor did she know how he would react when she stopped being the Sleeping Princess.

'Telling her about himself, Fyodorov mentioned more than once that he was a virgin, and she had grown used to respecting this. So much of his understanding of the world was based on the fact that he had never had any business with women and that she, whom he would save, free from her spell and bring back to life, would be his first. She didn't even know whether or not he would agree to become her lover.

'Externally nothing changed in their relationship, nothing at all, but with each day, each night that passed, she wanted him more. He slept, while she, desiring him, excited herself to a pitch of insanity. Forgetting about the glass, she thrashed against it, rubbed against it, pressed herself to it, shook all over. She was in a kind of constant hysteria, weeping without cause, not sleeping even by day, barely eating. And now, amidst all this, afraid of anything and everything – never had she known such fear – and no more able to make up her mind than she was before, while realizing that things couldn't go on like this or else she'd go mad, de Staël suddenly remembered the wet-nurse telling her recently that in Tambov a German chemist, Schlichting, had opened a new and very good pharmacy where a rare cold medicine was sold, based on morphine, or perhaps opium.

*

'The remarkable properties of Chinese opium, the opium dens of the East, and the sensations experienced by the person who takes this drug had been an occasional topic of conversation even back in the days of her Paris salon. Two of her acquaintances of the time, having spent many years in India, couldn't get by without it; one of them, the Baron d'Orsay, a sad individual with a yellow, almost Chinese face – a slow man, the type she now found herself remembering more and more often – once spent the better part of an evening persuading de Staël's guests that happiness, complete, absolute happiness, is close at hand and, above all, easily attained. Dirt-poor, hungry Indians are cleverer than their white masters, as they know only too well. They're prepared to work all day long, but not for the sake of food, money or power: all they need is a pipe filled with opium. Because whether you're young or decrepit, in good health or at death's door, a single pipe is enough for bliss to flood your body, for you to return to paradise, to return to a time when the Fall had never even entered anyone's mind. Opium wipes the dust off everything; if nature has aged, dimmed, lost its colour and freshness, now it returns to how it once was.

'You begin by identifying smells, then your other senses become sharper as well. You're like a child again, and God is taking you back again, back to the world as it was on the first day of creation. All around everything is blossoming, fragrant: trees, grass, flowers. You don't know their names, because not one of them has yet been given one; that day when the Lord will say to you, "As you name them, so it shall be," has not yet come, and names are not needed anyway. The colours are so bright, so striking, it's as if they have a separate existence, before anything else. Nothing dominates, nothing interferes. You can identify everything the world is made of, and not only what's outside, but even the air in your lungs, every drop of blood in your veins, every muscle. You're new and pure, like a firstborn, sinless man.

'But everything, alas, has its price: the moment of awakening, of returning to our world is terrifying and abrupt, the pain is immense – every cell in your body is aching, every piece of cartilage and bone, as if everything inside you has been trampled, broken, shredded – and so is the sense of loss; after all, nothing has faded yet, and you haven't had time to get used to anything, to accept anything, to forget. After the Fall, Adam must have felt the same way. There's only one consolation: paradise is easily regained.

'"The opium-smoker," said d'Orsay, "will never say whether the pipe merely grants him pleasurable dreams (in which case the price is surely too steep), or whether it really does carry you off into the world as created by God – I myself couldn't tell you even now. Sometimes I'm convinced that what I see is real, but the very next day I tend to think I was simply dreaming. In any case, when I'm smoking a pipe and someone starts talking to me, I hear, understand and reply perfectly normally, but it's all so mixed up with dreams that, even when I wake, I can't separate anything out."

'After this speech of long ago, she saw d'Orsay only a few times more; he soon left Paris for his estate in the Auvergne, where, rumour had it, he died a month later. Now, together with Schlichting and his pharmacy, all these memories came back to her. At first she was sad about d'Orsay, sad she'd paid him so little attention, but then, just like that, she thought that Fyodorov, too, might be given a small quantity of opium. He'd almost certainly never tried it, wasn't used to it, so a small dose (not for the world would she do Fyodorov any harm) should be sufficient: he'd fall asleep and, while asleep, become her lover.

'She found it very appealing and amusing to think that he would possess her, that his dream would come true and he would never know. Even leaving aside the fact that it would bring an end to his torment and hers, the idea was a very good one, and it occurred to her that in the past she might have written a novel on this theme with the very greatest pleasure, not to say lust. The plot, from their very first meeting, had been rather severe, rather strange, but there was a great deal of power and life in it, she could feel it, and the way it all came together was also perfectly natural. Above all, she knew that in the future, too, chance would have little say in this story; on the contrary, it could go on and on, developing and growing all by itself, perhaps even without the participation of either her or Fyodorov. She could follow the plot quite far into the distance, was convinced that at no point would it crumble and collapse – quite the opposite, perhaps: it would become ever steadier, ever firmer – but as for the dénouement, that, for the first time in her life, was out of sight.

'She had always felt, whatever she might be doing, that she was in the right, had never needed to go searching for justifications, and now she found herself suddenly captivated by the idea of turning herself into the heroine of a mysterious Russian *roman*, of becoming as much a prisoner of plot as the characters of her own novels. Recently – and Fyodorov had merely served to underline the fact – she'd been filled with fatalism; power not just over the world, but even over herself, had been slipping through her fingers, but she didn't mind, she was changing, suddenly discovering how good it is not to fight for anything, not to answer for anything, to accept at long last that your fate is planned out from start to finish, that it's pointless, stupid to try to turn off the highway. She'd gained a kind of peace, a calmness in her gait, her gestures, even her speech. She'd become fond of thinking that since this was how things were and there was nothing to be done, then she was innocent and without sin, or her guilt, at any rate, was miniscule, and this was ample reward for her resignation.

'The next morning she sent her old governess to Tambov, gave her a carriage for a speedy return, but then, with the medicine already in her hands, she was strangely slow to give it to him, putting it off for one day, then another. Some obscure fear had got into her; she'd suddenly become afraid of Fyodorov, afraid of their affair. Twice in the space of a week, when it all became too much, she even told the wet-nurse not to let him in, for the first time in a very long time. In general, ever since the appearance of the opium, his visits had brought her infinitely less pleasure than before; she was tense, cold, couldn't fall asleep, and the long wait for the morning, when he would leave, became sheer agony. Evidently, this was only to be expected; now, when their relationship was on the verge of changing, she was frightened by what she had got herself into and found herself thinking that if the affair were to peter out, she would be only too glad.

'But the very next day she would want him again, be unable once again to live without him, to live in wait for him. She'd tell herself that this was just her usual womanish fretting, her usual nervousness that always preceded either the writing of a major work, because you never knew how it would turn out, or a long liaison – because life would change, and who was to say whether for better or worse. And yet, even on days when she liked Fyodorov as much as before, the fear never left her; for the first time in her life she was about to step into a rut leading she knew not where, and from which, she felt, she would no longer be able to get out.

'She was used to being mistress of her life, which was why she'd never taken a husband in Russia, but now she had to renounce this freedom. More than that, she was plunging into something she knew nothing about and in which she was powerless. The change in her thinking in recent years and the fatigue she felt ever more strongly had prepared her to some extent, but still, accepting and agreeing to these new conditions did not come easily. For a fortnight or so she wavered and played for time; once she even tested the opium on herself, albeit only a little, but even that was enough to be sure that d'Orsay had not been exaggerating. Then, after appearing to have made up her mind, she couldn't think of a way to give Fyodorov the medicine without him suspecting anything. She had a quick, inventive mind, but now she found herself rejecting her own ideas one by one: there was always something wrong with them. Eventually it dawned on de Staël that all she had to do was mix opium into the candles on the lid of the coffin and Fyodorov would become intoxicated and fall asleep very slowly, almost as normal, and wouldn't notice a thing.

'Doubtless, this really was the best solution. To make the candles look as if they'd come straight from the factory, she ordered a selection of moulds to be bought in town – whatever could be found – but when they arrived she found none of them to her liking, so she instructed her own carpenter to cut new moulds in the form of the Ivan the Great Bell Tower, for reasons she couldn't have explained herself. She kept an engraving of the tallest Kremlin bell tower in her drawing-room, so the carpenter already had something to work with. Now, waiting for Fyodorov, she spent all day long melting the candles she'd bought in a deep dish, infused the wax with drops of opium, poured it into the moulds, and sat down next to them until the wax had properly cooled. It hardened very slowly, and often she couldn't resist the temptation to open the mould: it was still warm, as if alive, and gave a little beneath her fingers. She'd pick the candle up, stroke it, caress it. She bought expensive, fragrant kinds, and the smell would arouse her. She wanted to touch it with her lips, to kiss the bell tower she'd just cast, but, scared of spoiling it, she restrained herself and placed the half-finished object back in the mould.

'The day came when she realized she could retreat no further; several hours before Fyodorov arrived she herself fixed opium candles at the head and the foot of her crystal couch, then, as usual, she lay down, telling the maid not to light them – she wanted to be alone in the dark – until Fyodorov was already in the house. This was the first time she'd lain down in the coffin so long before Fyodorov. It was time to bid farewell to this naïve and pure story, in which everything was so beautiful: the candles, and the crystal, and the fairy-tale they'd played out, and though she'd deceived him from the very first day, his purity, needless to say, justified and vindicated them both. There was nothing in these two months of which she was ashamed, and there was nothing in her heart but gratitude towards him. Now everything had to change; she knew that from this night onwards she and her sin would be too strong for him, and he would become her toy – no more. If only she wasn't such a bad, wicked woman, if only he'd managed to reform her, or at least improve her, if only she had a little more purity and innocence, a little more of the love and devotion he'd offered her, and a little less lust. This wasn't self-flagellation, and it wasn't remorse; she knew herself too well for that. She was simply saying goodbye to the past.

*

'That evening Fyodorov arrived at his normal time, a couple of hours after dark; in fact everything was as normal, to the point that she felt aggrieved, on his and her own behalf, about his complete lack of anxiety and intuition, as if he couldn't hear, couldn't see that today she was totally different. He sat there telling stories about his childhood, even, it seemed, things she'd already heard before, but she found it hard to concentrate; he fell asleep very quickly, abruptly, the opium cutting him off in the middle of a word. Just to make sure, she waited a little longer, then she cautiously climbed out and, tittering like a girl, suddenly ran off to the bathroom, where the maid had already prepared her bath.

'When she was already lying in her bed, all soft and fresh, the wet-nurse brought in Fyodorov. Dragging his feet on account of the opium, and allowing himself to be pulled along by the wet-nurse, he looked every bit a child – sweet and clumsy. She felt an unbearable urge to take him into her bed, not as a man but as a child, to warm him, stroke him, give him the breast. The wet-nurse, supporting him with one hand to stop him from falling, began with the other to undress him; it occurred to de Staël to get up and help her, but she stayed where she was. Fyodorov, though short, had an elegant figure and she enjoyed watching him emerge from his rough clothes, most of which had been sewn by village tailors. Eventually, the wet-nurse brought him over to her bed and left.

'At first de Staël lay beside him, warmed him with her hip and didn't touch him, but then, as though remembering something, she started playing with him as if he really were her son; squeezing her arms beneath him, she started humming to him, rocking him, then gave him the breast. He began to suck it, straining himself and smacking his lips, but the breast was empty; he turned away and gave a plaintive cry. Then she realized that his childhood had come to an end, just like her milk, and it was time to stop being his mother – only his wife. She began to want him. All that had accumulated inside her during two months of abstinence, two months of this torment, when she lay beneath him in the glass box, feeling only his warmth, all this had made her impatient and brusque, scaring his flesh: her caresses were far too passionate. His flesh was untrained and didn't always respond to her promptly or appropriately. De Staël got angry and her hands became rough, hard. Even so, he entered her.

'On their first night, he couldn't do a thing without her help, but de Staël soon settled and managed to adapt to him; clumsy as he was, he had great natural strength. In the end, she was satisfied and regretted nothing. Her soul, her body, everything about her felt light; feeling famished, she resolved to order a bottle of champagne with her breakfast before taking a ride in her carriage. Towards morning the wet-nurse came in to dress Fyodorov. Helping her, de Staël set about wiping him with a sponge. It mattered to her that no trace of her should remain on him, not even her smell. By day, without her, he should be just the same as before – she mustn't let him guess that his night with her was no dream. She loved to stroke him like this, not with her hand, but with the sponge. She was aroused and wanted him again, but it was late and he could wake at any moment. Regretfully, she let him be taken downstairs. In the hall the wet-nurse placed him on the coffin, in the position he usually slept in – his elbow tucked under his head – and she herself fell fast asleep the moment she lay down on the couch; she didn't even hear him get up and leave.

'Even so, something stayed with him. His body, if not his brain, definitely remembered her, because with every night they spent together Fyodorov became more and more competent. If before he was like a child and she did everything for him, feeling every time that she was corrupting him, treating him as if he were a toy, now he was a fairytale hero – yesterday a boy, today a man. He learned to take her, possess her, desire her, enjoy her. What's more, it all happened so fast that sometimes it seemed to her that he was only pretending to sleep and not remember. And she, who before then had directed the performance herself, finally felt like a woman with him; she, too, learned to give herself to him, to lie in his arms, to be his.

'Previously he'd sat next to the coffin, guarding and protecting her, and only exhaustion would make him slump at his post. Fyodorov had been her knight, her groom, come to destroy the evil spell, to save her. She wasn't his, and he had no claim on her, couldn't even permit himself to think that she was his. If anything, she belonged to the old witch, and only a heroic deed, only a victory over the witch and the destruction of the spell, would give him a claim on her. That was the way he had looked at her, but now de Staël saw in his gaze ever more frequently that he had once possessed her a long time ago, then lost her; they were separated by the coffin, but the time would come when they would be together once more.

'She saw that he no longer looked at her as a bride, but as a wife. His eyes retained very little of the heroic craving that had so amused her, little of his readiness to take on all the forces of darkness, little of his other lofty desires; ever since that night, he simply wanted her. He himself must have noticed that there was something amiss in his thoughts about her, because he became embarrassed and kept blushing, not to mention the fact that as he fell asleep his flesh would rise at once – in other words, he wanted her constantly. She even noticed that it was no longer tiredness that made him sleep; on the contrary, he hastened sleep, sleep was his delight, for in sleep he was united with her. With every day that passed, his brain yielded more and more to his body, yielded so that he could possess her, de Staël. She enjoyed watching this struggle. Now, his flesh would sometimes rise and swell even when he was awake and she, observing his embarrassment as he tried to cover it with his elbow or the skirt of his frock-coat, could barely keep herself from laughing.

'Outwardly, they spent the hour or two until he fell asleep just as they'd always done. Both of them were now different and what they now shared was also completely different, but they deceived themselves and each other as best they could. He sat beside her as before, told her about this or that, while she lay without moving and with her eyes closed, leaving only an imperceptible slit through which to see him.

'The first days after Fyodorov became her lover were very happy ones for de Staël. She suddenly understood that no one before him had ever truly made her feel like a woman. She had always suspected that Talleyrand, and Barras, and Constant, and all her other lovers and husbands had been attracted to her by something else: her diverse talents, her intelligence, the fact that Germaine de Staël was always the talk of society, that to have her for oneself was a kind of trophy; and what terrified her even more was the old suspicion that within her, deep inside her, where she conceived and bore her children, lay the source of power, and people who craved power, who yearned for it, as if for food, were really after that, nor her. All this applied even to Rocca, whom she loved so much. But Fyodorov was pure, he didn't even need to explain himself, he was beyond suspicion, and the fact that he'd fallen in love with her, the fact that now, embarrassed and hiding his erect flesh, he kept looking at her as his lover, as a woman with whom he'd already slept and whom he still wanted, was proof that inside she was just an ordinary woman and that it was as the most ordinary of women that she was beautiful, loved, desired.

*

'But the gift he brought her was short-lived. After three weeks or so she suddenly noticed that even the way he spoke to her had changed. As yet there was nothing new in his words, just a slight change in the tempo of his speech, in his emphasis, but she knew that this was merely the beginning. She felt neither frightened nor depressed, except perhaps on the first day. Previously she had worshipped the opium that put his brain to sleep, but now she accepted as a matter of course that everything about her, not just her flesh, was open to him; she accepted it, and perhaps she had even expected it, hence the speed with which she came to terms with it all.

'Thanks to these three weeks of happiness she was ready to forgive everything and everyone, and of course him above all; even later she never forgot that it was he who had given her these weeks. Every day he surprised her more and more with what he said, he seemed to guess that she would soon bear him a son and that he would be a father, and spoke just like an adult – sometimes, she thought, ostentatiously so. Thoughts and sensations which until then had been vague and ill-defined started taking shape under her influence, acquiring a certain order; there was a foundation to them, no doubt about that, and at first she simply helped him: he merely took from her the tools by which to cut his ideas and gather them into a system.

'But Fyodorov soon became convinced that his world was not complete, that there were certain lacunae that he was unable to fill himself, and then, without the slightest qualms about his right to do so, he set about finding and borrowing whole chunks of her life. But we should give him his due: in contrast to the majority of her French lovers – who, with their blind belief in her genius, never dared change a thing, thereby joining themselves to her by such coarse, scrappy threads that she always ended up feeling sorry for herself – Fyodorov put his own stamp on everything. That's to say, he was never prepared to be a mere copyist, an obedient pupil; on the contrary, taking from her whatever he needed for the very rigid edifice he was erecting and, by the end of their life together, had eventually erected – some elements of this construction were generated by his jealousy, by his struggle with her and her world, others, on the contrary, by his struggle for her, but all of them were mixed with his own, crazed faith – he left her not one drop of freedom. De Staël could usually tell where he got his ideas from, though on other occasions he gave such a peculiar slant to whatever he took from her that she couldn't make head or tail of it and could only guess what lay behind his words. She found it all very interesting and observed what he was doing with her in rapt admiration. She was particularly struck by his jealousy.

'Coming to know de Staël as a woman, he simultaneously

came to know her entire past and hated every bit of it. As the Sleeping Princess, she was fated, intended for him and him alone; he had to destroy the evil spell and awaken her; she had to rise from the dead and be his. He'd been coming to her, sitting by her coffin, because she was his, because he believed that he, Fyodorov, not in a hundred years, but soon, even tomorrow, would say to her, as Christ once said to Lazarus, "Come forth", and she, like Lazarus, would follow him. But he'd learned that she had already been someone else's, that, in other words, she'd betrayed him, and he cursed the entire time when she had not been his, cursed everything that had corrupted her. Whatever had surrounded her, whatever had mattered to her before, whatever she'd known, valued, loved – all this was the world of sin and had no right to exist. He had a powerful, logical mind, he looked at the world in an almost mathematical way, he couldn't understand compromise and wasn't inclined to self-deception, but previously, before her, he'd lacked the experience and knowledge of life to find a definite, unambiguous answer to the question: why?

'Why is our world so terrible, so full of sin? His path to the answer was very slow and took many years,' Ifraimov said, 'so I'm condensing it all here, but he saw some of it straight away. The picture of sin he found in her overwhelmed him – sin had got into everything, everything was infected – and Fyodorov realized that life could not be reformed, that that was an illusion, a lie; evil had to be cut out, removed like a cancerous growth. Essentially, he was forgiving her; for the first time he'd grasped the power of sin and now he knew she couldn't resist it. He cast his eye over everything and deemed it all guilty: he repudiated not only the balls, receptions, salons, theatre, restaurants that she loved so much – these were just the last links in the chain – but also dressmakers and tailors, and all those endless manufacturers producing silk and cambric, velvet and muslin; he repudiated Gobelin tapestries, china, carved furniture, paintings, culinary rites and rituals, fine wines, all the relationships that bound her to human beings; her first marriage with the Baron de Staël and her second with Rocca were also sinful, and the children born from those marriages, they too were born in sin and for sin, and he repudiated the family, repudiated procreation; it was there above all, in procreation, that he found the root of everything from which sin grew and multiplied, and this sin, this flow of sin, had to be staunched, come what may; a limit had to be imposed; man was multiplying not himself, but sin, spawning not man, but vice.

'The image of God in which man was made had long been effaced. Try as he might, he, Fyodorov, could no longer see Him at all, only a diabolical grimace. Listening to him, she often thought what a marvellous illustration he was of Christ's words, "Your faith will save you." His faith and life were so pure and sincere that it was as if, she sometimes thought, he considered himself better than God; at any rate, he wasn't afraid that his teachings went against the Lord. For righteous people, in other words, the God who created a world in which there is evil and death, in which evil grows and grows must inevitably seem imperfect, and this is not a question of pride. Such people are unable and must be unable to accept the slightest injustice, but injustice exists, and because of it they retreat from God, they cease to understand Him.

'Why was the world created as it was? Why, for what possible purpose, was space left in it for evil? It all seemed to him like the outcome of a very strange, dubious deal. In respect of man it was clearly dishonest, and man, of course, was its victim. If God was simply conducting an experiment to see which was stronger – good or evil – then here, too, man was the victim. In the Lord's world, evil is manifestly stronger, and man was created by Him without the strength to resist it. Fyodorov was convinced, and said as much to de Staël, that the world had to be changed once and for all; prolonging suffering any further could not be justified. Tomorrow, and this was only the beginning, the world had to be radically simplified, clarified, defined. Most of man's woes were linked precisely to the world's complexity, thanks to which man was always confused, lost, incapable of understanding anything, of making sense of anything. The evil he did was often done out of ignorance, unintentionally.

'The greatest demonstration of the Lord's perfidy in Fyodorov's eyes was the fact that He had made man in His image and likeness, emphasizing thereby that He and man were commensurate, impressing on him that every man, every living human soul was as important to Him as the entire world, the Universe, that to save himself he had no need to seek out the help of others like him. Why should he, when he had God? Only his personal path to moral perfection, only his personal path from evil to good, to God, would raise him from the dead. The Lord had piled so much on the weak shoulders of man, who all life long, straining himself to breaking point, was meant, as God Himself had ordained, to earn his daily bread in the sweat of his brow and even to bring forth his own children, his flesh and blood, in pain and sorrow. Man, of course, was unprepared, unable to endure this conversation with the Lord on equal terms; he was far too tired, his life was without hope or cheer, and he soldiered on out of habit alone, dirty, unschooled, lost if anything went wrong, and the Lord who preordained such a life could instil nothing but fear in him. After all, even Moses, so as not to go blind, had to turn his face from the Lord when he spoke to Him – Moses, most righteous of the righteous, who spoke to God so often, whom God loved so much.

'God told man that he could and should turn to Him at all times, that He would always hear him and come to his aid if man's wish was righteous; but how often had He ever come? How much grief, how many deaths, how many people slaughtered through no fault of their own! Man was too scared to turn to God. God was far too menacing, far too great and terrible in His anger. He was prepared to lay waste – He already had – to everything He had built. Would a father really unleash a flood on his own house purely because his own children had not turned out the way he wanted? No, He was no father to them, but a lord, and they always saw Him not as the father who brought them into the world, but as their Master, who has the right to beggar them, scatter them, and even, ablaze with anger, to wipe them from the face of the earth. They were all children of Adam, all of the same blood, all brothers, but when, in harmony and friendship, they set about building the Tower of Babel, He could not rest until He had divided them, until He had made them foreign to each other, and man – for God Himself made him this way – had always been afraid of foreigners, had always considered them his enemy, had always been ready to kill them, to tear them to pieces. Since then, not one of them had ever understood his fellow men; each loved only himself, thought only of himself. Is that really how a father should treat his own children?

'As Fyodorov told her this, she, allowing her mind to wander, suddenly thought that even now he must retain a passionate faith in God, while beginning to hate Him at one and the same time. He'd already crossed the limit of his endurance and was no longer prepared to forgive; and it immediately occurred to her that atheism is a very bitter attempt to justify and forgive God: He is not to blame for human suffering, because He does not exist, and people repudiate Him to absolve Him of blame.

'"O," Fyodorov continued, "the confusion of tongues was far from the first of His ploys, nor even the most terrible. The Lord did everything in His power to prevent man from finding the path to heaven, from returning there. Why," he would ask her, "did He make the world so tangled? Why these myriads of plants, beasts, birds, reptiles, insects? What does any of this have to do with the quest for goodness? Nothing at all: it was thought up simply so that man would be bewildered, so that, as in a labyrinth, he would lose his way and never get out. And Cain? After all, the very reason Cain killed Abel was that he didn't know what offering would be pleasing to God. The Lord Himself had commanded men to cultivate the land, yet he rejected Cain's offering, the first fruits of his labour. But man," said Fyodorov, "did not wander blindly for long. He soon ceased to be a foolish child, soon tasted of the Tree of Knowledge of Good and Evil, so then, when the Lord understood that one day man, despite everything, would still return to the place from which he had been cast out, He began reducing his span on Earth. If the forefathers lived for many hundreds of years, and this was the normal span of a human life, we barely ever make it to fifty. No sooner is childhood over, no sooner does a man manage to understand and distinguish good and evil, to set out on the path of righteousness, than he must face his death."

'Fyodorov dreamt of an extremely simple, easily comprehensible life. Essentially he wanted people, whatever their trade – railroad construction, machine manufacture, farming – to become soldiers. The way soldiers lived, the way armies were arranged struck him as correct and almost perfect; here, at any rate, was a chance to be saved. He dreamed of "labour armies" that would function just like ordinary ones.

'Staël knew that this was far from being an abstract idea, that Fyodorov had a model in mind: in Russia, after the victory over Napoleon, military settlements were established in which peasants lived in precisely this way, and they still existed now. Several years before, near Novgorod, she herself had seen such a village, or rather regiment; she was taken there by Count Stroganov, a great admirer of both her and these settlements. She, too, had liked it: everything was clean and cared for; there were even flowers. The children, who in any other part of Russia would be in rags, filthy and unkempt, were dressed in tidy, well-fitting military uniform, and although they were only seven or eight years old, they marched with the bearing and boldness of true guardsmen. Nor did she see any crooked, chimneyless huts: Stroganov explained that as soon as a village becomes a military settlement, the old huts are immediately demolished, and in their place, enclosing a large square drill ground, barracks known as "links" are erected and divided into identical cells, one for each peasant family.

'The soldier-peasants, whenever they have a break from farming, march on the drill ground, learn shooting techniques and master the science of war. In the village you find neither drunkenness nor the slackness and slovenliness so typical of Russians; everyone is smart, everything is tidy. In regiment HQ a schedule is devised for drills and agricultural labour for every day of the year, so everyone knows exactly what he has to do and when. In the morning, at an officer's command, a bugler sounds the reveille, everyone gets up, lights their stove, lines up on the square, and then, to music, they head out in columns from the drill ground to the fields. Their tasks completed, back they come again in their columns to the village, then supper, a wash, and, at the bugler's command, lights-out. The labour of the peasant and the labour of the soldier are united, merge into a single life, thanks to which the military settlements produce virtually the best soldiers in the Russian army, an army, moreover, that can feed itself.

'Stroganov's passion for military settlements struck de Staël as perfectly natural at the time, especially since, as I've already said, she liked the village herself; by then she was quite used to looking at everything military through Russian eyes. She recalled that on her first visit to St Petersburg – it was the summer of 1809 – she was astonished by the enthusiasm and attentiveness with which locals observed a parade and she wrote in her diary that in this enormous boundless country, where each man treads a lonely path through life, often without purpose or meaning, and there is nothing to unite people except the fear of getting lost and vanishing without trace, the harmonious and precise movement of hundreds and thousands of men, gladly responding to each and every command, must seem the very height of perfection.

'"The army," said Fyodorov, leaning over her coffin, "is the last chance to arrange things so that man repudiates his lack of kinship, brotherhood, equality, his conviction that everyone else is foreign to him and he is different. In the army," he said, "everything is honest and fair, and there are no illegitimate children. The strength of the army is that it never indulges man's egoism: how he stands, how he moves, how he dresses – in all things he is just the same as everyone else.

'"If only you could have seen," he said, "how happy new recruits are after months and months of drills and training, when they have sweated out everything by which the Lord once divided them and they suddenly understand that they have become, as it were, one man, one creature, not a multitude of different, dissimilar people, that they are so tightly bonded that there is not a single gap between them and you can't even say where one of them ends and another begins. That is when they will finally march across the drill ground in exactly the right way, with confident step. Each of them now is a platoon, a company, a battalion, a brigade, a corps, a division, an army, and each of them rejoices that he will no longer have to speak to God one on one, that he will speak with Him only like this: as a platoon, company, battalion, brigade, corps, division, army. They've finally realized that they are not alone in the world, that none of them need be responsible for anything ever again. All you need do is be like everyone else, then you will always be right and free of guilt, whatever you do.

'"Even at war, when regulations permit them to abandon parade formation and scatter, they never forget that their life is merely a part of the common life, that on its own it is worthless, whatever the Lord might say; and yes, a bullet may strike you, but you are still alive, and vindicated, if your army wins. And for this newly regained brotherhood they are ready to die."

'An army of simplified, standardized people, Fyodorov thought, will understand by itself that it has no need of a world as complex as the one created by God, however beautiful it may be, that it only gets in its way, and then by our joint labour, within the space of just a few years, we will raze mountains and heights, fill up swamps, hollows, lowlands, turn rivers into straight canals and direct their current as man requires, not as He decreed. We will build a multitude of dams and artificial ponds, and nobody will need to pray to God ever again for rain, for there will always be water aplenty; no longer will the rivers overflow in winter and early spring, when the earth sleeps, nor, when it dries up in summer, ruining the crops, will they run shallow. Man will cut down forests and turn them into arable fields, irrigate the deserts and make them arable, too, and then, when the entire earth becomes one enormous level field and nobody ever goes hungry, when nobody has to think only of his crust, day in, day out, man will be able to take up his main task, the task of resurrecting his kin, the lofty task of transforming this world, mortal by nature, into a world without death – the Kingdom of Heaven.

'Fyodorov was no arid dreamer; his mind was pragmatic and precise. He understood that this could not be achieved all at once, and it didn't take de Staël long to guess that for the first phase it was precisely she whom he had appointed as the instrument of his transformations. He'd decided to pass life through her as through a filter and to cut out everything which evoked a response in her, everything she was sorry to lose and wanted to keep. In his new world nothing could be preserved except what she didn't care about, didn't know about and had never really noticed: simple, preferably homespun peasant clothes, equally simple, unpretentious food, the tools needed to produce it all, and not much else. For the time being Fyodorov was prepared to spare villages – life there was simple: good and evil could be told apart without too much difficulty – but not cities. Thanks to her, he'd conceived a hatred for cities; he yelled at her that they were disgusting, monstrous cobwebs of streets, courtyards, buildings, all brimming with vice. Like Sodom and Gomorrah, they had to be destroyed.

'The idea of saving and resurrecting the human race – every man, without exception, who had ever lived on earth – was more important to him than any other, and he had merged himself and her so fully in this idea that, as she listened, de Staël did not even try to separate herself off from him. During the first three months of their shared life together, having thought through all this with her help, blaming and all but cursing God, and burning all his bridges with Him, he suddenly became slow, like a man who has forgotten the way, shifts from foot to foot, then comes to a complete standstill. He discovered, to his astonishment, that he lacked the knowledge to save people, that he had nothing to say to them.

'De Staël had enough intuition to foresee the impending crisis, but could do nothing to help him. She merely noticed how, night after night, having drained her, as it were, to the dregs, he kept repeating one and the same text; and even before that, how their lovemaking was gradually becoming routine for them both. He slept with her now as you would with a wife who can no longer surprise you; today is the same as yesterday, and tomorrow will be no different – although at the time she thought that this was merely a reaction to the excessively tempestuous progress of their affair. He'd mastered her with such passion that in the space of a few months he'd managed to find and take from her more than all her previous lovers combined; she'd even become scared of him, frightened of how much he needed her, all of her, and how little she herself was left with. He'd scooped everything out of her, as if from a well – even the mud.

'By this time, though, de Staël was already carrying his child and could only be thankful that their relationship had become calmer, more even, that his ecstasy at possessing her, which was like nothing she'd ever known, had finally abated. His expectation that she should give herself to him completely, keeping nothing behind, had long exceeded all reasonable limits, and she wasn't prepared to indulge him any further. She'd taken it all far too lightly; meanwhile, the child she'd conceived with him, the child who was growing inside her, was crowding out Fyodorov, and nothing could change that.

'She reassured herself with the thought that after the steady provincial life to which Fyodorov had adapted and accustomed himself and which was the only life he could live, these three months, beginning with his first love for a woman – for her, Evgeniya Frantsevna Stal – and ending with his rebellion against God, had proved far too much for him; and when, having lost his thread, he suddenly realized that he had no way of helping people, that he would never manage to save anyone, that he, Fyodorov, was a sort of swindler, a fraud, the blow, of course, was overwhelming. But the thought that he might be on the verge of mental illness never even occurred to her, and what had happened did not really affect her. She felt sorry for him, of course, and even cried when she saw him at his worst, but her main preoccupation was still her child; it was her child she thought about and as for Fyodorov – well, it was his own fault: God had punished him for his pride.

*

'In the fifth month of her pregnancy, when she was already struggling to hide her condition, she packed her things in one day and, without warning anyone or taking anyone with her except the wet-nurse, left for St Petersburg. There, resting and reading, she whiled away the remaining months of her pregnancy in a small Finnish hotel on the edge of town. She gave birth to a son in the same place, suckled him for the first month, and then, leaving the child in the care of a good nanny, a very conscientious and upstanding Dane, set off back to her estate near Tambov.

'When she was already only half a mile from her home, Fyodorov suddenly emerged from a grove, walking straight towards her. It was July, it was hot and she was travelling in an open landau, lost in thought. When she saw him right in front of her she stopped the coachman in surprise and had already opened her mouth to tell Fyodorov that he had a son – she'd forgotten that he didn't even know he'd slept with her – but Fyodorov, without paying her the slightest attention or even seeing her, walked straight past and she realized once again that outside the crystal coffin she did not exist for him and that, however many times he might meet her, even if she were to start talking to him, this is how it would remain. On the day after her arrival, the maid admitted Fyodorov into the house as usual, just as soon as it grew dark, and their affair resumed according to precisely the same pattern as before.

'On reflection, his failure to recognize her left a bitter taste: she'd thought he had more love and intuition, that he should have at least felt her proximity. And the fact that everything picked up again between them as if she hadn't been away for these past six months, hadn't borne him a child, also upset her. He was so absorbed in his thoughts that it hadn't cost him the slightest effort to patch up the hole; he'd even begun from the same point, the same phrase, at which the opium had cut him off on their last night. But eventually she decided that this was all for the best, and certainly a great deal simpler.

'Meeting him on the road, she'd noticed straight away how much he'd aged, but he was gone before she could take a good look at him. Now, in the light of the candles, he looked for all the world like an old man: his eyes were lacklustre, and his speech, as he muttered away about some grievance or other, without even breaking his monotone, without the slightest excitement or inspiration, was slow and indistinct. He complained to her about God, said that God was confusing him, throwing him off course, and now he couldn't follow a single thought through to the end; that God was causing him almost daily headaches; and worst of all was the noise in his ears – sometimes a roar, as from a seashell, sometimes little bells that rang and rang, a lovely sound that made him forget everything else.

'He really did keep getting confused. Either he'd contradict himself from sentence to sentence or else, like a broken toy, he'd keep repeating one and the same thing. From time to time he'd suddenly begin to blaspheme, shout that God was a thief, that He'd stolen all he had, that it wasn't the Lord but he, Fyodorov, who'd come up with the idea that there is no death, that people will rise from the dead, both the righteous and the sinful, every single man – but God had stolen it for Himself. These flashes rarely lasted long, though, and faded of their own accord. And once again, until the opium did its work, he set about enumerating his grievances, one after the other: everyone was a swindler, everyone was a crook. He moaned and wept, and she was glad when he eventually fell asleep: nights with him had become even less pleasurable than just lying in the coffin. Their trysts continued by force of inertia and she knew she'd be glad if he never came again, while realizing that she'd grown so used to him that she couldn't break it off herself.

'But if they brought her no joy, these meetings did at least entertain her, every now and again. Occasionally, for example, he suddenly remembered what it was that had derailed everything and once again, seeing that he didn't know how to resurrect people without God, he started thrashing about, veering from one extreme to another, lending absurd significance to complete trivialities, then lambasting them with almost the same ardour as before.

'He would remember that first and foremost he had to restore the brotherhood of nations, to unite them in a single whole; only then, putting wars and strife behind it, would mankind be able to take up the task of resurrection. So then he discovered that the root of evil, its primary cause, lay in greedy, vile England – his hatred for England derived from her, de Staël – which, since the beginning of time, had been playing nations off against each other so as to profit from their blood. England's strength, of course, was her Indian possessions, so Russia, who was responsible for all, would have to send its fleet to India's shores. As a peace-loving country, Russia could not be the aggressor, even against England. But here Fyodorov made a subtle move. The Russian ships would have to cruise side by side with the English ships and wait, month after month, until the nerves of the English finally gave way and they opened fire. Now the aggressor would be England, the law would be on the side of the Russians, and they would seize the English vessels without any trouble, because Russian soldiers are the best in the world and their cause is just, after which the spoils would be fairly divided among the nations of the world and India would join in the common task.

'Having seen off England, he would start excoriating, at great length and with great malice, everything else that was impeding the unity of nations. One by one, taking each in turn, he derided Islam, Catholicism, Judaism, Protestantism, all of which were opposed to the true faith – Orthodoxy – and tore people apart. He spoke clumsily and much of what he said was far-fetched, but he had moments of inspiration. Essentially, she'd learned to accept his ravings and listened to what he had to say with pity and without hope.

'This went on for quite some time, almost a year if we include the period she spent in St Petersburg, and she found him more unbearable each day. She doubled, then tripled the number of candles, so as to make him fall asleep sooner but she still couldn't bring herself to end it all. Then, one night, she let her thoughts wander from the subject of her child – her only relief and comfort since returning to her estate – and suddenly felt happy with Fyodorov once more. She'd already forgotten when it was she'd last wanted him and now, feeling that she was all his again, that nothing should remain inside her that might be concealed from him and that, as before, not only their bodies but everything else had become one single whole, she realized that today he would finally come to his senses and move forward.

'Fyodorov began by recalling the reasons for his rebellion against God. He recalled that it was all because of her, de Staël. For two lifetimes the Lord had tempted her with power, placing its source right there inside her, but she had never possessed it, and all of this, like she and he, merged in Fyodorov with the conviction of the Russian people that the Lord had tempted Russia in just the same way for its entire existence, then cheated it just as badly. He had made Russia a new Holy Land and the Russian people, in place of the Jews, the new chosen people of God. He had entrusted them with preserving the true faith, with awaiting the Second Coming of Christ and the victory of the righteous. Russia had taken up the Cross. Nine centuries of unimaginable suffering and unimaginable patience, nine centuries of faith and willingness to accept Christ, to commit any sacrifice for the salvation of the peoples of the earth – and nobody, it turned out, needed any of it. So He was not the true God, not the All-Merciful Lord, but a mere tempter.

'No sooner had Fyodorov remembered the Cross than he immediately saw before him the path of resurrection along which he must lead the human race. It all happened in a flash: a year of illness, madness, worthlessness, delirium – and out of it all, like a sudden miracle, his own path of salvation, quite different from the path of the Church.

'"Truly I say to you," she heard through the glass (he was standing over her, with a voice like thunder), "every person deserves to be saved; even the very lowest sinner, beholding his crimes in horror, will undergo such torment, such suffering, that he will atone for his evil and be cleansed."

'Now, Fyodorov was filled with kindness and noble feelings, and felt moved to justify God in both her eyes and his own. He said: "All people are children of God, all of them are made in His image and likeness, therefore they cannot fall so low that they can no longer be saved. Man, the entire human race, every part of it, will be saved; not one man will be forgotten; not one will be cast out." In general, the more he withdrew from God, the more insistently he tried to forgive Him and justify Him. On another occasion he tried to persuade her that it was far from mandatory, even in the Lord's eyes, that the Apocalypse, the destruction of humankind and the Last Judgement that would crown this destruction should precede the resurrection of the righteous – it was no more than a warning. It was enough for man to reform himself and repudiate sin for the Lord, with joy and with love, to free him from suffering and spare him, as once He spared Nineveh.

'He even told her once, lest she think that he was forgiving the Lord simply out of pride, that all this could already be found in the Gospels, that the task of saving man had been bequeathed by the Lord to man himself. Christ gave us only the rudiments of a doctrine, only its seed, and if we prove to be good soil, well-moistened and loose, it will grow in us, ripen and bear fruit. He often recalled the words of Christ: "The works that I do (resurrection from the dead), shall he (whoever comes after me – i.e., man) do also; and greater works than these shall he do…" – and also: "Go ye therefore, and teach all nations…" So Fyodorov, who had already set his mind on the maddest of revolutions, on making a clean and permanent break with the entire world of the past, on breaking with the God Who begat both this world and Fyodorov himself, was desperate, nonetheless, not to be taken for an imposter; on the contrary, he began seeking in the Lord he was abandoning a sanction for his deeds, a root.

'De Staël had the time, the love and the patience to understand and appreciate Fyodorov. Night fused them into one. He opened up to her entirely, as she to him; merging in a single being, they could no longer tell which of them was which, and took from each other, as if from themselves, whatever they wanted. But at dawn they parted and once again she was able to see Fyodorov from the outside. It was the same in the evening: he arrived and sat by her coffin, they loved each other and were so close to each other, but between them was her death, and they could not break through it. Lying in the coffin, she heard him as if from afar, and both he himself and what he was saying seemed different, and she often repeated words once heard from her father: only death will tell. The distance separating her and Fyodorov permitted de Staël to judge him coolly and calmly, and she had long understood what it was that he couldn't forgive God for, why it was that he had rebelled against Him.

'The first thing was death: in making man mortal, Fyodorov thought, God had failed to understand, to appreciate his creation. Man by his nature was good, but life was short and so poor in joy and rich in suffering. There wasn't nearly enough joy to go round, and man couldn't wait – he was granted too little time – so he tried to snatch, to pinch at least a morsel of joy from his neighbour, shouting: How come you've got so much and I've got nothing! Death begat envy, spite, hatred; it turned people into enemies.

'If there were only a tiny bit more joy or if man's time on earth were longer, he would manage to make sense of things, to get his bearings, to separate the important from the secondary, to choose the good, understand it and love it. The truth could almost be touched. "You see," people would say, "this is good, and this is evil, and I no longer want what's evil, I want what's good, because the good is beautiful, and evil is disgusting," and they were walking towards the good, but they didn't quite get there. And their children – had they only managed to pass on to them what they'd understood – would not have known evil at all, wouldn't have gone anywhere near it, but He'd arranged things in such a way that the children had to begin from scratch. Although truth belonged to all people, to the entire human race, the Lord snatched it away from man, from his children, and they too, even if they found the good, died when they were only halfway there.

'Perhaps Fyodorov would have lived like everyone else and remembered about death only in his old age, having coming to terms with everything, having accepted and forgiven everything, but even love came to him through death. He loved de Staël as much as any human being can love another, but death and the coffin divided them. He came to her every evening and every evening he saw that she was beautiful and dead, and he couldn't fail to be horrified by death, couldn't fail to be staggered by its power. That was why his childish fear was still with him, the fear that life was fragile and could snap at any moment.

'The second thing was human inequality. At first she thought that Fyodorov's loathing of it was born of the French Revolution and taken entirely from her, de Staël, but then she realized her mistake: social and class inequality, the

175

inequality of wealth – all this barely interested him. His very first impression of childhood, the thing that had shaken and shattered him, was hearing his nanny say that his father, the father whose flesh he shared, whom he passionately loved and whom he should prolong and continue, was alien to him by law, that he, Fyodorov, was an illegitimate son and had no right either to his name or to his love. It was as if Fyodorov had no father. The chain of conception and birth that began with Adam had been snapped, all the roots had been chopped, and he was banished from the human race, cut off from God. A world where fathers permitted, and perhaps themselves established, such an order, where they deemed it just and pleasing to God, had no right to exist, so then – already then – he vowed to destroy it.

'The revolution conceived by Fyodorov would demolish the existing structure of this world, leaving nothing behind. As a first step he deemed all fathers unworthy of being fathers, unworthy of conceiving children and continuing the human race. He wanted, in his unchecked pride, to lead his entire generation, the generation of children, to the cemeteries, so that there, among the graves, having repudiated all that is transient once and for all, they might begin the great collective task – the task of resurrecting those who conceived them. The fathers, by committing mortal sin, had lost the right to conceive children; this right had passed by inheritance to the children, and now it was the children who would beget, restore, resurrect the fathers. Fathers among whom not one would be illegitimate. Then the fathers, like children, having inherited the blessing of their children-fathers, would restore their own fathers, and the slow path of resurrection, of the return of humankind to God, would have begun.

'Fyodorov did not desire any continuation of life; on the

contrary, he wanted to close it, reverse it. On the other hand, he did once tell de Staël that none of this would be mere repetition: the children, restoring their fathers from themselves, would live their fathers' life in a different way. The fathers had hurried through life without thinking, but the children would be meticulous and attentive. Nothing in the fathers' life would go unremarked, unappreciated.

'Mankind's backward path, according to Fyodorov, ought to be neither a circle nor a loop. The way Adam and his descendants had distanced themselves from God, deviated from good towards evil, then gradually abandoned evil and returned to the good – this wasn't even a case of turning back, as if generation after generation had walked further and further away from God before making their way back to Him. No: what you had to do was retrace your footprints while walking backwards. He spoke of the last generation's spirit of sacrifice, of how, its righteousness notwithstanding, it had repudiated procreation and was resurrecting its fathers, and of the terrible reproach to the fathers: just look at how you treated us and how we're treating you. He spoke of its chastity, of its immaculate conception of the fathers, of the birth of the fathers, cleansed of original sin. But Fyodorov would not resurrect women; he hated them. He told de Staël that it was precisely their lechery, their complaisance that brought illegitimate children into the world. He seemed to consider women even guiltier than fathers.

'Fyodorov had incredible faith. He had no doubt that his path was leading all mankind to heaven, that it was straight and short. How it was that he'd hit on it de Staël could only guess. Perhaps she again was responsible. By restoring and prolonging her mother, de Staël had dropped him a heavy hint, or else she had merely confirmed that the path he'd already chosen was right. He himself, after all, from the moment he caught sight of her on the country lane, had followed her because he knew, believed that he would be able to resurrect her.

'The resurrection in heaven which the Lord offers the righteous, said Fyodorov, is incomplete and defective, but resurrecting a man bodily on earth is an arduous task. The earth isn't even man's native home; it's his place of exile, his place of suffering and death. Man fell to earth; he was cast out here from his nest, from heaven; and he fell once again when death cut him down. To restore man, he needed to be returned to the cosmos. The sky – that is man's true home, the place where he was conceived, brought to term, brought to life. Only in the cosmos, where there is no gravity, nothing that weighs down life and bends it towards the earth, can all the atoms that once made up a man be found. Having once been part of a human being, said Fyodorov, these atoms remain alive forever, they are animated, and they remember who they once belonged to. In fact, Fyodorov was convinced that man can be reassembled bit by bit, and that, when this has been done, he will rise and walk. His soul, moreover, can be put together in exactly the same way, bit by bit; it, too, divides and fragments, before being assembled and becoming whole once more. He was a magnificent engineer and, though this was a world made of golems, Fyodorov's belief was such that de Staël also came to believe that he could save and resurrect all.

'I've already said that Fyodorov was very scared of being taken for an imposter; he knew that nobody would follow him if he was. And another thing: despite his belief in his vocation, fear never left him – fear of himself, of his pride, of Him against Whom he had set himself. Perhaps that was why disciples and fellow-travellers were always so welcome to him, why he sought people who were ready to walk the same path or had found it even before he did. Among those he told her about was Ham, son of the righteous Noah. It followed from the commentaries of Rashi and a few others he cited that Ham's guilt was not that, having seen his father naked, he'd called his brothers over to look rather than covering his father – that's a softened, smoothed-over version, merely a hint of what actually happened. In reality Ham, it seems, castrated his father. He castrated him after learning that the Lord had promised Noah that he would make him a new Adam, that Noah would begin a new human race with the sons, ignorant of sin, whom he would beget after the Flood. The Lord wanted to start human life afresh, he wanted everything that had happened between Adam and the Flood, this long, long story of man's retreat from God, of his lapse into evil, to be erased and forever forgotten. Human life, He said, was so fused with sin, so overgrown with it, that resurrecting it would mean resurrecting sin. The Lord told Noah that the memory of Adam and his descendants must die, that nothing from that life could be restored and returned. He sent waters upon the earth to wash away everything, to the last trace. Learning that the Lord had doomed the ancestors of Noah to definitive – resurrection-less – death, Ham rose up against Him.

'According to a different commentary, Ham, having supposedly seen Noah naked, lay down and copulated with him. Ham was not as pure as Noah and knew what sin was, even if, before the Flood, he had tried to avoid it as best he could. The only reason he was taken on to the Ark and saved from universal ruin was Noah. The life of the son, Ham, had been granted to Noah by the Lord as reward for Noah's righteousness, as Ham knew only too well. Ham also knew that his turn would come to resurrect his father. But he was naïve and he was scared of failing; after all, he wouldn't be able to restore Noah's most important qualities – his purity and sanctity – because he lacked them himself. So then, in order to know Noah, to know him fully, he united with him.

*

'Counting from the day of their first acquaintance, de Staël lived with Fyodorov for five and a half years, from 1849 to 1854. During this time she bore him three sons: on each occasion, no sooner did her waist begin to thicken than she left her estate for St Petersburg, gave birth there, suckled the child herself for the first month, then gave him into the care of the wet-nurse, the same Danish woman as before, after which she travelled back to Pine Ravine.

'Fyodorov's three sons were all strapping, handsome boys, blue-eyed and fair-haired, just the kind she liked, but the Lord had not fertilized their hearts, brains, bodies, and they remained as they were born, witless babes. She often wondered why Fyodorov should have such children by her. She knew of other people, too, who had been born already closed and complete, incapable of development – though not always as children – or when a man's development had ceased too early. She thought that the fate of these people might help her understand the kind of future that awaited Fyodorov's sons as well.

'Adam was created a grown man, therefore the Lord did not desire his development and immediately created him perfect, in so far as any man may be perfect. The first man, in other words, was not the first child; in fact childhood was not created by God at all, and man's path from childbirth to the state envisaged by God was visited on him as a punishment. But the soul of Adam was the soul of a child, undoubtedly, and this, perhaps, is the root of God's incomprehension of man, of the distance that separated them for so long. Red-haired Esau, the elder brother of Jacob, the favoured son of Isaac, the very same man who, by any human law, ought to have obtained the birthright, was deprived of it by God; the Lord tricked blind Isaac by having him bless Jacob, his second son, instead of Esau, because Esau's soul and mind were complete and his knowledge of God could advance no further.

'So the Lord acknowledged that man's path to God, his path from evil to good, is a boon and that man must walk it himself from beginning to end. God's knowledge of man, it would seem, was incomplete, and Christ, by taking on the sins of the world, Christ, with Whom, as it were, the life of the human race began afresh – until then God had been retreating further and further from man – now made the first step towards him, and this step was not His preaching, not His miracles or resurrection, not even Golgotha, but the conception of Christ by Mary His Mother.

'It was hardly likely, de Staël would say to herself, that the soul and brain of Fyodorov's sons remained forever dormant because Fyodorov, conceiving them, had been lulled by opium and they, as it were, inherited his sleep. No, God must have simply been afraid that the sons of the man who rose up against Him might repeat his path. Fyodorov's sin of pride was terrible, and his punishment extremely cruel. Fyodorov could not forgive any father a single illegitimate son, but all three of his sons were exactly that. He repudiated procreation forever because he knew that with it the sufferings of the human race would continue for yet another generation; he believed that it was with him that the backwards path would begin, but life continued through his sons.

'The task, the mission of the sons was the resurrection of the fathers, but Fyodorov's sons, who'd never seen him and knew nothing about him, would never be able to resurrect him, and Staël realized that Fyodorov, therefore, would not be able to resurrect his father either, and so the chain would stretch on and on. And yet, many years later, when she and Fyodorov had already parted, she realized that the Lord had not cursed Fyodorov with his sons – far from it: this was a blessing, for He had saved them from evil, arranged things in such a way that they would go through life ignorant of sin.

'After she broke off with Fyodorov, her life returned fairly quickly to its former rhythm; she took up husbandry again, had two large glass greenhouses built, but there were times when even the simplest tasks were beyond her and then, abandoning the estate for several months at a time, she would go to St Petersburg to visit her sons, or to Moscow, or to nearby Tambov. At first the change of scene did her good. In a new place she immediately felt herself again, slept long and well, ate with relish, delighted in what life had to offer, but this period soon ended. She suddenly realized that her vital energy had run out completely; Fyodorov had squeezed everything out of her, scooped it all out; she was empty.

'She didn't need a mirror to tell her that in a year or two she would be an old woman, and she knew that it was high time to decide whether to use the mandrake or simply to stop and calmly live out her days in Pine Ravine. She delayed and delayed, more afraid with each passing day of starting anew. This life, like her previous one, had brought her little happiness, and the temptation to end it all was very powerful. And yet, she prolonged herself. In Moscow, on 13 January, 1862, she gave birth to a girl, Ekaterina, who was herself. After the death of de Staël, which followed precisely two years after the birth of the child, the wet-nurse brought the girl to Pine Ravine.

*

182

'Bored of country life, sixteen-year-old Ekaterina Frantsevna Stal spent the winter of 1878 in Tambov in a small estate that looked out onto the town park and that had been bought in her name several years before. She loved this funny, perfectly toy-like little mansion, and through it she had also grown to love Tambov. That winter, her house even became home to a small, salon-like circle – visited by one Francophile after another – and she began receiving again for the first time since Paris.

'It really was a miniature Paris. De Staël didn't even change her days: Tuesdays and Fridays. She got out a lot herself, barely missing a single ball at the provincial assembly of the nobility. It was at just such a ball, towards the end of winter, that she met a charming young Georgian who had washed up in Tambov. They spent the entire evening glued to each other, dancing, drinking champagne, more dancing – he danced incredibly well. She'd fallen for him, no doubt about it; she felt happy and couldn't care less that she was breaking all the rules of etiquette. When the ball was over, de Staël, without stopping off at her mansion or warning anyone about anything, took him straight off to Pine Ravine.

'He stayed with her for seven days, during which they never left the bedroom; then she lost all interest in him, just like that. She told him – the Georgian's name was Vissarion Ignatashvili – that it was time for him to leave, that their relationship could not continue: she was irreparably compromised as it was. She also told Ignatashvili that she knew he wasn't rich, even though he was a prince, and that she wanted to be of use to him, to thank him for this unforgettable week. But the prince reacted proudly, refused the money out of hand and merely requested her permission to tell her a strange story. She gave it.

'The story went as follows. Vissarion Ignatashvili's father,

Georgi, came from an eminent and wealthy Svanetian family, but he was orphaned at three. By the time he could mount a horse and hold a weapon his neighbours had already managed to seize almost all the family lands; even worse, they had lured his people to their side. Georgi Ignatashvili had nothing to live on, fled Svanetia for Chechnya, spent what money he had on recruiting several dozen cut-throats and, returning to Georgia, soon made a name for himself as an outlaw, an *abrek*. No one could catch him: neither the government, nor the numerous local armed bands.

'By his fortieth birthday he had succeeded, largely by force but also, at times, with the aid of money, in restoring the ancestral possessions, after which he dismissed his band, having rewarded them handsomely. This was an unforgivable error. Precisely a month later, when he was celebrating his wedding with the renowned Imeretian beauty Salomeya, his neighbours broke in to his castle. The young couple had just retired to the bedchamber, while the prince's men, of whom only a few remained, were all drunk and offered no resistance. Georgi Ignatashvili, who hadn't even managed to get into bed yet, was seized naked, covered with a shirt, taken outside and hung on the spot.

'It all happened with improbable speed. Georgi was quick and strong; in twenty years of pillaging and plundering he'd seen just about everything, had come out of every scrape unscathed; but here he was, a man of rare courage, behaving as if he himself wanted to die. And to think that this was his own home, where even a wretched coward would fight like a lion; but he didn't even raise a finger, took it all like a monk.

'The bedroom was situated at the very top of the castle watchtower, where there had once been a wide open platform reserved for two cannons, but Salomeya, just as soon as the marriage had been decided, ordered the platform to be walled in and turned into a room: she adored the view of the mountains and the Ingur Valley. An extremely narrow spiral staircase led down from the bedroom, so Georgi could have been restrained by only one person – just occasionally, two – and of course he knew every door, every nook and cranny, not to mention the fact that the castle, as so often in Georgia, contained secret passages, one of which began in that same tower; so there was no reason for him to give up. The least effort on his part and his men might have come to their senses, but he acted, as people said later, like a lamb to the slaughter.

'He was, it seems, so overwhelmed by the disgrace of it all, by the bandits breaking into his and Salomeya's bedroom on their first night and finding Salomeya half-naked and him unable to defend her, that he really did lose all desire to live. Others in the castle said that he'd been too scared to flee because the bandits told him they'd have their way with Salomeya if he did; they only needed him, they said, and if everything went smoothly they wouldn't touch anyone else – but if blood was spilled or he made a run for it, he'd only have himself to blame: Salomeya would have as many husbands that night as there were strangers in the castle. They knew how much he loved her, and drove him into a corner.

'For all that he'd spent his life in the hills as a brigand, Georgi did not much resemble a highlander: he loved reading and collecting paintings, kept three artists from Tiflis at his own expense, was considered a connoisseur and patron of the arts throughout Georgia, so the idea of fighting naked with dressed and armed men in full view of his half-naked wife must have struck him as so pathetic and ridiculous that he decided he was better off simply accepting his death. And there was something else. He first got to know Salomeya in

Imeretia, when she was just a child and he a mere dependent in the home of his great-uncle. Salomeya's family was rich, and although they fell in love, as they say, at first sight (Georgi and she were both unusually good-looking) and had even vowed their fidelity to each other, there could be no question of Salomeya's parents ever agreeing to give their girl away to a destitute fugitive. But when Georgi was leaving, Salomeya's mother told him, half in jest, that if he ever got hold of as much land and cattle as his father once had, he should send over some matchmakers.

'So it was because of Salomeya that he'd taken up a life of banditry; otherwise, I suspect, he'd have accepted his fate without grumbling. The fact that a small band of men had been enough for him to recover his patrimony – when at times all Svanetia seemed to be against him – was, he thought, a sign from above. Brought up mainly by his mother, Georgi was deeply religious, observed the fasts, sang in the choir as a boy, and loved going to church even in adulthood – a rarity among highlanders. He himself was astonished that he'd never been seriously wounded, even though he always fought from the front, and this, too, he put down to Providence.

'As I've already said, he dismissed his Chechens the moment Svanetia acknowledged his claims on his ancestral lands. He considered banditry a sin and knew that he was up to his elbows in blood, including the blood of the innocent. He'd spent ten years waging war, and opportunities to ask himself who was right and who was wrong were few and far between. That Salomeya waited for him and was given to him in marriage meant, he thought, that God had forgiven him, and he intended to devote the years that were left to him to pious deeds: he wanted, for example, to have a hospital for the crippled built in Kutaisi. For the rest, he would lie low, pray and repent. But now, when the Lord, without even granting them a single night together, had taken Salomeya away from him, he realized that he had obtained her wrongfully, that the Lord had forgiven him nothing and was not minded to do so. So why live? Hence, he put up no resistance.

'Though they tried to restrain her, both in the bedroom and on the stairs, Salomeya ran out into the yard at precisely the moment when the bench was kicked away from under Georgi's feet. They wanted to stop her in the yard as well, but her appearance was so deranged that at the last moment everyone took a step back and no one even touched her. Running over to the sycamore, now a gibbet, she jumped up, grabbed her husband's neck and hung from him. Perhaps she wanted to hug him one last time, to remember his body, or perhaps she thought that her added weight would make the noose tighten quicker and cut short his agony. It was as if they had been hanged together. The sight was so horrific that every man in the yard froze on the spot; nobody even thought of going up to her, freeing her arms and carrying her back to the house.

'Barely had Salomeya pressed herself against her husband than she felt Georgi's flesh rise. It rose with such force that Salomeya suddenly felt that she didn't even need to cling on to his neck – his flesh would keep her there by itself. She pulled up her shirt with her teeth, parted her legs a little, and that was enough: she could feel right away that he'd entered her. Actually, Vissarion told Madame de Staël, one shouldn't be surprised – instances of erection during hanging are not unusual and are even described in medical textbooks: the rope squeezes the neck vessels, but the heart still pumps, and the blood, rushing down, fills the flesh. Then Salomeya realized that not only was her husband's flesh inside her, but his seed as well; she felt dizzy and, still clenching his body with her arms and legs, lost consciousness. Their orgasm merged with his dying convulsions and groans, and though there were a dozen people standing almost right under the tree, nobody noticed a thing. Georgi had long fallen silent when she was finally taken down and carried back to the house.

'The raid was over and the bandits, having stolen precisely nothing, rode off. Salomeya seemed to come to her senses at once; she was calm, assertive. She asked to be carried back to the bedroom, where that very same night she supervised the painstaking process of filling in the door and all three windows with stones. She permitted only two openings to be left, both the size of a brick: one in the window, to know whether it was day or night, the other in the door, to receive her meals.

'Six months later all the gossip about Ignatashvili's appalling fate began to peter out of its own accord, the members of the household tried to carry on as if nothing had happened, and attempts were even made to entice Salomeya out of the seclusion of her cell. To this end Salomeya's parents twice paid visits to Jvari, although Georgi's aunts were most persistent of all. There wasn't a man left in the house and they were terrified that, as in his infancy, everything would be taken away from them and they themselves would be driven out of their ancestral home.

'There was no lack of contenders for Salomeya's hand among the most influential Georgian clans, and both families stood to gain by giving her away in marriage once more. Initially her relatives thought that it would be easy to persuade Salomeya of the necessity of this step. Her life with Georgi had never even begun, and her bond with her husband could hardly be so strong; the further that night receded, the better she, a beautiful young woman, should understand that it would do neither her, nor even Georgi, the slightest good to give up on her life. Ultimately, that was all Georgi's mother and aunts wanted to say to her. But she had no desire to talk to any of them and eventually they left her in peace, deciding that time, as we know, heals everything, and one day she herself might wish to re-enter the world. For now, there was no point hurrying her.

'Not that this story was entirely forgotten; on the contrary, Salomeya was famed throughout Svanetia as a kind of saint. For this very reason it never even occurred to anyone to profit from Georgi's death and his aunts ceased worrying. Strangely enough, Salomeya was remembered more in the hills than in her own home. Twice every twenty-four hours a maid brought her the very simplest food: bread, cheese, some greens; for the rest it was as if she wasn't even there. The household grew so used to her self-immurement, to never seeing her or hearing her, that when, in the middle of December, for the first time since the wedding on the eighth of April, her terrible cries suddenly echoed through the house once more, the aunts decided that Salomeya had gone mad and dithered for some time before finally ordering the wall to be dismantled. This took longer than expected and by the time they'd forced a gap in the masonry large enough to enter the room, Salomeya had long fallen silent. They thought she'd died, so you can picture their astonishment when they discovered a newly born babe at Salomeya's side, the cord still uncut. Needless to say, neither Georgi's nor Salomeya's relatives were remotely prepared for such a twist, although no one disagreed about the identity of the son's father: the boy was Georgi's spitting image. The family decided, therefore, that husband and wife must have become intimate before the bandits even broke in to the castle.

'After the birth, Salomeya assumed her rightful place in the home; that is, she became mistress of the house and started educating her son. When he turned seven she told him every detail about the day of her wedding – the son already knew that his father had died then, but not why or at whose hand (the topic was taboo in the castle) – and she even told him how he was conceived. Then she made him vow that on the day he came of age he would start avenging his father and never stop until the last of his killers was in his grave. He promised. From this birthday onwards, she did everything in her power to ensure he grew up a man.

'The best *abreks* in Georgia taught him horsemanship, pistol and rifle shooting, the arts of wielding a sabre and a dagger. She made him take part in fistfights at every fair, and rejoiced if he won and brought home a prize. In the castle he was subjected to a harsh routine: he slept in rooms unheated even in winter, ate the same food as ordinary highlanders, wore the same clothes. She never forgot for one single day that she was raising him for revenge, and acknowledged only that which could facilitate this process. She wanted him to be strong and tough, so every summer he was sent out with the shepherds to drive flocks of sheep to their mountain pastures, or to hunt for months at a time. She managed to arrange things so that the only sustenance available to him at home was bread and wine – everything else he had to procure himself. When he turned fourteen, even this didn't seem enough to her, and so, following an old custom in noble Georgian families, she sent him for two years to an Ossetian aul, in the home of one of Shamil's henchmen, to harden him up even more.

'But Salomeya did not get her wish. On the contrary, by seventeen he had grown to hate death and blood; even hunting became a torment for him. Perhaps, having been brought to term and born in a cell, he was simply a coward,' said Ifraimov, 'although you'll remember that his father, despite his ten years of brigandage, was also different as a child: loved going to church, loved praying and reading the lives of the saints, was ready to accept his fate with a humble heart. It was only because of her, Salomeya, that he made for the mountains, after which, having recovered his patrimony, he also intended to live quietly: to pray and help the crippled, the orphaned and the poor. It was she, Salomeya, who thirsted for blood; it was she who could not forgive; but her son did not take after her.

'If Vissarion had not been an only child, he would have happily become a monk. Violence elicited such disgust in him that he was the first in his line to choose a civil, not a military career. By the time he came of age he and his mother had become completely estranged; she all but hated him. Knowing they could not live together, he left Svanetia for Tiflis and entered the civil service, but she followed him there a month later, made her home in the house opposite his, and came round every evening to demand that he keep his vow and start avenging his father. He dodged her demands for three years under various pretexts, and when he turned twenty-two she realized that all her hopes for him were vain: he would never avenge his father. She returned to Jvari and there, in the bedroom she'd once shared with Georgi, she killed herself.

'When Vissarion was told, he also considered taking his own life in despair, then decided to flee. He hadn't the stomach to see his mother in her coffin, or to remain in Georgia at all; but he changed his mind and turned back halfway, forcing himself to attend the funeral. In Jvari his relatives more or less imprisoned him, releasing him only after the prayers for the departed on the fortieth day. He never left home if he could help it: he only had to walk down to the village for his own peasants to start spitting in his direction, though even in the castle it was perfectly clear that everyone blamed him for

Salomeya's death. Later he left for Russia – he tried living in Odessa and St Petersburg – but everywhere he found people who knew him and his past, so he had to move on once more. Only in the countryside, in small provincial towns with few outsiders, was he left in peace.

'"There's no point denying it," Vissarion concluded his story. 'That man is me, as you've probably worked out for yourself. Such is my life: burdened by the constant memory of where and how I was conceived and why it was that my mother committed suicide. I would have followed her example long ago, but then neither Father nor she would have been avenged. Now, as for why I decided to confess everything to you: well, you resemble Salomeya very much, the same beauty, the same hardness and strength. I've never known another woman like you, and I'd like to venture one very strange request. A strange story and, to top it all, a strange request. May I?"

'"I'm listening," said de Staël.

'"Here it is," he said, getting down on his knees. "I beg you to bear me a son who will wash away our shame – my father's and mine."

'She'd been expecting something of the kind, but even so, when she heard it she couldn't restrain herself and laughed out loud. He wept, she laughed; then she calmed down, kissed him and agreed on the spot. She adored giving birth – it was the greatest and most accessible miracle she had known in her life. She'd often thought how good it would be if each one of her lovers left her a child to remember him by. Vissarion and she spent another month and a half together, until she was convinced she was pregnant. By that time she was utterly fed up with him and they had the coldest of partings.

'As usual, she spent the final months of her pregnancy in St Petersburg, where, on December 21, she was delivered of a healthy, sturdy little boy, whom she sent off to Georgia with the wet-nurse the very next week, without even christening him. At the station, she gave the wet-nurse the address in Tiflis which Vissarion had left her, along with some money, and never gave the child another thought. Then, when fate unexpectedly brought them together again, she regretted this bitterly and blamed herself for her son's difficult life.

'A year later the boy's father, Vissarion, made a good marriage, took a lofty position, through the good offices of his father-in-law, in the administration of Tiflis's governor-general, and didn't dare take Iosif – as he'd christened him – into his home. Vissarion did not hide the fact that he was the boy's father, nor did he hide the identity of the boy's mother, but he chose not to settle his son in Tiflis, nor even in Jvari with his aunts; instead he took Iosif to Gori and left him to be raised by a family with ancient ties to the Ignatashvili line. Two bastards from Vissarion's earlier liaisons were already living there, and to distinguish between them the locals named them after their mothers – so Iosif Ignatashvili became Iosif, son of Stal, or simply Iosif Stalin. You see, Alyosha,' Ifraimov concluded, 'Stalin, alas, is no myth, as Prochich would have it. Such a man really did exist, although the official version of his life, the version we know from books and textbooks, leaves a great deal unsaid.

*

'In 1879 de Staël turned seventeen; only recently she'd been an awkward, angular adolescent, but just as soon as she'd given birth she somehow softened: her voice, her gestures, her skin – everything about her became very feminine; she was young, fresh, and prettier, perhaps, than ever before. She was happy for the first time in years, brimming with life, so much life that she generated it herself: like those loaves of bread, there was more and more of it. A new feeling emerged in her, and only now did she realize how much she'd needed it: that this was something lasting, that God had finally turned towards her, remembered her, and now everything in her life would be just as she'd dreamt as a girl.

'She saw that the time approaching for Russia was her time, as if cut to her cloth, that it was not in vain that she had prolonged and prolonged her life. She had lost all faith, she was in despair, when suddenly here, too, in Russia, everything came to life, woke up. As if the Lord had taken her back a hundred years, to her French childhood, and given her another go. Life was everywhere; people had snapped out of their trance. Wherever she looked she recognized nothing: different books, different music, different plays. Just for fun, she ran through whatever she could remember, whatever had caught her eye out and about, and it was all new: even fashions were changing so much faster than before. In every home people were quarrelling, arguing, swearing, and speaking in exalted tones. They'd understood something terribly important, crucial, perhaps, for Russia and the world, and they could stay mute no longer; they rushed to say something, to shout something, no matter what, just so long as they were heard.

'Lawyers for the defence and the prosecution fought to the death; journals and newspapers were ready to slit each other's throats; there was a mushrooming of factions, parties, circles. There was even a real political underground, disciplined and created with terror and revolution in mind. Not only that: even civil servants could not see eye to eye with the government or among themselves, nor could the military, nor could the Church and its flock. Once, everything in Russia had been done by rank: decorum and status were what counted, and also, of course, obedience, the mother of all virtues. Whoever wanted to get ahead and make a good marriage had to know his place, know that there were certain principles that could not be violated, remember that simply to doubt them, never mind disturb them, would mean certain ostracism. Previously, people in Russia were calm and lived long, because they knew how to live. It was a simple science – live as your father lived, as your grandfather lived; hardly the worst of lives. On their death-beds each compared his wife's dowry with that of his mother, the rank he'd achieved compared to that of his father, and they met their Maker with peace in their hearts. They had sinned too, of course, but only timidly, furtively; in public, no one dared infringe the moral code.

'And then, just like that, Russia lost her taste for the life it knew. Everything began to seem stale, empty, unworthy; there was no dash to it, no sweep, and no God; no mercy, or even compassion. Was it really worth living for a dowry of a few thousand roubles, to work your way up to the rank of court counsellor and have children no different from you? And why should they walk the same path as you? In fact, why should they walk at all when you've already completed the journey yourself and you can tell them everything down to the last step, the last trick: how to draw up a document, how to curry favour with your superiors, how to take bribes?

'They suddenly discovered all the grief and unhappiness around them – the crippled, the hungry, the sick – and started turning towards them: wasn't there anything they could do to help them, relieve them? And then, before they knew it: how could this be fair? How could it be right? How could it go on and on? It was impossible to live like this, impossible to tolerate it a moment longer. Something had to be done, there and then. If such things were possible, then everything was rotten, so here it was, life's meaning – to change everything, and it was they who had to change it, they who had pulled the long straw. It wouldn't be easy, of course, but they were ready for sacrifice, ready for the prison camp, ready even for death, because their death would not be in vain; they would deliver the world from evil, free man from its grip. They would arrange things in such a way that everyone here, on earth – not in heaven – would be sated, content. Those who lived tomorrow, of course, would have it better, but they would never know the main thing – the joy of self-sacrifice, of giving your life for another, perhaps even for all humanity. And they envied themselves for having been chosen by God.

'De Staël knew what the French Revolution was all about, all that madness lasting almost thirty years, knew it from the opening bars to the official finale – the Restoration. Even before, few remembered that time as she did; she had always had an astonishing curiosity, an astonishing thirst for life. She knew how to look and knew how to see; she had none of the superiority of those who know the hidden mainsprings of events, and none of what happened passed her by. She knew a great deal, if not everything, from the inside, but never overestimated her role; on the contrary, she was struck very early by how little the outcome of the most magnificent schemes corresponded to expectations – even if the adversary was weak or non-existent, even if all possible contingency plans were firmly in place.

'Essentially, she had long tended to the view that revolution, whatever others might say, really is the time of the people, of its power. During a revolution the people is suddenly transformed into a strange, obscure lens, as fast-flowing and changeable as water, in which muddy but kind-hearted dreams of joy, clemency and love for one's neighbour are all mixed up with the hatred and bloodlust usually found only among maniacs. Adapting to this lens was impossible; nor could anyone discover what exactly had passed through it.

'De Staël had seen how the cleverest advisers first to Louis, then to all the governments that followed simply gave up; they began to see that it wasn't them, but somebody else, who was dictating events. That was when she deduced the most important law of revolution – that it is dark and mysterious, that nobody can know who it will choose, who, when and why it will bring to the surface, and in what circumstances: among people gathered in the evening in the former Church of Saint Jacques, or in her, de Staël's, salon, or perhaps its choice would fall on a little lieutenant from Corsica. Most likely of all, it would take a bit here, a bit there, and each of them – and others too – would be granted the role of conquerors, victors, but only a few, alas, would retain it for long. The people – creator of these rulers – would sort through them and shuffle them like cards. When would it get bored? When would it calm down and settle on someone? No one could tell. That was why the difficult thing in any revolution was not to seize power, but to hold onto it.

'Having spent the entire French Revolution in Paris, de Staël felt, in the Russia of these years, like a Pythian priestess, like an oracle to whom, as to a higher power, the future had been revealed. At times she felt sorrow and terror at what she saw, yet nevertheless she loved it all, loved it madly, lustfully, every day of her new life, prayed and thanked God that all this had been granted to her once more, that what had once been her youth had come back to her. And in order not to miss anything, she had to settle in St Petersburg – that was a given. St Petersburg was for Russia what Paris was for France. The rest of Russia, including the first capital, Moscow, could protest all it liked, but it was here that everything was being decided: what would happen to Russia, where it would go, what it would become.

'She had many ties with St Petersburg: she'd been received with great ceremony in the Winter Palace by Emperor Alexander, not the current one, of course, but the first – the conqueror of Napoleon, and was even favoured with several private audiences, each long enough for them to talk about all manner of things, to get to know each other well, and to develop a mutual affinity. Not one of the twenty-odd monarchs, major and minor, that she'd met in the course of her life had made half as good an impression on her as the Russian tsar, and she made no effort to conceal the fact. She was well received by St Petersburg high society as well and even became close to several families, despite the brevity of her stay. So the memories she retained of the Russian capital were pleasant enough and, sitting in her living room in Pine Ravine, she liked to sort through the scenes of that summer as if they were sacred relics. She knew that all of her acquaintances had long since died and nothing could be brought back, but she remembered both them and the life she'd lived with tenderness and sadness.

'Then there were her three sons from Fyodorov, who still lived in St Petersburg, as before, with that same Danish governess who'd come to Russia to save up some money, fully expecting to return to Copenhagen to marry, but had been living here for some fifteen years. She was careful, stingy and handsomely paid, so she must have collected her dowry by now, with plenty to spare, but she wasn't going anywhere and in recent years had stopped mentioning Denmark altogether. Staël could see how fond she'd grown of the children, that she considered them her own. The Dane liked the fact that they were still babes, and so did de Staël; they were fully-grown, good-looking, well-groomed, elegantly dressed, but as babyish as the day they were born. That was probably why she merely had to enter the house and sit by their beds to calm down at once, to cease worrying, waiting, wanting. Their souls were as pure as the souls of angels, and they lived like angels or the birds of the air; they did not sow, did not reap, yet were sated. The Lord fed them from his own hands. Staël often thought that, were a miracle to occur, were they to become ordinary boys, she would be greatly saddened. For as long as she continued to live in Tambov, visiting the children was a major enterprise; by moving to St Petersburg she'd be able to see them every week, so it was an easy decision.

'De Staël took a flat in a beautiful spot on Vasilyevsky Island, surrounded by water on three sides; across the water, to the left, was the Peter and Paul Fortress with its spire, and to the right, her beloved Winter Palace. The flat was large and cosy, chosen by her with great care, so that she would never have to move again. And yet, she did not remain in St Petersburg. She'd known a quite different city, inhabited by quite different people, and she kept confusing this St Petersburg and that one: the same surnames, the same given names, the same palaces. For her the old St Petersburg was more alive than the current one and, like an old woman, she kept putting her foot in it – calling the Emperor Alexander Pavlovich instead of Alexander Nikolayevich, or, even worse, mistaking her granddaughters for their grandmothers and taking offence when they failed to return her visits. This wasn't so terrible, of course: she soon got used to the new St Petersburg and became less muddled by the day, but then, all of a sudden, she felt an unbearable pity for what was passing away, for how little was spared; her memories were disintegrating, dying, and she suddenly wondered what on earth she was doing.

'Her health also suffered in St Petersburg: she kept catching colds and falling ill. Accustomed as she was to the far drier climate of Central Russia, she froze here, could never get warm and walked around her flat in furs. The doctor treating her advised her to leave: this city was no good for the lungs of a person like her, a southerner. But she wavered and when she did eventually decide to move to Moscow she did so not on account of her memories or the chill winds from the Gulf of Finland, but because something else was calling her to Moscow, something she did not wish to admit even to herself.

'In recent months word had begun to reach her that Moscow's Rumyantsev Museum now employed, as keeper of its library, a certain Fyodorov, an utterly extraordinary philosopher, a walking encyclopedia, and, what was more, a man of saintly habits who gave away his entire salary, every last copeck, to needy students – a true man of God. Fyodorov, of course, is a very common surname in Russia, so the librarian could have been anyone at all, but she was convinced that this was her Fyodorov, and she suddenly felt as drawn to him as ever before, wanted to see him all over again. She knew that if this was the same Fyodorov, it would be cruel to seek out a meeting with him; he probably wouldn't even acknowledge her, just as he hadn't recognized her before when he saw her outside the coffin. But if he did realize that she, de Staël, was the Sleeping Princess, it would be a terrible blow for him; it would mean that she, so young and so beautiful, had been brought to life and resurrected by someone else, not him, that he, Fyodorov, had lacked the love, the faith to destroy the evil spell.

'The risk was real and for that reason alone she ought not to have travelled to Moscow, but she knew she would end up going there anyway and looking for him on the very first day, and that only if she was proved wrong would she calm down. Only much later, in Moscow, did she finally understand what it was that had drawn her to Fyodorov so powerfully: their past – the crystal coffin, the candles, the alcove – was all left behind, and she had no intention of reviving any of it, but she suddenly felt that the source of the coming revolution, its true root, was Fyodorov himself. In relation to Fyodorov not just St Petersburg, but Russia – and everything else –was secondary; everything followed him; and if she wanted to be accepted by the Revolution, she had to come to him first of all.

*

'Madame de Staël's life in Moscow,' Ifraimov continued the next day, 'is virtually a closed book to me. And there are good reasons for that.'

This was uttered slowly and crisply, leaving me in no doubt this time that Ifraimov had come by not just for a chat – he was dictating a text to me. What was more, he was dictating it in the form that he wanted it to appear in the Memorial Book. Ifraimov's complete lack of ceremony (I'd never noticed this in him before), his tone, and the fact that I was being forced to write about people I did not know and could not love gave me every right to refuse him. But I obediently wrote and wrote, that day and the next, and all the days that followed, simply because I had no strength left to argue with him.

'The main reason,' Ifraimov calmly dictated, 'is no secret: for the duration of her stay in Moscow, de Staël was closely tied to the revolutionary movement, and these ties grew stronger with each passing year. On occasion, she even risked her own life, making sure, of course, that as few people as possible knew what she was up to. In the underground, an unnecessary witness is always an enemy. Not that her status was ever illegal; in fact, the Party needed her precisely as a wealthy Moscow noblewoman, as the owner of estates and a cotton factory (some thirty years before, her mother had invested a lot of capital in the manufacturing business, and the income which Staël now received from sales of cloth exceeded her earnings from land by a factor of ten). She was beyond suspicion and her irreproachable reputation was more important for the revolutionaries than the money she so generously gave to the cause.

'Arriving in Moscow from St Petersburg, she settled in Ordynka Street, in a modestly sized but very elegant merchant's mansion that had just been built by a reputable and prolific French architect, Dubois. She liked the house the moment she saw it, as well as the fact that it had not yet been occupied: the owners had decided it was too small for them and intended to build, or perhaps buy, another one. She paid for it without a second thought, even though by Moscow standards the price was very steep, and, having barely furnished it, moved straight in from the hotel. She'd never liked hotels, being very fastidious, and she was appalled by the thought of how many people must have slept on the same bed as her, used the same bath, the same basin... Good or bad, all hotels seemed to her as filthy and unwelcoming as railway stations.

'The mansion on Ordynka played an exceptional role in the history of the Russian Revolution, but it would be wrong to call it, as later happened, Revolution HQ. It was never a headquarters in the way that, say, the Smolny Institute was in St Petersburg, or else de Staël could never have lived there, largely undisturbed, for almost forty years. The Russian secret police was highly competent, illegals were arrested in their droves, and some parties struggled to muster enough members even for their central committees; yet her house was never even subjected to a proper raid.

'The house on Ordynka had a special purpose: this was where Russian revolutionaries first got to know each other, usually on Tuesdays and Fridays, the days when she, as all Moscow knew, opened her doors. Each time the house filled with a motley crowd, but, thanks to de Staël, those who needed to find each other did so easily enough, and it can be asserted with confidence that almost half of the anti-governmental parties and groups were born right there, in her living-room. The fact that for many years she was a member of none of these groups, that she was somehow both "one of us" and out on her own, saved her from danger; even if something did trickle down to the police, they didn't know what to make of her or her house, how they should be classified or categorized, so any intelligence about her ended up being labelled "miscellaneous" or dismissed as uninteresting.

'De Staël's mansion was indispensable for the Revolution for many reasons: we can hardly forget the money that, as I've already said, she gave so generously, but also, let me add, cautiously – usually through a second, or even third party. Far more crucial than the money, though, was the fact that two months after de Staël's move to Moscow Fyodorov moved in with her.

'In the years since she'd last seen him, Fyodorov had turned into the ideal revolutionary, and it was easy for her to see why any person who wanted to have done with the world as it was felt magnetically drawn to him. She appraised him calmly, soberly, no longer dwelling on the days, long gone, when they were lovers. She felt the same sympathy for him as before, even tenderness, but they were separate people now

– mere comrades in the underground. She remembered how forcefully he'd sucked out of her all she knew about the French Revolution, and how brilliantly, how skilfully, he'd refracted it, adapted it for Russia. But back then, at Pine Ravine, this was mere potential; he was still feeling his way, still prone to self-doubt; the future arrangement of the world was already clear to him in many details, but in its entirety it was still without form, still amorphous, and above all, he himself was unsure, unprepared, didn't know how to make people obey him, follow him. Now, all doubts were gone.

'One quality in Fyodorov struck her more than any other: he dreamed of destroying the world, of razing it to the ground, but both he and all he wanted were so deeply etched in Russia, flesh of her flesh, that the thought of revolution never even crossed the minds of his followers; on the contrary, they would claim that he had said nothing new, nothing that they, or indeed their ancestors, had not known themselves – all he'd done was make them see that the time had come. In other words, it was easy, very easy to follow him, it required no bravery on their part, no struggle; they followed calmly, without self-sacrifice, without suffering, without haste. It meant so much to them that he himself was just as they'd expected him to be. They could see he was saintly, ascetic; even to compare the purity of his motives to that so prized by the French in Robespierre would have been ridiculous. Rus was a holy land, a land chosen by God to show the path to salvation, to lead all the other peoples and tongues; they heard this from him, but they already knew it themselves; and they understood that just as they, the Russians, were chosen among nations, so was he chosen among them.

'There was not one to whom a single word he spoke could sound blasphemous, heretical. And this is what he preached:

men must overcome their lack of kinship and brotherhood, and society must be arranged as a life of togetherness in love. Christ entrusted us – His children, His disciples – with the transformation and transfiguration of Christianity from prayer to deed, and this deed must be the salvation and resurrection of every person who ever lived on earth; then sins would be expiated and sacrifices redeemed, and the world would return to the state of grace that existed before the Fall. For Christianity to become deed, he told them, they must go out of their churches and, united with all humanity, begin a global liturgy. The cemetery of the world would be the Holy Table, and all the sons of humanity, having become, as it were, a single son, would be the instrument of God's will, directing their forces and the forces of life-giving, life-depriving nature to the reconstitution and transfiguration of the deceased. And thus the transubstantiation of dust into living flesh and blood would begin.

'Nevertheless, barely had she seen him than de Staël could feel deep inside that it was not he who was fated to lead the approaching Revolution. He knew this, too; knew that he had not been chosen. For all his powers of prophecy – and she could see that any man who heard him even once would give up everything and follow him without a second thought – Fyodorov was an old man. Though he was not yet forty, he understood that the Lord had not bestowed His grace upon him. In his life he had loved one woman only. Day after day, year after year he had come to her coffin, in the knowledge that the Lord had not yet taken her soul to Himself, that she was merely asleep, not dead, that she merely appeared to be dead, yet even so he, who taught the universal salvation and resurrection of mankind, had not been granted the gift of breaking the spell, of raising even this one woman to new life.

Perhaps he also suspected that the Lord had not wanted him to remain pure, that there were children prolonging him, and therefore that the time to set out on the path he was preaching had not yet come.

'The circle of Fyodorov's admirers was very broad and followed him to Ordynka in its entirety. It consisted of quite outstanding people. Suffice it to name Tolstoy and Dostoevsky, though there were other remarkable individuals as well, Vladimir Solovyov among them; and each had his own retinue of disciples. Fyodorov, in other words, was the teacher of teachers, and all of them, let me repeat, would fill her house every Tuesday and Friday.

'De Staël had long admired the famous description of violence being the midwife of history, and in years to come she, when in a cheerful mood, liked to call herself the midwife of the Russian Revolution. It was scarcely an exaggeration. Remembering that it was granted to nobody to foretell which party would come to power and when, she sowed all these circles, groups, organizations and parties with the tirelessness of a good farmer. In general, whoever was unable to come to terms with the world as it existed found help and support in her. The HEURO group, which was developing its minimal and maximal programmes to increase the number of geniuses in Russia, was also her beneficiary.

'And yet, Alyosha, it would be wrong to accuse Madame de Staël of sowing discord in Russia, of spawning the Russian Revolution, and therefore of bearing responsibility both for that and for what came later. This would hardly be fair. It was certainly not she who conceived the Revolution; de Staël was quite right to call herself its midwife – she merely facilitated its birth. The people she received on Ordynka were so painfully aware of the imperfection of the life around them that they could no longer endure it; they would have managed without her.

'Of course, she too desired the Revolution, dreamed of the Revolution; and there was one other reason she was hastening it with such zeal: she was living her last life and could be prolonged, reborn, resurrected only together with the entire human race. She loved life, loved it madly, and did not wish to die. She'd grown used to being immortal. She was far from selfless, of course, but equally it saddened her that the people she loved, who'd been a part of her life, were dying and she was unable to save them. Fyodorov had reunited her with the human race, brought her back into its fold, and now she felt glad to be like everyone else.

'She helped these circles come into being, but she rarely knew what happened to them later. Some died of their own accord or through the efforts of the police, but the majority survived; the Revolution, after all, was a living tree. The circles propagated and multiplied (by dividing, budding and God knows how else), merged and split; the wind carried their seed across the length and breadth of the empire, and everywhere they put down roots. And their lives were all different, too: sometimes their strength really was in their roots – these were the most prudent, the most far-sighted; others, by contrast, reached for the light, for the sun, while in the shade they sickened and withered – these were the trunks and leaves; then there was a third type – these were usually obscure, tiny little groups, which would suddenly flourish one day though some unprecedented explosion, some brilliant act of terror, but their lives were short and they faded and died just as quickly as snowdrops. Did you know, Alyosha, that the hundreds of murder victims found in Siberia during the thaw are also known as "snowdrops"?

'And she loved them all – the desperate and the restrained, the reckless and the calculating, the modest and the boastful; loved them so much that her legs shook and her body convulsed. So many of them, after all, had been her lovers, and not one of those whom she loved and who loved her was forgotten by her, erased from her memory. In many cases their night with her was their last night with a woman: in the morning they had to throw a bomb or shoot a minister. Or the other way round: frightened, hounded, in a cold sweat, they would come running to her house straight after their crime, and she would shelter them for an entire day, or just a few hours – any more was dangerous; but even so, whether the man had already committed his fatal crime or was on the verge of doing so, both he and she knew, once he'd come, that there was no way back. The men were doomed, and she, their godmother, gave their deaths the blessing, so to speak, of her love, sanctified their Calvary. And from then on, for however many hours remained to them, they would think not of the end, not of the fact that they were dying so young, and not even of the Party and the Revolution, but only of her, de Staël, and of her presence in their life, which made everything right.

*

'For the first ten years de Staël limited herself to offering money to the Revolution and only occasionally, in extreme circumstances, shelter and refuge; that is, she rendered her personal assistance in accordance with the rules set down by Martov for the Russian Social Democratic Workers' Party (RSDWP). Later, however, after delving deeper into the mishmash of revolutionary factions and organizations, she sided definitively with the Party's infinitely more serious and resolute Bolshevist wing. In 1904 she gladly submitted to the rules now established by Lenin and entered, as a mere foot-soldier, one of the five-strong cells into which the Party was divided.

'She'd always felt a lack of risk in her life, a lack of life itself; in fact she was insatiable in both people and love, and perhaps that was why God ended up giving her not one but three long lives. So, as a member of her little cell, she readily acceded to all the Party's demands – there was no need to explain to her the meaning of discipline in an underground organization. Much later, after the Revolution, her secret Party reference stated that she had proved herself an enterprising and responsible comrade-in-arms, selflessly devoted to the cause of the proletariat and brilliantly carrying out the most perilous missions. Many times she acted as courier, bringing leaflets, newspapers and money from Finland and Sweden. The role of wealthy Russian landowner came easily to her – after all, that's exactly what she was. She was young, good-looking, witty, expensively dressed in the best Parisian style, and, needless to say, aroused not the slightest suspicion at border-crossings. Later, after the February Revolution, Lenin joked that, if only de Staël had been with them, the Bolsheviks would have had no need of a sealed train: she could have stored all the revolutionaries in her luggage.

'Eventually, though, de Staël passed through Swedish customs once too often, and the Party decided that it would be best if she laid low for a while. For the time being, she could be deployed in the South, in Odessa and Transcaucasia. She herself had long been meaning to visit Tiflis, having been invited there by several families she'd got to know in Moscow; she also remembered that she had a son in Georgia whom she hadn't seen since he was born – precisely twenty-five years before. The Party deemed that her contacts would prove useful, and she even wrote to Ignatashvili to say that she might be coming, but his reply never reached her, because two days later she was forced to catch the first train to Novorossiysk. A group of militants had just carried out a successful raid of a branch of the Russo-Caucasian Bank, expropriating several hundred thousand roubles for the needs of the Revolution, and de Staël was tasked with getting the ringleader, known among the Bolsheviks by his Party alias Koba, out of Georgia.

'The plan was for her to rent a first-class cabin for herself and her travelling companion on the *Elbrus*, a steamer belonging to the "Caucasus" joint-stock company which stopped at Batumi, Poti, Sukhumi and Novorossiysk. When the steamer was at anchor in the outer harbour at Poti, Koba would climb up a ladder from a boat and enter her cabin through the porthole. From there they would continue on their way, unsuspected, to Novorossiysk.

'In the event of unforeseen circumstances she could rely on the assistance of the captain of the *Elbrus*, a sympathizer, although he would almost certainly refuse, she was told at her briefing, to take part in the operation himself. But there was a sailor on board, an old member of the RSDWP, and she could count on him unreservedly; he was supposed to approach her himself with a password. And there was a back-up plan: if it transpired en route that the police had been warned and were waiting for Koba in Novorossiysk, they should alight at Sukhumi, hire some local guides, preferably Abkhazians, and cross the mountains to Nalchik.

'Everything went fine in Batumi: she reached the town in good time and took a cabin ideally equipped for their purposes, with a port-hole just three metres above the waterline. But, as often happens when things start too smoothly, unpleasant surprises soon follow. Near Poti the sea turned rough and the heavens opened, and although the captain delayed departure for two hours, risking the wrath of the passengers and the displeasure of the company, there was no sign of Koba or his boat. Standing on deck, with walls of water to both sides of her, de Staël trained her binoculars on the shore, but in vain – there was no boat, and even if there had been, she could not have seen it. De Staël spotted something only once the steamer weighed anchor and turned in the direction of the open sea. For a moment the wind rent the clouds, the rain ceased, and she saw two boats at once: a young Georgian, presumably Koba himself, was in the first, rowing for his life in the direction of the ship, while three officers sporting red cockades were in hot pursuit in the second.

'The Georgian was never going to make it, and he must have realized this himself, because the last thing she saw when the rain came driving down again was Koba jumping overboard. She wasn't the only one to witness the end of the chase: the captain, dismayed, joined her on deck and said that the Georgian would never swim to safety – he wouldn't last five minutes before freezing to death in the cold March sea. Nevertheless she managed to beg him to stop the engines and wait another half-hour: what if the Georgian miraculously resurfaced? They ended up waiting the whole hour; they'd both lost all hope, but they couldn't accept that their comrade was dead. Eventually the captain gave the order to weigh anchor, whereupon, at precisely the spot where he was meant to surface, they caught sight of a slowly drifting body. The deck was deserted on account of the rain – there was only her, the captain and the sailor who was meant to help her bring Koba to Novorossiysk; it was he who caught him with a boat-hook, pulled him towards the boat and, with the captain's help, lifted the Georgian on deck.

'Everything suggested that Koba was dead. For a long time they pumped away at his heart, almost crushing his chest, and tried mouth-to-mouth resuscitation; all the water he'd swallowed came out, but the little mirror they kept pressing to his lips remained clear. Even when the sailor was trying to catch his body with the boat-hook, she suddenly recalled that Koba, as far as she knew, also had another alias – Stalin – and she'd even heard him being named as such in St Petersburg. Now that he was lying on the deck before her, dead, she realized that this was her son.

'Her son, that is, whom she had never put to her breast, not once. Tears streamed down her cheeks with the rain as she looked at him, her son, whom she had seen but twice – after giving birth to him and now, straight after his death. She knew nothing of his life or how he'd spent it; all she could infer, having been sent to shield him, was that the Revolution had united them, brought them together. The Revolution had brought him back to her – not for life, but in order that she, his mother, should close his eyes.

'She wondered: had the possibility occurred to him, even once, that he had made himself a revolutionary precisely in order to return to her? Had he ever thought that the Revolution was the only way to reach her? She wanted to tell him that this was not so, that she had come to him not just as a Party comrade; no, she had long been missing him, regretting not having kept him for herself, not having placed him with Fyodorov's children. She had to tell him all this, had to tell him they were together – whether or not he heard her. She wanted his last warmth to go into her as he took his leave of earthly life; for him to be warmed by her, by the warmth he'd known only in her womb.

'She told the captain quite calmly that in Norway there had been cases of women offering the heat of their bodies to sailors cast ashore after shipwreck, and that she also wanted to try. She had Koba brought to her in the cabin, diligently prepared the bed, undressed him, undressed herself, and then, placing him next to her, embraced him with her whole body and began to warm him. She wept, told him that the Lord had reunited them, the Lord and the Revolution, that she'd been on her way to him but never reached him, never made it to Tiflis, so instead they'd met here. She said that she had always loved him and always suffered, that her life had never been complete because he, her son, had not been with her, and now here they were together; she talked and wept, talked and wept, asked why he'd been taken away from her and wept again, before finally falling asleep. There was a storm, the *Elbrus* was rolling, the wind was against them, and the steam engines only just managed to pull the ship through. She didn't know how long she'd been sleeping, several hours or several days. She would wake up, fall asleep, wake up again and say: "My darling, you've come back to me, your life was brief, you died young, but you died in your mother's arms, and you should know," she said, just like Fyodorov, "that every human being will rise from the dead, every single one, so your death is not final, it's not for ever" – and she wept, and blamed herself, and comforted him once more.

'In this half-sleep, half-oblivion, she realized that he was inside her again, that he'd listened to her and returned to her, entered her, and to keep him there, to discourage him from ever being born again into this terrible, cruel, unjust world, she instinctively clenched her legs. She could feel him growing, hesitating, turning about inside her, could feel how big he was, how alive he was, that he was hers, all hers. And he grew and grew, and there was never enough space for him, and she kept giving way to him, giving in to him, letting him go wherever he wanted, opened herself up to him entirely. And all she could do was clench her legs tighter and tighter, to stop him abandoning her, going off into this life. She begged and cajoled him not to be born, to remain inside her; she wept and explained how cruel this world was and what good was it to him anyway? Wasn't he fine where he was, inside her? Wasn't there enough space for him there, enough warmth, enough caresses and tenderness? She stroked him, kissed him, caressed him with all her flesh, her entire being.

'And he, already aware that she was his mother, already entering her, coming back to her, also wept and wept, complaining: "Mummy, mummy, why did you give birth to me then? I don't want to come out of you, mummy, I want to remain inside you. Don't let me go, don't give birth. The world's evil and cruel, if only you knew how awful it was for me without you. Why did you have me?" He said to her: "Mummy, darling, don't chase me away, you're mine, mine, you're with me again, I've come back to you again. Mummy, mummy, how long I've been without you." And then they both understood that everything bad had ended, that he was inside her again, for all time, that once again they were one being, with no more births or separations, and they fell silent.

'Directly before setting sail from Sukhumi, the captain knocked on the door of her cabin: he'd just been informed by radiogram that the port at Novorossiysk was under strictest surveillance, every vessel was being searched from hold to masthead, and this Georgian of hers would do well not to show his face in town. She thanked him for his help and warning, asked him to pass on a beautiful silver cigar case to the sailor who'd helped them, after which she and Koba, having stuffed her things into trunks and suitcases, disembarked. In St Petersburg, as I've already mentioned, the possibility of their getting no further than Sukhumi by steamer had already been foreseen; now, the contingency plan came into force: the evacuation of Stalin from Georgia by mountain trails, over the peaks to Nalchik.

'Following advice from the Centre, they hired an elegant, pink-and-white carriage outside the passenger terminal – the only one in Sukhumi with pneumatic tyres, or so the coachman told them – and, playing a young couple on honeymoon on the Caucasian Riviera, rode on to the Abkhazian village of Lykhny. Stalin had some comrades there and fully expected to find a trusty guide or two who knew the mountains inside out.

'But news of the Tiflis bank robbery travelled fast, thanks to its political implications, and the order soon came from St Petersburg to block the mountain trails one by one and not let the militants out of Georgia. The task was entrusted to local Svanetian and Abkhazian clans who were promised a considerable reward for every captured militant. Custom forbade Stalin's contacts in Lykhny from going against their own people, and Stalin did not even ask them. With the greatest difficulty, and at huge expense, de Staël and Stalin managed to strike a deal only with a fifteen-year-old shepherd, and even he wavered for a long time, wondering whether he'd be better off just turning them in. Eventually, since they were offering three times more than the Russian tsar, he agreed; but de Staël would remain convinced that it was him, the cunning little shepherd, who, having pocketed the advance, deliberately led them straight into a mounted patrol of local militia. Either way, no sooner were they stopped than he instantly vanished and she never saw him again. The patrol caught them completely by surprise – they were going along slowly in a squeaking ox-cart, and she and Stalin, having entered fully into the roles of newlyweds, were locked in a passionate embrace.

'Staël could never take these highland patrols very seriously; her money, not to mention her bearing and charm, disarmed even the best professional policemen, and in different circumstances, she and Stalin might well have been simply waved through; but not this time, for the man at the head of the detachment was Vissarion Ignatashvili. He rode up to the ox-cart slightly ahead of the others, instantly recognized them both and, addressing himself exclusively to Ekaterina, commented ironically that, just as he'd written in his letter, he welcomed her arrival in Georgia and had been waiting here since the previous evening in order to meet her and take her to his estate, a mere ten versts away.

'De Staël immediately took exception to his tone. The pose in which he had found them left few doubts about the nature of her relationship with Stalin, but Ignatashvili feigned indifference about the fact that the woman who had once been his lover and whom he loved even now was sleeping with her own son, conceived moreover from him, Vissarion Ignatashvili. None of this augured well. Stalin, who knew his father better than she did, seemed to be thinking the same thing. In any case, he jumped down from the ox-cart and, with the composure for which he was so renowned in the Party, walked straight up to his father and the mounted patrol; Ignatashvili, scared that Stalin might start shooting, had just rode back to the safety of his detachment. Stalin was advancing so confidently that the horses carrying the militiamen even began retreating and parting before him. But he stopped before his father and, playing with a slender whip – his sole weapon – addressed the detachment with the following words:

'"Perhaps Vissarion Ignatashvili has already told you

himself that I am one of the militants who robbed the bank in Tiflis. If not, then I, Stalin, am telling you so now, and I'll tell you something else. I, Stalin, aka Iosif Dzhugashvili, am his eldest son, so, like the good highlander he is, my father is guarding this road for a specific purpose – to deliver his son's head to the government. Such love does not surprise me. His father, my grandfather, was the renowned *abrek* Georgi Ignatashvili, that very man who was captured and hung by his enemies on his wedding-day. Georgi's wife was a true highlander: knowing, that her husband's soul would not rest until he had been avenged, she managed to conceive from him when he was already swinging from the rope. But Georgi's son, Vissarion Ignatashvili, your leader, was born a coward; too scared to punish his enemies, he fled Georgia. When his mother Salomeya Ignatashvili realized that Georgi would not be avenged, she committed suicide. Then this man came to my mother, Ekaterina Stal – she is sitting on the ox-cart before you – and said to her: 'I'm as timid and cowardly as any woman. All Georgia mocks and despises me. So I beg you for a son as brave as my father, to wash away our family's shame.'

"'Ekaterina Stal took pity on him and bore him a child – me, Iosif Stalin – but he did not even acknowledge his son. And now that I've begun to avenge, now that I've vowed that not one of those who killed Georgi Ignatashvili will escape retribution, he wants to hand me over to the tsar with your assistance. Well, what can I say – a nice job you've found for yourselves."

'Stalin was as straightforward and natural with the highlanders as if he were standing before a crowd of workers in Baku; he spoke softly, calmly, with none of the pathos so characteristic of other Party orators, but the effect of his words was overwhelming. Before he'd even finished his account the detachment surrounding Ignatashvili had dispersed of its own accord: the majority turned their horses round and galloped off up the road, while two others simply crossed over to Stalin. Vissarion Ignatashvili was left in the middle of the road all alone. Fear drenched his face in sweat; his hands trembled on the reins. Stalin looked at him with great calmness, even sadness. Then, without a word, he flashed his whip under the horse's snout. The horse shied, reared up and, throwing off its rider, galloped away down a ravine, through hazel bushes.

'The two horsemen who had come over to Stalin's side helped the couple cross the hills and only once they were entirely satisfied that he and Staël were out of harm's way, on the outskirts of Nalchik, did they turn back to Georgia. They subsequently joined the RSDWP and, never once deviating from the Party line, remained Stalin's loyal associates and friends to the end of their days.

*

'Fyodorov was a prophet, but he was not the Messiah; the Lord had not conferred his grace upon him, and it was not for him to save the human race, to raise it from the dead. His was a humbler role: like John the Baptist, he had to prepare the soil, to plough and nourish it, and then, after giving his blessing to the man who was greater than he, step aside. But Fyodorov delayed. Perhaps he thought that the choice had not yet been made, that the Lord might still choose him, or that the Lord Himself would give a clear indication that he had no more need of Fyodorov here on earth: he'd done what he was sent to do, what he was given to do, and now he had to clear a space for someone else. The Lord could have called Fyodorov to Himself long ago, but He was in no hurry, as if He really was

218

unsure, and Fyodorov delayed as well: the hope that he might still be the Messiah, the saviour of men, had not died in him, and he clung to his disciples as best he could.

'And these disciples, for as long as Fyodorov was alive and among them, exhibited not the slightest independence; they merely competed with each other in their adoration of their teacher, their loyalty towards him. With dismal consequences: life ground to a halt, and the Russian Revolution began almost twenty years later than it should have done. Among those who visited Madame de Staël were several far-sighted people who understood all this no less than she did. Lengthy debates ensued about the need to sacrifice Fyodorov in the interests of the Revolution. Many argued that if Fyodorov really did believe what he preached, then he should accept and approve this, realize that he himself had become the main obstacle to the task of resurrecting the human race. One man was even prepared to take the murder upon himself: apparently, this was Fyodorov's oldest disciple from Tambov days – the first man ever to have followed him.

'Whether for good or for ill, bloodshed was avoided: Staël succeeded, at the end of 1903, in persuading Fyodorov to leave. In collusion with the doctors, they acted as follows: on the twenty-eighth of December Fyodorov was admitted to the Mariinsky Hospital for the Poor with a diagnosis of double pneumonia, before which Staël had turned all visitors away for five days running, saying that Fyodorov was too sick to see anyone. All this time she and the doctors were waiting for a corpse to turn up in the hospital morgue that might be passed off as Fyodorov's. It eventually appeared and Doctor Sergei Alexeyev, a former student of the Medical-Surgical Academy and an active member of Zaionchkovsky's Populist group (de Staël had been on close terms with him for some time), immediately assigned Fyodorov to a special ward for the dying. That same day, towards evening, Fyodorov was confessed and received the sacrament; two hours later Alexeyev and another doctor bearing the strange surname Skripok, also a Populist, certified death from asphyxiation.

'Next, Alexeyev and Skripok put Fyodorov's body on a trolley themselves and began pushing him towards the hospital morgue, some five hundred yards away from the main hospital building. Halfway between the hospital and the morgue was de Staël's carriage, which, for conspiratorial purposes, was being driven not by her coachman but by the aforementioned disciple. When the trolley drew level with the carriage, Fyodorov climbed into it without any assistance, and he and de Staël set off at once. That very same night she sent him off to Pine Ravine, where a special little house had recently been built for him by the windmill on the river bank. Two days later, despite the freezing weather, a large crowd followed the coffin to its grave at Skorbyashchensky Monastery – Fyodorov's popularity was truly astonishing. The man who took his place in the coffin was a holy fool, famous throughout Moscow, who went by the name of Sashka and froze to death in the street. In both appearance and way of life, he was Fyodorov's spitting image.

'After Fyodorov's funeral, his disciples were in ferment, their souls now freed from the dead weight of obedience. Each considered himself their teacher's true follower and everyone else to be heretics, apostates or, even worse, traitors. In each there was an abundance of energy and life; everyone was in a terrible hurry, quarrelling, fighting; nothing lasted, and at times Staël could barely understand who was on whose side. There were endless conspiracies and intrigues, and once (had they gone mad?) there was even a spate of duelling – an absurdity, of course, for any self-respecting revolutionary. Staël often tried to guess which of them would end up as leader, because they were drifting ever further apart and it was obvious that there would be not just one, but several schools of disciples. But every time, she guessed wrong.

'At first she assumed that Fyodorov's cause would be taken up by Tolstoy, who himself had no lack of admirers in Russia, wielded immense authority and was cut out to lead. Essentially, it was to clear a space for him that de Staël had shown such persistence in removing Fyodorov. But, to her astonishment, Tolstoy immediately stopped attending her salon after Fyodorov's funeral; he never explained himself, and she felt almost insulted. Only later did she learn that he had been attracted less by Fyodorov's ideas than by his personality. For Tolstoy alone, it occurred to her, the substitution of Sashka the holy fool for Fyodorov was no great deception.

'Tolstoy's supporters left with him, and the ranks of Fyodorovists thinned out; but this was no crisis, just a purge of random, unstable and dispensable individuals. And indeed, most of the remaining disciples soon gathered around the poet and philosopher Vladimir Solovyov, one of Fyodorov's earliest followers – and one of his favourites. Solovyov was a rather strange, lonely man, and it took de Staël some time to understand him. This is what he taught:

1) Global catastrophe is already at hand. Apocalypse is nigh. The age of the antichrist has arrived.

2) The complete fulfilment of truth and justice must begin forthwith.

3) The starting point of human history is original sin; the Last Judgment and victory over world evil will be its endpoint.

4) (after Fyodorov) The world as created by God was imperfect. Life is not a gift. With the Act of Creation, the world fell away, so to speak, from the Absolute, and original sin was

the natural consequence. But the Act of Creation was justified by the fact that the world was moving towards perfection and sooner or later would return to the Absolute, merge with it again, and return to the "new earth" and "new heaven".

5) (against Fyodorov) There can be no personal and social salvation of mankind, and no return to heaven, outside collaboration with God.

6) Every particle of the universe is alive, distinct, animated; there is no particle without memory; so the restoration and resurrection of everything that has ever lived on earth is possible.

7) The realization of this is near at hand. The world has already completed the greater part of its journey. Previously, it abided in a perverted, chaotic state, but now: a) chaos has been gathered up into its original totality by the force of gravity; b) this totality has been harmoniously dissected, so as to render possible the intimate reunification of the universal body (via electromagnetic forces); c) life has appeared – the organic unity of newly created matter and light; d) man has been created.

8) Man's Messianic mission is to cultivate and improve nature, to save it, liberate it, and, bringing History to its completion, to return to the Absolute.

9) The Fall was man's attempt to do all of this on his own, without the collaboration of God; the result: chaos, destruction and the triumph of evil. But this did not nullify man's mission – it merely postponed it.

10) The aim of world history is the unity of God with non-divine nature directed by man.

11) This unity cannot be achieved without the divine-human organism of the Universal Church – the foundation and embodiment of the voluntary solidarity of men.

12) Russia's historical mission is religious mediation between West and East, their convergence and eventual reunion as a World State, to be led by the Russian tsar (secular power) and the pope (spiritual power).

13) The State itself, not personality, or even the commune, is to represent the human principle in theandric unity; personality must accept that its true freedom is to renounce itself.

'After this programme was promulgated one more group split off, but not before committing a severe breach of Party discipline and publicly charging Solovyov with heresy and with the distortion and betrayal of Fyodorov's teachings. Not without reason, it must be admitted. The faction was chiefly made up of young intellectuals of common birth who joined the Party in the last year of Fyodorov's life; nobody, including de Staël, knew very much about them, so it's no wonder that they immediately vanished from view. De Staël found them again only two years later, by complete chance. By then they had named themselves the Fyodorov Faction and entered the RSDWP, which was headed by a certain Georgy Plekhanov.

'De Staël was well-disposed to Plekhanov, an old acquaintance of hers, funded him, and several years earlier even hosted a meeting of his Populist splinter group Black Repartition at Pine Ravine. At first Plekhanov gave a warm welcome to Fyodorov's disciples. They included many strong, talented people and the workers' movement stood to gain a great deal from them; but soon the Fyodorovists began picking arguments with Plekhanov, too. The ostensible reason for their disagreements was a trivial question of tactics, but that was just on the surface; in reality, they agreed on almost nothing. Formally speaking, the Fyodorovists remained within the Party, but together with Lenin they formed an independent faction: the Bolsheviks.

'Neither then nor afterwards were they Marxist. They viewed Marx with irony and took no pains to hide the fact. His vision of socialism and communism; the role of the working class in history; the fact that the Revolution would begin not in Russia, but in one of the most advanced countries of the West; and above all, his notion of the meaning and purpose of man himself – all this struck them as quite astonishingly naïve. But Lenin, to whom they readily deferred, was forgiven his infatuation with Marx. Lenin impressed them as a man who could take decisions and get things done, and they had no doubt that in the end he would abandon Marx and cross over to Fyodorov. That time had not yet come, and this was no fault of Lenin's; it was simply that the nations of the world were not yet ready to hear the Word of Fyodorov, whose revelation was given to man too soon. For now it could survive and be preserved only as a secret, esoteric doctrine. Marxism would become the shell that saved it.

'The Fyodorovists' influence on the Bolsheviks was multifold. In particular, it explains why Lenin, contrary to his clearly stated wishes, was not committed to the earth after his death, but placed in a glass coffin for public display. Fyodorov told his disciples more than once about his efforts over several years to save and resurrect the Sleeping Princess. For him, this was the start of the common task of resurrecting all the people who had ever lived on earth. Failure, it seemed, had not disheartened him: in the cosmos, where there is no gravity towards earth, only towards heaven, he would have saved her without the slightest difficulty.

'In 1924 it was the Fyodorovists who insisted on protecting Lenin's body from decay, on leaving him to sleep, as it were, in his glass coffin, until Russia had built him a rocket. One of them, Konstantin Tsiolkovsky, devoted almost thirty years to its construction. The rocket was meant to take Lenin to space, where, freed from gravity, he would rise from the dust and become once more the leader of world revolution. The Fyodorovists were also responsible for another idea whose consequences for the Revolution were, quite possibly, decisive. Given that death was not final, they said, the correct and even essential thing to do now was to destroy, for their own good, everyone whose existence hindered the common task.

'But to return to Solovyov. As far as can be judged from the sources, he was unperturbed by the split and defection of the Fyodorov Faction. Over the course of several weeks he created an underground party out of those Fyodorovists who remained loyal to him (by now they were weary of freedom and only too willing to sacrifice it for the sake of dissolving in a larger organization). This party struck de Staël as highly promising and she gladly lent it her financial support. When the cost exceeded her means, she recruited several gold magnates from the merchant families of the Rukavishnikovs and Silantyevs.

'The grass roots were subjected to the strictest discipline: the whole party was divided up into groups of three (troikas), the members of which knew their commanding officer and no one else. The commanding officer was part of the troika on the next level, and so on all the way up to Solovyov. But this principle, essential for any underground organization, was not observed at the very top, by the personal caprice of Solovyov himself. Solovyov was the Party's organizer, its acknowledged leader; he had developed both its philosophy and its programme. But he believed that the Party should be led in collegiate fashion and decided to share his authority as leader with Nicholas II's former personal adjutant, now military commander of St Petersburg, General Dragomirov, and with the celebrated religious activist and preacher John of Kronstadt, whose canonization was only a matter of time.

'Perhaps, just like Fyodorov, Solovyov doubted that he had been granted God's grace, that he was chosen. Or perhaps the problem was the infrequency of his visits to Moscow; he spent long stretches of time staying with his friends in the country, and especially with the philosopher Trubetskoy. Only on Trubetskoy's estate was he really able to work; he went for long walks, slept without bromide, thought clearly and wrote fluently, and sometimes even brought back poems. He knew, of course, that the Party should not be left to its own devices for months at a time, without any leaders at the top, but why, realizing this, he was unwilling to change his way of life and deny himself the pleasure of at least some of his trips, is beyond me,' said Ifraimov. 'The destiny of so many people depended on his decision; so much was at stake. I simply cannot explain it.

'But we should give Solovyov his due – the team he chose was a powerful one. The most influential and powerful forces in Russian society – the army, the Church, the intelligentsia – were represented there, and by prominent figures. It was easy to predict the enormous popularity a party led by such men might command, but even if it didn't, it could still seize power at the drop of a hat, given the forces at its disposal. John of Kronstadt and Dragomirov had both been recruited by Solovyov, and both, as I've already said, acknowledged his primacy and would have submitted to him readily. But here, too, Solovyov insisted that governance be divided into three spheres, and even declared that each of them should govern their own sphere independently; only decisions concerning the world as a whole should be taken jointly and unanimously.

'A system like that could lead to nothing but idiocy: instead of a disciplined, battle-hungry underground organization, all they achieved was a likeness of the Polish Sejm. It didn't take long before both Dragomirov and John of Kronstadt began to think themselves tsars in their own fiefdoms, not even bothering to execute decisions accepted by the majority, unless they themselves were in favour. This was no way to survive in the political underground, of course, as all three of them quickly realized, but no one was in any hurry to change. The Party seemed bent on its own destruction and, I dare say, they all breathed a sigh of relief when it finally came.

'The pretext for the split was Solovyov's demand that the Party attract more Jews. Solovyov claimed that, contrary to the received wisdom, the covenant between God and the Jews was not ripped up by the New Testament; nor had it been replaced. Quite the opposite – it had been reinforced and renewed by the millions of sacrifices with which the Jews had paid for their loyalty to the Abrahamic faith. Victory over evil and the salvation of humankind would be possible only through the conjunction and combined actions of both of God's chosen people: the people of the Old Testament – the Jews, and the people of the New Testament – the Russians.

'Dragomirov agreed with Solovyov in principle, but John of Kronstadt was categorically opposed. He maintained that the entire worldview of both the Russian Church and the Russian people was based on the latter being God's only chosen people. Granting it His special grace, the Lord had chosen Russia alone among all the nations of the earth; she alone was the Messiah-nation. Even if Solovyov was telling the truth, this truth had to be hidden, for the Russian people would never accept it. And if it did accept it, its faith in both God and itself would be destroyed, and Russia would be forever lost to the Revolution.

'In the end,' Ifraimov continued the next day, 'all this

makes for a very sad story and, viewed from the outside, a very monotonous one: a long, long line of men, peoples and countries all convinced that the Lord has entrusted them with a special mission, the story of their faith and readiness to accept any sacrifice, any suffering, and then, at the end of their lives, when it's already too late to start over again, their realization that neither they nor their exploits are of any use to anyone, in the present or the future, that everything was in vain. And the torments and bitterness of their last days: whatever God has left unbroken in them they break themselves, convinced that there can be no sin greater than their own, that they are impostors, chosen by themselves, not God. So it was with Russia, and with de Staël, and with Fyodorov, and with Solovyov, and with many, many others, not least the person who will be discussed below. None of them were called.

'And yet,' said Ifraimov, 'we shouldn't rush to judgment. After all, their faith was so pure and so selfless, their devotion to God so unmistakable, that the Lord – even if, in their ignorance, they had taken a wrong turning, even if they had misheard Him – was simply obliged to acknowledge this, to explain himself, to help them. For five centuries in a row, year after year, battle after battle, Russian victory after Russian victory, He had confirmed that yes, it was all true: the Russians really were God's chosen people, Russia really was the Holy Land, the land where God's Spirit had found its refuge. So how could Russia ever have doubted that she was chosen?

'Overall,' said Ifraimov, 'I tend to the view that the Lord really did choose them all; not very firmly perhaps, not definitively – just provisionally, as it were – but still, they had been promised, and therefore they were without sin, not culpable of anything. But then, and not for the first time, the Lord's plans for mankind changed. In her angrier moments, de Staël would accuse him of having deliberated tempted his followers – as the Devil had once tempted Christ in the desert – with sacrifice, heroism, holiness, power; but I doubt this is true: He probably simply forgot us. He thought far too much about the fate of the entire race of Adam; but as for individuals, there just wasn't enough of Him to go round. So those were all mere words: that one human being, one human soul, was more important to Him than the entire world. Too much indifference had accumulated in him, too much apathy; we and the lives we led did not actually interest Him all that much. So He may have not even noticed that He was doing us wrong.

'The dispute about the Jews made it perfectly clear to Solovyov, John of Kronstadt and Dragomirov alike that their party could no longer exist in the form in which they had made it. Either everything had to change or they had to accept that it was not for them to lead the Russians – and others in their wake – along the path of salvation. They were obliged to resurrect and raise the Party, but they no longer had the strength.

*

'De Staël saw that all of them were tired, all Fyodorov's disciples: twenty years of hope and faith had worn them down, and they were no longer any good for anything. Most of the Fyodorovists had left the movement entirely, others continued to attend her salon from sheer inertia – conspiracy and Party membership were the only life they knew; but they'd given up, they'd aged, and they were merely making a pretence of youth and self-sacrifice. They only got together out of habit, like old friends. They'd accumulated their fair share of mutual resentments and suspicions, of course, but even these had lost their edge. As a belligerent Party, they were a spent force, having achieved precisely nothing. And how typical this was of Russia: such eagerness to turn the world upside down, to attempt any and every possible feat, and nothing comes of it except lofty talk. She hadn't given them any money for more than a year, although for some reason she never turned anyone away from her house.

'At that time in Russia, the first Revolution was already in full swing. To the astonishment of the police, the party of Fyodorov-Solovyov turned out to have nothing to do with it. Once again, things went no further than discussions and statements, demands not merely to participate, but to lead the revolt: the Party had such experience behind it, such powerful forces and such brilliant theoreticians that without it the common people would be wandering in darkness. The Fyodorovists simply could not understand why the Socialist Revolutionaries and the Social Democrats were not turning to them for help, but they were too proud to make the first move themselves. All this at a time when what was needed was action, action, action, when the Russian throne, thanks to the war with Japan, was virtually being handed to the Revolution on a plate, when everything was already rotten to the core and falling to bits. Staël, whenever the Fyodorovists came up in conversation with one of her comrades from the RSDWP, liked to repeat that there is an age for everything, that Solovyov would soon understand that the stage of life his party had attained was not maturity, nor even old age, but senility. In those years she was already actively helping the Bolsheviks, and for conspiratorial purposes it suited her well that the police still had her down as a Fyodorovist. It became an excellent cover.

'Later, though, de Staël often mourned the fact that the 1905 Revolution had passed the Fyodorovists by: blood, plentiful blood, might have revived them, especially given their considerable influence in matters of theory, both then and later, on other revolutionary movements, not least the Bolsheviks. This influence was transmitted through Fyodorov's erstwhile disciples and through de Staël herself. Evidence of this can be found in the miraculously preserved fragments of the transcript of the RSDWP's Theoretical Conference, which took place on May 10-13, 1910, at Pine Ravine. The participants were Lenin, Plekhanov, Zinoviev, Bogdanov, Trotsky, Axelrod and Tübing, the German manager of Staël's estate.

'Lenin: "The sacrifice of the Russian people has proved surplus to requirements. A thousand years waiting for the coming of Christ, a thousand years expanding the territory of the true faith, millions of human lives expended to this same end, serfdom, starvation, epidemics, self-immolating schismatics, peasant uprisings – all for naught. (Moving on) Man has long desired to return to heaven; he has never asked for anyone's help in this task and set about building the Tower of Babel all by himself; but the Lord took fright and tore it down when it was almost complete. The Lord has always pursued His own selfish aims. He craves the Absolute, but in nature, which depends on equilibrium and the balance of good and evil, there can be no such thing. It is contrary to human nature, contrary to nature *tout court*; it's woven from the likeness of angels, not man, and for the sake of this abstract Absolute, mankind is doomed to unthinkable and eternal suffering.

"'Man suffers from birth, before he's even done anything wrong, and he continues to suffer all his life on account of some mythical original guilt – the sin of Adam. Which, by the way, he committed without his knowledge, childishly, thoughtlessly, and only after being tempted so persistently by a serpent. All this is simply incommensurable, simply ridiculous, without measure or meaning; it betrays nothing except disappointment in the human race, revenge against it for not living up to expectation, and jealousy towards it for being so talented, for being able to return to heaven unassisted. Conclusion: We must renounce all hope and all trust in God, in His fairness. Perhaps we are victims of His lack of love for us, or perhaps we are just a toy, a stake in a vicious argument between God and the Devil: To what extent can human nature be changed, purified, angelized? To what extent can man's spirit be separated from the body? It follows from the above that we must convince the rank and file of the Party to renounce God for good. Without disregarding for one moment the religiosity of the Russians, I see no insuperable problems here: all that's needed is for the workers to realize how the Lord deceived and betrayed them, how He poked fun at them, and all their illusions about Him will disappear."

'Zinoviev (spontaneous intervention): "I have a compromise solution: we will tell the proletariat that there is no God and never has been; man simply invented Him. In this way, we will remove God from the firing line. He will understand our intentions and feel nothing but gratitude towards us. Secretary: Kindly note in the minutes that I do not share Comrade Lenin's extreme position, his desire to multiply our enemies. I believe that in some further twist of the Revolution, God will once again be of use to us."

'Tübing: "The Revolution will be followed, as has already been mentioned, by the total rule of the soviets, which I envision housed in a specially dedicated edifice built in the shape of the Tower of Babel – an upward spiral that narrows with every twist, to be crowned by an enormous, mile-high statue of the Leader of the Revolution – Comrade Plekhanov, perhaps, or Comrade Lenin, or someone else chosen to lead the proletariat. This statue will rise up like a mountain peak, and everyone will see that the man it depicts has already reached the sky, reached heaven. And there's something else I must emphasize, something crucial, without which we will fail once again to build the Tower of Babel. Back then, the Lord, to prevent people from finishing their task, mixed up their languages; they became different nations, began fearing and hating each other. Now, we must do more than merely proclaim internationalism as our aim – rather, the international education of all working people must be at the centre of our work. We must, at all costs, unite humanity once more into a single whole. Only then will we be able to begin and successfully complete our labour of construction."

'Bogdanov: "Comrade Plekhanov, I have a different concern: if God promises man eternal salvation, we can only offer him a very brief interval of heavenly existence – his human life. This is a serious shortcoming and will, I fear, drive many proletarians away from us. People will accept any torment so long as the prize is truly worth suffering for, but here, though the prize may be easily attainable, the benefits are far from convincing."

'Plekhanov: "Eternal heaven does not and cannot exist; we will explain this and the masses will follow us, so Comrade Bogdanov need not worry."

'Lenin: "No, Comrade Bogdanov is right, this is a serious problem; but, according to Fyodorov – and the country's leading physiologists agree with him – there is nothing to prevent us making human life eternal, nothing at all, and we will make it our overwhelming priority. Let the workers know: whether on earth or in space, we'll put an end to disease and, for that matter, death. Whoever deserves to will have eternal life, and not the life of some mawkish, anaemic angel, but real, human life, with women, wine and good food; in short, with all the pleasures of the flesh."

'Trotsky: "The motive force of the Revolution and of the future construction of the Tower should be the fusion of two messianisms – Jewish and Russian. The potential of both is vast, but until now it has mostly been wasted on the conflict of Jews and Russians between themselves. The Lord played them off each other by vowing to each group that they and they alone were God's chosen people."

'Lenin: "God Himself became human long ago, and expects humans to become angels – that's absurd. Take, for example, that old chestnut about divine Providence: that the exile of the Jews from Palestine and their dispersion throughout the world was a blessing, for it enabled the true faith to spread. God thinks like a general or a politician: if I've lost a thousand men and my enemy two thousand, then everything is as it should be and I'm in the right. In other words, He has long accepted that good is mixed up with evil, long realized that evil is often the shortest and only path to the good. Such is the world we live in and neither He nor we, at least for now, can do anything about it."

*

'Solovyov, Dragomirov and John of Kronstadt all seemed to have accepted with perfect equanimity the fact that they had not been blessed, and their dispute about the role of the Jews did not give rise to any struggle for power; it was as if they were only too happy to put their underground lives behind them. Withdrawing from the Party, they behaved less like revolutionaries than well brought-up English parliamentarians. Announcing their collective retirement, they smiled and shook each other by the hand. When someone asked them about the

cause of their differences, they replied that it was a purely
personal affair, and that it would be unethical to disclose
the details to outsiders. Regarding the truth of Fyodorov's
teachings, they had not the slightest doubt even now; the
blame rested squarely on them, so they would remain in the
Party, but only among the rank and file. These, of course, were
just words. Never again were they seen at de Staël's.

'John of Kronstadt spoke after Solovyov. He confirmed that
this was their shared interpretation of events and added that all
three were of the view that the principle of Party leadership
needed to be changed: one-man rule should be restored and
he proposed the young but already well-known composer
Alexander Scriabin as leader. This proposal shocked everyone
– first and foremost, de Staël. But Party discipline was still
in force, and the proposal was passed unanimously, without
a single query or objection. So it was that on December 13,
1905, Scriabin became the Fyodorovists' official leader. Later,
de Staël marvelled more than once at the intuition shown
by Solovyov and John of Kronstadt: to see in someone so
young – Scriabin entered the Party only on December 12 – an
outstanding leader, and not a rather ridiculous novice, was no
mean feat.

'He had, after all, given plenty of cause for ridicule. Only
the day before Scriabin was asked to lead the Party he took part
in a musical evening at de Staël's, whose circle he'd recently
joined. He played a short, but highly entertaining fragment
from, as he put it, an immense opus which he had only just
begun. The first part of the evening went well, despite her
concerns, when inviting Scriabin, that the Fyodorovists would
accept neither him nor his music: they had become ever more
withdrawn and developed a cordial dislike of outsiders. But
they clearly took a shine to him. They even persuaded him to

play one more early prelude, which many of them knew. The applause that followed was especially fulsome. Scriabin would always take his time at the end of a piece; now, he sat with his back to the audience for a good long time before he eventually closed the piano lid, turned round, got up and, stopping the applause with his hand, said in a high-pitched, but serene and beautiful voice that he, Scriabin, was the Messiah, that he had come to give them the good news, to tell them that the rebirth of humanity was nigh, that he would accomplish it himself through the magic of art, and more in that vein.

'This outburst, needless to say, was largely ignored: some of the guests were chatting, others were moving into the dining-room, where the table was already laid. Offended, he suddenly shouted for all to hear: "I am the creator of a new world. I am God!" whereupon sharp-tongued Uzdin, who was standing next to him, tapped him on the shoulder and shot back: "How can you be God – your voice hasn't even broken!"

'Scriabin seemed to wilt on the spot. She could see that he was almost in tears, and felt excruciatingly sorry for him. De Staël had known Scriabin for some time now: her old friend Belyaev was his passionate admirer and patron, it was he who had published Scriabin's first works, and four years had already passed since he started pestering her with invitations to hear this genius musician. Eventually she went along to one of Belyaev's Wednesdays, and didn't regret it. She was astonished by Scriabin's music, by how he played, and most of all, perhaps, by Scriabin himself.

'Scriabin was still very young then, but everything about him – his countenance, his demeanour – was erotic through and through: his fine, languorous features, the sensual dimple on his chin, his intoxicated gaze, and that same languor and lust in the way he moved, the way he touched the instrument:

Balmont rightly said of him that he kissed sounds with his fingers. His fingers really did move smoothly and tenderly, as if taking their time, even lingering, so as to draw out the pleasure. He caressed every key, only for the piano to give birth to spasmodic, convulsive rhythms, to sounds that were broken and twisted, and you began to understand that this was not merely a caress, but slow, refined torture, and that only by tormenting himself and the instrument did music exist for him.

'He must have taken notice of her, too, because they met again the very next evening, exactly seven days before Pancake Week. That was when their tempestuous, almost insane affair began. It was brief and broke off unexpectedly quickly for both of them, just as suddenly as it began – on one and the same day. Scriabin was unpredictable, but astonishingly spontaneous; he alone, of all the people who had crossed her path for many years, knew how to have fun, just like a child. Once, when she herself was a child, she'd been like that too, but she'd lost and forgotten this skill a long time ago; now, he brought it all back to her. Pancake Week was in full swing and they spent virtually every waking hour at the fairs, visiting one booth after another, riding on merry-go-rounds and sleighs, watching the jugglers, jesters, trainers (Scriabin liked the performing cats best of all), magicians, rope-walkers. There were carnival processions every day, and he would procure the most extravagant masks, usually something so demonic and so terrifying that once, when they left their house already in costume, a policeman reached for his whistle in fright and was about to have them locked up. When the policeman finally realized that this was not the devil incarnate, with a witch in tow, Scriabin laughed himself sick, and so did she.

'But what Scriabin loved most was dancing. As performed by him, any dance immediately turned into a kind of orgy;

entering the round, he fell into a state of ecstasy and, forgetting about everything else, would force her – roughly, almost violently – to join him in his endless, frantic dance. Only when the music stopped did he come to his senses; then he would buy them both a glass of vodka, with a marinated apple on the side, before setting off in search of a new round. In the evening they either partied the night away in a restaurant (despite his languorous appearance, he had energy in spades), or else she took Scriabin home with her. He loved life with a passion, while asceticism irritated him beyond measure, as if there were something of the corpse about it. He loved excess in all things: feelings, sensations, caresses, suffering, pain and joy; loved sounds, colours, smells – the list goes on – and made her just like him. With him, she never tired of delighting in life, never tired of having fun; she felt young and beautiful.

'But at home, with a roof over his head, she remembered a quite different Scriabin; there, he was always feminine and effete. She particularly enjoyed observing him at his morning toilette. He'd be late for the Conservatoire, would insist that he was in a tearing hurry, yet still he could spend a good hour before the three-leaved mirror, perfecting his moustache and his hair. Such pampering evidently brought him a great deal of pleasure. He had a particular weakness for French *eau de toilette*. In fact, his obsession with hygiene bordered on madness: he was scared stiff of infection and dirt, and the *eaux de cologne* with which he continually rubbed his hands were his only salvation.

'Once, when she let slip how many affairs she'd had, the severity of his reproaches almost reduced her to tears. Only later did she realize that his reaction had nothing to do with jealousy, though there was no doubting his love for her; he simply disliked the fact that so many different men had touched her and, no doubt, soiled her. His concern, in other words, was purely sanitary. Realizing this, de Staël flew into a rage, but she soon calmed down and forgave him: one of her girlfriends might have told her off in just the same way.

'This was far from the only occasion, during the early days of their affair, when she felt confused: at times he really did behave like a woman dressed as a man, and she opened up to him as she would have opened up to a friend. It reminded her of the bath-house – everyone is equal, everyone's a friend, nobody feels shy – and that was when he took her. As if he'd been waiting for precisely that moment. Despite his youth, he was astonishingly experienced and refined, knew women as only a woman can know them, that is, as one can only know oneself. Surrendering to him, she felt that she was all his, that she was laid open before him; whatever she wanted to give him, whatever she was able to give him, would be appreciated, accepted. Nothing would be lost, nothing wasted.

'After making love to other men she usually felt sad and often cried; their possession of her was at best provisional – they did not need all of her, did not want to know all there was to know about her, substituted strength for subtlety, could not understand what else she could want, why she was not satisfied. Perhaps she, by her nature, was too subtle for them, and they were incapable of knowing her as she was. She chastised herself for not adapting to her partners, not playing up to them – so if she was unhappy, she only had herself to blame – while realizing that this was not the point: she was a precious cup, but they didn't know the first thing about art and thought she was only good for drinking from. There was a time when she even thought that only lesbian love could give her what she wanted, but this was a purely abstract notion: she'd never liked women, never been drawn or attracted to them. Essentially, she'd accepted her fate and it was a long time since she'd asked God for anything – then along came Scriabin.

'When he was alone with de Staël for the first time, he was very tense, as though unsure whether she would understand him, accept him. For a long time he held back, playing for time, but then he began talking with a terrible conviction that instantly communicated itself to her as well. She was like Mother Eve, he told her. Her feminine, passive principle was waiting, still merely waiting, to be given form, and as such it was hindering him. She found herself inwardly agreeing: she really was cold, uptight. That was when he took her by the hand and ordered her to relax, and she understood, felt her body soften to his voice, and no longer resisted.

'"Every animal, insect and blade of grass," he told her, "bears the countenance of the impulses of our spirit. Each one is created by the same caresses with which man caresses woman, and so it has been since the days of Adam. It was not God but Adam who, caressing Eve, begat and named with his caresses all that surrounds man in this world.

'"Here are birds," he told her, barely touching her nipple with his lips or his tongue, "they are winged caresses. Here are twisting, serpentine caresses – they are caresses wandering at large," he said, the tips of his fingers sliding up from her little feet, up and up, and then along the very edge, so that she froze in fear for him; he circled the entrance, the dip which led inside her, then carried on up over the stomach, between the breasts, wrapping his fingers around one, then the other, as if framing them, before straightening up once more over the hollow of the clavicle and up the neck to the earlobe and hair.

'Then he started mauling her, mauling her slowly and savagely, with the caresses of every wild beast on earth. He tormented her flesh with the caress of tigers, pecked and tore it with the caress of a thousand eagles, stung and bit it with the caress of hyenas, and when she was already losing her mind, yelling from pain and passion, he soothed and calmed her with the cold, slippery caress of frogs, after which the breath of a warm breeze seemed to travel up her body – these were flowers come to life, and butterflies and insects brushing against her with their light little wings. The caress of the revived flowers came just before he and she, dissolving one in the other, were already entering oblivion, and the last she heard before she sank into herself and into him was his voice as it whispered, "This is the final dance, everything is about to end... soon already, soon... and now we will shatter into millions of butterflies and cease to be people, ourselves becoming caresses, beasts, birds, snakes."

'Only with him did de Staël finally discover who she was and how much she had in her, understand how perfect an instrument God had made her. Only with him did her body fill with sound and song; she saw it, heard it, was astonished and amazed, and saw that he understood this, too. He could draw every conceivable melody from her, every harmony; like Eve, she gave birth beneath him to the languages of this world, its music.

*

'Sadly for de Staël, Scriabin was like this rarely. I've already said that he was very unpredictable. More and more frequently, he came to her depressed and morose; he just sat there, not wanting to go anywhere himself or for her to go anywhere either. De Staël had to miss one engagement after the other. She was a woman of her word, always punctual, and she found all this utterly infuriating. His sorrow soon communicated itself to her as well, as did all his moods. With him, she really was a passive feminine principle waiting, as he put it, "to be given form". Such dependence on him further irritated her – she was accustomed to being self-sufficient, to being the demiurge of all that surrounded her. For as long as she could remember, everything had always revolved around her, and the role which he had accorded her and which she, by his grace, carried off so naturally, could not fail to wear her down sooner or later.

'He'd given her a great deal and she knew it; there was enough fairness in her, enough intelligence, to acknowledge this. But now, when Scriabin had shown her, revealed to her, what she really was, when he had exposed and brought to completion everything that the Lord had put into her, everything He had given her, she wanted once again to be free. Naturally, she did all she could to drive away his gloom, but her efforts were in vain; often he didn't even notice them, and only once, when she kept nagging him with one and the same question – How come he had been so cheerful just the day before and the two of them had been so happy, but today he felt like killing himself? – he told her: "If only you knew how hard it is to feel the entire burden of world history! I feel such envy when I look at people just walking along the street…"

'And yet, in fairness, de Staël fought for him not nearly enough, as she herself was only too keenly aware. The closeness between them dissipated with almost hurtful speed. Yes, she wanted freedom and she was weary of him, but even so, she ought not to have told Scriabin that he should stay at home if he felt miserable, and she had even less right to turf him out.

'After they separated, she thought of him often. For as long as he was beside her, love and love-making had dominated, all else was secondary; now that they had left each other for good, she suddenly began to see him differently, so differently she even surprised herself. With each passing day she became more and more convinced that in the figure of Scriabin fate, perhaps, had brought her the most brilliant of all the revolutionaries to have crossed her path. It was a gradual process. One day she recalled the occasion when, happening to wake earlier than usual, she saw him praying. He was kneeling by the window and whispering loudly: "Despite everything I'm alive, alive, and I love life, I love people, and I love them all the more for the fact that through You, God, they too are suffering. I am going to them to proclaim victory, to tell them not to rely on You and not to expect anything from life other than what they can do and provide themselves. Lord, I thank You for all the torments, all the horrors of Your trials. You have allowed me to know my infinite strength, my limitless might, my invincibility. You gave me my triumph…"

'On another occasion he told her that as a child he was exceptionally religious and loved attending services. There was a Church of the Ascension on their street with a very intelligent, knowledgeable priest and a fine choir, and he visited almost every day. At home, too, he prayed often, for hours at a time. He'd wanted to be a concert pianist for as long as he could remember and knew that this required an enormous amount of work, though practice came easily to him – he enjoyed everything about the piano, even the scales that others hated so much. He was twenty years old, negotiations were under way for a contract and a concert tour around the south of Russia, but then, literally a week before he was due to leave, he sat down at the piano one morning and discovered he could no longer play: he'd overworked his left hand. His life fell apart before his eyes. That was when, after taking his time to think it all through, he conceived a hatred for God and cursed Him. A few months later he regained the use of his hand, but this happened too late to change anything in his relationship with the Lord.

'Recalling this story now, it occurred to de Staël that Scriabin's revolt against God and his path to revolution were unusually direct and organic. If the participation of others frequently puzzled her and struck her as a matter of chance, and if, naturally enough, she was always unable to trust such people to the end, with Scriabin it was quite the reverse. It suddenly became clear to her that he was more dependable and more devoted to the task of revolution than even she was herself. This was like a turning-point, after which her recollections of Scriabin flowed one after the other, and she, even while she was merely sorting them out and putting them together, already knew that the final result would be that single, whole, uniquely truthful doctrine for which they had all been searching: she, Fyodorov, Solovyov, and thousands upon thousands of others – the doctrine which only he had found.

'Twice Scriabin told her in passing that he was the Deity come to earth, doomed, as Christ had been, to pass through unthinkable torments, to sacrifice himself for the salvation of mankind. He had a calling: a beautiful, but arduous vocation which he had no authority to refuse. He was the Messiah of the races that appear in the eras of transition at the end of the *manvantara* in order to perform the Mystery and unite humanity with the Deity, the World Spirit. His precursor was Christ – a kind of little, everyday Messiah. He explained to her firmly and calmly that the end of the world, the time when every prophecy would be fulfilled, was nigh, but that the beginning of the end depended on him, on Scriabin, and this date was not yet fixed. Through the Mystery the One would be reunited with the world that had fallen away from It in multiplicity and fragmentation.

'"In the past," he would say, "I thought I would accomplish everything myself, that my sacrifice was all that was needed, but I came to understand that this was not so, or not necessarily so. The fact is that my 'I' is reflected in millions of others, like the sun in a spray of water. Integrated, collective personality can be obtained only by gathering everything into one, with nothing forgotten, nothing lost, and this is the mission of art, of music. I will describe everything in a new Gospel, which will replace the old one, just as the New Testament once took the place of the Old. The end of the Universe will be sublime coition. Just as man, during the sexual act, loses consciousness at the moment of orgasm and every inch of his body experiences bliss, so too the God-man, experiencing ecstasy, will fill the Universe with unthinkable happiness and spark a conflagration. The Mystery will be the final holiday of mankind. Its centre will be a sublime orgy, a rite, a kind of global frenzy. A dance without end, ecstatic, extreme…"

'Scriabin said that his *Mysterium* would combine poetry and music, music above all: for it is music that possesses eternity and can bewitch, even stop it, and rhythm that casts a spell on time. To notate the *Mysterium* he would have to create an entirely new language. He would have to invent the means to notate dances, smells, tastes, movements, gestures, glances. Just the slightest inaccuracy and all harmony would be lost. The *Mysterium* would end with an enactment of the Universe in ruins, of global conflagration, and this very image would provoke global catastrophe. To follow: the death of mankind in the God Who Rebelled, though how this death would occur he could not yet say. Would the reunion of the brothers in the Father happen at the beginning or later? He did not know. Scriabin told her more than once that the human race was blameless and always had been; it was without sin and always would be, whatever it might do. In fact, there is no truth in the world, no good, no sin. It is we who create truth which, whatever form it may take, excludes the one thing that really exists, that is truly good – freedom. The whole world, the whole Universe is within us; we, not God, are its sole creators; and when we stop, when we cease creating, it will perish right away. The physical world, he told her, is only the gleaming of our spirit.

'Once she asked him what he thought of socialism. Scriabin replied that there was a time when he had been filled with enthusiasm, thanks to Georgi Plekhanov, who impressed him so much that he even considered joining the Social Democrats, but then he realized that a system built on equality is a pure absurdity: no contrasts, no distinctions. Whatever remains is monotonous, linear, infinitely dull. Creativity, all ups and downs, cannot survive under socialism. Yes, there would be a time when materialism would triumph on earth – the world, on its path to the Mystery, would inevitably pass through the era of socialism, when materialism would reach its peak – but this would be a short, transitional stage, like a necessary evil.

'"The lifespan of socialism is extremely brief," Scriabin repeated. "It will pass in a flash. In the space of a few months of appalling shocks and convulsions the entire world may become socialist, but even that is not necessary – it will be enough for socialism to reign in one corner of the globe to clear the way to the Mystery."

'Socialism's triumph would leave no taste; spiritual life would wither and nothing would remain save the terrifying tedium of machines, electricity and mercenary interests. Socialism would be a pause in the war between Germany and Russia. Of course, there would be many other combatants too, but only as fellow-travellers: war would simply grab them and draw them into its circle, like a dance. Germany was materialism taken to its furthest extreme, the utter abandonment of the spirit and unthinkable exaltation of the flesh. Russia, on the other hand, had preserved a residue of spirituality. Russia would eventually emerge from this war as victor; the spirit, in other words, would prevail. So war would be salutary, no doubt about that.

"'But now,' he added, "socialism, like every other project aimed at rearranging the world, holds little interest for me. Everything is leading to the Mystery, leading to the end, and only that has any meaning."

'She had one other brief conversation with him about war. It took place in the Metropol, where they lunched together almost every day. At the time the newspapers were full of the disturbances in China. After reading a very vivid report from Peking in *The Moscow Gazette*, he exulted: "Things are stirring there, an awakening, a real awakening! China, you know, is a huge force, not so much politically – politically, it's weak – as mystically. Before the Mystery there must be a universal awakening, when everything will open up and be revealed. There will be a new migration of peoples, enormous wars, a truly universal world war. It will begin, I think, in Europe, then spread to Asia and Africa...

"'War and death should not be feared, you know. There are times when murder is the highest virtue, when the murdered experiences the very greatest pleasure, even more, perhaps, than his murderer. War should supply feelings of extraordinary strength and power. The mere possibility of killing people – that, you know, is something very special, the rarest and most vivid sensation. It does you good, every now and then, to shake off the shackles of so-called morality. Morality is far broader than what we understand by that word; in fact, it doesn't even exist. What we call sin in one context is an act of highest virtue in another. We are on the cusp of a time when killing will become moral. Besides, we should remember that our wars and social convulsions are merely the reflection of events on the astral plane, so it's idiotic to reproach ourselves, to repent, to be shocked by the evil afoot."

'But did it not worry him, de Staël asked, that if Asia and Africa rose up, European culture would all but disappear? He calmly replied that this was perfectly possible, even probable, but so what? Culture had already had its say. Besides, Europeans had always killed mysticism with culture, while in the East it was the other way round, so the arrival of the barbarians from the Orient would bring liberation. In fact, a true mystic should always welcome war: it's the path to transfiguration, to ecstasy. After all, only great shocks, a global conflagration and carnage can give birth to the Mystery: they are its font.

'Her affair with Scriabin lasted little over a month. He was an unusually open man, reluctant and clearly unable to conceal anything, and she began to think that he must be very lonely: the only people he ever named in conversation with her were his uncle and aunt, who had raised him virtually from the cradle. She was convinced that the world he moved in was entirely empty, and she was quite astonished to discover that she was wrong.

*

'A week before their separation Scriabin invited her to his apartment – the first time she'd ever been there – for a musical soirée. Later, she learned that he gave concerts at home twice a month, for an audience that hadn't changed in years. That day he played a large fragment from a piece that he intended to include in the *Mysterium* – the "Theme of the Bells". It appears never to have been written down. Observing the guests as they listened to him, she realized that she was attending a meeting of some kind of Scriabinist sect. It was all very reminiscent of the rites of the Flagellants: the guests were intoxicated, stunned by his music. He performed in a state of perfect ecstasy, and they were in exactly the same state themselves. Brass harmonies, full of dread and doom, flowed forth like a tocsin. Mankind was now ready for the terrible and joyful hour of its final reunion, and Scriabin was bidding it farewell.

'The sounds he drew from the piano controlled these people as if they were puppets. His every note transformed their faces: torment, unthinkable suffering and fear instantly gave way to bliss and purely infantile joy, but then once again it was as if the ruin of the whole world had been suddenly unveiled before their eyes. There could be no doubt that he was their God, that they believed in him, that they professed him as their Messiah, and any one of them, being summoned by him, was ready to cry, "Truly you are the son of God," and follow him. When he finished playing, he leaned back, but his hands hovered over the keys as before. He whispered something as he watched his fingers fly through the air; perhaps he was trying to persuade them, for he clearly lacked the strength to stop and becalm them himself.

'Like everyone else, Staël was waiting, transfixed, to see if he could bring his fingers under control, when all of a sudden Scriabin thundered: "Ah, if only these bells could ring from heaven! Yes, they must ring from heaven! It will be a summons. Mankind will respond to it, follow it, to the place where the temple will stand – to India. To India and nowhere else, for that is the cradle of mankind. It is from there that mankind emerged, there that it will complete its circle."

'Later, over tea, when the guests had left and the two of them were alone, he told her, "It's time for me to get ready. I don't know where my initiation awaits me – I expect I have to go to India," before adding feebly: "After all, it's also time to prepare those who will occupy the central rungs of the hierarchical ladder, who will be closest of all to enlightenment." Now, she understood why he'd invited her. Scriabin went on: "I have to choose my apostles, my disciples, and it seems to me that they are among the people who were here just now, that they should come from this circle, but I'm uncertain and wanted to ask your advice. You, as far as I can tell, are a good judge of people." Staël asked him what mankind's preparations for the Mystery would consist of and what responsibilities his disciples would bear.

'"The Mystery," he said, "is remembrance. Every man will have to remember everything he experienced since the creation of the world. We all have this experience, it's preserved in each and every one of us – you just need to learn how to summon it. I've already tried: it's as if you return to a state of primal undividedness, as if you merge with everything, like waters during a flood. At first there's nothing, and it really is like a flood of waters upon the earth, from one end to the other; no mountains, no forests, no life, only water, and you can't say where it begins and where it ends. The Jews say that as a token of His vow to Noah never again to send a flood upon the earth, the Lord struck out the year of the Flood from the days since the creation of the world – after all, there was no life that year, except on the Ark. Well, it's exactly the same here: it's as if everything has gone back to how it was and once again there is nothing in the world except matter, except the feminine principle, inert and resistant. But it's from this that everything is built, it's here that the creative spirit imprints itself, and our task will be to experience this imprint, to re-experience, as it were, the act of creation, followed by the entire history of the human race – in short, to experience everything anew. And in this combined experience the collective spirit should be born.

"'I've already planned this year out from start to finish," Scriabin went on. "It seems to me that the only people ready for the Mystery are you and Alexei Lvovich – you must have noticed him, that tall, fat man who was sitting on your right; and then the doctor, the one with the eyeglass and a big ring on his finger – isn't he a treasure? He's known me longer than anyone, I love him dearly, and he's so very keen. The fourth, Ivan Semyonovich, is the one with the curly black hair – he dotes on me like a mother and he'll be terribly offended if I don't take him. But I have some doubts about the fifth, Sergei Lvovich, and wanted to ask your advice. You probably noticed his shifty eyes. He, too, is a very good man who's long been close to my heart; he used to be my John the Baptist, but I fear he won't be able to take part in the Mystery: for that, you need to be completely sound of mind, or the consequences could be serious. The doctors say he's very sick, and he often complains himself."

'Seeing her out, Scriabin said: "I don't want to rush you; I understand that you need to think it all over, but of course, the sooner you decide, the better."

'The conversation was never continued; a week later, as I've already mentioned, they parted. But the conviction steadily grew in de Staël that Scriabin was a revolutionary of genius, blessed, as they say, with God-given talent, and she kept wondering whether or not to resume their relationship. The prospect of his becoming her lover again frightened her – she knew that she was at fault before him, but still considered their affair to be well and truly over. Her designs on Scriabin were of a different kind. Aligning herself with the Bolsheviks and collaborating with them ever more closely under the leadership of Lenin, she virtually abandoned the Fyodorovists, merely observing from the side as this party withered by the day. By now she had tried any number of means to help them. In particular, she'd discussed their plight repeatedly with Lenin, proposing either to merge the two parties into one, or to bring the Fyodorovists into the Bolshevik tent as an autonomous group; moreover, she pledged whatever funds would be required to finance this union. In their final conversation Lenin overcame his previous uncertainty and refused outright, even though he himself was strapped for cash. It was hard to argue with his reasons: he said that after some research he'd come to the conclusion that the Fyodorovists were terminally ill and anyone who entered into an alliance with them risked becoming ill themselves.

'And yet, de Staël clung to her faith that the party of Fyodorov-Solovyov would revive; she'd tried everything, and the only hope that remained to her was Scriabin and his sect. Somehow, she'd succeeded in convincing herself that this was the new blood that would bring the Party back to life. Her plans vis-à-vis Scriabin remained purely theoretical for more than a year, and that's how they might have stayed – she hesitated to write to him or invite him over – were it not, as so often, for sheer chance.

'An old friend of de Staël's, Baron Grünau, took her along to a concert, the first half of which was given over to Scriabin's Third Symphony. She'd already heard it once before, with Scriabin himself conducting, and it had made quite an impression. While studying the audience through a pair of opera glasses – Grünau had a box in this theatre – during the interval, she picked out Scriabin's face in the stalls and, on the spur of the moment, sent him a warm note, thanking him for the enjoyment his music had given her and suggesting, without the slightest pressure, that he call on her.

'Scriabin replied the very next day, unable to hide his delight at the invitation. He said he would come the next Friday and that, if she so wished, he would play for her guests all afternoon long, until dinner. His fame in the Russia of those years knew no bounds and she was touched by his courteous gesture, which, perhaps, is why she was shocked when the Fyodorovists, after listening to his music for two hours in her home, suddenly began mocking him unsparingly. But she was even more shocked when, the next day, Vladimir Solovyov, John of Kronstadt and Dragomirov, paying not the slightest attention to the previous day's scandal, unanimously proposed the candidacy of Scriabin as their party's leader.

'The only one of the three she subsequently kept in contact with, and sporadically at that, was Dragomirov, and one day, many years later, she asked him why their choice had fallen specifically on Scriabin. Dragomirov was taken aback by her question and replied, as if it were something utterly obvious, that they had always been astonished by Scriabin's mighty symphonic gift, his ability to score for dozens of different instruments in such exhaustive detail that in the end their voices merged into a perfect unity, in which, furthermore, everything was so complete, so polished, that to break up and fragment this voluntary concord seemed quite impossible. He himself, for example, could not bear, after hearing Scriabin's First Symphony at a concert, to stay for a solo violin recital after the interval: it seemed to him that all the other instruments had all died, that only the violin was left to sob and beg for salvation. So they had been considering Scriabin's candidacy for some time and believed he had many of the qualities needed to lead the Party. And then, at the première of Scriabin's Third, with the composer himself conducting, they were even more astounded by the inspiration, even rapture, with which a flute or oboe played its modest part beneath his guiding hand. He was their true leader, he was their God: wherever he called them, whatever he commanded them to do, they would obey at once.

'But the hopes that both de Staël and the former leadership of the Party invested in Scriabin were realized only in part. Externally, the life of the Fyodorovists changed little with his arrival. As before, the practical preparations for the Mystery were carried out by Scriabin within his sect; the Fyodorovists remained on the margins. Suffice it to say that not a single one of them was introduced into the inner circle of Scriabin's closest disciples. Nevertheless, the disintegration of the Party ceased, as did all the whining – Why fight? Why live? – that had long been a source of irritation to de Staël. Now, on the contrary, each had the sense of being a part of something, something, perhaps, that would decide the destiny of the universe. None of them doubted the path chosen by Scriabin.

'Before, they would blame anyone but themselves for the Party's failures, but now they grasped the reason they still remained in the shadows: their knowledge and understanding of Scriabin's music was still very poor, infinitely worse than that of his old disciples. They tried to make up for lost time, never missing a single concert where Scriabin was performing, not only in Moscow but even on tour. So, although not even his rise in the Party was enough to cause terrorism, strikes, rallies or demonstrations, a cult of Scriabin flourished among the Fyodorovists, who competed with his closest disciples in love and devotion for their teacher.

'All this de Staël observed from the sidelines. The years leading up to the war had drastically altered her life; executing various tasks for the Bolsheviks, she made only sporadic, brief visits to Moscow. She remained on affectionate terms with Scriabin and corresponded with him when the need arose, though these exchanges were mainly concerned with the interests of the Party and were devoid of sentiment. Only occasionally did they come to life. Thus, in 1914, when rumours began to reach her from Russia – she was in Stockholm at the time – that Scriabin, despite his failing health, was set on going off to the front, she wrote him a long, confused letter, imploring him to change his mind.

'He replied swiftly and in the highest spirits: the war had begun, he wrote, and the path to the Mystery lay open. The day that he and mankind had awaited for thousands of years had arrived. He could not understand her sadness, could not understand how she could fail to see that the hour of joy and triumph, of merriment and jubilation was upon them. He went on to tell her about his new friend Nikolayev – it was the first de Staël had heard of him – who'd been called up just two months before and wrote that he was simply drunk on war and blood, that for the first time he was living life in all its fullness and colour, that he felt unlocked, unshackled, sharpened in all his senses, even crazed; that he'd understood what it meant to be human. In a postscript Scriabin added that he, too, would have gladly joined up, but he could achieve a lot more here, on the home front, so her worries were unfounded. "I also have my fair share of explosives," he concluded, "but they are of a very different kind."

'Three months later, two more letters from Scriabin arrived in fairly quick succession at the same Stockholm address (the second, posted from Switzerland, she read only in 1916, by which time Scriabin had already been dead for a year). In the first he reported that he would soon be leaving for Switzerland

– the last patch of peace, now squeezed between two warring blocs. Mankind, he added, was now ready to accept the good news he was bringing, and it was in Switzerland that he had decided to begin his preaching, his *Via Crucis*. From there he would be heard by all. The second letter, sent from Geneva on the tenth day after his arrival, was very strange. In it, Scriabin wrote to de Staël: "I swear to you: if only I could persuade myself that there is someone else greater than me, who could create such joy on earth as I never could, then I would immediately retreat and make way for him, while I, of course, would cease to exist."

'And this, Alyosha,' Ifraimonv resumed after we had drunk our evening kefir, 'is where the story of Professor Trogau comes in: what he did, why he died, and why the Institute for Natural Genius was disbanded. Music scholars know that Scriabin was always surrounded by people, always fairly open with them, and that the life he lived is relatively well-documented; but that month in Geneva is a complete enigma. What happened to him there? What crisis did he experience? What did he understand? All is darkness. On first reading, the letter from Geneva might lead one to think that he had begun, for the first time, to doubt that he was the Messiah, and subsequent events would seem to confirm this. But why did he lose faith in his mission? Thanks to Trogau's efforts, the external outline of events has been reconstructed: where Scriabin lived in Geneva, what kind of life he had there; but the main thing – what happened in Scriabin's soul – will, it seems to me, never be known. And perhaps that's for the best: there are some things so painful that they should follow a man to his grave.'

*

'It's well-known that there were plenty of political émigrés from Russia living in Geneva in 1914; most were Social Democrats, but there were others too. Having been scattered all over Europe in the years leading up to the war, they had now gathered in neutral, peaceable Switzerland. Here, in their attempts to agree a common position, Russian socialists held interminable discussions, conferences and negotiations with the socialists of other European powers about their attitude to the war, what should be done and how, and above all, what would ensue once the war was over. Hundreds of police agents also followed their charges to Switzerland. The governments of the belligerent states were all alarmed by widespread socialist activity, surveillance was unremitting, and Lenin and Zinoviev conceived the idea – before anyone else, it seems, though it was later copied – of hiring a little boat whenever they had something particularly important to discuss and rowing a hundred metres or so from shore. Occasionally, as if to tease the snoops, they would cast a line into the water, although, legend has it, they never caught a single thing in four years of war.

'The frequent hiring of boats was an expensive business, but fully justified in the interests of secrecy. Deep in conversation during one of these conferences on Lake Geneva they failed to notice that the current had taken them right up to the shore. They were brought to their senses by the voice of a well-dressed gentleman standing knee-deep in the icy November water and yelling something at them. Zinoviev, never the bravest of men, fancied that this was all a provocation to have them thrown out of the country, but Lenin, for some reason, was intrigued.

'The stranger spoke with exceptional fervour, though without any great coherence. Furthermore, having evidently mistaken Lenin's and Zinoviev's nationality, he was trying to make himself understood in German, but his grasp of the language was poor and it was hard to understand him. Perhaps Lenin was intrigued by the fact that the words the stranger was yelling at him – world war, carnage, the death of the old world, revolution, socialism, the last days – were precisely the words he and Zinoviev had been exchanging a moment or two earlier, but given such an unexpected spin that they could not fail to amuse him.

'Much harder to understand was why Scriabin – for it was he – had chosen such an unusual place and method to reveal himself to his fellow men. I think he was influenced by the coincidences between his own fate and that of Christ, coincidences which both he and his disciples had been vigorously emphasizing for some time – not least the fact that he was born on Christmas Day. Everything else had followed of its own accord: he was strolling along the shore, saw Lenin and Zinoviev in a boat and, having decided that they were Swiss fishermen, began preaching to them as Christ had preached to the fishermen of Galilee.

'But even this probably wasn't the most important thing. Right from the beginning, far more had been revealed to Scriabin – the apostle and prophet of the new world – than to ordinary people. All his life, from the very day of his birth, he'd been guided by a higher power. It was this power that induced him to leave wartime Russia for quiet, neutral Switzerland, where, on the shores of the astonishingly beautiful Lake Geneva, he was to find and bless Lenin, as John the Baptist had found and blessed Christ.

'Once he was convinced that he had Lenin's attention, Scriabin, still talking, kept on wading through the water in the direction of the boathouse, and Zinoviev, who was holding the oars, had little choice but to paddle after him. After mooring, he immediately said his goodbyes, while Lenin offered to accompany Scriabin to his home on Rue de Plessis. Here, he received Scriabin's calling card and an invitation to lunch the next day.

'Lenin accepted, and for the next four weeks he and Scriabin met daily, from lunchtime until deep into the night. This has been confirmed by numerous sources, not least the memoirs of Scriabin's landlady, which are held in the Museum of the Revolution. Madame Troyes, as she was called, writes that at her lodger's request she had a grand piano installed in his room, rented by her from Shtutzer's, and that Mr Scriabin would play the most peculiar music on this piano until the middle of the night for another gentleman, whom she had since identified, from photographs published in Swiss newspapers, as the current head of the Russian communist state. Madame Troyes goes on to say that she might have paid her lodger and his guests not the slightest attention – she didn't like poking her nose into other people's business – but Mr Scriabin's neighbours kept complaining that they couldn't sleep on account of his playing. For this reason, and despite the fact that Scriabin paid handsomely and punctually, she was eventually obliged to turn him out.

'The landlady's testimony seems unremarkable on first reading, but if we recall how sensitive Lenin always was to any attempts to drag him away from his work, how he hoarded every spare minute for his articles and theoretical tracts, and if we further recall that Lenin, according to those who knew him well, didn't enjoy or understand the music of his time – his favourite composer was always Beethoven, whom, by the way, Scriabin couldn't stand and didn't even consider a real composer – then there can be only one conclusion: Lenin could have changed his life so drastically only for the very weightiest of reasons.

'On this basis, Trogau surmised that all month long Scriabin played Lenin sections of his *Mysterium*, accompanying them with the most detailed commentary – how, where and when the work should be staged. The fate of Scriabin's *Mysterium* is something of a puzzle: it's well known that he spent many years writing it, but music scholars have failed to unearth a single fragment. Scriabin's friends unanimously maintain that only once did he play an extract from the *Mysterium*, ten years before his death – those very same "Bells", although even they were not written down. The scores for the other sections have disappeared without trace.

'So what made Scriabin choose Lenin of all people for the first airing of the *Mysterium*? And why did he refuse his old admirers this privilege? For Trogau, there could be only one explanation – Scriabin knew that he had not been blessed, that he would not become the Messiah; the intentions of the higher powers had changed and their choice had come to rest on Lenin. Lenin it was who would lead the peoples of the earth to universal ruin, so that afterwards, cleansed by fire and death, they might be resurrected, reborn. Scriabin had been told that the revelation which allowed him to peer into the very depths of being and write the *Mysterium* was not false – everything would come to pass just as he had written, but his own role had come to an end and the *Mysterium* had to be handed over to Lenin, for it was he who would stage it.

'Trogau's next move was to surmise that among Lenin's manuscripts dating from the end of 1914, whether published or not, some trace must have remained of Scriabin's *Mysterium*, though for a long time he was unable to find any. Only in 1927, while talking to Nadezhda Krupskaya about something else entirely, did he discover that Lenin had developed his own, very cunning shorthand system, which permitted him not only to transcribe at great speed, but also to encipher what he heard. Lenin had concealed the key to this code even from his wife, fearing, presumably, that she might betray his secret under torture. Trogau would have to search for it. Had he entertained even the slightest doubt about Lenin transcribing the *Mysterium*, he would hardly have bothered.

'One day,' said Ifraimov, 'Trogau told us with a laugh that two things had put any lingering misgivings to rest: Lenin's comment that revolution is a form of art, and the words of Lenin's adversaries, who said that he had performed the Revolution note for note. It took Trogau four years of strenuous labour to decipher the code, after which it became clear, for example, that Lenin's famous work *The State and Revolution* is, from start to finish, nothing other than a meticulous transcript of one of the principal themes of the *Mysterium*. Decoded samples of other texts by Lenin gave a similar picture. In fact,' said Ifraimov, 'Trogau was of the view that all Lenin's late writings, up to and including the articles he wrote on his deathbed – "On Cooperation" and his political testament, "Letter to the Congress" – are sections of the encoded score of the *Mysterium*.

'As I've already mentioned,' Ifraimov went on, 'Trogau's work was cut short early on. Nevertheless, two of the fragments he decoded – one from the prelude, another from the main theme – escaped confiscation and miraculously survived. I have them with me today; perhaps you'll find them useful.'

So here, in my Memorial Book, I cite without alteration Trogau's transcript of Lenin's shorthand.

*

'Smells are a constituent element of Scriabin's score, on a par with all others, and in some discrete sections they even come to the fore, pushing both the lighting effects and the music itself into the background. The sounds slowly cool and grow cold. The whole *Mysterium* is a tissue of deaths, and Scriabin traces the throes with almost clinical precision. Sometimes, though, it's only a false finale and the theme goes on and on, exhausted, twisted, wracked with pain, but these are not yet the throes; a long struggle with death is underway, life hangs in the balance, then the theme rises once more. He puts more and more into it, and that's how it is with people, too. A man can endure a great deal – actually, it seems he can endure just about anything – and it's precisely this ability to know no limits in filth, abomination, baseness, suffering, humiliation or evil, that Scriabin deems to be the apotheosis and triumph of life.

'As a rule, however, these themes are weak and melodic; they keep dying on him, they don't last, and, like old women who have prepared themselves and already lamented their own passing, they slip away quietly. And it is always then, once Scriabin, having accompanied the theme on its final journey, as if to its burial, muffles the sounds almost to the point of silence, that the smells come into their own and run wild. This is their time, even if, in the first chords, whose subject is St Petersburg, they still exude weakness and death. Scriabin combines smells in the most whimsical way, with no thought for harmony. His favoured device is to mingle the smells of the high-society salon, of perfume and flowers, with the smells of the abattoir and the rubbish-heap.

'If in music the laws of harmony still retain their importance for him, and if the melodies, now breaking off, now reappearing,

stretch almost to the end of the *Mysterium*, then the smells
are a cacophony, the direct negation, murder, immolation of
harmony, and he loathes them, like an asthmatic. If there is
any madness in Scriabin, then this is where it lies – in the way
he treats smells. His olfactory palette, despite this mishmash,
is bracing and violent; the smells, in whatever combination,
are exaggeratedly pure, unrelated, unclouded. They will never
add up to even the lousiest of bouquets; they merely stop one
another from living; they scoff at each other. So when music
emerges once more from amid this delirium, very quietly, as
if from nowhere, it seems softer and more tuneful than ever,
however tragic the theme; it brings calm and peace.

'In music, for all his innovation, Scriabin undoubtedly
remains within the bounds of tradition, albeit of the very
broadest, freest kind; in smells, he denies not only tradition,
but culture in general. It's the destruction and negation
of everything, first and foremost of organized, man-made
bouquets, whether cheese or perfume. Yet still, in the
cacophony of smells that permeates Scriabin's score, two
interwoven themes can be clearly distinguished: the city in
its St Petersburg guise and the Russian South – the beginning
of the Mystery's progress to India. Both themes are treated at
ostentatious length, and through them, through the smells, it
becomes easier to grasp how Scriabin imagined the course of
the Mystery than, strangely enough, through the music itself.

'St Petersburg: war and gradual weakening, the dying away
of the smells of normal, manicured life, of confectioner's
shops, restaurants, bakeries, where every custom – who should
smell, how and where – has been fixed a long time ago. In
their place are the smells of men engaged in the primordial
labour of war, leaving for the front, briefly returning home
from hospital, leaving once more; the artificial smells of the

sick quarters: iodine, spirit, carbolic, ointments of various kinds, all mixed up with the smell of a body rotting alive, of excrement, urine and the rich, abundant sweat of the wounded and the dying; the smell of the desperate and hopeless struggle for life, the smell of your body being cut into pieces like meat, the table where you are carved up (a part of you – an arm, a leg – is already corpse, yet you cling to life). The sweat of deadly fatigue and deadly labour. And also: the smell of freshly laundered bandages, which take the place in this world of freshly laundered linen; the smell of a rotting wound and of a newly applied, white, medicine-soaked bandage. Yet stronger still is the smell of corpse, stronger and stronger; you can't get rid of it. It's the definitive, terminal smell of man, the end of life.

'The theme of the sick quarters seems almost deliberately drawn out, and then suddenly, Vladimir Ilyich, when everyone least expects it, just here, a new theme starts up: unrestrained jubilation from the opening bars, fireworks, fun, dancing, the tsar overthrown, the future beautiful and cloudless. Everyone is kind, everyone is loving, everyone is beside themselves with joy. All doubts are gone; no sorrow, no grief. Just here, the theme of sadness seems to flit past but is immediately forgotten (flashes, and is gone), and once again everyone is carefree, euphoric. It's the Revolution, the first days: people were afraid, they were terrified, but it turned out so easy, so simple, and there aren't even any casualties, or hardly any, and it's just like when the French were dancing in the place where the Bastille once stood. Look, now the dance melodies begin, and then the firework explosions – a touch of parody, a cheerful imitation of the explosions of war (there's a war on, after all), and people shudder with fear before immediately realizing: no, it's just a firecracker, and now they're really having fun (after firecrackers there's always a burst of fun), and the music becomes more deafening still, even though the orchestra is stretched to its limit and, you would have thought, can play no louder. And the smells also seem to come from the old life: good cooking and bountiful fresh produce, gluttony and restaurants, perfume, champagne, subtle sauces –a burst of life before death. Cinnamon, incense, cardamom, the overpoweringly rich and saccharine smell of thanksgiving services in Church – and then, suddenly, the bracing cold and frost. Tomorrow, it seems, the war will end; everyone believes that, everyone is hopeful.

'The town wakes up gradually, the mills and factories start working, it's all very rhythmical, mechanical, crisp, harmonious, with almost no extraneous sounds, and here, in these rhythms, lies a massive force, and nothing, it seems, is beyond this force. The triumph of materialism. Spirit is almost absent here, it's not needed and only gets in the way, popping up here and there and always sounding off-key. It goes away on its own, for its time has not come. It soon will.

'The holiday ends: hunger, cold. See how quiet and slow the music is, like the way people walk when they're cold and hungry, when they're saving their warmth and their strength. But no one is angry with anyone else; it's what everyone wanted. Once again, the slow weakening of life and the dying away of the old smells. First to disappear are the rare, refined smells, but they've already become foreign to you anyway and you're glad they've gone; next to go are the perfectly ordinary smells, but also slowly and gradually, so that you barely notice – they don't so much go, they are muffled.

'Women, too, start smelling differently: there's no wood for the fire, no hot water, and it gets harder and harder to wash, but there's still an abundance of perfume, rouge and face powder;

trying to kill off the smells of their own body, the feeling of dirt, they lay it all on much thicker than before, but the perfume and sweat merely make one another stand out more strongly, and the women start to smell cheap. The smells combine so sharply, so vulgarly, that the women increasingly resemble the prostitutes of old, and the men sense it, like it, feel aroused, and their excitement communicates itself to the women, and now they actually want to smell cheap, feel cheap, be cheap, be loved and taken like cheap girls. This is a rejection of culture, of convention, rules and etiquette, a return to nature and to the search within for one's own fate, for meaning. This theme will last to the end, merely growing in intensity and complexity.

'There's less and less warmth in people's homes. Only recently it still felt warm everywhere: it wasn't just the stoves, hearths, fireplaces and lamps that smelled of warmth – no, the warmth came from the walls, and the furniture, and people, too. The warmth intensified certain smells, but it was the same wherever you went, so everyone got used to it and, unable to separate the smells, they would just say: it smells warm. Now, when most of the warmth has gone, but it's still warmer indoors than out, all the smells inside faintly but unmistakably change. Especially wood, and especially the wood nearest the earth – the floorboards that creak with damp. Before, it was warmth that brought smells to life; now, it's damp. Hence, the smells of must and age and stagnant water; the smell of rot and lilies. Before, the warmth forced everything foreign to it beneath the floorboards, behind the wallpaper, beyond the windows and walls; now, all that is returning into the home, and only around the portable stove does the old smell remain. The room is split into these old and new smells, and during the day you are constantly passing from one world into the other, as if you keep leaving home and returning. You want to be at home and not go anywhere, but you are already a nomad, a rolling stone. It's your fate.

'The boundaries of warmth are shifting, weightless; they are not walls to keep you in. The men just back from the front find it easier and barely notice the change. Then the smells become fewer, the strong smell of rotting thins out and dissolves, and you begin to smell faint old-womanish decay. There's hardly any waste. It's been a month or two since the municipal services went on strike day after day, when the rubbish wasn't collected and everything smelled of rot; now, the city is purging itself, everything joins in, everything clean and cold.

'All that lives is leaving; there's almost no horse manure, so pungent against the winter snow. Hallways don't smell of the street, doors are kept locked, people rarely go out. They walk slowly; most lie in bed, saving warmth. You're still alive, you're still not frozen. There's a cult of live smells in the city, a cult of warm clothing, preserving the smells with the warmth.

'The smells of the main and tradesman's entrances are hard to tell apart now. The women are no longer hiding their natural smells, nor trying to hide them. Only occasionally does a piece of Swiss cheese, or a bottle of good wine, tasted and lamented at great length, burst into this world as a strange reminder. Earlier, during the raiding of the royal cellars, an explosion took place, an apotheosis of fragrant wines from all across Europe. Pink rivers streamed through the city, melting the snow, washing away last year's dirt, pouring under arches into courtyards and cellars; summer in the middle of winter, a harbour, the sea, and everyone walking around drunk. As a memento of all this: a bottle picked up who knows where.

'Then, even natural odours grow faint; to prolong their lives, people keep them inside themselves, barely sweating, barely smelling. Like mummies, they dry out before death. Somehow there's less of the city now than there was before; the town centre is cold, fresh and smells of the forest; there's no smoke from the factories or the mills. Urban warmth, which used to force foreign smells out beyond the gates, is all but gone, like human warmth. Bit by bit, the surrounding world with its sea and forest, its flowing and stagnant water, reclaims the town.

'At home, expensive garments exchanged some time ago for bread and potatoes are replaced by old, mothballed clothes, and for a long while everything bears this strong, sharp smell, even food, but it too goes away. Now the city smells only of damp and neglect, of creaking floorboards swollen by moisture, and it's this very smell of wood on stone that will last the longest.

'The South of Russia. The same forcing out of hot, unclean factory smells and the return to the town of the smells of the steppe, of the pungent smell of wormwood, which grows stronger and stronger, because many fields are not sown and the earth lies idle. Here, too, there's a rejection of culture, of agriculture, and a return to how things once were, before humankind. Wrapped up in mutual violence, people forget about nature, and it rises up. Even when, during battle, a forest or a field with ripened wheat catches fire, nature apprehends this as a part of itself, as something elemental; shell bursts are just as sharp and fleeting as lightning, there's no system here, no planned, methodical destruction, and the trees, accepting the fire as their fate, do not complain. In Scriabin, it must be said, there are occasions (the gentle fading of life, or an explosion before death) when the beginnings and ends of the two categories – music and smells – come together, but here, too, he emphasizes that in one case life obeys harmony, however veiled that may be, and in the other, discord.

'The South, once again; looks like the Civil War already. Retreating and advancing units keep swapping places. Those advancing are calm and confident: the thrill of the chase. Those retreating smell like sweating, hounded animals, like game. They run themselves into the ground and, like offerings given up for sacrifice, accept their death as a mercy, as liberation from deathly fatigue. Primitive life has returned: the Fall is still recent, not yet forgotten. The times of Nimrod, if not earlier: bivouacs and encampments, hunting exploits, strength, intelligence, cunning and luck. Men who are indefatigable in love, free from convention and subordination, from all the old customs. Power is seized in a flash by those who really deserve it, who smell of strength and can prove their right with their own hands.

'Life is free and beautiful, with nights in the field, horse-bathing, bonfires, the familiarity of death and food, where everything is a hunter's trophy, where everything is prey. Once again you are the man you really are, and this is the life, the happiness, the freedom and will for which one part of a nation offers up another to God, like a lamb, and believes itself to be Abel and its sacrifice to be pleasing to the Lord. And the whole earth, the whole steppe is an altar, and its wormwood smell is condiment and spice. One part of a nation leads another to slaughter and the smell of the offering, the fragrance of the offering, brought with faith in truth and justice, with unwavering readiness, goes up into the sky. It's a return to paganism: the enemy is sacrificed, and God catches the scent of triumph and victory.'

The second fragment deciphers part of the third chapter of *The State and Revolution* – "Experience of the Paris Commune of 1871":

'Now listen up, Lenin: here are the opening bars. There's

a lot of uncertainty, the rhythm keeps being broken, people are tearing around in all directions, scouring, searching, and every now and again there's a cry of jubilation: they've found it! But no, that's not it either. The weak give up quickly, very quickly, in total confusion and despair; they've thrown in the towel. Just listen to this, it's as if the sounds are all tangled, the apathy growing and growing, while the strong... the strong... No, here comes another surge – it takes more than that to stop the strong. But what are they after, Lenin? What can't they find? The Mystery is a sublime sexual act, sublime coition. The amorphous feminine essence, which has never been given form, should be impregnated with the strong, unbroken masculine principle. This act of impregnation is the Mystery, and the Mystery is the new birth of the Universe. Passing through death, ceasing to be anything at all, dissolving in this boundless feminine principle, humanity, and with it the whole world, is reborn for a life that, this time round, is eternal and beautiful. And here is the music of this life. See, Lenin, how effulgent, how bright are its harmonies! The feminine principle is Russia, an immense, boundless country, a meaningless plain, on which there is nothing except inertia and resistance; but where is the masculine principle that will impregnate her, where is the creative spirit that will leave its imprint on her, that will make her conceive? Where?

'The strong seek the strong; and so did I, long and hard. Lenin, I expect you think it's the Revolution, that the Revolution will make Russia pregnant, but that's not the case at all. Yes, you're right: Russia, in fact, is already pregnant with the Revolution, she has already conceived, and the Revolution is her fondest, dearest child; so the creative spirit must already be leaving its mark, but who is it? The Revolution is a child who can't do much on her own, though she quickly, very quickly, becomes a woman, beautiful, decisive, ecstatic, passionate, a woman who at times will behave like a man, but remains a woman nevertheless and, like her female comrades, soon runs out of steam, gets tired and is incapable, unwilling, to try anything new. Power, too, is a woman…

'Lenin, I have gone over these words time and again, I have tried them all out, and found only one with the masculine principle: rebellion. But rebellion is short, fleeting, chaotic. Dealing with woman is beyond its resources and it will never last long enough to leave its imprint on Russia; it will sink in her and vanish without trace. I searched long and hard for this masculine essence, searched and searched and eventually found it – yes, Lenin, I found it! It's terror; that is the mauling, crucifying principle, indefatigable, ubiquitous, sexual, that I was seeking.[3]

'The executioner and the victim, their union, their bond – it's erotic through and through. See how terror is made: insane cruelty today, a softening tomorrow, and if one day the hangman's a sadist, the next he's lenient, full of sympathy and understanding, and the joy when they stop beating you and let you catch your breath, and the hope, and the love, and the purely feminine conviction that everything is as it should be, that the executioner has every right, not least the right to torture, and there is no greater sin than to doubt this. And the constant desire to justify, the faith that grows the greater the cruelty, meaning that cruelty is for good, not ill, the faith that terror is all-powerful, that it's the main tool for building whatever is radiant and lofty, that there can be nothing without it – truly, it is the creative spirit. And most important of all: the profound mystical eroticism of terror, its sexual appeal – after

3 While revolution is a feminine noun in Russian (*revoliutsiya*), rebellion (*bunt*) and terror (*terror*) are masculine. (Tr.)

all, it even arrives in the guise of a woman, Revolution, and wears her clothes, and only when the act is under way does she turn into a man (this is eroticism of a very particular kind.) And the equally mystical, indissoluble bond of executioner and victim, the impossibility, imperfection of one without the other, their inseparability, their fusion, infusion, like man and God in Christ.

'Terror and terror alone deserves pure, loyal love, terror alone can screen off everything else that has happened in your life, force you to forget it all, and Russia will give herself to terror unreservedly, selflessly. Terror grips you, dominates you, body and soul, you can't think about anything else, only terror and fear. Any day they may enter and take you, and all you can do is wait, shuddering at every rustle or squeak, every careless word or hint, and when the terror suddenly weakens it seems to you so mild and tender, so kind and generous! You thought ill of it, but it proved better, milder, so who are you now if not a scoundrel, a bastard?

'Later, when terror's soft caress gives way once again to cruelty, you seek the blame not in it, but in yourself, only yourself, and everything is as it should be. You are full of remorse and die in the knowledge that you deserve it all, that your death is recompense for your sin. Actually, Lenin, terror is not an executioner but an investigator who, trying to get at the truth, interrogates a woman. Only necessity can make him kill.

'This woman has always been devoted to the Revolution, to socialism; she's no enemy, she's "one of us", but here she is being arrested and taken away, and she finds out that she is one of many, so many. The interrogations begin. They extract utterly unthinkable confessions from her about outrageous, crazy things that, needless to say, never took place: it's all nonsense, madness, but who knows what it might lead to? She's asked to testify against her husband, whom she loves and who is also devoted to the regime, and against her children. Just picture her: she loves the Revolution and keeps trying to explain this to the investigator, who for her is the embodiment of the Revolution, and she never blames him for anything, nor will she, whatever he may do to her and to her nearest and dearest: he can beat her, torture, rape, even kill – whatever he likes, because if he is guilty, then the Revolution itself must be guilty, for he is only a part of it; but that means her arrest is justified, that she is an enemy, and all hope is gone.

'The fact that she's locked up with so many female comrades just like her only goes to show how cleverly the enemy disguises itself, how difficult and impossible it is to expose the enemy, what an important and responsible job the investigator has, how loyal and devoted he is in protecting her and other honest souls. It's quite obvious that he can never be respected too much, and even if he may not be entirely right in her case – well, never mind, it's only to be expected, and only right, given the sheer quantity of enemies. It could hardly be any other way and merely proves that he's alive and not a machine, that humans make mistakes, and she, a woman, likes the fact that he is alive, and now she's understood him, and actually everyone in power is so alive, so human, her nearest and dearest.

'She grows to hate her cellmates even more for selling and betraying power, for dressing up as power while being its enemies; so only they are guilty, while he, the investigator, is the innocent victim of their deception. And she is sick at heart to think that she, too, behaving like these enemies, helped them, as it were, to disguise themselves, hid them. She hates them just as the investigator does, with exactly the same hatred. So now, beginning with the very first interrogation, she wants to tell him that she is as open as an unclenched fist, that she's not hiding anything, that she presents no threat.

'And she searches herself, even more thoroughly than the investigator does: perhaps she really is less than squeaky clean, perhaps she really is guilty of something, and he is right? After all, she knows that the "organs" are always right, that any mistake on their part is almost as unthinkable as a mistake by God; so now she tells the investigator all there is to know about her, the whole lot, far more than she ever told her husband, and what she is really telling him is "I love you", because you are the Revolution and I can't tell you apart; you are her human countenance, her human hypostasis, you are fused with her. She has bared herself before him, she is naked, and her every word is "I love you". Heavens, she will do anything for him! She is all his and only his, and for his sake she forgets both her husband and her children.

'Initially, when she tries to convince him that she has been loyal to the Revolution, perhaps she really does want to save her own life, her husband's, her children's, but not afterwards – no, afterwards she loves only him and forgets all about them. You see, Lenin, she can't be true to her husband while telling the investigator that she is true only to him, the investigator. She's split in two, and weak, and guilt-ridden; soon, she forgets about everyone except the investigator, and if she dies, then in the knowledge that she is guilty.

'He's interrogating her and she can't stop fretting that she is poorly dressed, that she's worn out and exhausted, that he might not find her attractive, might not respond to her love. She does all she can to look after herself, to keep clean. Her terrible moral filth before him (he thinks her an enemy) is matched by her bodily filth; they fuse into one. She thinks only of him, dreaming or waking speaks only to him, seeks the right words, intonation, seeks her own guilt, and sooner or later she finds them and understands that she is guilty, not as guilty as her comrades, but still guilty, and she thinks how merciful he is, believes he will forgive her. Oh, how kind he is. And if all hope of leniency proves vain, then still, even as she dies, she understands that he is right: she, and only she, is to blame for her death.

'Lenin's article "On Cooperation" has exactly the same theme. Sometimes, during interrogation, he changes his tone, becomes affectionate and compliments her, and she's delighted he's finally paying her some attention. Once again she feels like a woman, feels happy to have pleased him, at least a little. That way he has of humiliating her, of interrogating her, has nothing to do with indifference – only eroticism, the same eroticism that permeates everything between them. She's alone with him, he's stripped her bare: she's told him everything about herself, listed everyone she's ever had. She's turned herself inside out, she's all his; and he draws out the pleasure. First he's cruel to her, then soft, then cruel again, and she catches even the faintest change in him, gives herself to him, holds nothing back, but he delays, keeps readying her but not entering her, and it's an orgasm that never ends. She can no longer think straight, can't hear, can't remember, but the main thing is still to come. There's such lust here, Lenin. She's never known or seen anything like it, never known such a thing could exist. And it's like this day after day for hours on end, and when he tires and leaves her, he gives her to another man, his colleague, who continues in the same way; and this infidelity of hers, the way he gives her away to be desecrated, is also erotic, and what she has with these two men is like nothing she's ever had before, however many men she went through.

'And when he beats her, she knows why: because he thinks she's betrayed him, she's been unfaithful to him, she's taken her cue from other women who betrayed their men, the women she shares her cell with; he's convinced she's just like them, and she does everything she can to show him that she's not, that she's faithful, that she loves him more than life itself, and only him. There's no need to explain to her that the reason he's torturing her day and night, trying to make her confess that she's betrayed both him and the Revolution, is that he loves her, that if she's been unfaithful then for him it's a tragedy, it's death. So all this, all the blood, is mixed up with love, only love.

'When he does manage to extract a political confession from her, she doesn't understand it, or rather, she understands it all as a kind of allegory, because love and jealousy are all she knows, her only explanation. Tragedy is impossible here, even if she dies from torture or hunger, even if he kills her; for behind it all is love, immense love. It's a tragedy only for the executioner, who for the rest of his life will torment himself with the question "Did she really betray me?" while knowing that he can't have her back: he's killed his love and stained his soul with sin.'

*

'After the October Revolution,' Ifraimov resumed the next day, 'de Staël immediately assumed a fairly elevated position in the communist hierarchy. By December she was already one of the section heads in the Department of Science of the Central Committee (CC), while working simultaneously in the Agitation and Propaganda Department, as well as the Female Department, so her timetable was worked out to the minute. She accepted these endless chores with relish, with a kind of animal ecstasy. Flat out from morning to night, giving speeches at political rallies almost daily – her comrades held her oratory in high regard – or attending the no less obligatory Party sessions and meetings, she was able to forget the fact that this third life of hers had, in the final analysis, proved as futile as the previous two: supreme power would elude her in Russia, just as it had back then in France.

'Bearing in mind everything she'd done for the Bolsheviks – from the money she'd given them (there were years when only her help kept the Party going) to the underground work she'd carried out since 1903, risking everything, even her life – she might have counted on a great deal more; her revolutionary credentials were almost unrivalled. But Staël was clever enough not to delude herself. She saw that the positions she was being thrown, like bones to a dog, carried no real influence, despite their imposing titles; these were dead-end jobs – prestigious sinecures, at best. A quite different breed of people was getting ahead now, most of whom had done almost nothing for the Revolution, and she knew that this was how it would be in the future too, only ever more blatantly.

'It was sad, of course, but she understood that these were different times and different people; so it had always been and so it would always be. And yet, returning home (she'd given away her mansion in October to a group of former political convicts, leaving herself only a cosy two-room loft that resembled an artist's studio in Paris, decorated by her in the same style), de Staël recalled with regret how they'd all been before the war. Much of what had become normal today would have been out of the question back then among Party comrades. Not that they'd always seen eye to eye, but the squabbles and slanging matches she witnessed now would have been unthinkable just a few years before. Still, it occurred to her that she might be mistaken here as well – she'd been more independent back then, so she might have simply not noticed such things.

'At the beginning of 1918 her mood improved, not because she'd come to terms with these changes, but because the entire CC and Council of People's Commissars (CPC) were moved to Moscow and her relations with Stalin resumed after a ten-year break. She'd been scared of seeing Koba again and felt unsure how to act towards him, but he came to see her himself on the very first day after his arrival and, dropping everything, spent a day and a night with her. They were inseparable, just like that first time on the *Elbrus*, and when he finally ran out of strength and lay down beside her in exhaustion, eyes closed, she wept with joy.

'She marvelled at him and couldn't get her fill of his open, noble face, his handsome, high forehead, his strong yet slender figure; he'd become so manly while still remaining her child, her son. And she had every right to be proud of him: soon after his move to Moscow he'd been made first General Secretary of the CC, so the practical task of developing and organizing the Party had, it seemed, been entrusted specifically to him.

'But here, alas, disappointment awaited her. After attending two sessions of the Politburo (on both occasions the subject in question was the state of scientific research in the country) and observing Stalin and his CC colleagues, many things became clear to her. Stalin was a man of uncommon honesty and decency who revered the old guard, especially those reputed in the Party as orators and theoreticians; for them, he nurtured an almost childlike love. It was those same people who had proposed him as Secretary of the CC, because nothing would ever make him stoop to their bickering or convince him that

278

such things were even possible among former comrades in the political underground.

'His notions of friendship, honesty and dignity were different – he was an idealist to the core. This was well known inside the Party, and the likes of Trotsky, Kamenev, Bukharin and Zinoviev, who were gathering their strength for a decisive battle, had given him the General Secretaryship as a temporary measure. During Politburo sessions, whatever their platform, they made fun of Koba quite openly; he was the odd man out, the village idiot, and they couldn't forgive him for being better than they were. Stalin himself never noticed their mockery. On the contrary, he hung on their every word and delighted in retelling witticisms aimed at him. When he did so, she felt like crying.

'On several occasions when he spent the night with her she tried to open his eyes to the situation, but it was a thankless task: he had always been deaf to any criticism of his comrades. Convincing him that a single one of those who'd experienced hard labour and exile with him had acted dishonourably was simply impossible. No proof was sufficient; he'd just laugh, kiss her and tell her that bad people were taking advantage of her gullibility.

'Staël loved him as only a woman can love a man. After all, he was her son, her flesh and blood, her child, the son she'd saved near Poti when she gave birth to him, as it were, all over again. The Lord, in other words, had forgiven her for renouncing Stalin after he was born, as if he were a stranger to her; for never giving him the breast and sending him off to that scoundrel, Ignatashvili. The Lord had let her save him, brought him back to her. Not only that, He had made him her lover, a man she loved even more strongly, perhaps, than Scriabin. Nights may have been more enjoyable with Scriabin than with

Stalin – Scriabin was more refined, more skilled – but, taking everything in the round, it was Stalin who gave her more.

'And so, seeing his so-called comrades make fun of him, she vowed to herself that she would pave Stalin's path to power, real power, and immediately realized, somehow, that God would not refuse her. All her life, or rather, all her lives, she'd been begging God for power, but now she thought that, were Stalin to receive the same absolute power – unfettered by anything or anyone – that she'd been requesting for herself, she could still forgive God. She would forgive Him even though He had tempted her, even though He had placed the source of power inside her and teased her with it day after day, year after year; anyone could drink their fill of it, anyone but her. And never mind that Stalin, too, had drunk from that source and would acquire power only for that reason – on her death-bed she would still grant the Lord her forgiveness. Now, once again, de Staël had a reason for living, but for a long time she didn't know where to begin. Stalin was as deaf to her words as before and wouldn't respond to any of her efforts. There were days when she lost heart completely and, like a little girl, sobbed from dusk till dawn. Then chance came to the rescue.

'In the spring of the following year, 1919, Stalin left for a lengthy assignment in the South Caucasus, where the Mensheviks were organizing putsch after putsch. The talk in Moscow was that he would almost certainly remain there, and Staël was in two minds about whether or not to follow him. Experienced Party cadres were sorely needed in Georgia and she could have got herself sent there easily enough, even without Stalin's assistance. Bored in his absence and hesitating whether to go or to stay (she was well aware of how difficult it would be for them in small, provincial Tiflis), she gratefully accepted an invitation from her old friend Yakov Sverdlov to meet up and, while they were about it, to see *The Miracle of Saint Anthony*, directed by the young and unusually gifted Vakhtangov – another Georgian, apparently.

'It was an impressive production, especially in its contrast with the Moscow of 1919; discussing this subject during the interval – contemporary Moscow as the backdrop for *The Miracle* – they left their box and stretched their legs in the foyer. Sverdlov, who had been keen on her since even before the war (she had lost none of her appeal and many of the most famous people in the country were in love with her, openly or otherwise), eventually tired of the topic and, giving her his arm, started whispering compliments into her ear. At this very moment, Koba walked into the foyer. Later she learned that he'd been recalled from Tiflis to Moscow for an urgent meeting; he'd kept it quiet, wanted to surprise her and, hearing that she was at the theatre, went straight there.

'He was a terrifying sight. The blood drained from his swarthy face, leaving it completely white; his eyes looked crazed and his hands shook as they groped for something at his waist – his holster, as she realized only the next day, thanking God that he hadn't taken his revolver. The entire scene lasted only a few seconds before Koba turned and walked out. Sverdlov was too busy flirting to notice him, but she accidentally caught sight of herself, through Stalin's eyes: she and Sverdlov were walking towards a mirror that covered half the wall. It was a long time since she had been given such a fright.

'Disturbed by the incident, she couldn't countenance the thought of staying on for the second act, made her excuses to Sverdlov and went home. She decided against telephoning Stalin: she was better off giving him time to cool down. The next day, he travelled back to Tiflis without seeing her, and she, after pondering what had happened for a week or so, realized that he had the blood of a true highlander and that, if she could only take advantage of that, she had every chance of getting what she wanted, of her prayer being heeded.

'The tactical approach taken by de Staël was simple enough: without even telling him, she made a clean break with Stalin and started having flings with whoever stood in his way at the top of the Party. Her targets were easily identified. She'd known them all for years, had no illusions about any of them, including Lenin, and above all she, just like Stalin, belonged to no faction and observed everything from the sidelines, so she saw the situation as it really was. To provoke Koba all the more, de Staël publicized the ins and outs of every affair. No more was required of her. Stalin set to work straight away.

'The men Stalin sentenced to death were no longer old comrades – they were rivals who'd stolen his girl and they could expect no mercy. Staël now discovered a different Koba. Wreaking vengeance, his grandfather, Georgi, must have been just the same, and she was astounded and horrified by her son. To her dying day she could not forget the depths of madness to which Stalin sank on hearing, in that same year, 1919, that Sverdlov had died of tuberculosis – just like that, in his own bed, and there wasn't a thing Stalin could do about it. He barely left his Kremlin apartment for an entire fortnight.

'But there was no other route by which to bring Koba to power. Staël understood perfectly well that the people she was taking into her bed, whom she permitted to love and caress her, to whom she declared her own love, were doomed. Jealousy made Stalin not merely cruel, but resourceful and patient to an extraordinary degree. Like a good huntsman, he could wait years and years: as he and de Staël both knew, his prey was going nowhere. And so it proved. His enemies died in car crashes, on operating tables, beneath trams, from poison, or from the bullets of hired assassins. Later on, he simply entered their names into the NKVD lists and took great pleasure in watching them being tortured over the course of many months, before finally sanctioning their execution. Even in the thirties, even in the fifties, long after the end of her liaison with Stalin, when they were both in old age, he, remembering them all, went on killing her lovers, and if someone, like Sverdlov, managed to elude his grasp and die in his own bed, he would settle his scores with his relatives, in merciless fashion.

'For all this, remorse visited de Staël rarely, if at all. Yes, she knew that she was leading the men who loved her to their slaughter, sleeping with them only so that Stalin could kill them later, yet the moment they were in her bed she loved them passionately. Her talent for love was simply astounding, and Stalin, of course, had every reason to be jealous. As for her, she thought that they, having once known her love, had not lived in vain and shouldn't grumble, just like the young Populists she'd once known. It was Stalin who worried her most. She understood that no one could live long with such hatred, such tension, year after year, and in order to help him, to let him recover his strength, she introduced a kind of rewards system: after disposing of another rival and thereby reasserting his claim on her, Stalin could have her for an entire week. They would travel out to one of the government sanatoriums in Yalta or to his beloved Lake Ritsa, or – most often – they would cut themselves off from the world in the dacha at Kuntsevo, just outside Moscow.

'The system worked without a hitch, and within the space of just five or six years de Staël had cleared Stalin's path to the very summit of power. Only once did it fail. In '27 she had a stormy fling with Trotsky, who was the last to offer any threat to Stalin. When the time finally came to end it, she suddenly realized that she had fallen for Lev quite badly and didn't much like the idea of Koba killing him. Trotsky, of course, was a problem for Stalin, a very big problem – that's why she went to bed with him – but now she wanted Stalin to keep him alive, to get rid of him some other way. She knew how stupid it would be to broach the subject with Stalin, not to mention dangerous (he'd never understand her) and so, biting her tongue, she made out that her affair with Trotsky was nothing serious, a mere fling. In fact, she was already pregnant with Trotsky's child and was counting on having it; she changed her mind only at the last moment, realizing that Koba would kill this child, come what may.

'Stalin had his own, supremely efficient spy ring. From their very first conversation both she and Trotsky were under surveillance, so he knew everything that went on between them, where, when and how often, yet he was so used to believing her, so used to her not concealing a single one of her lovers from him all these years, that, exhausted by his own uncertainty, he eventually had Trotsky thrown out of the country. Only at the end of the month did he realize the true state of affairs, when he was denied his usual reward. He came to whisk her off to the Caucasus, only for her to spill all the beans, like an old gossip, and he had no rest until Ramón Mercader plunged an ice-pick into his enemy's skull in Mexico, 1940.

'They stopped seeing each other after Trotsky's exile. She thought the NKVD would come for her, had no doubt she'd be tortured, and begged God in advance that He not prolong her suffering, that He grant her a quick death. But Stalin didn't touch her, as if he'd forgotten all about her. By that time he'd acquired a real taste for power and was clearly in touching distance of what she had been asking God to give him. Hatred and vengeance had hardened him and made him a man; even so, de Staël was still unsure that he could become a ruler worthy of the great country of Russia without her help.

'Thanks in no small measure to Khrushchev, it's become a truth universally acknowledged and repeated that the essence of the Stalin cult was the unrestrained, unlimited praise lavished on the Leader; but this is nonsense. The aim and meaning of the Stalin cult, which was also de Staël's child (she began shaping it in the hugely popular Soviet magazine *Worker Woman*, of which she was the editor and to which she contributed copiously in each issue, before her lead was followed by thousands of others: poets, artists, composers), was quite different. In fact, it was the direct opposite.

'The image of Stalin created by her and others with such zest was the ideal for which Stalin should strive while ruling Russia, whatever it cost him – through gritted teeth, if necessary. This image, in other words, was not a eulogy but a constant reproach, a public demonstration to the people of how imperfect he, Stalin, still was. The image surpassed him in every respect: it was wiser, braver, more beautiful, decisive, ruthless, far-sighted and, last but not least, younger and healthier. And Stalin, hating and cursing his cult, just as de Staël had foreseen, strained after it all his life, until the strain finally became too much. He was chasing a leader he could never catch.

'How he despised himself when, standing on the Mausoleum during the parades, he ordered a little bench to stand on, while knowing that this was a fight he could never win. Stalin was getting old, his strength was ebbing bit by bit, but he remained as young and healthy as ever. How ashamed he was, how he hated himself – old, sick, with a withered arm. Eventually the double more or less hounded Stalin into seclusion: he became scared of leaving the Kremlin and eventually moved away altogether to a nearby dacha, where he wouldn't even venture out to the garden. He'd become utterly pathetic and knew that if he so much as dared come out and say that he was Stalin, he'd be dealt with like an impostor. It was the cult that ruined him: if at first it was reasonably well-disposed to Stalin and tried to raise him to its level and teach him something, taking pleasure in his successes, then later, realizing that Stalin was no longer good for anything, that he'd run out of steam, it destroyed him.

*

'You mustn't think, Alyosha, that de Staël's only occupation after 1917 was to help Stalin climb to the top,' Ifraimov continued. 'That, of course, would be untrue. The lion's share of her time was spent not on Stalin but on work connected with membership of the venerable HEURO group, the very same group that dreamed of turning Russia into a country of geniuses. In the twenties HEURO was in deep crisis. Back in the day, when it was first formed, the decision had been taken that it should remain a closed, secret society – fear, as they say, has big eyes – and after Tkachev's betrayal the resolution was passed not to accept any new members at all. This was a serious mistake and the consequences were not slow in coming. By the time of the Civil War – the time for which the group had existed all along, for which it had been waiting and praying – only two functioning members remained: de Staël and Trogau, the psychiatry professor. All the rest had died, been killed, or had turned into decrepit old men.

'De Staël had long been trying to rescind this absurd regulation and put the issue to a vote seven times between 1910 and 1920, but she never gained a majority. As a result,

HEURO quietly aged and weakened. Even so, for as long as Trogau and she were alive, the group survived as well, and both did all they could to enable the "maximum programme" to be fulfilled.

'The Revolution and the Civil War – the main trials, according to HEURO, which the country had to undergo – were now in the past, and Russia had earned the right to lead the forces of good, to begin the very long, historically decisive battle which, according to the Book of Revelations, should culminate in the final defeat of the forces of world evil and the victory of the righteous. De Staël knew that in the impending struggle the soul of man would be cleansed and freed of original sin, that he would abandon and reject all evil and return once more to God, to be united with Him once more – this time, for good.

'The hopes invested in the Revolution by HEURO proved well-founded. Having razed the old society to the ground, having mixed up everything and everyone, again and again, having arranged things so that the people who were once at the top had plunged to the very bottom, to hell, to the abyss, to be replaced by complete nonentities, the Revolution had infinitely enriched the experience of the nation: hunger, cold, cholera, typhus, the execution of hostages, the killing of brothers by brothers, fathers by sons, had all become part of normal, everyday life. Even more importantly, the Revolution had freed us from all the previous rules and conventions, shown the illusoriness of the old world, its astonishing, incomparable fragility (hadn't it collapsed in a single day?), the astonishing weakness of the fetters that constrained the brain and soul of the genius, telling him: "Do this but don't do that; never, under any circumstances."

'And now the genius, knowing that he was stronger than

society, that he was entitled to do anything he wanted, opened up and walked free. What celebrations, what fireworks – a true bacchanalia of genius! But unfortunately, the Bolsheviks couldn't make the most of it. Consumed by the struggle for power, they didn't even notice the geniuses dying of disease and hunger: in times of crisis, they and their children always come out worst. Even worse was the completely gratuitous execution of thousands of their fellow geniuses, for no better reason than, as they said in the Cheka, sticking their head above the parapet. Most unforgivable of all, though, was the fact that the Revolution gave them permission to leave the country, or even forcibly expelled them; this was a betrayal, an act of sabotage against the forces of good.

'Trying to save what could still be saved, de Staël, beginning in January 1918, literally bombarded the CC and CPC with letters; she also made a direct appeal to Lenin, demanding immediate action. Many seemed to agree with her – the situation, they said, was indeed intolerable – but every time more pressing problems were found. She was on the point of giving up and even told Trogau one day that she would never ask anyone for anything again: she had no strength left.

'Only in 1922, out of the blue, did Lenin call her at home and say that if she had concrete ideas for the creation of an Institute of Natural Genius, they could be heard in a week's time at the next session of the CPC. But, he added gently, she shouldn't be under any illusions: the chances were slim, for ideological, as well as financial, reasons. All the same, he'd do his best to support her; Stalin, too, had said he would vote in favour.

'The rationale for the Institute and a draft of its charter were prepared by de Staël and Trogau in the space of three days. They wrote it day and night and, despite all that happened afterwards, this copy has somehow survived – you can find it in the hospital library. Externally, and indeed internally, it differs little from other such documents, and it's hard for us now to understand the indignation provoked by the Institute at its inception. The rationale consisted of three parts. After an introductory passage stating that the catastrophic shortage of geniuses would inevitably lead to the failure of forced industrialization and bring the Revolution to its knees, it was argued that the State needed scientific criteria of genius, that such idiocies as "Like – Don't Like", "Good – Bad", were no longer sufficient; it needed to know for sure what was just a simulation of talent (to be determined as a court determines the simulation of madness) and what was real. Just think of the amount of money this could save on art alone!

'Next came an explanation of the very phenomenon of genius. It is wrong, wrote Trogau and de Staël, to see mental illness and other pathological manifestations as purely detrimental; that's how it is seen by doctors, who approach geniuses as if they were ordinary people or, more precisely, ordinary patients. We need to examine pathology dialectically, see its positive aspects. To remember at all times that genius is a cross between two biological lines. One line gathers an enormous quantity of hypostatic energy, known in common parlance as talent, but this is not yet genius, merely its potential. For a genius to open up and his energy to be freed, a special mechanism is needed, a trigger, as it were. That is the role of pathology, which the genius inherits from some other ancestor. The normal apparatus of consciousness, Trogau and de Staël emphasized, is a hindrance to genius. Like every norm, it is opposed to the abnormal. The creative process, in fact, lies outside the sphere of stable consciousness; it's delirious in origin. In conclusion, they set out the main aim of the Institute:

to prevent geniuses from going unrecognized and unused, to find them, understand them, open them up, then develop them in accordance with a fixed plan.

'The task was to be divided into a series of stages and tendencies. The initial priority was to study all matters related to genius, including the scientific testing of both geniuses and their works. Moreover, Trogau and de Staël insisted, particular attention should be paid to those who, through lack of education or for any other reason, were unable to manifest their genius. This, they commented, was an enormous resource, a veritable Klondike. Exhibitions, museums, editorial offices, publishers, competitions for technological innovation accumulate, year after year, a quite astonishing quantity of examples of pathological creativity; a good number of these are the work of geniuses, and our task is to prevent them from passing unnoticed, from sinking into the Lethe.

'There's a second resource: dreams, visions, states of hypnosis, trance, passion and hysteria, hallucinations of various kinds. All these, wrote Staël and Trogau, contain in the purest, most perfect form that which is commonly known as genius; sometimes, one single dream is enough to turn our conception of the Universe on its head. Expert analysis of the dreams and visions of geniuses would in itself justify the Institute's existence.

'Prisons and clinics for the mentally ill represent the third resource. Such places, de Staël and Trogau noted, always attract a great number of talented people, so it's only natural that these establishments should also enter the ING's sphere of interests. Knowing the laws of creative pathology, the State will take a different approach towards the abnormal, often asocial manifestations of genius, stop condemning such people to hard labour or locking them up in the madhouse; instead, it will hand them over to the ING, where their creativity will serve the good of society.

'In connection with this, though not exclusively, Staël and Trogau proposed that a 100-bed home be built at the ING, as well as a special school for two hundred pupils. The beds would be given to the patients of mental homes and to prisoners, as well to those not-so-numerous geniuses who, drawing purely on themselves, can only create in hothouse conditions. Such specimens, Trogau explained at the CPC, tend to lead secluded lives and very rarely socialize with their equals. There were also beds for geniuses wandering at large: weakened by hunger, cold and disease, they would be given the chance to recover their health and their senses in the nursing home. As for the special school, de Staël's intention was for it to be attended exclusively by child progidies.

'The Institute was also to include a special research department to test various methods of stimulating pathologies, including artificially provoked tragedies, shocks, pain, hunger, cold, deaths in the family – whatever might assist in liberating a genius's accumulated creative energy. As it expanded, the ING would become the nucleus of an entire complex of institutes tasked with fully developing the abilities given to man by nature, and above all, with attaining every variety of genius, including eternal youth and immortality.

'The draft, as I've already said, met with no objections from the CPC and was approved without difficulty, but Trogau and Staël's celebrations proved premature: only a year later opposition to the ING among the Party aristocracy – the old underground activists and revolutionaries – was such that the Institute seemed doomed. It all began with the school for prodigies, which de Staël and Trogau had intended as little more than an appendage to the Institute. No sooner did it come into being than rumours started circulating in the Party to the effect that vacancies in the higher nomenclatura would henceforth be filled by its graduates. Where these originated is not known. Once, at a closed session, Lenin really did say something of the kind, but that was just a slip of the tongue; he was merely trying to explain why any special schools at all should be needed in a country where the Revolution had triumphed.

'Previously, the ING had not a single enemy. On the contrary, everyone tried to help it, support it. After all, it had to be built from nothing, in the midst of devastation and hunger. De Staël, of course, made the most of this good will, but once, in conversation with Trogau she let slip her suspicion that they were viewed in the way that tutors to the heir to the throne had once been viewed. It did not even occur to Trogau and Staël that this assistance was not disinterested, that everyone who had ever done anything for ING was convinced that they were owed a debt of gratitude. It was a typical instance of ordinarily intelligent, worldly-wise people not noticing what was right under their noses. Despite blatant hints aimed in their direction, de Staël and Trogau noticed nothing for over a year, and the virtually unanimous CC directive to liquidate the Institute came as a complete shock to them. A sense of outrage had been mounting for some time and was easily explained: de Staël really had made sure that only prodigies were admitted to the school, while the Party aristocracy was convinced that, for the Revolution to survive and keep to the true path, the home needed to be filled with the children of Old Bolsheviks, their children.

'A compromise,' said Ifraimov, 'was perfectly possible: all she had to do was admit two or three dozen offsprings of CC members and that would have been the end of it, but de Staël dug her heels in. As a result, the Institute became the object of serious political accusations. On 13 March, 1923, the Central Committee passed a secret resolution stating that the ING had become a breeding-ground for the reactionary and essentially racist theory of Mendel-Morgan-Weismann and was upholding the primordial inequality of men, a hereditary inequality that was implanted in man by nature herself, and that even under communism could never be overcome. Doubt was thereby cast on the fundamental communist ideals. Were this theory to reach the masses, millions would desert the Party and the construction of the new society would be indefinitely postponed.

'Even more frightening was another accusation: analysis of the pupils' dossiers revealed that more than eighty per cent of the child prodigies came from noble families, the bourgeoisie and the priesthood – class enemies, in other words, of Soviet power. This was set alongside the noble origins of de Staël herself and the conclusion was drawn that the real aim of the ING was creeping and silent – hence especially dangerous – counter-revolution. The creation of the Institute was an act of sabotage jeopardizing the very construction of communism in Russia. The campaign against the ING was well-organized and the pressure applied by the Party aristocracy so strong that neither Lenin nor Stalin could resist it and the Institute's activity was frozen. Only five years later, when Stalin really came into his own, did the ING resume its work.

*

'By then the Old Bolsheviks had become visibly weaker and for them, as once for Lenin, the pull of death had become ever stronger. Lenin, as a faithful disciple of Scriabin, knew that the Russian Revolution was merely the beginning, the prelude to universal ruin and Apocalypse; the world, always and everywhere, was evil and foul. Only by passing through death and thereby cleansing itself of all-pervasive evil could humankind be reborn and resurrected for new life.

'But by 1927, hopes for worldwide revolution and universal ruin had evaporated and the Bolsheviks, realizing that their lives were ending in failure, that they were destined never to see that for which they had struggled, for which they had accepted every possible sacrifice, set about hastening their own deaths as best they could. A different generation of communists was coming to power – orthodox Fyodorovists, for the most part. These staked everything on life itself, on eternal life and eternal youth; they could not accept death in any of its guises. Stalin was their natural, decisive leader, and when, in 1927, the Institute was restored, nobody objected. The Party aristocrats gave in; their only remaining hope was that their children, if not they themselves, might succeed in bringing the peoples of the earth to their deaths.

'Their attempts to secure places for their heirs in the special school at the ING now acquired a humiliating and often comical flavour. In the belief that this would intrigue de Staël, the Party high-ups supplied their offspring with meticulously documented medical histories (these were drawn up in return for bribes by the best psychiatrists of both capitals), from which it followed that they, their parents and all other relatives on both the maternal and paternal side, not only possessed hidden talents – we all have the right to blow our own trumpet every now and again – but, most importantly, suffered from mental illnesses of every kind; in short, they were mad. So there was not a single act, including the Revolution (in fact, especially the Revolution), for which they could be held responsible. The Revolution, they wrote with complete certainty, was sheer delirium, delusion, and the fact that they had taken any part in it, that they had carried it out, permitted only one explanation: their continuous state of insanity and affect dating back to 1905.

'A belief in the inheritance of acquired characteristics,' Ifraimov explained, 'was shared at that time by all the Party élite. As early as 1922, the famous biologist and vehement opponent of genetics, Paul Kammerer, had moved from America to Russia, where he received an ecstatic welcome. Ten years earlier Kammerer had studied two groups of the Italian working class – specifically, Genoese bakers and dockers – and proved that it wasn't only the obvious, easily distinguishable features of a person's face or figure that were handed down: in fact, children, grandchildren, and great-grandchildren all inherited, with not a single discrepancy, the school marks of their ancestors, as a result of which Genoese teachers were even considering dispensing with school record books.

'This piece of research,' Ifraimov went on, 'dealt a crushing blow to Mendel, but still the enemy would not surrender. Mendel's ally, Weismann, tried to save whatever might still be saved. Over twenty-two generations he mercilessly cut the tails off mice in his laboratory, and since the descendants, loath to learn, continued to be born with tails on, he deemed Kammerer's theory disproven. Kammerer repeated Weismann's experiments once he was already in Moscow. The results were awaited with bated breath. It transpired that yes, over twenty-two generations, mice do continue to be born with tails even when their parents' tails had been chopped off (for nature, wrote Kammerer, this is far too short a term to draw any conclusions), but after amputation the healing process is quicker and less painful with every dropping.

'It's interesting that even Stalin, who ought to have known from the history of his own family what's inherited and what isn't, remained convinced until the end of his days that the moral health of the nation demanded that precisely Kammerer's theory be upheld (even if it was just a beautiful fairytale, an ideal as far removed from life as the teachings of Christ), and not the cynical teachings of Morgan-Weismann. Otherwise, the attraction of the good would wane to nothing: why all the sacrifices, why the arduous, agonizing path towards perfection, if the children would have to start from square one whatever you did?

'In 1923, therefore, Stalin co-authored a book with Lenin on genius under socialism. Lenin was gravely ill that year, on the brink of death, and in all likelihood the book was written by Stalin alone (Lenin merely approved it). The question of the inheritance of genius is treated there with unusual evasiveness; in fact, it's virtually ignored. The only statement on the subject is that after the October Revolution the essence of true genius lies in unwavering, purely intuitive and frequently irrational compliance with the Party's General Line, and in keeping well clear of any oppositionist activity; everything else is secondary and insignificant.

'For a long time Stalin shared Kammerer's delusions, so eager was he to believe that acquired characteristics were inherited and that the children of his most loyal comrades in the struggle would take all that was best from their fathers. He didn't want to see what everyone else could see, what de Staël had been saying to him day after day: that the Old Bolsheviks and their children were no longer any good for anything, that they were holding the Party back, that all the stagnation and apathy was due to them. How many years had she been telling him, again and again, that it was high time to kill them all off, that the Party needed new people, new blood, rejuvenation? She would ask him: is the Party a living entity, or is it a corpse? If the former, then it must submit to the laws of nature. Every gardener knows that unless you prune the old branches in autumn, the garden will run wild and cease to bear fruit. A vegetable garden, she told him, had to be weeded, and weeded often, or nothing would grow. If you spare the weeds and whatever else chokes and saps the useful plants, whatever deprives them of sun and water, then there will be no harvest, no matter what you do. But he didn't listen, didn't want to listen, and brushed her away whenever she started harping on that theme. He was a very good, very kind and slightly sentimental man; needless to say, he was better than everyone around him, but for the Party of that time, the country of that time, kindness was not a blessing, but a curse. There was nothing she could do. Jealousy alone could liberate him, jealousy alone gave him strength, but she could hardly go and sleep with half of Russia.

'At Kuntsevo they often took walks in the park together. Stalin liked listening to her talking about bugs and butterflies, about the grass and the flowers. Staël made the most of it. Returning to the garden at the dacha, she was able to illustrate, with one example after another, that revolution is a natural phenomenon, that it's organic and always right, and that if fate had made him its leader, then the laws of nature were the only ones to which he, Stalin, should submit. Death, she told him, is a part of nature, a tool by which to speed up life; outside it lies stagnation and lethargy. Death cuts away all that is barren, all who are no longer capable of developing, of adding anything new. And this is true of everyone, of the entire country, not just the Bolsheviks. If he wanted to build communism, he had to kill and kill; whatever tried to stop, hold back or hamper their common task had to be mercilessly destroyed. Communism would be formed by perfect people; imperfect people would never manage to build it – they would only get in the way.

'He agreed with her and knew all this himself, but he would answer sadly that there was nothing he could do about it, that he could not bring himself to kill a man; in fact, he sometimes even regretted killing her lovers. De Staël chased away the thought that perhaps he was simply not made to rule, that he lacked the force of will, the decisiveness to be a real leader, and that he should make way for those perfect people she told him about every single day. She'd already despaired of persuading him that repressions, mass repressions, were an absolute necessity for the nation, when suddenly – it was May 1, 1929, a national holiday – she found the words to convince him.

'On that day she told him that the death experienced by those killed on his orders was not a real death, but a sort of mock death, like in a fairytale. When communism finally arrived, and the dead would no longer be an impediment to anyone, then, just as her teacher Fyodorov used to tell her, they would all be returned, resurrected, raised from the ashes. Perfect people would shoulder the terrible weight, the entire burden of building a new life, while these small, defective, pitiful specimens would be rewarded in the most generous way possible, simply for having agreed to depart this life temporarily, so as not to make the cross even heavier. They would fall out of non-existence into a world more beautiful than any that had ever existed on earth, a world of happiness and harmony, eternal youth and beauty, love and joy. They would return to the paradise from which Adam was once expelled for his sins, the paradise they continued to dream about, generation after generation.

'That May-day conversation determined the fate of the country. After it Joseph Stalin finally became the real Stalin, the Stalin we all know.'

*

298

Stalin and the Institute for Natural Genius turned out to be the final topic of my week-and-a-half long series of nocturnal meetings with Ifraimov. At first I'd been gripped, afraid every evening that he wouldn't come, and when eventually he did, I was happy. I'd become very fond of him, too. But at a certain point I ceased to understand why, for what possible purpose, he was telling me all this about de Staël.

He knew that every day until late, I listened, took down and transcribed the confessions of the men on our ward, and he knew why I was doing it. Perhaps my relationship with God (I held nothing back from Ifraimov), His retreat from me and the others, and the love by which I intended to save the old men and the entire world struck him as naïve; but he couldn't fail to see how crucial these memorial records were, both for me and my fellow patients. He couldn't fail to see these decrepit old men lining up first thing in the morning, one behind the other, even though, at their own request, I'd carefully registered them all a long time ago and stuck up the order of confessions next to the staffroom. They knew that every man would be heard at the given time, in the correct sequence, and yet there they were every day, never leaving their posts, never even squatting.

I used to think that Ifraimov's attitude towards me was one of respect, even affection, but now I understood him less and less. After all, he could see that I was taking down what he said, just as I did with the others; but why de Staël and her lovers needed to be entered in the Memorial Book, why they needed to be preserved, was something he never explained.

This hardly seemed right. Every night I spent three or four hours taking shorthand, which I then had to transcribe and go over – at least six hours' work all told. I never got enough sleep; in fact at night I barely slept at all, sitting down to transcribe just as soon as he'd left, scared of forgetting a single detail. I didn't sleep in the morning, either: meekly, wordlessly, the sick came over to me, forming a queue from the very head of my bed. That was that – I had to get up, take pen and paper, and start writing all over again.

Thanks to Ifraimov, the queue moved twice as slowly as it might have done. De Staël took up as much of my time and energy as all the others put together, but to what end? He knew I was trying to record only that which pertained to the hospital, to our old men; I had no strength left for anything else. I should have talked to him about all this ages ago, of course, but I hadn't dared, I'd felt awkward, and I was always waiting for him to tell me himself, to explain himself. One day I very nearly did ask him, but he suddenly got up and made for the door; it felt stupid to shout out after him. A week and a half of this had exhausted me, and all I could think of was a good night's sleep, so the day when Ifraimov finally cut short his tale came as an immense relief.

On that first night without any talk of de Staël I slept like the dead. I woke up fresh and cheerful and had a full day of good, solid work. I saw four people – double my usual number – and the queue shuffled forward. I was pleased, of course, and the sick cheered up too. They had lost all faith, all hope, especially the ones at the back, but they had the same determination as those queuing for bread during the war. What if today was the day? The day for a miracle? At home such a miracle was out of the question, but not here. So the queue began to move, a head-count was taken, and it turned out that if it could only carry on like that, I'd get through almost everyone by the end of February. Those at the back infected the others with their faith; after all, this meant that God needed every human life, every single one, not just the lives of the righteous and the chosen.

Fearing that God might change his mind, I began to hurry, writing faster and faster. For now, though, I still had the tact not to rush anyone. Just like before, I heard the patients out and recorded everything, word for word. Not that there was any need to crack the whip; they'd long been shy of taking up too much of my time and they were also ashamed before each other, those standing next to them. Urging themselves on, they started keening and gabbling, chewing up their words, swallowing whole lumps of life. In the end I had to slow them down and, if I lost their thread, stop them in their tracks and make them turn back. There was so much meekness in them, so much nobility of feeling. Every man who confessed thought less of himself than of the fact that, if some other man did not manage to have his say, a life would go unrecorded, a life that might mean more to God than his own. They felt newly culpable and they repented, asked for forgiveness. Deep down, they wanted one thing only: to make peace with those standing next to them and quietly leave.

The old men, of course, did not resemble an ordinary queue: they took no pleasure in reaching the front. They understood that the life of one man is just a tiny piece, that to survive, to be saved, they had to become one whole. I even doubt it was the fear of losing their place that made them stand there from dawn till dusk; no, they wanted to show themselves, and me, and God, that it was only before that they were separate people, separated from one another by life and by illness, but now they were together, and they would always be together, and there was no going back. They valued fairness, but it seemed to me that if someone had asked to be let through, they'd have agreed without even asking why, by what right. They'd become very kind, very affectionate, very tender to one another. After all, they were queuing for love; they knew that only love can save, that there should be more and more of it, enough for everyone. And they themselves were prepared to love.

Things carried on like this for several days. It was all going very smoothly, unusually so. My shorthand was becoming ever more professional, with tricks and refinements all of my own, and the transcribing went quicker too, so I got a lot more done, without even getting too tired. And then, one evening, when I didn't think anything bad could happen, when such thoughts no longer even crossed my mind, fear entered me once more.

It wasn't the quantity of work that frightened me, though I'd got through no more than a fifth of it. I'd suddenly understood something, suddenly been shocked by the fact that it could even occur to me, that I could even believe, that I, and I alone, had enough love for all these people, enough strength to love them all. Wasn't this the task I'd set myself? Wasn't this what I'd promised God, and not just a record of their confessions? I saw how little love there was in me. I simply wrote and wrote: sometimes I found it interesting, and then I listened and wrote with pleasure, sometimes I felt bored. I was well-disposed to the sick, I felt sympathy for them, I was proud that those who intrigued me and those who didn't were equal in my eyes, but was this really love?

And I immediately understood that all of them, the entire queue, had long been aware that I was an impostor, that I did not have and could never have so much love; that I was an ordinary man, no better and no worse than the rest. Yet still they would not disperse, still they stood there, day after day, by my bedside. And I knew why it was that they would stand there until the very end. Even now they were hoping for a miracle. After all, the Lord could give me this love if He chose to. They could see that it was all the same whether He had abandoned man for good, or whether He was still retreating;

in either case, He was further and further away from them, and they ever further from Him. Yet still they waited, believing that the bread of love would come their way, that same bread with which the Lord had nourished man since the time of Adam, but which had made man no better, so much evil did he have inside him. And really, what would it have cost the Lord to vindicate me, to arrange things so that I was no longer an impostor? After all, I really did want to do good. But even if there was to be no miracle, they felt warmer together – not to mention the fact that they had already begun to love each other, that they feared separation. They had lost far too much in life, far too often, not to fear this.

Strange though it sounds, only now did I understand how differently they and I viewed the world. My dream was to save them, to show God how much love a man can have, even for people who are utterly remote and alien – old, filthy, misshapen old men. Lord, I seemed to be telling him, You decided to leave them, to abandon them, but I've gathered them up, I've taken them under my wing. I was reproaching Him, of course, as if I were telling Him: I'll be your teacher in love. And I was rebelling against Him, too. Why is it that the moment we want to be better than nature made us we instantly go against God? Can it really be that there is a limit even to our goodness, a boundary we must not cross?

The sick, meanwhile, trusted only in God. I don't know whether they prayed to Him or how they prayed to Him – most, after all, were atheists – but I heard them tell God that I was a very good man, that I wanted to love them all and that perhaps I could be helped, at least a little. After all, I'd already given them a great deal of love, and this love was still in them now. It was through my love, they told God, that they had learned to pity each other. My love, in other words, was neither false nor sanctimonious, and they asked God to perform a miracle that would only be just – to give me enough love to go round them all. Everything that had love in it, everything that I wanted myself, they left untouched; they only got rid of what I would have got rid of, too: my reproach, my pride, my rebellion. No longer would this be the love of man for man, but the love of God for man, revealed through man.

*

Who knows, perhaps the Lord really did hear the prayers of the sick, but they were less about me than they were about them. He was waiting for me to turn to Him, to ask Him myself, but I had no strength left either to live or to believe in miracles. I carried on working as before, while finding it harder every day. Apathy took hold of me. Recording the confessions became a matter of complete indifference, as if I'd forgotten the meaning of my labour, as if I was doing my daily homework – no more.

Or perhaps this apathy and indifference could be explained simply by the fact that a new fit was approaching? My earlier fits, before I was even admitted, had been preceded, a week or so in advance, by similar moods. A fit did indeed arrive, but not the usual type: my consciousness dimmed slowly and gradually, unevenly, as if it were flickering. At times I had a clear idea of where I was – I could even speak – but then awareness ebbed once more. It wasn't a rupture, it was more like those days when they started stunning me with heavy doses of medication and I just couldn't get used to them.

For so long now, only one thing had really frightened me – loss of memory – but in my current state a fit became a blessing. I wanted to leave everything behind, to forget it all; nothing else could help me. Fear weakened first, leaving only the notion of it, the understanding that it existed, but not the fear itself. I'd been granted a respite, a chance to sleep, to step aside. So I wasn't being accused of anything; on the contrary, I was being promised lenience and mercy. And the last thing I remember is this: I wanted to ask everyone for forgiveness and to forgive everyone myself. I was convinced that everyone would be forgiven, that everyone, not just me, would be vindicated, that everything would be exactly as if I'd succeeded in doing what I wanted to do – with all the love that required.

I said all this to the other patients in my room, glad to be able to lift their spirits, then I went out into the corridor to give my good tidings to the others as well, and ran straight into Ifraimov. Reproachfully, though without attaching any blame, I said: 'Why did you tell me about Madame de Staël? For what purpose? Why this long, sad story?' As I said this, I realized that until it was finished, until I knew its meaning, I would never truly be able to sleep or forget.

He replied sadly: 'Alyosha, you mean you don't remember all those times you asked me about the elegant, straight-backed old lady in the next room along? You were even surprised that you couldn't work her out: was she one of the ordinary patients here, or one of us, the ING alumni? Well, that's Madame de Staël, the same Germaine de Staël I've been telling you about; and in the flesh, to boot. The story of her life, I believe, has every right to be entered into the Memorial Book. And the old man in love with her is the famous philosopher, Fyodorov. It seems to me that both he and the soldiers the Sisters sleep with should also be mentioned. After all, they're not actually soldiers at all, but Fyodorov's children by Madame de Staël, those children deprived of reason whom she bore him in St Petersburg and whom he never saw in his youth. He didn't even know he had them. To this day he won't accept they're his sons,' Ifraimov said, after which I remember no more, as if these really were the only words I needed to fall asleep. Did I do anything else? Speak to anyone else? A complete blank. All I know is that I was ill for a very long time, almost an eternity.

I lay unconscious for more than a month and a half all told, but this time I recovered my senses easily and without loss. I came to as if I'd simply fallen asleep then suddenly woken up. Not only that: I fell asleep while talking to Ifraimov and the first thing I remember after the fit is him standing next to me by the window and scratching something out with his nail on the frosted glass. Just as the blade of a knife will not pass between well-laid stones, so here there is no room even for night: we were talking in the corridor, then I felt like going to bed, then we moved to the room. But this fit was not my first. I know it happened, I know I spent a long time unconscious, that my conversation with Ifraimov about Madame de Staël, Fyodorov and the soldiers did not happen yesterday, and nothing will make me change my mind.

People who live smooth, day-to-day lives rarely notice change. After all, change accumulates like drops. For such people, today is just like yesterday, and tomorrow, no doubt, will be the same. Their life has only one beginning and only one end. Their memory does have some footholds, of course, but not many: a few scenes from childhood, getting married, having children, etcetera. But those of us who suffer from the same form of amnesia as I do must begin from the beginning over and over again. Our existence is sharply circumscribed by our illness, divided into autonomous parts, and we don't even try to fill in the gaps, we don't even pretend that nothing has happened.

After my third or fourth fit, I, like many others, began to

appreciate this broken rhythm. I'd adjusted to it, begun to enjoy the freshness, the brightness, the fact that there were so many colours and so little routine, that life tasted different – after all, you were virtually back from the dead. But the first days after the fit are always tough. As a rule, you're wary about what you say and what you ask, you rarely enter into conversation, you just watch from the side, listen in and try to get your bearings. After all, nobody wants to make a fool of themselves, to be taken for a madman. Each time, I was astonished at how much had happened since my fit. In order to remember everything, to get up to speed, I'd have to spend almost three months for every month I spent unconscious. It was like in a war, where one year is worth three; and just like in a war, danger felt near at hand. Especially when I came across something I couldn't understand. I could see the danger at once and there was no need to warn me.

But this time was different. When I came round I felt that it wasn't just me, that even those who hadn't lost their memory were clueless, afraid. This was a new sensation: life without routine, without anything fixed or stable – only fear. Fear was everywhere, to the point that I should have guessed that it was not my fear alone; but I'd never known anything like it and to begin with I couldn't believe it, I decided I'd been unconscious for a year or more, so of course I was astonished when, steering my conversation with Ifraimov towards this topic, I learned what day it was. That was when I finally grasped that only to a very small extent was the fear my own. Everyone was afraid, though I didn't know why.

Outside, snow was falling. There was no wind and it fell in big, thick flakes, landing on the trees, the earth, the flowerbeds. A thaw seemed to have set in over these last few days, and at first the air, warmed by the earth, drifted upwards; the snow would stop and sometimes even rise slowly with the air. It was as though the flakes were tied by fine threads to the sky and someone, still undecided, was letting them fall, only to regret it afterwards and pull them back. But this didn't last long. The earth was cooling fast and, as night drew in and large yellow lamps were lit on the hospital grounds, snow covered everything. Snow, only snow. Even the black branches of the trees were visible only as white against dark.

I already knew that today was March 28 and I said to Ifraimov: 'Must be the last proper snowfall. There was no snow this year until January, so I've skipped a whole winter.'

'No, Alyosha,' he replied sadly. 'This isn't the last snowfall. It will snow for another forty days and forty nights. The snow will fall and fall…'

'That's impossible,' I objected. 'When has snow ever fallen in Moscow all April and half of May?'

'True enough,' said Ifraimov. 'Nothing similar has ever happened, but this year isn't like previous years. When the forty days come to an end, a blizzard will rage for five months, for a hundred and fifty days, a snowstorm so powerful that from the highest peaks to the lowest lands, from north to south, everything will freeze, drown and be hidden beneath the snow. Only next spring will warm weather return, only then will the snow finally thaw and the water flow down to the sea.'

'What you're describing,' I said, 'is a kind of flood… So who will come out of this year alive?'

'A flood's exactly what it is,' Ifraimov confirmed.

'But that other flood, the first one,' I asked, not yet believing him entirely, 'what was the reason for it? Why did the Lord want to destroy us? And now, why does He want to do the same thing again?'

'The Lord,' said Ifraimov, 'made the earth just as perfect

and beautiful as paradise. Everything was at its peak, in bloom, including man; but man's soul was the soul of a child. It had been born only yesterday, and only yesterday had it begun the long path which the soul of man has to travel to discover what is good in the world and what is evil. Adam was a child, a grown-up child, and, having tasted the fruit from the tree of the knowledge of good and evil, having received the highest gift, the gift of creation, he began fooling around with it, like any child. In all he did he was fearless, carefree; his soul had not yet been schooled, and he knew no sin.

'Banishing Adam from paradise, the Lord gave him the entire earth for him to manage on his own, and stepped aside. But man did not cease increasing his knowledge, he didn't baulk at his gift; he was, I repeat, as fearless as a child. The world around him was as one; everything was united with everything else. There was ecstasy here, the rapture of mutual possession, of understanding that nothing was alien to you, that everything belonged to you, and you to it. You were not alone, thanks be to God; you were merely a part of the whole, not answerable for anything. All flesh had corrupted its path, and even the angels started coming in to the daughters of men on seeing their beauty. Living things forgot the Lord's commandment: "And the earth brought forth grass, the herb that yields seed according to its kind, and the tree that yields fruit, whose seed is in itself according to its kind. And God saw that it was good." Soon the world was taken over by monsters and mongrels the likes of which had never been seen before. From a semblance of paradise, the earth became a cabinet of horrors filled with murder, atrocity, rape, and the Lord was appalled by the world He Himself had created.

'But the most terrifying creature spawned of man was the centaur of good and evil. Still fooling around, Adam crossed them as a child, and the result was evil that gives birth to good, good that leads to evil, and a great multitude of variations thereof, in which no one can tell where one ends and the other begins, so deep is the confusion and contamination. Bringing a flood of waters upon the earth, the Lord meant to cleanse the world, to return it to its primordial state, and most of the monsters did indeed drown; but this mutant was indestructible. Having no body, it lived on in the soul of man, even in that of the most righteous man, Noah, and, finding its way onto the Ark, survived.

'Even Christ, the Son of God, the pure good given by the Lord to man to redeem his sins, given as forgiveness, as a chance to be cleansed and raised to new life with God, even He was mixed up by man with evil. How much blood was shed in his His name, how many wrongs committed, how many innocent killed! The Lord, though, had no illusions. When the waters abated, He said:

'"I will never again curse the ground for man's sake, although the imagination of man's heart is evil from his youth." In other words, He did not believe that man could be reformed. Living creatures, having managed to preserve their God-given nature, could still be found at the time of the Flood, but pure good could not – it was all mixed up with evil.'

'But, although He already knew this, the Lord still vowed not to bring another flood of waters upon the earth to destroy all life,' I said. 'So why has He gone back on His word?'

'He hasn't gone back on anything,' replied Ifraimov. 'This flood is not God's will. He has merely seen fit to answer the prayers which the human race has been offering up to Him for many thousands of years. If before the Flood man, ignorant of sin, did evil without a second thought, then after the Flood, after Noah, he understood how sinful he was, how far he'd retreated from God. Sin began to cause man unthinkable suffering, like scabies, and everything was drowning in evil. Even then there were those who managed to find a path to God, who managed, amidst all the evil around them, to remain righteous. It was only thanks to their prayers that the scales wavered for so long. At times it even seemed that by their life, their teaching, their prophetic gift, good would gain the upper hand, but then people gave up completely.

'Once, man had thought that he could save himself, without the help of God, that he could return to paradise all on his own, by building the Tower of Babel; but now he remembered that he was created in the image and likeness of God and decided to imitate Him in another way too – by summoning a flood and putting an end to evil.

'This idea hardened in men until the time eventually came when they could no longer think about anything else. It became an obsession. They were convinced that what they wanted was pleasing to God, and they didn't hide the fact that their flood would be crueller than His; they knew where evil was rooted. It was rooted in them, in every human soul, and they started beseeching the Lord for death, for everyone to die, the entire human race; no one, even the most righteous of the righteous, should survive. And the beginning of the Flood was the Revolution.

'A flood,' said Ifraimov, 'is not always linked to water – far from it. "A flood of waters", says the Torah about the times of Noah, while the word "flood" itself, in the original Hebrew, means the "mixing up of all things", like during an avalanche, or a torrent of mud. A great mass of stones, sand, clay, earth and, yes, water, pours down the valley from the peak to the bottom, as if down a gutter, with a thunderous din. Whatever crosses its path – houses, gardens, people, fields, cattle – is ground up like porridge. Who lived here? Anyone? Everything is covered in mud: the roots and bonds between people and between things are hacked away. Where did you come from and when? All is erased, forgotten, levelled, muddled.'

'When did all this begin?' I asked. 'How long ago did man start wanting his own death and decide that he could no longer cope with evil?'

'That's hard to say with any precision,' replied Ifraimov. 'Probably impossible, in fact. It was a slow, slow process. We had one patient here, not for long, mind you. Ilyin was his name. Well, he would say that it coincided with the coming of Christ. But I wouldn't put a fixed date on it; I'm not in favour of saying that today can be one thing and tomorrow another. Although there's no denying that the coming of Jesus Christ on earth marked a boundary.'

*

'That, said Ilyin, was when the Lord had the idea of saving the human race and sent Him, a second Adam, into the world, giving people to understand that their sins were forgiven, redeemed, that everything bad was forgotten and life could begin afresh. The Lord did not repeat his mistake: Christ was conceived on earth and, unlike Adam, was meant to live a full human life right here, from birth to death. Infancy, childhood, adolescence. But, said Ilyin, even before Christ could walk, His birth ceased, by some strange circumstance, to be a secret and changed the world. Everything changed: the very structure of life, the commensurability and correlation of its parts, its edifice – and even notions of right and wrong; yes, right was always right, and sin was always sin, but nevertheless, in the gap between them something was disturbed, displaced, distorted. Many lost their way, confused by the lodestar that guided the Magi to Christ. The aim these people had set themselves, people who'd known what path to follow since time immemorial, who knew that they could only do so much, suddenly disintegrated and could no longer be true, at least not while Jesus Christ still walked the earth.

"'I'm reluctant to say this,'" continued Ilyin, "but it would seem that when Christ appeared on earth, only one path remained in the place where He lived, in Israel: the revolutionary, lightning path walked by the Son of God and His disciples. The Magi and the shepherds, who lived beneath the stars, were the first to notice this disturbance in the natural order of life, and to see how powerful it was: God had come down into a world where man was meant to look after himself, and it proved too cramped for Him. This disturbance of the normal way of doing things, this overwhelming advent of God on earth (remember that nothing similar had ever happened before, or has ever happened since) inevitably altered the fate of His chosen people, and not only theirs.

"'What remained from the three years that Jesus spent walking and preaching in Israel was not only that which He told His disciples and which came down to us through the Scriptures; no less important was the knowledge gained by Christ Himself during his time on earth: that only miracles can help man. Christ does not console the crippled and the sick; He has no words for them. Nor does he exhort them to accept their lot – He heals them. And that is the whole point. The fate of the crippled, the maimed, the mad is so awful that words without salvation are nothing. The sheer number and variety of miracles performed by Christ on earth shows how essential miracles are; there's no getting by without them. Miracles are worked by the Lord in the conviction that the world is terrible, that He, Christ, has been sent to save it."

'This same Ilyin claimed that all the disputes between Christ and the Pharisees come together in the parable of the labourers in the vineyard, where one path to God competes with another: the master hires labourers for a denarius (eternal salvation); when midday passes, he hires others, and an hour before the end of the working day he hires a third group, and he pays them all the same wage – one denarius, and when those who have worked since the morning object, he says to one of their number: "Friend, I am doing you no wrong. Did you not agree with me for a denarius? Take what is yours and go your way. I wish to give to this last man the same as to you. Is it not lawful for me to do what I wish with my own things? Or is your eye evil because I am good? So the last will be first, and the first last. For many are called, but few are chosen."

'Here we see that miracles and mercy are greater than justice, greater than long, slow, arduous labour, greater than anything. Good is at the core of everything that Christ, filled with the Holy Spirit, does on earth. Having lived for so many years among men, having seen so much evil, He, ceasing to be a man, becoming the Messiah, becoming God once more, cannot help doing good, as much as he possibly can, good for the weakest and the maimed, and for sinners too. Essentially, He violates the way of doing things that He himself established: not the slow path of man's repentance and reform, not the slow path of salvation from sin and, as reward, eternal bliss, but simply mountains and mountains of good, whole sackfuls of good, and the worse off you are, the weaker, the more sinful, the more deserving you are of goodness and mercy. For there to be more good in the world He sends His disciples in all directions, telling them: "Heal the sick, cleanse the lepers, raise the dead, cast out demons," and then: "Freely you have received, freely give," lest they pause to ask themselves whether or not to do good, whether or not the man beseeching them is deserving of mercy.

'Christ, Ilyin would say, is God's joy – the great joy of the God who is able to do good and can finally do it, who no longer has to wait for man to be reformed, to look at all the endless woe and sorrow of human life, who loves man as His child, for what is man if not His child, His continuation, made in His likeness and image, and in His suffering too? God simply cannot bear to look any longer at the woes of man, to see evil spawning evil, more and more of it each day. Is this really how God's world should be? And does He not remember how and when evil first entered the world? It entered when man was a child, when he could scarcely answer for his actions. And anyway, can the evil done by that child really be compared to what followed?

'Hence the Son of God: full of love, full of desire to forgive, craving an end to evil, craving equality. Why should some have everything, even righteousness, while others have nothing? Doesn't everyone stem from one root, from Adam? So to those who have nothing – the poor, the sick, the maimed, the dead – he gives the miracle of forgiveness and deliverance. But in that case, said Ilyin, the purpose for which God created man, to whom it is given to do good and evil and who one day, so God believes, will reject evil and freely choose good, thereby proving the truth and goodness of God's world, must remain unfulfilled, and all that came after the birth of man – all that evil – was pointless, merely evil spawning evil. And the deeds of the righteous are also pointless, and God is alone, and above all good is no better than evil, for men have not chosen it. Either they didn't want it, or they ran out of time. So then, Christ stops.

'The Hebrew faith, Ilyin said, is a faith of children, not disciples; Christianity, on the other hand, is a faith of disciples. Christ had no children; the thought never even occurred to Him. He Himself was the Son of God and even to imagine Him leaving His Son on earth in His place, as He ascends to heaven and sits at the right hand of the Father, is impossible. It would be a completely different faith. Christ's children are His disciples, the disciples of His disciples, and so on. This was, of course, an alien, unnatural and, therefore, strangely rapid way of spreading a faith. Sometimes it took just a single day for an entire city to convert to Christianity or, as in Russia, an entire people. Christ's disciples were in a terrible hurry, they believed that His second coming and the Last Judgement were at hand – in twenty years' time, perhaps, or even less. They were trying to save as many people as possible; they could think of nothing else.

'The Church of Christ was an enormous Ark, which alone could save and preserve whoever found himself beneath its blessed canopy. Christianity spread through the earth like a forest fire. The Word of God reached the farthest-flung quarters, sometimes even in advance of the apostles themselves. An almost tragic tempo was set for world history. The destruction that was so close at hand, that was bearing down so fast made this tempo justifiable, permissible, even comprehensible. What was the point of sparing anything from the former world, if that world was doomed?

'The disciples made Christianity the faith of the eve of the end; a very brief, almost transitional faith. In this faith, it turned out, history was built on miracle; everything about it expressed the great disillusionment in the path previously taken by man, and the greatest trust in God: the belief that He would help and save. And the belief that if, in the space of a single day, man could cease to be pagan, convert and know the One God, then the human soul must be soft, pliable, easily reformed; so then it would be even easier to make the world anew, to shake off the dust of the past from one's feet, begin afresh, and build paradise on earth.'

'But surely,' I asked Ifraimov, 'the world is not so flimsy that one snowfall can be enough for it to perish, for it to be covered and drowned in snow?'

'It is,' he confirmed. 'Man was given more freedom than he could bear; he became confused, entangled, and lost his way.'

'So this time no one will survive? Everyone will perish?' I asked.

'No. Just as during the first Flood, there will be an Ark, and several men will be saved. After the Flood, their life will be prolonged.'

'So where is this Ark?' I asked.

'It's our ward,' Ifraimov replied.

'And the Lord,' I asked again, 'won't preserve anything? He won't want to spare anyone, except this dementia ward? Can He really believe that only those who are here deserve to be saved?'

'Yes,' said Ifraimov, 'only those who are here, and not all of them, either. The Ark is overladen; unless most of the sick leave of their own accord, it will sink.'

'So even on the Ark the pure will be separated from the impure, the impure will perish, and the pure, though saved only at the expense of the impure, will still be righteous in the eyes of the Lord?'

'Those who leave,' repeated Ifraimov, 'will leave of their own accord; or at least that's how it will seem. In fact, it will be hard to restrain them. They find themselves here purely by chance. They did not come to the Ark, they were brought here by force. For them, this is a prison; they dream only of freedom.'

'And they'll know what they're letting themselves in for? They'll know that the world is about to perish, that they, too, will perish if they leave the Ark?'

'Not necessarily, no. It would probably be fairer to say that they'll be tricked, but there'll be no force here, none at all. And don't bother asking any more questions: there's no one to blame here. This is a case where God decides everything, not man. The Lord removed the year of the Flood from human history; you won't find it in the tally of years. Man had no say about anything then: that was the time of Divine, not human history.'

'And yet,' I said, 'I've heard that there's a Talmudic commentary in which two men – one a scholar, an expert on the Torah, *Talmid Chacham* in Hebrew, the other ignorant of the Scriptures, a "man of the land" (*am ha'arets*) – are dying of thirst in the desert. There's only enough water left for one of them to get to the well and be saved. So the Talmud says that all the water should be given to *Talmid Chacham*, because otherwise knowledge of the Torah may perish with him. But, the commentary notes, *Talmid Chacham* cannot deprive *am ha'arets* of his water, because if he does, he will be taking an entire human life as the price for learning, and isn't righteousness the only reason why anyone need know the Torah? A man who takes someone else's life cannot remain righteous before the Lord. The path of the scholar and the path of the man of the land should be one and the same, so either they die together in the desert (says the Talmud), knowing that both are God's children, that both were created in His image and likeness, that God loves them both, or else the Lord must bestow a miracle on them equally, just as once he saved Joseph.

After Isaac, no one can sacrifice the life of a human being.'

'Yes,' Ifraimov agreed. 'But this is different. Here, no one has any say.'

'So who is Noah?'

'Nikolai Fyodorovich Fyodorov.'

'Fyodorov?' I was astonished. 'But you said yourself that he virtually rose up against God, that he began building the Tower of Babel from scratch?'

'True,' replied Ifraimov, 'but that's not all. The Jews had long accused Noah of not praying for forgiveness, of permitting the destruction of humankind. Even though he was without sin, even though he was a prophet (God had spoken to him more than once), the Jews maintained that his righteousness was remarkable only by comparison with his peers, who were so depraved that, according to Genesis, the Lord condemned them to death. He was, in other words, the best of a bad bunch, and in Abraham's generation he wouldn't even have been noticed. Yes, they said, Noah built the Ark in plain view, without concealing a thing, so anyone could follow his example, and yes, it was true that he told his fellow tribesmen more than once that the Almighty would soon be bringing a flood of waters upon the earth; but this was hardly enough. After all, it was his own family – his brothers and sisters – who would die. It's as if he himself thought they should die: all of these sinners were beyond redemption, none of them would take the road that led to God. And he made not a single attempt to turn them away from evil, not a single attempt to persuade the Lord to postpone punishment, to spare, at least for a while, the descendants of Adam.

'This terrible accusation had hung over Noah's head ever since the Flood. He stood accused before God not just by his children, his direct descendants, who had survived thanks only to him, and not just by the hundreds of scriptural exegetes who tried to understand why he'd been saved and others condemned, but even by the dead who'd perished in the waters. Accused of abandoning them, of not interceding, thereby condemning them to death. Year after year, age after age, millennium after millennium, he bore this cross, but then he rose up against God. In the presence of his disciples he vowed to resurrect everyone who ever lived on earth, to save them and return them to life, because death was unrighteous, death was evil, and there was no sin on earth for which a man deserved to die. And the Lord understood him, understood that the burden with which He had saddled Noah was heavy even for the righteous, that Noah was moved by faith, love and compassion for human beings, and so He did not blame him.'

'And de Staël? In what does her righteousness consist?'

'The Devil once tempted Christ with power over the world, and Christ passed the test; He did not give in to the Devil. But he was the Son of God. Madame de Staël, meanwhile, is just an ordinary woman. The source of power lay within her, not outside her. Power over the world was invested in her by God, it seemed to flow out of her, it was hers by every human law – yet she never obtained it. The Lord acknowledged that He had tempted Germaine de Staël all her life, without giving her the resources to overcome this temptation, and so He forgave her both her lust for power and all the other sins that gave rise to this lust.

'What's more,' Ifraimov went on, 'the children of de Staël and Noah will also be saved. The Lord arranged things in such a way that their souls were not fertilized at birth; they lived more than a hundred years as dumb creatures of God, ignorant of good and evil, and sin could not touch them. True, Noah hates them all the same. He's convinced that, for all their ignorance, they are flesh of the flesh of the old world, children of lust, born of sin, and that's that. Noah has always wanted to bring the past to completion, not to draw out man's retreat from God. He was prepared to put up with sons, but their lives could only be justified, he thought, if they began the task of restoring their fathers, thereby reversing life's course.

'But who could these three idiots ever restore? They don't even know that Noah's their father. Besides, Noah is terrified that it was through them that evil entered the Ark, that if these three succeed him, if his life continues through them, everything will be in vain – just like the first time. Noah is begging God to give him another son from de Staël after the Flood, the son of all the people ever born on earth, and for this son – pure and unstained, like Adam before temptation, ignorant of sin – to begin human history afresh.

'The three Sisters will also be spared – the wives of Noah's children. Just as soon as it stops snowing, they will turn into doves on consecutive mornings and fly round the earth, seeking a place where the snow has melted and the water has sunk into the soil. They will find a dry hillock and start building their nest.'

'And that's all?' I asked. 'No one else will be taken into the Ark?'

'Yes,' Ifraimov confirmed. 'That's probably all.'

'So none of the sick will be saved? So my love did not suffice to save even one of them, not a single one?'

'I suppose you're right,' Ifraimov concurred.

Returning to my room, I realized that everyone here, down to the most decrepit old men, long incapable of making head or tail of anything around them, knew that the Flood had begun or was just about to. A flood as in the time of Noah, sent by God to destroy the world. Where this knowledge came from is hard to say: perhaps the Lord, depriving them of their reason and turning them into children, brought them closer to Him at the same time, revealing to them what others could not know? Or perhaps here on the Ark – the only place in the world He had protected from the elements, removed from the general order – this knowledge was given to all, and that was the whole point?

*

Our ward, as has already been said, was far from straightforward: most of Kronfeld's patients had once been Party functionaries, the nomenclatura; they'd worked in the Kremlin, in the CC, in the CCC (Central Control Commission), or nearby, in secret police HQ. At the very least, they'd occupied positions of authority in the ordinary ministries and, needless to say, they retained their old contacts. As a result, the moment anything went wrong on our ward, bulging denunciations were dispatched to the powers that be. There was no postbox in our building, and relatives visited rarely, but the patients, as if in memory of their previous lives, paid bribes to get their reports out into the world.

Just like his predecessors, Kronfeld spent hours trying to explain to the nurses and attendants that, by passing on the letters, they were putting themselves in jeopardy: each wave of denunciations was followed by a visit from a special commission, and although the Ministry of Health would always warn the hospital who would be inspecting and when, the result was always the same: a frantic, last-minute clean-up. The washing, laundering, scouring and scrubbing was done by those same nurses, of course, but they didn't like planning so far in advance, and always preferred three roubles in hand to long-term benefits.

The denunciations contained much that was true:

indescribable filth, especially in the toilets, sheets unchanged for weeks, rude attendants. Good food – meat, cottage cheese, fruit – was systematically filched, and there were no oranges at all this year, not even for the October holidays. This was all mixed up with a familiar litany of complaints: the sick were being deprived of their right to vote in elections for the Supreme Soviet, no one was collecting their dues and they were cut off from the Party, lecturers were never sent over, their experience and knowledge was not being tapped for the edification of the young, etcetera, etcetera.

But the denunciations and the complaints were merely a prelude to the main point: accusations of sabotage. The abuses were listed one by one: treatment, diagnosis, incorrect dosing. Ever since Kronfeld was put in charge of the ward, the topic of doctor-saboteurs and Judeo-Masonic conspiracy immediately reared its head: the counter-revolution had built its nest in the department and was being served by the medics, who were deliberately destroying tried-and-tested Party cadres. It was almost an exact replica of the Doctors' Plot of 1953.

Kronfeld, who took a professional view of the denunciations, was astonished at how accurately their memory, despite all the damage, had preserved the past. He, too, remembered that time very well: in the spring of '52 he graduated from medical college, and '53 was the first year of his independent career. But there was something else going on here – in fact, it would have been stupid to compare his memory and theirs. There was something inhuman about the way that they repeated, like a carbon copy, all the accusations of that time, the exact wording and phrasing, deviating not a jot in syntax, tone or style. The present was no object, and the past, cleansed of all that followed, was brought back to life.

Since the old men, though sick, were considered perfectly

competent citizens – technically speaking, ours was not a psychiatric ward – and since they wrote to the old addresses, where their friends and those they promoted still worked, the commissions were uncharacteristically prompt in arriving. But that was not the worst of it. Their findings were summarized with almost personal hatred and serious measures were proposed.

On the one hand, everyone seemed to realize that the authors of the letters were unwell, that they were incapable of answering for themselves or what they said, and that their denunciations were just the usual ravings. As such, they ended up in medical history books, and no one seemed to mind. On the other hand, every point, every detail was verified several times over, and each time it was said that there's no smoke without fire, that there must be something behind the accusations. The upshot was that the commission found examples of widespread neglect, gave the head of the ward yet another ticking-off, and made itself scarce. Kronfeld's two predecessors each managed to survive a year of this pressure before succumbing to heart attacks, after which Kronfeld was sent here, as if into exile – in exchange, let it be said, for a trouble-free defence of his doctoral thesis.

Most of our old men saw the Flood as a gift. For many years all they had begged for, all they had dreamed of, was to be needed by the Party once more, and now, at the point of despair, fate had taken pity on them. A believer would have said that their prayers had been answered; and perhaps the Lord, bringing a flood upon the earth, really had been thinking of them. Aren't we all His creation? Aren't we all His children? Not one of us can be a stranger to Him. So now their hour, their time had come. Everything had been done in accordance with their prayers, in accordance with their faith that the country, the Revolution, would still need them, that it was too early to write them off.

By divine mercy they really had ended up at the very heart of events. At the beginning of the century Lenin had argued, with great passion, that the centre of the revolutionary movement had shifted to Russia, that it was precisely in Russia that the fate of the Revolution, socialism and the world would be decided. Many disagreed with him, and at times even he entertained doubts about Russia's mission – and therefore about his own mission too; nevertheless, he felt there was joy here, delight, a licence that made him always right, that gave him the strength to do what he did.

And just imagine the strength this gave to all the Bolsheviks on our ward! After all, none of them could doubt any longer that the fate of the world, of all humankind now depended on them alone. What was being decided here was infinitely greater and more important than what had been decided in 1917, and just try comparing their ward – a small dementia ward – to the enormity of Russia! It's not even a dot on the map. Think how much energy was gathered here! How much had been poured into all these men!

They knew that they were on the Ark, that they too had been chosen, that the Lord had added their names to the list of those who could be saved. All they had to do was state openly and freely that they wanted to remain here, on the Ark, that they were ready to break all ties with their former life, ready to forget it entirely – the life that He had condemned to destruction. But in fact – and we must acknowledge this openly – not one of the sick ever entertained the possibility of his own individual salvation, ever imagined that his comrades were condemned, doomed, along with all that they had built, known, loved, their entire world – and not only theirs – and that only the chosen, for some unknown reason, would survive. This thought, to their credit, never entered their heads. And even if it had they would have deemed it blasphemous, because they had only thing on their minds: to forewarn the Party, their comrades, the 'organs' about the terrible danger ahead of them.

They wanted to live, but only if the Party survived too. They belonged to it, and life outside it was unthinkable. In their own eyes, they were not God's chosen, they were spies, intrepid scouts, who found themselves on the Ark by will of fate, in the enemy camp. Many among them now began to understand why their relatives had renounced them and consigned them to a geriatric ward, why the Party had allowed this, not protected them, not preserved them. They reappraised the last years of their lives, all they'd been through; they forgave and justified the actions of all those who'd brought them here. After all, they could do so much more for the Party here, on Kronfeld's ward, than in their brightest dreams.

Danger elevated them, ennobled them. The denunciations which they dispatched from the Ark were filled with restraint and dignity; they were precise, considered, calm, no hysteria, no frenzy – just facts and sober analysis. They informed the 'organs' that, according to the reliable information at their disposal, God, having hardened His heart, intended, in the nearest future, to drown the human race in snow, thereby destroying the world's first state of workers and peasants. They wrote that this dagger in the spine of the Revolution should have been foreseen a long time ago. An obvious error had been committed: the struggle with religion, with God the Father, had not been carried through to the end, for all Lenin's encouragement. Vacillation, compromise and occasional out-right flirtation had allowed the terrible hydra to recover and rear its head once more.

As if armed with signed copies of the Lord's plans, the sick listed when, where and for how many days the snow would fall, for how many days the blizzard would rage. It had already been decided, they wrote, that the entire world, not excluding the very highest mountains, would be plunged deep in snow. No one would be spared, not a single man, except those who had been taken onto the Ark by His special decree. The Ark chosen by the Lord on this occasion was the geriatric ward of the Korsakov Psychiatric Hospital. Let me repeat: I still do not understand how the old men were so certain of these details. Perhaps I really was the only person in the hospital not in on the secret? Having chosen those He would save, having singled them out and taken them into His confidence, the Lord divulged to them his plans for the human race, a race which the survivors should prolong and extend. But I don't exclude the possibility that God had nothing to do with it. Perhaps He didn't say anything at all, and the sick wrote purely at the prompting of their own class instinct.

They went on to note that although the situation was critical and any delay would be tantamount to death – never before, not even during Denikin's march on Moscow, had the Revolution been in such danger – victory was still possible, and the first step towards it was the immediate arrest of Noah (Nikolai Fyodorovich Fyodorov), Madame de Staël (Ekaterina Frantsevna Stal) and their children.

Their arrest would be sure to stop the Flood in its tracks, since for the Lord the continuation of life on earth was bound up with the fate of Fyodorov's family; He'd staked everything on them. By kidnapping Noah's household, though under no circumstances killing Fyodorov and de Staël (that would merely provoke Him: a world deprived of the righteous would not be spared for even an instant), they would force the Lord to change his plans. In this way, by alternating threats with shows of repentance, as in the days of the Treaty of Brest-Litovsk, the Party would buy itself some time; and if this time was put to good use, the Lord would simply revoke his decision to unleash a flood.

This all seemed sensible enough: a simple, clear plan that required no complex preparations. And indeed, the nurses delivered denunciations of God to the outside world just as punctually as they had previously delivered denunciations of Kronfeld. Even the price remained the same: three roubles. For twenty days commissions continued to arrive, so for almost three weeks, until Moscow's roads became snowbound and impassable, the 'organs' continued to receive the most detailed information.

But this time nobody believed the sick old men; no one even wanted to listen to them. Their denunciations were dismissed as the usual ravings, and Kronfeld, once again, was held responsible. The commissions' findings stated, like a carbon copy, that this new bout of delirium, shared moreover by all the patients, was manifest proof of inadequate care on the ward. What it all came down to – professional incompetence or wrecking – remained to be seen. As Jesus Christ once said: many are called, but few are chosen. Nobody heard the old men, nobody answered their call, when something, perhaps, might still have been done. The earth was on the verge of becoming a snow-bound desert, but they continued to cry, unheard, in the wilderness. What further proof is needed of the madness of our world!

*

To all external appearances, Fyodorov's trysts with de Staël continued in much the same fashion as before. I'd been observing them for some time, in fact they were the first people I really paid any attention to on the ward, not least because only one bed separated Fyodorov and me. But although Ifraimov's stories had clarified a great deal, I couldn't notice anything different.

Sometimes their meetings were idyllic from beginning to end, similar to the ones that took place at Pine Ravine, as described by Ifraimov, before there was any talk of political parties, before anything at all. She would come and lie down on his bed, and he would arch himself over her, like a bridge. Fyodorov was a master of the 'air cushion effect', well-known to psychiatrists, whereby the head and the body, assuming their normal pose, seem to turn to stone; now, too, he lay over her, but not on her, as if he and de Staël were still separated by a crystal coffin. They passed many hours this way, chatting about something very quietly, very tenderly, his head hovering over her breast. In hospital, I noticed that Fyodorov had learnt to recognize de Staël outside the coffin as well, but even so, each part of their relationship was closed, complete; there was no point of intersection, no influence between them.

De Staël was never less than elegant, even on our ward, but in the coffin circumscribed by his body she became still younger and prettier, her wrinkles smoothed away. She lay there with a relaxed, almost indolent air, tucking up her right leg and smiling softly, as if in her sleep. She still retained her rare allure. Like any two people who have known each other for a very long time, they spoke about anything and everything – the hospital, books, the remaking of the world, the weather – but eventually Fyodorov would seem to tire of this ordinary, unforced conversation, of the tone they had struck, and he would return instead to their former relationship, talking as if nothing had happened in his life or hers since the days of Pine

Ravine, as if nothing had changed.

Again and again he told de Staël that he would save her and resurrect her, that she would be his and his alone, that she, the princess lying in her crystal coffin, was meant only for him. A scene like this could continue for days: I would sleep, wake, go off to eat, come back again, and nothing would change – she'd be lying on the bed like before, and he would be thrown across her, like a bridge.

Unfortunately, such conversations rarely ended well. It's hard for me to say which of them was more at fault, but Fyodorov would suddenly change the subject and begin trying to persuade de Staël that after the Flood, when she had risen from her coffin, she would bear him a son who knew neither sin nor evil, who would begin human history all over again. What had been, had been; everything would be rubbed out, eternally erased from memory; the time that had passed was the time of man's retreat from God, and it had to be forgotten. I'd heard it all before from Ifraimov.

His words, his gestures – it was as if he'd never had a single child by her. First she pretended not to notice and she answered calmly, with an almost exaggerated mildness, that her breasts had dried up and withered, that the way of women had long ceased in her. But her words merely provoked him. 'Remember Sarah,' Fyodorov would tell her, 'Wasn't it just the same for her? Was she any younger? Is anything impossible for the Lord? Sarah believed and Sarah conceived.'

De Staël would admonish him: 'But Sarah had no children by Abraham and the race of Abraham would have had to be extended by Eliezer – a servant, an outsider – when the Lord answered her prayers and worked a miracle. Our case is different; in fact, it would be a sin even to compare you to Abraham: I've already born you three righteous, sinless sons

– what more do you need? The Lord has chosen them; after the Flood He will fertilize their souls, and they will extend the human race. What right have we to ask Him for a new miracle, for more sons?'

Hearing these words, he would straighten up and start yelling that he didn't want these sons, that he didn't acknowledge them and never would, that they were the fruit of sin, the fruit of her violation of him, of her debauchery. Having put him to sleep, she'd copulated with him as if he were an animal. He hadn't wanted them; by rights, they couldn't even be counted his children – they were precisely children of sin. These outbursts rarely lasted long. He would gradually calm down and once again begin expounding his cherished idea about the purpose of children: to remember, restore, resurrect their parents – something which the sons conceived at Pine Ravine were manifestly incapable of doing. This argument seemed so persuasive that Fyodorov even cheered up, and then she would finally snap. It was if she suddenly became possessed, though I can hardly explain why – after all, she'd heard him say these things hundreds of times before. Never had he concealed from her what he considered to be the most important thing in life.

Different things were involved here, I suppose. His refusal to acknowledge the sons she'd born him, even to hear about them, could not but be interpreted by her as a diminution, a deficit in his love towards her. Any other time she might have agreed that she hadn't always done the right thing, but not now, before the end, when all of this should have been left behind. Now, any explanations had lost their meaning and she couldn't but suffer, knowing that he, who loved her so madly, did not love their children, defective though they were. Fyodorov, it seemed to de Staël, had betrayed her. Needless to say, there was no shifting her in her conviction that whenever she had brought life into the world, whatever the circumstances and whatever may have followed afterwards, she had done something good. And the thought did not leave her that, by refusing to acknowledge his children, Fyodorov was trying to show her that she, unlike him, was not righteous, that there was nothing in her but lechery and lust, and that she had only ended up on the Ark as his wife, the wife of Noah.

For de Staël this was especially painful. She was very fond of her sons by Fyodorov, she was proud of their passion, their physical power, and she loved to talk about their strength with their Sister-brides. In many ways, she was their ideal mother-in-law, and it flattered her that their relations with her sons were an almost exact replica of her affair with Fyodorov, that this made them happy. It was as if her old life was multiplied in them, presenting itself to her now in three different copies. After all, the Fyodorov she had loved was not the Fyodorov of now, but the boy from Pine Ravine, that naïve and funny little boy, her child, her toy, not a man chosen for his righteousness by God so that he, and he alone, could extend the human race. She wanted the old Fyodorov, the one who resembled their sons, and she envied the Sisters. The Sisters could see all this, they felt for her, and they too paid for love with love.

De Staël had always had a strong maternal instinct, and she loved her children by Fyodorov just the way they were: she liked the fact that they hadn't grown up, hadn't become adults, hadn't left her like other children. They'd remained just as foolish, just as ignorant, just as uncomprehending as if they'd come out of her womb only the day before. There's no doubting how proud she was that it would fall to them to extend the human race. Once, during an argument, she even told Fyodorov that the Lord had chosen them not because they were his, Fyodorov's, sons, the sons of a righteous man, but because they themselves were righteous and innocent, as if it were the first day of creation and evil could not stick to them – they didn't even know what it was. It was to such children, Christ said, that the Kingdom of Heaven belongs. Saying this to Fyodorov once, in the heat of argument, she immediately took fright; but actually her thoughts had long been tending in this direction.

Love, and hurt, and fear for her sons' future exacerbated the irritation that Fyodorov had long been causing her. She couldn't forgive him the fact that for him she was as dead as ever, dead in her coffin; a woman who, however madly he loved her, had to be resurrected and brought to life once more. But she'd been alive since their very first meeting, everything about her was alive, and it was as a living being that she wanted to be loved.

She was sick and tired of the chasteness, the detachment of their relationship. It maddened her. She desired him often, to the point of spasms and pain, but she couldn't make up her mind to sleep with him. She was desperately afraid of conceiving and bearing him a fourth son, a son who – she was certain – would deal with his brothers as Cain had dealt with Abel. All this worked her up into an indescribable frenzy and, losing all self-control while lying there beneath him, she would begin, without the slightest pretext, to scold him with obscenities. She'd say: 'Why this stupid act? Have you really forgotten what you did with me? Do you really think you're so pure and innocent?'

She'd ask him where it had all gone – all those times he'd slept with her – and say: 'No, you know what women are like, you know what it means to lie on a woman, not as you're doing now, but properly, you know what it means to want a woman, to enter a woman, to lust for a woman.' She'd tell him:

'Your flesh knew what it wanted well before I came along – just remember how it rose when you lay on my coffin – but I taught you a lot: have you really forgotten what it's like when a woman comes and thrashes beneath you? Darling, you're lying, you remember this and much else besides. My efforts weren't in vain.'

And she began describing to him how he slept with her, their first night, the nights that followed, and more, and more, in the dirtiest, filthiest way: what his penis was like, how he took her, how often. And again – how she wanted him and how he wanted her: 'Your brain may have slept when we were together, but your body, your flesh didn't sleep, it desired me, called me, it was intelligent, strong, clear-eyed. Your flesh was never violated, so these children are yours, your lawful children, and they will be your heirs.'

Hearing all this, he was in unimaginable pain, but not once, as she lay there beneath him, did he answer back, not once did he object. As if de Staël had hypnotized him. Even for an outsider like me, it was hard to watch her mocking Fyodorov like this, so I usually left the room straight away, returning only once he had come to his senses and fled.

Deep down, de Staël understood Fyodorov perfectly well. She was aware that his time was at hand, a time which filled her with a desperate fear. He was literally obsessed with the idea of everything beginning anew, but she was not prepared for such a break; she thought that the old life contained much that was good, that should be preserved and saved from the Flood. An attempt, at least, should be made.

The same distrust that separated her and Fyodorov whenever they spoke about the world of the future and about her sons also affected their conversations about the sick. De Staël was convinced that everyone on the Ark should survive the Flood;

God's will could hardly have been expressed any more clearly, or else why would they have all ended up here? The reason that they, like the righteous, had been taken onto the Ark – whether it was because they had become foolish children, poor in spirit, whose kingdom was heaven, or whether the Lord had other reasons of His own – was, she told Fyodorov, a matter of complete indifference to her. They were on the Ark and they should be saved. Just like him, her and their children. His argument that the Ark was overladen and dilapidated, that it couldn't bear the weight and would disintegrate, drowning everyone – so why shouldn't the oldies, good or bad, wander off? – was one she had no wish to hear.

He told her that there was no sin here, that everything was as it should be; not one of the sick had come here of his own accord, and all of them had been duped. For them, this was a ward in a madhouse, almost a prison. She replied that the Lord had more than enough power to perform a second miracle and stop the Ark from sinking, however many people it contained. If it was possible to feed five thousand with five loaves, with bread to spare, and if he believed that the Lord could arrange things so that she could conceive once more and give birth to a son, then it was also in His power not to let the Ark disintegrate, however decrepit it might be.

There was more to her anxiety than this, of course: the sick, after all, were Old Bolsheviks. For de Staël it was important that the Party, at whose origins she stood and which, after the triumph of autumn 1917, had mercilessly, hurtfully shoved her aside, should now be saved thanks to her. To her, the Party was sacred, it could not be at fault; and de Staël bore no grudges. She loved the Party, worshipped it; the cord between them had not been cut. She had known nothing purer or finer in her long life, despite all the dirt that had stuck to it during its years

335

in power. And so what if the Party had forgotten her? It was still her child, and de Staël was its mother, as forgiving as any other. All she knew was that her child had come back to her and was begging to be saved – who could resist?

Germaine de Staël understood that if the Party survived the Flood, she – and no one else – would become its leader, finally obtaining what she had dreamt of ever since she was born. Just as soon as the waters abated and the earth dried out, she'd be able, thanks to the Party, not merely to rival Fyodorov but even, if she so wished, to crush him. And it would make no difference whether the Lord took his side or hers. Still, the main thing here was not cold calculation, but the purest altruism. It was her old comrades, her old brothers in the struggle, who were on the Ark, and Party ethics, Party solidarity obliged de Staël to prevent their destruction.

Fyodorov was not blind to the danger. From the very first snowfall, he did all he could to drive the Bolsheviks from the Ark – they were interfering with his preparations for the Flood, jeopardizing everything; but each time, de Staël blocked his path. He tried to explain to her that Party solidarity and brotherhood were irrelevant here – the people she was protecting were senile morons, ballast, damaged goods, for the country, the Ark and the Party itself. His arguments were persuasive. He told de Staël that if they really did want to stay, if they really were prepared to serve the cause of the proletariat after the Flood as they had done before, then they would have transferred their Party membership from their old places of work a long time ago and re-registered here, on the Ark.

This question, by the way, was discussed at the very highest levels, in the CC. The response was positive and a Party cell was formed on the ward a year before the Flood. But nobody, save the unfortunate Kronfeld and two attendants, who had once been accepted into the CPSU under orders from above, transferred here. The sick clung like grim death to their old Party cells, and it wasn't hard to understand them: that had been their entire life, and most importantly, they hoped, believed that they would still return there. At their old places of work they and their relatives still received the occasional extra ration, bits and pieces that were in short supply, trips to the sanatorium and medication, not to mention the fact that for as long as they were still on the books there, no one could deprive them of their rights to a prestigious cemetery and a funeral with military honours.

Fyodorov exploited this. Look, he told her, here you are praying for the old men, here you are prepared to go under with them, taking him, Fyodorov, and her darling children with her (he never forgot to mention her children, when the need arose), while the sick had only their own interests at heart. Formally speaking, they might still be CPSU members, but in reality, Fyodorov told her, the time when you could still call them Bolsheviks had long passed: they'd gone to seed and dropped out of the Party, indifferent to the needs of the working class. There was some truth in this, of course, and de Staël realized that for as long as the old men were still turned back to the past, to a world condemned to death, living out its final days, for as long as she was unable to make them re-register here, on the Ark, she had no chance of helping them. So then de Staël made up her mind. Everyone was against her: Fyodorov, God, the old men. They were all unable to understand her, they all considered her a traitor, and no one more so than her Party comrades, but she would not accept that.

*

How many days did she waste flattering the old men, trying to explain to them what was happening, where the world was headed – but they wouldn't listen. De Staël's words struck them as just another ruse to deprive them of their well-deserved benefits and privileges. But still she would not give in: she fought for them tooth and claw, and her one single weapon was love, only love.

Having chosen a soul which she intended to convert and save that same day, having chosen a Bolshevik who, she thought, would eventually promise to re-register as a Party member on the ward, de Staël would buy clean linen from the nurses, obtain fresh, crisp sheets from God knows where, and make the bed for her chosen one. Then, if he was hungry, she would feed him, and if he was full, she would treat him, in no particular hurry, to some sought-after sweets, which the oldies liked as much as children. She slowly unwrapped the gold foil and placed the sweets in their mouths with her slender fingers: truffles with rum and cognac, prunes filled with whole nuts and drenched in chocolate, candied fruit. Then, when she could see by his eyes the pleasure she'd brought him, she undressed her lover, undressed herself and lay down beside him.

The old men accepted all this without grumbling, in silence: the hospital had long become their home, they'd got used to the local mores and they knew that nobody would ask them about anything – they'd just do whatever they had to. And nobody was embarrassed by anyone else. Illness, like a blind wall, screened them off from everyone else. No sooner had it begun to take root in them, many years before, than they started running away from it into their past. It wasn't just that they didn't see, didn't notice their neighbours on the ward; they weren't really with them at all. So she got into bed with them, pressed herself against them and began to warm them.

Warmth was the main currency in this world, what they'd always lacked more than anything. And these last few days had been the worst of all: freezing outside and freezing inside. The coal had almost run out: it was spring and the hospital was barely being heated.

Her love was devious, ingenious. Warmth was the only thing they let in without fear or caution, the only thing, in fact, that they asked for and wanted, and so she came to them at first not as woman but as warmth. And, as once with Stalin on the *Elbrus*, so now she hugged them close, warmed their beds like a hot-water bottle, and then, without rushing, warmed them as well; and thus, as warmth, she entered them. She softened and soothed their shivering old bodies, and in gratitude they let in her warmth, her smell; they thought she was from there, from the past, that distant past which they loved and trusted, the past where they were so happy and so warm, where they loved and were loved, and where women smelled like her.

And now, were anyone to tell them that she was the wife and accomplice of Noah, the wife of that same Noah who had contrived this flood, for whose sake, by whose prayer, the Lord had decided to destroy them all, destroy everything they held dear, everything that mattered to them and was meaningful to them – in other words, that she was an enemy, a terrible, sworn enemy – they would not have believed it, they would have said that she came from the same place as them, from the same past, that they'd known her for many, many years and could vouch for her as a trusted comrade.

She was already one of them. She became first their warmth, then their memories. It was a very slow, uncertain process. The old men had firm, solid defences, without a single gap, but de Staël gradually penetrated them, seeped in, and only then, having become a part of them, someone they'd already known before, did she begin to caress them. Her caresses were also slow and careful. The old men's flesh was feeble and easily scared, even more suspicious, perhaps, than their minds, for it had long lived by memory alone, and the slightest clumsy movement could ruin everything. But de Staël was undaunted, she would not give in; again and again she began from the beginning, taking ever more care.

Every time it seemed impossible to me that she could achieve anything, such was the old men's infirmity, such was their incapacity, yet she succeeded. Sometimes it would take three hours, sometimes seven, sometimes almost the entire night, but she got what she was after. And so, when they already wanted her so badly that they could think about actually taking her, they began, with the greatest difficulty, to kindle, as slowly as damp wood, and only then did a flame begin to rise, a flame that needed to be constantly assisted and supported, lest it die. But now the fire was catching, they already wanted her, all of her, her breast, her groin, her lips; with twisted, rigid fingers they stroked and caressed her skin, her hips, her stomach, legs, spine, buttocks; their bodies were still too scared to trust themselves, scared to believe that they were capable of anything, but they were capable, and in fact they could no longer do without her, de Staël. So then she, not letting them inside her, took their flesh with her lips, their newly revived, risen flesh, and began to torment it.

Now they wanted her even more. Weeping, they begged her not to delay, not to draw it out, but she, neither allowing their flesh to fall nor allowing them to come, demanded fiercely, categorically, that they, before uniting with her, before entering her, swear on their Party ticket, swear by the name of Lenin, that tomorrow, and no later, they would re-register here, on the Ark. They continued to resist, but she kept kissing them, caressing them, flattering them, complimenting them on their manliness and their skill with women, lamenting the fact that she could only sleep with those who'd already registered their membership on the ward, because she only yielded to men from her own cell – that was her rule. She enticed them, lured them with promises of important positions and assignments after the Flood – after all, they were the pivot, the anchor, the guard, and the powder had not run out in their flasks.

After the Flood, she explained, the Party ranks would thin out dramatically; it was inevitable. Few of the Old Bolsheviks, the regular fighters, would survive, and the ones that did would be worth their weight in gold. Life's not over, she told them; it's just beginning. After the Flood, the Party would be needed even more than it was now. Just recall, de Staël urged the old men, how difficult it's been for you all these years, to build a new world, a new man, how sluggish progress has been; but after the Flood, she repeated, everything will depend entirely on you, on the Party: whether we take the path we took before, where there was nothing except man's exploitation by man, except tears, suffering and hatred, or whether we set out on the true path right from the start. It all depended on them, the Old Bolsheviks, and if they refused to re-register here, if they consented to the Party drowning in the waters with everything else, they were not worthy of the name communist – they were pathetic cowards and deserters who'd betrayed their ideals.

Eventually they gave in, made vows, even signed statements, and only then did she yield to them. How to describe what followed? I'm strongly tempted to compare it to the throes of death, and yet, despite everything, this was life. The old men were on the point of expiring, the old world was on the point of destruction, and, without doubt, this night with de Staël was their last night with a woman, like a night beyond the end. For

families and friends, they were already dead, when suddenly –
this gift. And this gift was love, not death.

De Staël resurrected them and returned them to life. They
stopped fearing the present, stopped running away from it
into the past. They came back here for her; to live with her,
near her, in her time. For her they rejected their last remaining
things, their benefits, extra rations, privileges – everything was
heaped up at her feet like a gift, offered for one single night.
She was queen, tsaritsa, and the entire world was hers. She
knew this, and for her, too, this was love – not work, not duty,
not cold calculation. No, she understood the gift they were
offering, understood how big it was, understood that nobody
had ever loved her like this and surely never would again,
and she whispered: 'Darling, I'm not deceiving you, trust me.
Really, it's better this way. Darling, I love you, I want you, I
need you alive, I want to save you. Darling, I want you to live,
for us to do this again, and again, and again…'

Love gave birth to love, and together they were happy.
But the aftermath was painful. An hour later, typing up their
statements for re-registration, she came for their signatures; but
either the old men really had forgotten everything – sleeping
with her, making vows – or else they were cunning enough to
pretend. Either way, they refused to even look at the papers she
brought them, and de Staël left empty-handed.

So it went every time. Looking in from the outside, I knew
the outcome in advance, and for a long time I was unable to
understand why she couldn't see this either. Then I began
to understand that she, like they, was led through life not by
reason, but by instinct; she seemed not to notice failure at all.
At any rate, she responded to these setbacks with apparent
equanimity and, like a bee, flew from flower to flower,
beginning all over again. But I already knew that her next

lover would also make a vow to her, promise her whatever she asked him, even convince himself that he would do it, but then everything would sink into oblivion.

Fyodorov knew this too. Our rooms had glass doors decorated with wooden lattice-work, like the ones that open onto dacha verandas. The doctors and Sisters liked it that way, while the sick – with the obvious exception of Fyodorov – couldn't care less. Fyodorov could see what de Staël was doing in bed, all of it; as for me, I've never seen anyone suffer quite so much. He looked at de Staël and her nth lover unflinchingly – his eyes frozen, his face drained of blood, his body turned to stone, save the faint twitching of his hands.

We knew how jealous he was, how madly he loved her, and when she had someone with her we tried to shoo him away, but he wouldn't move; we had to literally drag him away and carry him off – his own legs would not move by themselves. And despite all his love for her, not once did he try to interfere, to stop her. It was as if he understood that whatever was happening was a matter between de Staël and God, and only them, and that she was not betraying him, for the Party's entire existence was at stake. In other words, he felt that de Staël was acting on full authority and that her success or failure depended solely on the Lord. He believed that the Party, like everything else, was doomed and would die, but he wasn't sure and feared that the Lord might, for whatever reason, want to save it.

Fyodorov understood that now was the time not of man but of God; of all the people on the Ark only he, in my view, had really grasped this. But de Staël's zeal was killing him. When after yet another failure she emerged, exhausted, from her room, he made a dramatic show of sympathy and even stroked her arm; she was drained, scared of being left alone for even a minute and glad of his company, even though she'd lost all illusions about Fyodorov a long time ago. They walked to her room, she lay down, and he, sitting down next to her on a chair, asked her how many times he had to explain this: that the people she was trying to save were corrupt egoists and liars, that they were the ones who had destroyed the idea, who had arranged things in such a way that man could no longer be saved. It was because of them that the Lord brought a flood upon the earth.

'But you,' he'd say, 'want to beg God to forgive them, you want to save their lives, so that all this can carry on and on. You've tried everything possible, but what have you gained? They still behave like animals, and anyone can see that they're doomed, that they've doomed themselves to ruin. Just look at them,' he insisted. 'Are they really in any fit state to help the Party? They're damaged goods, a stone around our neck. Just think how much you're sacrificed for them! A true heroine...' He tried to suggest that he didn't blame her for sleeping with them, that it wasn't a betrayal of him, but a sacrifice: 'Has a single one of them ever renounced his privileges, his extra rations, and thought about the common good?'

Fyodorov, of course, was very clever; he knew how to get through to her. Eventually, just as she had once done with Stalin, he found the right words, the words to convince de Staël that all the love she had would not be enough to save the Bolsheviks, and with them the Party. And when, seven days later, he got what he wanted and turned the old men out onto the street, into the snow, she, for all her screams, was inwardly prepared – she'd already accepted it.

What he told her was this:

'The patients on our ward are not the point here. The Party does not live by them, and even if they die, the Party will not.

The Party is immortal. The Party is like God and will last forever. For as long as you are alive, it will live through you, through you alone. That's to say, it will survive the Flood, it will not drown in its waters. It will be saved in your person and be prolonged, then it will continue in your children, so you needn't be afraid. And that's all I want to tell you...'

After lights-out she went back to her room and, calmly thinking over all she'd heard (Fyodorov did not rush her), agreed with him and realized he was right: her love, as once my own, had not been sufficient to save even one of them. They really were doomed, if nobody's love could help them.

*

Late one evening, a week after this conversation, when Fyodorov already knew that de Staël was no obstacle, a steady shuffling sound, almost indistinguishable from a distant rumble, started up in the ward. Perhaps it was the night of a full moon, when the oldies' usual syndrome – 'packing their bags' – always recurred with particular force. From under mattresses and pillows, from bedside tables, from behind radiators and skirting boards, and from other, much stranger places, they collected all the bits and bobs they'd stashed away for a rainy day, every last thing: old crusts of bread, chocolate wrappers, rags, odd little hooks and springs, decomposing leaves and flowers from the year before, and other junk; cautiously – in fear that they might be noticed and stopped from leaving – all this was tied and packed up into paper bags, little bundles and boxes, and then, shuffling along the floor in their slippers, they emerged from their room into the corridor.

Together with the shuffling – it would be impossible for me to say which came first: what was the cause, and what was the consequence – there came the piercing sound of Fyodorov's falsetto. Bounding up and down the stairs like a faun, tearing this way and that along the corridor, never even brushing against the oldies lined up on either side, darting in and out of the rooms, he shouted joyously, at the very top of his voice: 'Last day for Party dues... Non-contributors automatically excluded... Closed Party meeting... Attendance of all Party members strictly compulsory... Non-attendees automatically excluded... Excluded!... Secret resolution of the Party CC about a worldwide flood... Only Old Bolsheviks allowed... Retaliatory Party measures... We are ready for the struggle!... Under "Miscellaneous",' he proclaimed from the other end of the corridor, 'the dossier of Khorunzhy, Party member since 1916... Moral disgrace... Forty-year affair with his secretary ... Two children... Khorunzhy's wife exposed him... Can we tolerate such people in our ranks any longer? I don't think so! All members must state their view!...'

Then, all of a sudden – I couldn't understand how – Fyodorov appeared on the ground floor, by the entrance, where almost half the ward had already gathered and where de Staël, the Sisters and nurses, all in tears, were clinging on for dear life to the legs of the old men and managing, for the time being, to keep them inside the building.

This seemed to suit Fyodorov, because at this point he, still cackling, still soaring above them, cried out in ecstasy and triumph: 'Nobody will be let out! Don't you dare let anyone out!... Everyone knows Kronfeld's orders: no walks in winter... Who's going to let you out now, especially in this weather?...'

Only afterwards did I realize that Fyodorov was simply playing for time. He was just waiting for all the sick to gather downstairs. But the oldies could not know this and they were frightened by Fyodorov's yells about Kronfeld and by the fact that the Sisters clearly supported him. Earlier, without speaking or raising their heads, they had stubbornly tried to force the medical staff and de Staël away from the entrance and almost succeeded, but the appearance of Fyodorov ruined their plans. Losing hope, the sick started babbling excitedly and their pressure abated.

But not for long. The old men were also resourceful and cunning, and now, realizing that they couldn't force their way out, they decided to play on the Sisters' heartstrings. They grabbed them by their uniforms, kissed their hands, shoved the customary three-rouble notes into their pockets and in orderly fashion, as if after numerous rehearsals, wailed in a three-voice canon: 'Let me out, let me out… Our baby's not eaten for two days'; 'My milk will run out, and the child will die…'; 'I left with the stove still going – my little one will burn alive…'

These words about unfed children abandoned at home were repeated by all the old men; they were the main words and could still be made out amidst all the other noises, which merged into a drawn-out groan. Transfixed by this strange chorus, we, unlike Fyodorov, were not counting the sick and didn't notice that all of them, even the feeblest, had already made their way downstairs and that the shuffling had finally come to an end. We only grasped this when Fyodorov appeared by the door in the blink of an eye; none of us managed to block him in time, he flung it open, and the wind and the cold sucked the old men out so quickly that not one of them had time to scream.

Fyodorov immediately tried to slam it shut again, but the wind had pressed the door against the wall of the building and by the time we managed to close the front door again, all pitching in together, the corridor was half-filled with snow. We all spent half the night shovelling up the snow and throwing it out of the window; then Fyodorov, de Staël and the Sisters went to bed while Ifraimov and I finished the job. After clearing the snow, we sat down on the stairs – we had no strength to go up to the rooms. We sat next to each other like that for a good long time, catching our breath, before I eventually asked him: 'And what will become of us?'

'I don't know,' he said. 'For now, it looks as if we've been preserved as a memory of that life. If God decides to prolong it, we'll stay; if He begins from the beginning, we'll leave. Just like the others…'

1988–1991